MW01631696

Sears Point

A Novel of Cape Cod

By Jim Coogan

Harvest Home Books
P.O. Box 1181
East Dennis, Massachusetts 02641

www.harvesthomebooks.com

This is a work of fiction. References to real people, events, establishments, organizations, or locales are intended only to provide a sense of authenticity. All other characters, incidents, and dialogue, are drawn from the author's imagination and are not to be construed as real.

Sears Point. Copyright 2016 by Jim Coogan. All rights reserved. Printed in the United States of America. No part of this book may be used or reproduced in any manner whatsoever without written permission except in the case of brief quotations embodied in critical articles and reviews. For more information, address Harvest Home Books, P.O. Box 1181, East Dennis, Massachusetts 02641.

Coogan, Jim
Sears Point by Jim Coogan
Summary: A century of change affecting Cape Cod is seen through the eyes of one man who experiences his community's transformation from a small rural town to a modern municipality.

Harvest Home Books
P.O. Box 1181
East Dennis, Massachusetts 02641

Visit our website at www.harvesthomebooks.com

Cover design and text layout by Kristen vonHentschel

Printed in the United States of America

First printing: October 2016

ISBN: 978-0-9893073-5-2

Sears Point

A Novel of Cape Cod

Cover painting "Sears Point" by Karen North Wells.
See page 234 for more info.

Dedicated to my parents, who gave me Brewster

The Brewster Flats, 1907

The sound of a fish horn drifted across the mud flats from the small beach landing. Nathan Sears swung the last of the day's catch of mackerel into the back of the beach cart. With the incoming tide, some of the outer sand bars were losing their twice-daily battle with the sea. The heart of the fish weir already had about four feet of water in it. It was time to head in. The trap fisherman looked shoreward and saw the small figure of his seven-year-old son, Freeman, the source of the horn's blast, waving across the half-mile expanse of channels and grass-ringed tidal pools. The boy's excited cries were muffled by the noise of the gulls.

The horn had broken through the eerie solitude of the flats, where a man could lose himself even when the world had a different schedule. Nathan stowed the net in the back of the wagon and climbed aboard for the ride back to the beach. Overhead, terns dove and wheeled, their cries competing with the gulls. The sorrel horse began to retrace the familiar track across the hard-packed sand, a route that had taken generations of local trap fishermen out to the weirs for as long as anyone could remember.

There were two possibilities for the summons. Nathan's father, Joshua Sears, was on his deathbed. The old man had been in decline for most of the summer and Doctor Cummings hadn't given the family much hope that he would see another Christmas. "Best we can do is just keep him comfortable," was the advice from the physician. Perhaps, thought Nathan, his father's time had finally come.

The second likelihood was that Nathan's fourth child had been born. His wife, Mary, had been in hard labor for almost thirty hours, and when he'd left earlier that day to follow the retreating tide out to the weir, she was weak and exhausted. Before leaving, he'd sat on the bed and applied a wet towel to her forehead. Both wondered why this child was so reluctant to leave the womb when the previous three had been born in just a few hours. Strange how life was, Nathan thought. In one room a life was ending. And not far away in the same house, another soul seemed reluctant to let life begin.

Nearing the beach, Nathan looked to see if his son's face held a clue. The old timers always claimed that no one ever died on an incoming tide. Nathan didn't know whether he believed that, but if his father had indeed passed, it could never be said that the old man had been cheated in life.

Joshua Winslow Sears had lived a full measure, and God knows, thought Nathan, there had to be a better place to fly to than the coughing sickbed that had grasped his father tightly for the past five months.

Like most people in Brewster at the dawn of the new century, Nathan's view of life was grounded in the practical and held together with a kind of spiritual anchor. Death was part of life, and when God summoned, you answered up and moved on. It was like a door that everyone eventually went through, an acceptable and predictable part of some eternal plan. Some few departed early and others, like Joshua Sears, hung around for the full extension. What was on the other side of that door Nathan didn't care to speculate, but since it was the fate of everyone, there seemed no reason to trouble one's mind beyond that.

"What is it, Freeman?" Nathan shouted as the wagon neared the beach. "What's all the commotion?"

"Ma's got a new boy," the youngster grinned as the wagon reached the eel grass. "You should see the size of his ears!" Nathan swung the child up next to him and clucked to the horse, encouraging the animal up over the hard clay scarp into the low stubble-covered moors that rose above the beach. The house at Sears Point was just a short distance down a sandy road in the lee of several large sand dunes. Father, son, horse, and team headed home.

Joshua Winslow Sears

The Sears family homestead lay with its front exposure facing south, the traditional arrangement for Cape Cod houses. The seventeenth-century structure was covered with salt-bleached pine shingles, and since its initial construction the house had experienced a number of alterations and additions. A ramble of Castilian roses, planted by some forgotten ancestor, climbed up one side of the house. At the seldom used front door, wisteria and morning glory vines draped themselves on latticed arbors. At the time it was built, British colonial authorities had prohibited the cutting of all trees measuring more than two feet in diameter. The house featured wide board floors, some over twenty inches in width, but not a single one reached the two-foot limit. Those "illegal" boards were always used in the outbuildings where animal manure hid them from the king's inspectors. They were still as good as new.

On the east side a porch provided views of Namskaket Creek and the Lower Cape. Eastham's sandy shoreline stood out clearly in the far distance. Just below the frontal dunes was a scattering of large rocks that had been deposited by the glacier eons ago. A wooden figurehead from a wrecked ship once owned by one of Nathan's distant cousins was mounted high on the bluff to the west of the house. The so called "White Lady" had formerly been attached to the clipper ship *Imperial.* Now long retired from the sea, she faced toward Boston as if awaiting the return of her lost ship and crew.

A forest of pine and oak trees marched from the house down a hill to the shore of a nearby pond. There was a small apple orchard and a large barn that sheltered a menagerie of farm animals. The property at Sears Point consisted of a bit less than seven acres and included a small cranberry bog. Cora and Augustus Thorndike's "Pinecroft" farm shared the dirt track that reached the promontory from Lower Road, and several Cobb and Nickerson family woodlots made up the rest of the adjacent property. The imprint of the Sears family on this piece of ground went back almost three hundred years. Richard Sears "The Elder" had arrived around 1640 when it was part of the town of Yarmouth, and had purchased a large tract of upland and marsh from the original grantees. With a fecundity that was remarkable even by the standards of the other prolific settlers of the time, the Sears clan begat and begot, spreading their lineage into Harwich, the north section of which eventually became the town of Brewster. In time, the Sears clan became one of the dominant families in the region. Their line was interwoven with branches of Crowells, Winslows, Halls, Fosters, Crosbys, Clarks, Bangs, and Bakers until it was a veritable bramble bush of cousins.

There seemed to be a Sears family connection to just about every important happening in the area, starting from the earliest days. Samuel Sears set the boundary between Harwich and Yarmouth along Squatcum Creek in 1717. Edmund Sears, another relative, helped throw tea into Boston Harbor in December of 1773. The Sears family was represented at Lexington and Concord in the presence of Judah Sears, who had been born in West Brewster in 1734. Freeman Foster, an uncle by marriage, was one of an eight-man committee that unsuccessfully tried to negotiate a reduced ransom payment with British Commodore Richard Raggett when he threatened to blow up the town's salt works during the War of 1812. And in the nineteenth century, Willard Sears made a name for himself as an ardent abolitionist.

Nathan and his father had both been born in the house, along with Nathan's brothers and sisters. Save for the three years when Joshua had gone south with the 45th Regiment of Massachusetts Volunteers to serve in the Civil War, the old man had never known any other place. And he was quite content to have it that way.

A Maxwell automobile was parked outside the house. Descending from the wagon and instructing the boy to take care of the horse, Nathan entered through a side door. Dr. Cummings and Mrs. Higgins the midwife were sitting in the kitchen.

"Congratulations, Nathan. You have a fine, healthy son." The physician, his sleeves still rolled up, moved to shake Nathan's hand. "He was a bit late in getting here, but things look fine and Mary is resting comfortably." The doctor's hands were soft and still warm from washing in the basin on the stove.

"You get a chance to look in at the old man?" Nathan asked.

"It'll be soon, I'm afraid," the doctor responded with a nod. "His coughing is much worse. I'll let Ben Fessenden know so he can have things ready. When you think the time is close, have someone call me and I'll come down right away. Meantime I've given him something to make him a bit more comfortable."

The physician picked up his bag and moved toward the door. "I'm sorry, Nathan. But there is that healthy boy." He put on his hat and went out into the gathering darkness.

Before going up to see his wife and new baby, Nathan paused at the door to his father's room. Unlike his more illustrious brothers and cousins, Joshua Winslow Sears had not followed the sea in the clipper ships and schooners that had been built in nearby Sesuit Harbor. Instead, he'd become one of the many weir fishermen who harvested herring, squid, mackerel, whiting, and butterfish in the abundant waters of Cape Cod Bay. In the years after the Civil War, there were several dozen weir traps between the harbor at East Dennis and the flats down toward Orleans.

Each March, the nets and ropes were tarred and the hickory poles painted. Using a flat-bottomed scow, the deep water trap men set their poles six feet into the sand in a pattern that took advantage of the habit of schooling fish that would come in with the tide, feed parallel to the shore and then, as the water ebbed, seek deeper water. With a long line of poles and nets placed fence-like to intercept the track of the school, the fish would end up in the heart section of the weir, and then, as the tide dropped even further, they would swim into the bowl. At low tide, the fishermen could net the fish and bring them ashore to be iced up in barrels for shipment off Cape.

The spring run of menhaden required a lot of men to harvest the silver fish. Fishermen knew that when the buds on the oak trees were as big as a mouse ear, the squid were in. It was the same when the shad bush blossomed. When the mackerel were running, fishing schooners from Provincetown and Gloucester would anchor off the Rock Ledge four miles offshore and the trap fishermen would ferry the fish out to them. The schooners would be heading out to the Grand Banks to fish for cod and haddock and they needed bait.

The weirs on the lower end of the bay could be reached by horse and team at low tide across the exposed sand flats. In good years when the market was glutted, a trap fisherman might barely make expenses. When for some reason the fish absented themselves from the bay, the fishermen made nothing. In the new century, the demand for kippered silver hake and spiced mackerel had seen some new weirs built. Fred Young had a trap off Robbins Hill just west of Nathan's and a bit further west toward Paine's Creek; and Freeman Atwood and his partner, Jim Corrigan, had another large one nearby. Gilbert Ellis and his brother Frank had put up a new weir off East Brewster. It was always the hope of the trap fishermen that the demand and supply balance would be sufficient to keep a family out of debt.

Joshua Sears had been able to do that. He and his wife, Bethia, Nathan's mother, had never really prospered but their seven children hadn't gone hungry. They were, as people said of those days, "Cape Cod poor." What little cash they made came from selling cranberries and whatever was realized from the weir. The vegetable garden supplied large amounts of potatoes, beans, turnips, and other root crops that were stored in the circular cellar under the pantry. In season there were beach plums, raspberries, blueberries, and strawberries to put up for the winter. Apples were sliced thin and dried in cloth mesh bags in the loft attic. When the family butchered a fatted calf, the fresh meat was shared with neighbors. The neighbors in turn repaid the Sears family when they did their own slaughtering. Late fall was the time for killing hogs, which provided the family with lard and pork. The cold weather made for good storage of the meat. In the spring, herring were taken from the creek and the shiny fish were smoked in a small shed over apple twigs and sweet fern. In September they harvested the small cranberry bog and stacked and split the dry wood cut the previous spring. The manure pit in the barn had to be cleaned regularly and the droppings spread on the garden.

A small flock of chickens, several hogs, and the milk from two jersey cows added to the family food supply. Eggs were preserved in a crock filled with just enough salt water to float a potato. Almost anything that lived in the sea was eaten. Fresh fish of some sort or other, often speared at low tide with a pitchfork from the grass-filled tidal pools, was a regular staple. Some would be salted and hammered, hard as boards, to the wall inside the barn as a food of last resort. Eels were caught in pots in the tidal streams and cooked for breakfast.

If a person got sick, there was Father John's Medicine, and Atwood Bitters helped move the bowels along. A piece of salt pork spiced with a bit of pepper and hung around the neck was the common remedy for a cold. People who couldn't care for themselves ended up living with Betsy Small, who supervised the almshouse. Each winter, Joshua and his neighbors cut ice and stored it packed in sawdust in a double-walled building on the north end of nearby Cobb's Pond. They used the ice to pack the fish that would be shipped to Boston. Joshua and his sons regularly visited the family woodlots in back of the Mill ponds to cut the fuel that fed the big two-burner Glenwood stove in the kitchen. There was a hand pump for water and an "outie" was attached to the back of the house. What little trash the family generated was dumped in a pit on the property. There was no town dump. Wealthier houses in town, like Homer Clark's place on Stony Brook Road, had a large windmill that pumped water into a tank where it was fed by gravity into the house below. Most families didn't have such a luxury and hauled their water from wells or cisterns.

The time after the Civil War saw the economic fortunes of the Cape ebb as the great age of sail slipped into history. By the turn of the new century the average income of a family in the United States was about four hundred dollars a year. But few in Brewster ever saw that kind of money. The populations in most Cape towns declined as young people left to find work in places like New Bedford, Fall River, and Brockton. Two of Nathan's brothers had done that, but when Joshua asked if Nathan would stay on and help with the weir, he hadn't hesitated. At Sears Point, as the land around the small homestead came to be known, he had a roof over his head and an outdoor life that suited him far better than anything a city might offer. Nathan had courted and married Mary Foster and started his own family in the same house. He'd worked alongside his father for almost two decades before the old man had shown signs of consumption two years ago. As his father's condition worsened, Nathan worked by himself, never making quite enough money to hire another paid hand.

Now, watching his father struggle for breath, Nathan felt quite alone. The old man had always been there to give advice and point a direction. The two had shared the grief of losing Bethia in1894. Their relationship had been typically undemonstrative. Nathan could not remember ever even touching his father. But the bond between the two of them had nonetheless been genuine, and important. Even now, at thirty-nine, Nathan still deferred to Joshua as head of the family. He moved to the bed and pulled the quilt up to warm the dying man. He patted the frail arm and quietly blew out the lamp. Only then, after closing the door carefully behind him, did Nathan Sears start up the stairs to meet his new son.

A Birth and a Death

Washington Foster Sears was emerging from a short nap when his father entered the bedroom. The Aladdin kerosene lamp gave just enough soft light to illuminate the bedstead. The baby commenced to make a case for dinner, and his cries nearly came close to rattling the sashes much as would happen in a winter nor'easter.

"Sounds like a healthy one," said Nathan to his wife, who was already maneuvering the small and struggling bundle to her breast. "That's if we can judge him by the strength of his lungs."

He watched the small fingers of the baby rhythmically opening and closing in the pleasure of his mother's warmth. "He doesn't look like the others," Mary said. "Freeman and David had dark hair. This one is almost blond. And he does have big ears!"

"Took his time getting here, that's for sure," said Nathan. "But I guess these things happen in God's good time. Doc says you came through it well enough. Is that so?"

Mary looked up at him. "I'm tired, but no more than with the others. I feel well enough. And it's good to be holding a warm one close."

Nathan knew that she was referring to the stillborn child that had come a year before, and he nodded toward her. "I guess he can make all the noise he wants. Just as long as he quits when I'm ready to turn in."

"There's the spare room across the hall," Mary smiled, and pointed with the arm that was outside of the coverlet. "If he squawks too loud, you can go over there."

"I don't think so," Nathan said, as he sat on the bed and gently caressed his wife's face. "There's not a man born, large or small, who's going to come between me, my wife, and my own bed." Their fingers touched. All the while the baby's own tiny fingers continued to open and close.

Three days later, Joshua Winslow Sears died. He was laid to rest in the family plot in the Red Top cemetery, next to the weathered and boarded-up church off Stony Brook Road, west of the old factory village. The building had once housed the Reformed Methodist Church. Now, with its original congregation long disbursed, it was used as a cranberry storage building. The shadows were long across the graveyard by the time everyone had passed the burial plot. The main character in the day's somber tableau had been a popular man. But there was no wailing or weeping. Joshua Sears had been granted more than the average run of years. You paid the debt of nature when your time came, that's how it was.

It occurred to Nathan as the family rode silently down Lower Road behind Ben Fessenden's black hearse that it would have been more convenient to bury his father in the graveyard at the foot of Swamp Road. But that resting place, fronted as it was with a proper granite and pipe fence and sporting expensive obelisks and marble stones, held Brewster's gentry, sea captains, ministers, and lawyers. Even in death, people of property and status, not Brewster's working class, had possession of the town's prime burying ground. Ordinary folks like Joshua Sears didn't end up there. True, there were members of the Sears family in that rarified spot, but they were distant relations. As the coffin was lowered into the sandy soil, the wind picked up and blew in from the bay. The dirge of the surf was magnified as it echoed through the surrounding cedar trees.

In the hours just before the old man slipped away, Nathan brought his three boys into the dark bedroom. Only Freeman, at age seven, seemed to have any sense of what was happening. Three-year-old David played with a yarn spool on the floor. Nathan carried the sleeping newborn into the bedroom and laid the child on his father's chest. Neither the baby nor the dying man moved or made a sound. But somehow, in those last moments of his father's life, Nathan felt that something important had passed between all of them in that room. There would always be Sears in this place, he thought. And they would be connected through history and time – one and all, the first and the last, by the land that surrounded them.

A week later when Nathan entered the town clerk's office, Tully Crosby struggled up with some difficulty from his chair by the stove. Crosby was substituting for Frank Crocker, who was at home with a broken leg after a balky horse had pitched him off his dray. Crosby was a good-sized man and the effort to coax his substantial body to become vertical made him wheeze. As the official moved toward the counter, the aroma of a recently smoked cigar lingered in the room.

"Come in to register the new one, Nathan?" The clerk reached under the counter for the ledger that housed the town's vital records. "Yours'll be the twenty-third child writ down this year. With this bein' October and two other women scheduled to foal before Christmas, it looks like we'll have at least twenty-five new citizens for 1907."

Nathan didn't like the clerk's use of the term foal, but since Crosby raised horses in East Brewster, it was probably natural that the word had slipped out. He wrote: "Washington Foster Sears, born October 13, 1907. Father: Nathan Winslow Sears. Mother: Mary Foster Sears." The birth had already been recorded in the family Bible and in the First Parish Church records. This final act satisfied the less important civil requirement.

Crosby pressed the blotter on the page and continued talking about what a good year this had been for babies. "Yes, sir," he said. "That cold snap last winter seems to have moved things along right well in the baby department. Musta been twelve inches of ice in School House Pond in December, if I recall. I remember Charlie Briggs drivin' down here from the depot with a bunch of Christmas packages for William Knowles at the post office. Cold as a frozen mackerel he was. As he was gettin' the larger boxes off his wagon into the building, the hangers-on heard him say, 'By Crimíney, Willie, this is one of them days that I wished to God that Jesus Christ had been born in July!'" The memory of the story crinkled the clerk's eyes, even though he'd told it countless times. "Yours is the sixteenth baby listed in the book this month. I guess there's truth in what we tell them summer folks when they ask if there's more going on in the winter down here than just fishin' and fowlin.'"

Crosby extended his pudgy hand across the wooden divide. "I'm sorry for your father's passing. He was a good man in this community. And, by the way, that'll be fifty cents."

Growing Years

Washington Sears entered on the scene as Brewster was slumbering through a long period where not much seemed to be happening. Most residents weren't sure whether it was the calm before the storm or maybe the aftermath of the tempest. One woman who had arrived from the city to work at the Nickerson estate in East Brewster told a summer visitor, "This is the last place God made, and He's not finished with it yet."

By 1900 Brewster had roughly the same number of people that it had counted a half century earlier. The town that had produced so many master mariners during the great age of sail surprisingly possessed no natural harbor, and the artificial reef and wharf, built in the 1840s for the packet boat, lay in ruins. Unlike the south side of Cape Cod, which was beginning to attract upper middle class residents seeking escape from the crowded cities, Brewster still retained its rural flavor. In 1907 it was a homogeneous community of painters, shore men, paperhangers, carpenters, poultry farmers, and cranberry growers.

If Brewster could claim anything that was close to noteworthy, it would be as the birthplace of popular novelist Joseph Crosby Lincoln. But he had departed as a teenager and was subsequently linked more with his summer home in Chatham than the town of his birth.

William Winslow Knowles and his son ran the dry goods store in the center of town that included the post office. The sign out front announced: "Dealers in dry goods and fancy wares." The store was also one of the few places in town that had a telephone, and it was where Washy's mother purchased her sugar and flour. George T. Foster had another store in East Brewster and a mill out back for cutting laths used for wall plastering and for bracing the bases of weir traps. A little further east where the railroad crossed the main road, Herbert Foster ran a grocery store with everything from fresh ground Berry and Dodge coffee to cider that came from apples in the orchard behind his house. Mrs. Samuel Chapman operated the Brewster House at the head of Lower Road, a bucolic rutted track that some referred to as Lobster Lane. In the summer, with its easy walk over the mostly denuded hills to the beach, the establishment had a good following. From September to June, it was mostly old bachelors who lodged there. Another place that took in boarders was the Brier House on Brier Lane in West Brewster.

Over by the Dennis line stood the Breeze Hill Inn run by Walter Gorham. Andrew Rich also ran a summer boarding house near the cemetery on Lower Road. Hiram Rowe was the town dentist and the doctor, Irving Cummings, took care of the town's medical needs. Thomas Sears was overseer of the poor. As to the spiritual requirements of Brewster's citizens, there was a Baptist church on Main Street and a new Catholic church in East Brewster. Faith Bickford, who ran the Sea Pines School, donated some land on the corner of Foster Road for a Christian Science Church. Unitarians occupied the First Parish Church in the village center, where Washy's family attended services. Family lore had it that all of the Sears clan in Brewster switched from being Congregationalists when one of the sea captains in the family returned from a long sea voyage to find that the church had rented out his pew after he'd left strict instructions that it be held for free use by some of the less financially fortunate members of the congregation.

The Methodists, remnants of the original Red Top church in West Brewster, now had to achieve their salvation in Dennis. In the hierarchy of social class in that time, Unitarians were on top and Baptists were at the bottom. Catholics were too few to amount to anything.

Brewster had no formal police force at the dawn of this new age. Edwin Hutchins was the elected town constable, but no one could remember when there'd been much of a need for him to do anything. There had been the murder of Sadie Hassard at the hands of Freddy Alexander in 1896. A lover's quarrel, it was said. Alexander had taken his own life the same day, drowning himself in Snow's Pond. Nathan was one of the men who had pulled the young man's body from the water. The Irish-born Hassards were star-crossed. Only six years earlier, nineteen-year-old John Hassard had been accidentally shot and killed by a friend while hunting ducks from a dory in the bay.

Aside from these misfortunes, Brewster was a quiet and peaceful place and doors were never locked. Politically, the town, like the rest of Cape Cod, was solidly Republican. Other than some seasonal Irish laborers and the Catholic priest from the Fall River Diocese who made a monthly circuit to serve the few local families of that sect, Democrats didn't exist in Brewster.

A lot of the men in town belonged to the Satucket Tribe of the International Order of Redmen. Women socialized as members of the Daughters of Pocahontas. Many men and women were members of the Brewster Grange #272, and the Masonic Lodge had a full register. The railroad depot about a mile southeast of the center was a hub of daily activity and a gathering place that drew Brewster men for business and gossip. The big coal stove in the main room was surrounded by a half dozen beat-up chairs and a brass cuspidor that occasionally was a successful target for tobacco juice. The daily weather forecast provided by the Department of Agriculture was posted outside the ticket office.

The depot area contained a coal yard and a grain storage facility. The Nickerson Lumber Company had a small spur off the main track for unloading boxcars. Several daily trains from the New York, New Haven and Hartford Railroad ensured that a gathering of unofficial overseers would be present to see who and what would come off the cars. No one arrived in Brewster without the surveillance of the hangers-on at the depot, and within the hour a visitor's presence was known in every household on Main Street. It took a bit longer for intelligence to reach the outlying farms.

In the early days of the century, Brewster was a wonderful place for a boy to grow up. With two older brothers and a younger sister born in 1909, Washy Sears lived like a Cape Cod version of Huckleberry Finn. The children roamed the hills and dunes near the house and camped out on summer nights along the shores of the Mill ponds, falling asleep to the sounds of whippoorwills and awakening to the shrill call of bobwhites. They played Cowboys and Indians, harpooned honeysuckle whales with bean poles, hunted frogs and fished in School House Pond for perch and sunfish. Baseball was played on the big field west of the old Seabury place and behind Captain William Freeman's house. In winter the children skated on the bogs and ponds and slid down Cannon Hill behind Cordelia Keith's Elm Tree Inn. Mothers made popcorn balls and molasses candy for skating parties. On winter evenings the boys played Whist and Hi-Low Jack, absorbing the warmth of the stove into their bodies before heading for their unheated bedroom upstairs.

Once a week the boys went to the Brewster Ladies Library and checked out books from the stern-faced librarian, Alma Rogers. A movie was shown in the upstairs of town hall every Saturday night, accompanied by the piano playing of Doris Chase. A roller skating rink at Greenland Pond in South Brewster was the site of family picnics in the summer. There were plum porridge suppers with Uncle Seleck Sears playing the violin.

The boys also helped their father with the weir, and Washy grew to love the solitude of the flats and its ever-changing vastness. The morning fog and the pungent odor of marine life in all its forms created an atmosphere like no other, with the silence broken only by the ageless cries of gulls.

School was in a two-story building on Main Street across from School House Pond. Washy walked, if his bicycle had a flat tire, and brought his lunch in a metal pail. A wagon driven by Joe Doyle brought children from outlying farms near the Punkhorn or from Poverty Lane in South Brewster. Another one took care of a section of East Brewster called "Blood Village," where it was said that you could play a nine-inning baseball game and be sure of eighteen fights.

Some children brought more than their lunches to school. Head lice were a constant problem. When Washy's mother detected nits, the boys were marched to the barn and had their scalps scrubbed with kerosene. This stinging product was also used to clean cuts if there wasn't any Sylpho Napthol in the house. A lot of the boys ended their schooling before entering the high school, working as jobbers, laborers, or heading to New Bedford or Fall River and the mills. A few stayed and went quahog dragging. Girls studied domestic arts such as cooking and sewing, and hoped they were attractive enough to eventually find husbands among the ever shrinking pool of eligible local males.

The Caddy

One summer when Washy was about ten, David got a job as a caddy at the golf links in East Brewster. He brought home fifty cents at the end of a day carrying golf bags for wealthy tourists staying at the Consodine House. When David spread the coins on the kitchen table, Washy was sure that his brother had found the secret to becoming a rich person.

"Can I go with you tomorrow?" Washy asked his brother.

"You're too small for carrying those bags," David said. "I think each one is bigger than you are. Besides, you have to be at least twelve to caddy."

But Washy persisted, and his brother finally gave up his objections. The next morning they were on their bikes at 7 a.m. and headed for the caddy shack in East Brewster. "What happens," explained David to his younger brother, "is that we sit in the shack until someone comes and asks for a caddy. Anybody asks, you are twelve. You have to wait your turn and hope that you get someone who is a good tipper."

It was almost ten o'clock before two men, accompanied by two ladies, came looking for caddies. David agreed to carry the men's bags and Washy was assigned to the women. When they went out to the big Auburn car in the parking lot, David pushed the women's bags toward Washy.

"We get twenty-five cents a bag for nine holes. Here, sling each one over each shoulder."

The bags, filled with shiny clubs with wooden handles, were almost as tall as Washy. It seemed as if each weighed at least fifty pounds. Once on his shoulders, they felt to Washy like two large bags of cement. As he walked toward the first tee, the bottom of each golf bag dug a furrow in the sand behind him.

The men hammered long drives down the fairway and David immediately headed out to spot the location of the balls. The two women smacked their shots about thirty feet into the rough. It took Washy some time to find each ball in the heavy grass and wild raspberry. The men waited patiently as each woman took seven or eight shots to reach the first green. In every case, Washy had to put the bags down, look for the balls, sometimes removing them from places with poison ivy, take out the requested club, re-shoulder the bags, and then repeat the procedure. When they finished the first hole and the brothers had a chance to talk to each other, David asked, "What do you think? Are you starting to get the hang of it?"

Washy looked at his older brother. "Hang of it? I've already earned my fifty cents and we've still got eight holes to go!"

That night, with muscles aching, he bathed with yellow soap, hoping to prevent the poison ivy from setting in. But in the morning he was covered with it, and it took more than a week before he stopped itching.

Another time, David came up with a scheme to retrieve golf balls from the pond at the ninth hole. The problem with the plan was the presence of Elbert Robbins, the club's maintenance man. Robbins sported a tattoo that said "U.S. Navy" on one of his large biceps and had a mustache that curled on both sides of his nose. Rumor around town said that the broken nose had come from his prior work as a prizefighter. Robbins had little use for the caddies, and said that any golf balls lost on the course belonged to him. If the boys found any they were supposed to turn them over to Robbins. Selling balls to players would get a caddy barred from working at the course.

Neither David nor Washy had any intention of giving up balls to Robbins. Out of his sight, they quietly sold the good ones they found to players. But it was difficult to find balls around the course in saleable condition.

Sol's Pond, which bordered the ninth hole, was undoubtedly loaded with balls, but getting to them presented a problem. The pond was home to several big snapping turtles. Neither boy wanted a close encounter with one of the creatures. David suggested a plan to avoid both the snappers and Robbins.

"What we'll do," he told Washy one afternoon, "Is get a mess of herring and let them cure outside for a while. Then we can take them to the pond and dump them in at one end. When the snappers come to get the fish, we'll be down at the other end picking up the golf balls."

"What about Robbins?" Washy looked skeptically at his older brother. "He's supposed to have a shotgun loaded with rock salt to scare people off the property. Did you think of that?"

"Of course I did," replied David. "We are going to get the balls just after sunrise. We'll do it on a rainy day. There won't be any golfers. Robbins ain't awake until at least nine in the morning when it's wet out. By the time he's up, we'll have the balls and be long gone."

And so the plan was launched. The boys caught a hundred or so herring in Stony Brook and took them home and put them in a barrel beside the barn. In about ten days the odor of the decaying fish was such that it caught Nathan's attention. "Those fish stink something awful. What are you doing with them?"

The boys explained that they'd made a deal with a lobsterman from Sesuit Harbor to supply bait for his traps.

"He's giving us a penny a fish," said David. "We'll have them out of here soon."

The rain came later that week and the downpour was steady throughout the night. David and Washy were up before dawn. With the very ripe fish in sacks slung over their shoulders, they rode their bikes down to Snow Road and entered the woods near the golf course. There were no players and no sign of Robbins. The boys emptied their malodorous cargo at the pond's east end and then backtracked to where the water met the fairway. In theory, at least, every snapping turtle in that pond was now heading away from them for breakfast.

The two put on water goggles, snapped mesh bags on their belts and entered the frigid pond. Even though they were still wearing pants, the first cold bite of the water took their breath away. The boys spent almost an hour crisscrossing the bottom without success. There was not a golf ball anywhere. It was as if the pond's floor had somehow been vacuumed clean. They headed home cold and discouraged.

In the cluttered maintenance shed that served as his home, Elbert Robbins luxuriated in the sleep of the just, snoring to the rhythm of the raindrops. Beside him on a small table were four egg cartons filled with shiny golf balls that the hired man had extracted from Sol's Pond the previous afternoon. When the sun came out later that day and the golfers arrived, Elbert Robbins made himself a nice bit of extra cash.

Rumors of War

During these years there was talk about the country getting involved with the war in Europe. People discussed it in the post office and Washy heard strong opinions when the adults gathered after church. He didn't know much about Germans, but from what he'd heard, he didn't think he liked them very much. In April of 1917, the United States formally entered the conflict. At school, as the children learned about nutrition, Mrs. Baker had them plant vegetables as part of a class project. She taught them a little poem as they worked. "With God's good aids, the rain and sun, we plant the things that will beat the Hun."

There was one German family, the Heinrichs, who lived in South Brewster. Washy was in school with Emma, one of the daughters. As far as Washy could tell, she and the rest of the clan of Huns seemed pretty much like his own family. Aside from the fact that they were Lutherans, they appeared to be just like anyone else. Still, that spring, a resolution was introduced at the annual town meeting that called for denying any town office to people expressing pro-German sentiments.

With the United States in the war, the town mobilized its small population for the effort. Mrs. Roland Nickerson headed up the surgical dressings committee. For the first time that Washy could remember, his father flew an American flag outside of the house. He watched as his oldest brother Freeman, along with Ernest Black, Augustus Ellis, and Ray Tubman, boarded the train at the depot on their way to recruit training at Camp

Devens. The enlistees, who were still not much more than boys, were given a rousing send-off, accompanied by the town band and a patriotic speech by the chairman of the board of selectmen. One day in spring there was great excitement when a number of airplanes flew across town toward Chatham where there was a new naval air station at Nickerson's Neck.

Washy's Boy Scout troop sold Red Cross tickets and collected used clothing for relief efforts in France and Belgium. The boys also practiced marching and camped out regularly on weekends, supervised by scoutmaster Ernest Chase. With wheat in short supply, the Sears family got used to eating "war bread" made with barley meal and rye flour. They consumed more rabbit and less beef. The national campaign to save fat meant fewer baths with soap. But that wasn't so much a bother to young Brewster boys as it was for the ladies in town.

Freeman Sears never got overseas to fight the Germans. He spent most of his military service in Philadelphia, where he was hospitalized during the influenza pandemic that eventually killed thousands of Americans. He survived his contact with the infamous "Spanish Lady" and was mustered out in the spring of 1918, returning home by train one day in May to little fanfare.

The other war-connected incident of local significance was a German submarine attack on a tug and barges off Eastham in the summer of 1918. Reporters streamed through Brewster on the way to interview the survivors. When the train came back through town carrying John Ainsleigh, the young boy who had reportedly saved the American flag from a sinking barge while under enemy fire, Washy was envious. But at his young age, there hadn't been all that much that he could do for his country. In November, with the war finished, things went pretty much back to normal in Brewster. As for the Heinrich family, they were gone. They'd left town in the late summer of 1918. The blackened cellar hole and the foundation of their farmhouse was all that was left from the fire that had mysteriously burned them out just after the July 4th town picnic.

The Artist

During these years, the Sears family became acquainted with some new neighbors who had moved into the old Cobb homestead on Lower Road. Harrison Calderwood and his wife, Mildred, were artists. He was of the paint and pallet variety. She created gray pottery with swirls on the outside. The couple had moved to Brewster from Provincetown where, as Mrs. Calderwood often remarked, "It was just too crowded and noisy." There was no worry about that in Brewster. The town was still largely dirt roads, and farm animals outnumbered people. The largest crowd that anyone could ever remember assembling in town had occurred back in

1890 when Albert Crosby was forced to liquidate his art collection to satisfy creditors who had thought the former Chicago liquor baron was long dead. The auction of the interior furnishings and artwork from Crosby's mansion, Tawasentha, had brought in several hundred people on the train.

Harrison Calderwood was an artist of some reputation. He'd been a member of the Provincetown Art Association and for more than a dozen years had assisted Charles Hawthorne in his summer school for young painters there. The arrival of the two artists sparked much conversation in the Sears household. Everyone agreed that it was nice to see lights on again in the old Cobb place.

All the family talk about the new neighbors pretty much passed over Washy's head. He knew little and cared less about art. As for credentials, Harrison Calderwood's English accent, which was heard loudly in the mornings at Knowles's store, made Washy think that the man could never be a real artist like some of the illustrators whose pictures were in the magazines he read at Nate Black's barber shop on Red Top Road.

All this changed one warm spring afternoon when David screeched his bicycle into the yard in a cloud of dust and shouted for Washy to meet him behind the barn. David was still out of breath when his younger brother came around the corner.

"Wait 'til you hear this." David could hardly get the words out fast enough. "Calderwood, you know, the artist in the old Cobb place. He paints naked ladies in his studio. I'm not kidding. I heard some of the men talking about it at Knowles's store. They said he has a college girl who comes up from Provincetown on the train every Tuesday and she poses for him! And she doesn't wear any clothes, not a stich! Me and Luther Eldridge are going to spy on them tomorrow. Want to come along?"

Up to that point, girls hadn't figured much in Washy's thoughts, and certainly not girls without clothes on. He'd seen his younger sister, Clara, getting a bath in the kitchen but she was really just a child, not a girl in a real sense. The girls Washy knew always wore so many layers of clothing, even when swimming, that it seemed that this was their natural state of affairs. On washdays, frilly items hung in great abundance from clotheslines behind the houses where girls lived. He had no idea of their function. Washy could never imagine girls swimming naked like he and his friends did on summer afternoons at Sheep Pond. He figured that girls his age and older probably wore clothes even when they took baths. Now he was presented with the opportunity to see a real live one with no clothes on, and not just any girl, but a college woman, and from Provincetown, no less. Whether she would exhibit any qualities that might differ from the girls of his own age, Washy wasn't sure. He didn't really know what those qualities could possibly be, but it seemed like a good idea to find out.

The sun was out in full force when the boys put their spy plan into operation. They slipped through the pines along the west side of Cobb's Pond and set themselves up, hidden from view, in a thicket of brush with a good view of the artist's house. David had a pair of binoculars focused on the large studio window that took up the entire wall of an extension off the summer kitchen.

"I can see them," David reported, "but they're just sitting at a table. Ain't nothing happening. Don't look like he even has any paint out. And she's got her clothes on."

For almost a half hour, the binoculars were passed back and forth between the boys, who were growing bored watching two adults drinking coffee.

Finally, the artist opened the door at the back of the studio and led the girl down a path to a small studio just in back of the dunes. Calderwood's safari hat bobbed up and down like the flight of a moth in the evening. The girl trailed behind.

The boys followed, keeping in the woods and crawling silently through the bayberry and honeysuckle to a point on a sand dune about forty feet from the shack. They watched as the artist went inside to get his easel and paints, followed by the girl, who emerged wearing a white bathrobe. The artist and his model walked down the path to the secluded beach.

Inching closer to the rim of the dune, the three boys hid just above where Calderwood was setting up his easel. There was no need for binoculars now. As she waited for the artist to be ready, the girl busied herself smoking a cigarette and making designs in the sand with one of her toes.

Washy was watching a cricket move through the sand when he suddenly sensed that neither David nor Luther was breathing. He looked up and saw his companions fixed on something that had temporarily ceased the flow of air from both of them. The girl had taken off her robe and was standing with one foot on a rock looking out to sea. She was as naked as the day she'd been born.

The three boys watched dry-mouthed as Calderwood repositioned his model in different poses. The boys observed the scene for perhaps fifteen minutes, until Luther decided he wanted to move closer for a better view. As he wiggled forward, the dune, which was riddled with swallows' nests, gave way.

In a rush of collapsing sand, clay, and bayberry roots, Luther was pitched from the top of the dune to land in a tangled heap at the foot of the startled artist. Just before he went over the edge, Washy felt his brother grab his shirt and bring him back from the brink. The model shrieked and ran for her robe. Calderwood was so stunned that his pallet landed face down in the sand and he fell, upsetting the easel.

Without waiting to see what was going to happen next, David and Washy backed away from the edge of the traitorous dune and ran wildly back toward Sears Point. The fate of Luther Eldridge, their hapless companion, was of no concern to either of them at that moment.

That evening, a car came up the long dirt road into the yard. It was Harrison Calderwood. Nathan went outside for a chat and the two men shared a smoke and some conversation. At one point, there appeared to be some laughter coming from both men, but Washy, who was watching everything from his room upstairs, couldn't be sure. At length, the car drove away and Nathan came back into the house.

"Boys, come down here – *now*." There was a hard edge in the command that wasn't to be ignored. David and Washy trooped down to the kitchen. When they got there, they found their father seated at the table.

"Mr. Calderwood tells me that you boys seem to have quite an interest in art." He looked across at them. "That was quite a lesson you two had a part in today, I'd say."

Neither boy looked at their father. Their feet shifted under the table and their eyes avoided each other.

Nathan continued. "Calderwood says he's lost his model. The young lady's not coming back here to pose anymore. He's not happy about it. Now he's got to take the train down to Provincetown and bring all his paints with him. Seems like that's the only place on the Cape now where you can get girls to take their clothes off while you paint 'em. You boys are responsible for that."

Sipping some coffee and fixing both boys with a serious look, Nathan let his words settle in. "Here's what I'll say. I'm not surprised that you wanted to see what the other side has to offer. I probably did something like that myself when I was your age. But if you want any more looks, I'd suggest that you ask Nate Black for some of the magazines that he keeps in the closet at the barber shop. They've got everything in 'em but the instruction manual. And you won't really need that when you are old enough to get your hands on the real thing. It'll come natural. Right now I want your word that you won't spy on Harrison Calderwood anymore."

The boys looked at their father, who was trying hard to hold in a chuckle at the thought of Luther Eldridge falling off the dune and Calderwood's model running for cover like a scalded Salome. The brothers agreed they'd leave the artist in peace, and both went up to bed more than a little thankful, and certainly surprised that they had gotten off so easily.

Nathan used a handkerchief to stifle his laughter as the boys departed up the stairs. He wondered how it had gone with Luther when the boy's mother, an ardent deep water Baptist, found out what he'd been up to. Later, he and Mary shared that laughter as they lay in bed and he told her how Harrison Calderwood had revealed the boys' new interest in art.

"That Calderwood's not such a bad fellow," Nathan said. "He wasn't all that mad. He did wish, though, that the girl hadn't been so spooked.

Reminds me of the time when me and Alpheus Foster hid in the dunes near the Consodine bath houses to watch the girls from Camp Wahtonah get into their bathing suits. We were about twelve, I think." Nathan smiled at Mary. "I'm sure our boys had the same thoughts today that Alpheus and I did then – what on earth do those strange things do?"

There was a playful poke in his ribs and a tender voice close by. "If you can't remember, Nathan, perhaps you need to be shown what you've apparently forgotten." The sound of the surf washing against the beach outside the house was soon joined by muffled laughter within.

Turtle Hunter

In his early teens, Washy got a job working for Azariah Eldridge, who had advertised for help with his turtle business. "Riah" Eldridge was a trapper and hunter, and when the snapping turtles went into the mud in the fall to hibernate, he would pole for them. When he wasn't occupied with turtles, he was killing seals, bringing the snouts to collect the state bounty of two dollars for each one. He also painted houses, delivered ice, and sold clams to the Nobscussett Hotel in Dennis. On the morning when Washy got to Eldridge's house, the turtle man was already sitting in his truck, a cutaway Ford Model T with a wooden platform attached. The truck was almost as old as Eldridge, with slick tires and a cracked windshield.

"Where ya been, kid? I've been waitin' a half hour already." The old trapper was puffing vigorously on a pipe, and as Washy got in, he spat a dark stream of juice out the window. Eldridge was a short, stocky man and his face exhibited a host of cracks and fissures that resembled a bird's eye view of the flats. His remaining hair was long and gray and wispy ends billowed out from under his cap. "Git in! We got to git them turtles when they's asleep, you know." And without another word, he jammed the gearshift forward and the truck jounced out of the yard in a cloud of blue smoke. Following some dirt roads, Eldridge turned down a narrow track near some cranberry bogs and an isolated pond. They stopped in a grove of white oaks. Walking around to the back of the truck, Eldridge handed Washy a long pole and a burlap sack. The pole had a crook at one end and a metal hook at the other.

"Now you watch me, sonny," the trapper gestured. "What we do is wade in the shallows and probe the bottom ahead of us. When we hit a turtle, the pole will make a thunkin' sound. They's all buried up for the winter but once we've got one, we can use the crooked end of the pole to pry him out. Turtles this time of year are pretty much asleep and we just lift 'em into the sack and bring 'em back to the truck."

It wasn't easy to tell the difference between the shell of a snapping turtle and a rock. Several times Washy called Eldridge over, only to have the old trapper laugh after it turned out to be a good-sized boulder. But then the boy put his pole down and heard a different sound, definitely a thunk.

"You think you got somethin' this time?" Eldridge paused about twenty feet away.

"It's different," Washy shouted. "Sort of hollow but still solid. It's ain't a rock."

"Maybe you got a log. Put your crook under it and see if you can turn it over."

This time there was some give to whatever was down there. Washy could feel the thing coming loose from the muddy bottom.

"Hey, I got one!" Washy stepped back as the white undersides of the turtle came up to the surface, its four clawed feet flailing about. "It's a big one."

"Well, grab him and put him in the bag," Eldridge shouted across to his young partner.

"But how do I grab him?" Washy looked up at Eldridge.

"By the tail! Stay away from his head!"

Washy had had enough experience with snapping turtles to know that the mouth of one of these creatures could be lethal to a finger. It was clear that this turtle was not happy about being awakened from its semi-dormant state of winter rest. As he lunged to grab it, Washy suddenly lost his balance and went forward right on top of the creature. Now turtle and boy were splashing around at the same eye level and it was hard to tell where one began and the other left off.

"Grab the Gawdamn thing or we'll lose him!" Eldridge was still too far away to be of any help. Washy, now on his knees in the muddy water and trying to avoid the business end of the turtle, was able to turn the thirty-pounder enough to pull its tail out from the shell. After a bit more wrestling, he got the turtle into the now thoroughly soaked bag.

"What do we do now?" The apprentice turtle hunter looked toward his mentor.

"Where there's one, there's got to be more." Eldridge resumed poling. "Turtles is like old married folks. They like to sleep close together when winter comes. Rest of the year they stick pretty much to themselves. We'll work this spot awhile."

Fortunately, it was one of those fall days that can feel more like late summer, and Washy's outer clothes dried quickly. The warm air, however, also had the effect of waking up the turtle, who in short order was very much recovered. The bag flopped on Washy's back as the angry terrapin struggled to escape, and at one point the boy had to take off his jacket because the turtle had bitten through the bag into it.

The two hunters took another six turtles between them before returning to Eldridge's house. That's when Washy learned about storing turtles.

"Ain't we going to take them up to the railroad station for shipping?" he asked.

"Naw, ain't enough yet to make it worthwhile. We'll keep 'em in my cellar until we can fill a barrel. Then we'll ship 'em."

Eldridge led Washy down a steep stairway into his cellar. It had a dirt floor, and in the reduced light Washy could see a number of other turtles that had partially buried themselves, happily asleep as they would have been in any muddy pond.

"It takes about fifteen of 'em to fill a barrel," Eldridge said, as he re-lit his pipe for about the tenth time that day. "And they got to be shipped live. We'll pack 'em up and send 'em to New York where the fancy restaurants make soup out of 'em. I get twenty cents a pound. They keep real good down here in the winter, sleep all day and night. Don't have to feed 'em nothing. You know, you can predict the winter by these turtles. The deeper down they're buried in the mud, the colder the winter's goin' to be. That's the truth. The only problem I got now storing 'em in the celler is when it rains for a few days. If the wife can't get outside, she hangs the laundry down here to dry. She raises some hell with me if she ends up steppin' on one of 'em."

The Deer Drive

Every fall the men in Brewster looked forward to deer season. One of the rites of passage that served to transform boys into men was to be taken by their fathers as fully fledged members of the deer hunting party. Washy was in his first year of high school when Nathan called to him one morning.

"Deer hunt's going to be next week. I took David last year and I think you're ready to go with us. What do you say?"

For Washy, this was a badge of honor to hunt with the older men. Freeman had been hunting with his father for several years now. Washy had chafed when David took part the year before. Now it was his turn.

Autumn days always brought vibrant colors. The white and red oak leaves changed to red and gold. The cranberry bogs and surrounding uplands were a blaze of color complemented by a vault of blue sky. Even the poison ivy decked itself out in beguiling shades of crimson and yellow.

It was on such a day that the hunters met just after daybreak. Someone had prepared a steaming pot of coffee. Truck doors slammed and rubber tires screeched as a caravan of old cars and trucks headed into the woods above the Mill ponds. Several pheasants crossed ahead of the group but no one bothered with them. The eastern white-tailed deer was the quarry on this day.

Freeman was driving with Nathan seated beside him. David and Washy rode in back. Shotguns were stowed in the trunk. "Will we all start out together?" Washy asked.

Nathan turned and pointed at the line of vehicles moving down the dirt road. "There's too many of us to start as a group. We drew straws at town hall to see who will be the shooters and who will be the beaters. Half the group will go on ahead to the west end of Walker's pond. They'll start driving the deer back toward us. We'll set up out of sight just above that big cranberry bog over there. Today is our day to take deer. Tomorrow everyone will switch and we'll be the drivers."

This far back in the hills of Brewster there were few houses. But it wasn't unknown country. Everyone knew the dirt roads because they led to the cranberry bogs, and many of the families had woodlots nearby. There were large stretches of open space where wood had been cut in more recent years. From the place where Washy and his brothers were sitting, they could see the deer coming across these open areas where they'd be silhouetted against the pines. The shooters' line was extended enough so that there wouldn't be any doubt about who'd shot a particular deer.

It was about ten o'clock and the sun had warmed things up enough for the shooters to shed their outer jackets. Suddenly a single shot rang out in the drivers' direction.

"That ain't right," Nathan said, as he walked over to where everyone was anxiously looking westward. "The drivers ain't supposed to shoot unless they have some deer doubling back on them. We'd be hearing more than just one shot if that happened."

After a few minutes, two men could be seen running across the cleared area in front of the shooters. "Hold your fire!" cried one of the runners, waving his arms excitedly. "We've got a man down."

John Berry, one of the runners, explained that Alton Baker had been wounded when he tried to cross a stone wall after resting his shotgun against it. As Baker had started over, the loaded weapon had fallen and hit a rock, discharging directly into the unfortunate man's stomach.

"He's bad. Gut shot. Lost a lot of blood," said Berry. "We got to get him out and run him to a doctor."

Before anyone could bring a car up, a group of men emerged across the open area with a body on a makeshift stretcher. Small knots of hunters began to come out of the woods. The face of the man on the stretcher was covered with a jacket but no one needed to be told that it was Alton Baker. And it was clear that he was beyond the help of any doctor.

They brought the dead man down to Constable Frank Campbell, who called the undertaker and went to break the news to Baker's wife. After some milling around in the town hall lot, most of the hunters got into their cars and quietly went home. There would be other deer hunts. But Washy never forgot his first one, the time that Alton Baker didn't come home.

The Noble Experiment

In 1920, the nation "went dry." The "No-Funs" and "Shouldn't Do's" had won the day with the passage of the Volstead Act. It was a noble gesture born of good intentions and high-minded optimism, but from the start it was doomed to failure. Like the rest of the nation, the majority of Cape Codders didn't like the idea of government getting its hands into personal behavior. It was a tradition in social settings that men openly oiled their conversation with whiskey or some variation of "flip." The women, as well, liked their "tea," slipping small amounts of liquors into their cordials and taking more substantial amounts in patent medicines like Lydia Pinkham's Elixir.

The first awareness of what Prohibition would mean for Brewster came one dark night in the spring of 1921, when a truck slipped quietly down to Paine's Creek landing. It was high tide and the driver had his headlights off, guided only by a flashlight held out the passenger side window by his companion. Once parked on the crest of the dune, the driver turned on his lights, blinking them quickly three times. From out in the bay, there came an answering three-light acknowledgment, and shortly thereafter a fishing boat moved in close to the narrow creek channel where three men jumped off, securing the vessel to a small pier. In short order, a number of cases of Canadian whiskey were on their way to the cellar of a prominent restaurant owner in Hyannis. The entire procedure took about a half hour.

Cape Codders moved quickly to exploit the situation. Countless isolated channels and coves could be used to bring liquor onto the Cape for transport to cities like Brockton and Taunton. Vessels left ports in Cuba, the Bahamas, and Canada and anchored just outside the twelve-mile limit, where local boats would arrive and transfer the liquor to shore. There were a couple of slimmed down high-powered cruisers in Sesuit Harbor, one a thirty-eight footer with a Lathrop engine that had no obvious connection to the fishing trade. The other sported a twelve-cylinder Liberty engine that gave the boat a thirty-knot capability. When asked why he needed such a fast boat, the skipper joked, "Never know when you have to chase down a tuna."

On Slough Road near the Dennis line there was a place called "Rum Corner," where empty five-gallon jugs were left in the woods each morning. By late afternoon, they were filled with liquor and picked up by their owners. One morning as Nathan followed the ebbing tide out to his weir, he found some boxes containing straw-wrapped bottles of Double Eagle Pure Rye Whiskey just east of his trap. They had been ditched the previous night by rumrunners fleeing a Coast Guard boat. Three men later came out from shore and tossed the boxes into the back of a wagon. Nathan didn't recognize them. The men retreated with their cargo to Saint's Landing where a large truck was parked. Soon after, they were gone.

Following his brief war service, Freeman Sears had not fared well. He'd worked a short time for Charlie Bassett at the Bay State Freezer Plant in Yarmouth Port and married Ida Howes from East Dennis. The couple leased a small farm on Sesuit Neck. But the farm and freezer plant yielded barely enough to live on, and when the marriage failed, Freeman moved to New Bedford.

His letters home indicated that he'd landed a good job in the Whaling City. Nathan was surprised one morning when he found an envelope waiting for him at Knowles's store containing a carefully wrapped hundred-dollar bill. The amount was so large that Nathan hid it in a drawer, fearing that if he took it to a bank there would be all kinds of questions. Many families in Brewster never saw a hundred dollars in an entire year.

A month later, Nathan heard a car coming up from Lower Road. It was a new Pierce Arrow and Freeman was behind the wheel. What had brought this sudden prosperity for Nathan's eldest son became clear later when Freeman told the family that he was working for a New Bedford shipping company. The owner, Francis Collins, had been a big wheel in Boston before branching out to New Bedford. When the two met in a club that Freeman frequented, Collins had offered him a job with a wage that could only be dreamed of in Brewster. Details of what exactly Freeman did were vague, but David and Washy were convinced that their older brother was going to be the next John D. Rockefeller.

Nathan knew that Freeman wasn't making all that money working a regular job. Information had passed between father and son that the source of Freeman's new-found fortune was clearly the liquor business.

Several more months passed, and on a crisp April morning in the spring of 1923, Nathan was alerted that someone from the New Bedford police department wanted him to call the city, and he walked to Knowles's store to use the phone. The operator put him through to New Bedford and the police department.

"You got a boy named Freeman, Mr. Sears?"

Nathan told the police dispatcher that he did have a son by that name.

"I'm sorry to tell you that we've got his body here and you need to come and claim it."

There was a stunned silence as Nathan tried to comprehend what the speaker had just said.

The dispatcher continued. "He was washed up on Nashawena Island yesterday along with six other men. We identified him from some papers in his wallet. It doesn't look like your son died from drowning."

Nathan blurted out, "Freeman? Dead? What do you mean? He's only twenty-three years old."

"Well, he's here in our morgue and he's got four bullet holes in him – very dead sir, I'm sorry. Get over here as soon as you can."

The earpiece of the phone somehow got put back on the hook and Nathan left without speaking to anyone else. He couldn't even remember if he'd said good-bye to the police officer. All he knew was that he'd not had the chance to say the same thing to his oldest son.

Graduation Day, 1924

The tragedy of Freeman's death had no impact on the regular pace of life in Brewster. Nor did it cause the Sears family to cease participating in the activities and affairs of their small Cape Cod town. Mary Sears continued to attend monthly meetings of the Woman's Alliance at Dawes Hall where progressive causes were championed and debated. There were whist parties and Grange meetings, and in May the men's club of the First Parish Church sponsored an Old Time Medicine Show. A committee headed up by James Burgess, Henry Allen, and William Consodine started a letter writing campaign to see if electricity could be extended into Brewster. Boys and girls had organizations like the Junior Poultry Club and the Junior Canning Club. A survey by the state Department of Labor and Industries noted that farming continued as a mainstay of the Cape's economy. "No better potatoes are raised or more bushels to the acre than here, corn is successfully raised, and apples are abundant," said the report. Eleven-year-old Catherine Ellis of East Brewster won a Cape-wide poetry contest about just how well things were going:

> "The girls are darning stockings and the boys are feeding calves.
> The Cape Cod kids keep busy and they don't do things by halves.
> We're going to stay right on the Cape and never roam abroad.
> There's nothing there for us you see, that's better than Cape Cod."

But the truth was, young people were leaving for the cities. There was excitement and a sense that a person could make something of himself where the buildings were made of brick and the streetlights stayed on all night. Brewster's population, which had been over fifteen hundred people in 1840, numbered less than eight hundred only eighty-four years later.

So in June of 1924, when Washy became the second member of his family to finish high school, after David, there were decisions to be made. On an evening that was unusually hot for early summer, he walked proudly across the second floor stage of Brewster Town Hall and received his diploma from Superintendent of Schools Alton Small. Audience members temporarily put down their fans to applaud the scholars. There were nine girls and four boys in the class, and after the recitations and singing, friends and families disbursed to their homes to salute the graduates and drink fresh-squeezed lemonade. For all of them it was both an end and a beginning.

A Guilty Conscience

The phone rang in the kitchen. Washy picked up the receiver. The year 1925 had come in with blustery winds and a cold spring, and he was glad that he no longer had to go up to Knowles's store for a phone message. The Sears family had gotten their own phone the previous fall, a magneto and hand-crank affair. The local operator said she was holding a call from New Bedford, and when Washy answered, a gruff voice came on the line.

"Your father home?"

Washy found Nathan outside splitting wood. "It's somebody from New Bedford."

"Nathan Sears?" The voice came through the receiver.

"Yes, what do you want?"

There was a low growl, almost a cough, and the voice responded. "It's not what I want, Sears, it's more about what you might want."

"And what would that be?" Nathan asked.

"Information about how your son Freeman died the night the rumrunner *John Dwight* went down two years ago. I'll tell you what I know, but not over the phone. Can you meet me in Mattapoisett tomorrow?"

"I can be there in the morning. Tell me where," Nathan replied.

There had never been a satisfactory explanation about what had happened the night that the *John Dwight* was lost. The Coast Guard investigation and the work of police departments in Newport, Rhode Island, and New Bedford fleshed out the story enough to satisfy the general public. But the Massachusetts Attorney General admitted that questions remained on what had led to the violent deaths of the ship's crew.

Freeman Sears and nine other men were aboard the 110-foot wooden steamer when she'd left Newport on the evening of April 1, 1923. Speculation was that the ship was headed out somewhere into Block Island Sound beyond the twelve-mile limit to rendezvous with one of the whiskey ships. A few days later, the *Dwight* was seen anchored off Nashawena Island, north of Cuttyhunk. Watch standers at the Coast Guard station there who caught a brief glimpse of the vessel noted that the ship appeared heavily loaded and low in the water.

Sometime in the early morning hours, at least one strange whistle was heard in the vicinity of the *Dwight*'s anchorage, and there were reports of gunfire. As dawn broke and the morning fog lifted, the *Dwight* was seen down by the stern and sinking. By the time the Coast Guard could get a closer look, the ship had disappeared.

Investigators thought it especially strange that the *Dwight* had gone to the bottom with most of her valuable cargo still aboard. Had she been scuttled? Could the ship's sinking have been a message sent by one bootlegging syndicate to another that encroachment on one's territory would not be tolerated? There had never been any clear answers.

Nathan could only wonder if the mysterious caller would finally provide them.

A Startling Revelation

Murphy's was a hole-in-the-wall eatery just off the state highway in Mattapoisett. On this dreary spring day, the place needed a coat of paint as much as it needed customers.

In the corner away from the windows a figure sat silhouetted in cigarette haze. He made no move to get up when Nathan approached.

"You want a drink?" The greeting was curt. Nathan declined the offer. The face that looked back at Nathan was expressionless and gray. The man's eyes were cavernous, framed with wrinkles and crow's feet. His teeth were stained yellow with nicotine.

"Your son Freeman was not supposed to die that night. It was an accident."

"What do you mean, an accident?" Nathan stared at the man.

There was a fit of coughing before the man replied. "Mr. Sears, I'm not all that sure why I bothered to come here this morning. I'm not a sentimental man. But there's a couple of things I thought you ought to know about what happened aboard the *John Dwight* the night your son was killed.

"When the *Dwight* left Newport, she met the Canadian schooner *Sadie A. Nickerson* about 15 miles southeast of Block Island. Almost 640 cases of ale were off-loaded and the *Dwight* headed up Vineyard Sound to meet some local rumrunners off Falmouth. The fog set in and the ship dropped anchor off Cuttyhunk to wait for morning and continue through the channel into Nantucket Sound.

"A bit before dawn, a second vessel came near the *Dwight*'s anchorage following a homing signal that had been planted aboard. Your son Freeman had carried it aboard in Newport.

"Freeman was working with us," the man continued. "The *Dwight*'s captain, John King, was supposed to be carrying a hundred and fifty thousand dollars in cash in the ship's locker. We had Freeman on the inside to get us to the *Dwight*'s anchorage so we could steal the money. We didn't care about the booze. In fact, by sinking the *Dwight* with her cargo still aboard, we were hoping it would look as if some rival operator was making a statement about who could do business in Buzzards Bay. It was the money we were after."

"You were there that night?" Nathan drew closer to the face on the other side of the table.

"Yeah, that's right." The man turned away and began coughing again. "I was one of three men who boarded the *Dwight*. Freeman was supposed to go off with us after we'd gotten the money and set the ship to sinking. But we couldn't get into the captain's cabin and the noise we made alerted the watch stander, who hit the signal horn. Freeman tried to get to the pilot house and took a couple of bullets from the watch stander. He was dead when he hit the deck.

"Our ship moved away into the fog, fearing that the gunshots would bring someone around to see what was going on. Somehow the *Dwight*'s anchor line got snagged with our ship and she lurched to starboard. With the big rush of water over the stern quarter, she began to settle quickly. The three of us lowered a boat and rowed to Naushon. At first light we stole a sailboat and made it to Vineyard Haven."

"So the money went to the bottom with the ship?"

"Wherever it ended up, we didn't get it. The only money that anyone ever reported was some small bills that came from the pockets of the dead crewmen."

It was an incredible revelation. Freeman Sears had died in a hail of gunfire aboard a rumrunner. Nathan sat back, not sure he was relieved that at last he knew what had really happened or whether he was simply numbed by the awful truth of its conclusion.

"There's more to why I came here." The man started coughing again. "Maybe it's the bit of conscience that I have left that I feel some guilt about what happened. There's something else you should know." Sucking on another cigarette and exhaling toward the wall, the man leaned forward until his face was just a few inches from Nathan.

"Freeman left a kid behind, a little boy. He was living with a Portugee woman in New Bedford for about six months before he signed on aboard the *Dwight*. She's a Cape Verdean, a real darkie. She got pregnant and didn't tell Freeman before he left on the *Dwight*. She had the baby about seven months after the sinking. He never knew that he was going to be a father."

The man let the information sink in and watched as the color drained out of Nathan's face. Reaching into his coat pocket he pulled out a handwritten card. Along with the street location in New Bedford, was a name, Sylvia Medeiros.

"Here's where they live if you're interested. He flipped the card on the table and just as suddenly was up and gone from the room. It took a while before Nathan picked the card up.

Finally rousing himself from the table, Nathan had already made a few decisions. No one would ever learn the circumstances of how and why Freeman Sears died aboard the *John Dwight*. That information Nathan would take to his grave. The other secret that would never come out was that Nathan's first grandson was a colored child growing up in a decaying section of New Bedford. More than Freeman's death as a criminal, this was something that shamed Nathan above all else. When he got back home, Nathan took the still crisp one-hundred-dollar bill from its hiding place. He put it in an envelope without a return address and addressed it to Sylvia Medeiros in New Bedford. The next day he drove to Hyannis and dropped it in the post office. It left the Cape on the evening train.

The Forest Fire

Washy stirred in his bed. It was about four in the morning and he could smell smoke. Looking from the window toward Eastham and Wellfleet, he saw a bright glow. He could hear stirring below in the kitchen. Obviously, Nathan had been awakened by the same smell. A big fire was burning down Cape.

When he came down, he saw his mother and father were fully dressed. "Looks like a good fire going down in Eastham," Nathan remarked. "They'll be needing people to go down there and help fight it. I just called over to the constable and he said that a train will be coming through a little after six this morning and men can hop on and ride out there to cut fire lines."

It was understood that every able-bodied man who could carry a shovel would be on that train. With just a few formal fire departments existing in 1927, most Cape Cod towns relied on volunteer manpower to handle the many woodland fires that always accompanied dry weather. This year had been drier than usual, and from what Nathan could judge by the glow to the east, the pine forest that covered much of the outer Cape was burning.

When the train arrived at the depot, about twenty men got on board. The same thing was repeated at the East Brewster station. At Orleans a much larger contingent clambered into the cars. Someone had brought an urn of hot coffee, and a lot of the men recognized friends they hadn't seen for some time. The train took on the atmosphere of an excursion to the county fair.

The fire was centered in South Wellfleet. A fire break had contained it somewhat near Le Counts Hollow, saving property in Eastham, but the worry was that the afternoon southwest wind would push the flames north into areas where people lived. The firefighters assembled at Brackett's store to get rides up to the lead edge of the blaze. Washy got into a truck with about ten other men and they headed north.

Just below Paine's Hollow the truck stopped. Flames were jumping between the crowns of pitch pines and the dry undergrowth was smoldering. The tar road itself was ablaze, and black smoke filled the air. A large man, face smudged with soot and wearing a torn shirt, came down the road toward them. "Any of you know how to operate a bulldozer? It's hot enough that we have to run the machines in shifts. You can't stay near the fire for more than fifteen to twenty minutes. We're trying to cut a fire break from where the railroad tracks cross the county road, over toward Gull Pond and the backside. If we can't stop it there, it will move into Truro."

Washy stepped forward and held up his hand. "I can run it. Take me up there and I'll do it." The others looked at him. Washy was the only volunteer. It didn't matter that he had never been on a bulldozer in his life.

The man who had sought volunteers pointed Washy toward a truck. "Sam Holway's going up there, get in with him."

At a clearing off Gull Pond Road, they found a crew working with three bulldozers. Some of the men were felling trees with axes, trying to open a break to prevent the fire from crossing the road. The bulldozers, all Holt model 60s, were scraping away the underbrush and pulling stumps. One of the operators slid down from his machine and came toward Washy and Sam Holway. "Who's going to take over?" he asked. Washy nodded and headed toward the bulldozer, which thankfully was still running. He climbed up and noticed that the metal frame of the machine was hot to the touch. A water bag was slung next to the controls. "Don't drink it," shouted the man who had just gotten off. "Slosh it on the hand controls every once in a while to keep yourself from getting burned. There are no brakes. Use the track levers to stop. Keep your eye on your watch. Fifteen minutes max and you're off." The man disappeared in the smoke.

Washy assessed the control levers. Two controlled the tracks. There was an accelerator lever to move the machine. The front blade was raised and lowered by still another horizontal lever. Gingerly, Washy engaged the left and right tracks simultaneously and pushed the accelerator lever. The bulldozer moved forward. He discovered that he could change direction by stopping one track and letting the other continue. Hopefully he wouldn't need reverse. He had no idea how to back up. The blade initially went down too hard and the machine spun momentarily. Washy pulled it up so it had about a foot of clearance. The big machine once again lurched ahead.

Twice Washy rammed the blade into a large oak stump, almost stalling the machine. He never looked at his watch and was surprised to see his relief standing out ahead of him and waving through the smoke.

"Hey, man! You've been running that dozer for about a half hour. Time to get down and take a break. I told you, fifteen minutes max."

Washy climbed off the machine and headed to the relief station. He'd scraped maybe fifty yards of material from where he'd started. It must have been good enough, because no one said anything to him while he took a brief rest before mounting another dozer.

The fire crews worked into the early evening. By midnight, it was clear that the worst was over. What was left of the blaze south of the fire break eventually burned itself out. A few trucks came over around noon with sandwiches and cold drinks. It was the first food that Washy had seen in more than twenty-four hours.

As Washy sat on a log eating his lunch, a man came over and joined him. The stranger put his hand out and smiled. "Nice job you did there with the dozer. It made a big difference to the rest of the boys having you pitch in like that. Where are you from?"

"I'm glad I could help. I'm from Brewster."

"You've never been on a dozer before, have you."

"Was it that obvious?" Washy looked sheepishly at the stranger. "How'd you even know with all that smoke around? I figured no one would be paying much attention."

The man chuckled. "Well, for starters, you never put the dozer in reverse the whole time. And you always went to a machine that was running." He smiled and pulled a cigarette from his shirt pocket, offering it to Washy. "I'm from East Orleans. Name's Sparrow Higgins. What's yours?"

A New Friend

Sparrow Higgins turned out to be the owner of a small construction company. He was ten years older than Washy and had served in the war. Unlike Freeman, Higgins had been sent overseas in the spring of 1918 and was in the final allied push that led to the November armistice. After returning home he'd purchased a couple of Graham half-ton trucks and started to do work extending the electrical lines on the Cape. When not doing this, Higgins had his crews digging sand and spreading it on cranberry bogs. A state program of ditching the marshes to get rid of mosquitoes offered more work. Occasionally he was called to put in a foundation for a new home. A new airport in Hyannis was being developed and Higgins had a piece of that, too.

Washy was surprised to learn that Higgins still lived with his mother in a house on Barley Neck Road. "I got married when I came home from the war," he explained. "Within a year, we pretty much knew that it was a mistake. When she asked if I'd let her go, I didn't make much of a fuss. My father had died in the meantime so I moved back in with my mother and I've been there since."

In the weeks and months following the fire, the two men spent a lot of time together, becoming good friends. Sparrow showed Washy how to operate every piece of equipment that he owned. His young pupil was a quick study, and in time the older man came to rely on Washy as one of his best workers. With many Cape roads becoming macadamized, Washy went on jobs from Yarmouth to Wellfleet. Sometimes, when working on the outer Cape, he stayed with Sparrow and the two played cribbage late into the night, talking about life over cigarettes and coffee. Higgins introduced Washy to places like Jacob's Garden in the woods of Chatham and the Owl Inn in South Harwich, where, if a man such as Sparrow Higgins was known to the owners, he could get a drink and spend time with some local women who made friendly introductions of their own. It was all a very new world for Washy, who admitted to himself that it was a world he liked very much indeed.

"I can't believe you never went to a place like the Owl Inn before," Higgins said to Washy as they drove back to Orleans late one spring night. "Don't they have establishments like it in Brewster?"

"Well, sure they do," replied Washy, looking across the front seat at his friend, who was having a hard time keeping the car on the right side of the road. "But most of 'em are operated by my relatives, and they cater mainly to out-of-towners. Like we are when we're in Harwich. Nobody in Brewster would ever go in one of those places in the same town. You'd never go to the Owl Inn if it was in Orleans, would you? Everybody'd know you. So Brewster is off limits for kicking up my heels. I don't want to have to do any explaining to my parents."

Sparrow slowed the car. "By gorry, you're right, Washy. I hadn't ever thought of it quite like that. I guess it wouldn't seem right to be in church on Sunday and seeing the girls that we'd been diddlin' the night before. I'd catch the Devil enough from mother if she knew I was sneaking off with you to raise hell in the woods of Harwich. Guess it's better to be out-of-towners."

The Indian

On one of those fine late fall afternoons when Cape Cod provides an excuse for artists to get outside with a fresh canvas, Washy was finishing up a foundation hole for a new house on Indian Neck in Wellfleet. The excavation was pretty much completed when Frannie Cash, who was loading a truck with stumps, ran up waving his arms.

"Stop! Stop! There's something on the edge of the pit." Cash pointed to a corner that had just come loose as the blade of the steam shovel had scraped through.

"What is it?" Washy looked down at the wide-eyed truck driver.

"Bones! Lots of 'em! And a human skull! Someone's buried here!"

Washy slid awkwardly through the sand to the bottom of the pit. Half suspended in the debris near the top of the excavation were some obvious human remains. The intact skull, its hollow sockets embedded with clay, was canted slightly over on its side, its teeth clearly visible. What looked to be the long bones of the individual's lower legs were tucked up close to the skull.

It was clear to Washy that the bones hadn't gone in the ground recently. A closer examination showed some arrowheads and what looked like a stone pestle near the skull. Washy surmised that these items had probably been placed near the grave by the individual's friends to accompany the deceased on his final journey to whatever spirit world awaited him.

"Looks like we've hit an Indian grave." Washy pointed to the remains as Cash reluctantly came down into the pit for a closer look. "I uncovered one like this about a year ago in Harwich."

"Shouldn't we call the town constable?" Cash was hanging back, hesitant about getting too close to the bones. "Suppose you're wrong? One of the Holbrook boys went missing about eight months ago over near Crowell's cranberry bog. Supposedly he was trying to hijack some bootleg whiskey from a truck parked in the woods. A friend who was with him said that some men came out of a nearby barn and shot at them. The two split up and he never saw Holbrook again."

Washy shook his head "This ain't no hijacker body, Frannie. Look at the bones. They're old and yellowed. And there's no sign of any clothing, not even shoes. The bootleggers wouldn't have taken the time to strip Holbrook naked. And if he'd just been wounded, he would've stayed by the road hoping someone would come by. Besides, the bones were about two feet under the surface of the ground. I'm telling you it's an Indian grave. We've got to call Sparrow."

Cash headed to South Wellfleet to use a phone at Dave Butekin's store. Washy had made it clear that Cash should keep his voice down and say nothing to anyone about what they had stumbled onto.

Higgins arrived an hour later. By now, the shadows were long and a flashlight was needed to illuminate the grave. As the beam of light hit it, the skull seemed to leer at the three men. Cash came up with an excuse to climb out of the pit to make sure his truck was all right.

Once Higgins got a look at the bones, he agreed that it was an Indian grave and not the first that he'd come across, either. "Jesus, Washy, this is a problem. We'd have been better off if it had been the Holbrook kid. In that case, the constable would just have come up here with the medical examiner and identified the body and taken it away for an autopsy. With Geronimo here, we've got something else entirely. If we let anyone know that we've uncovered an Indian grave, we'll have all kinds of people up here, archaeologists, historical commissioners, and people like Professor Willoughby from Harvard. You remember him from the Indian burial that Sam Harding stumbled over in Chatham last summer? Willoughby will quarantine the job site and start looking around for artifacts. There'll be more digging, and a hell of a lot of egghead types running all over our foundation hole. The man that has hired us to do this job won't be happy if we tell him that his house project is going to be set back six months. And we don't get paid until the job is done."

"So what should we do?" Washy looked at his friend.

"We're going to rebury this guy in a new hole that we'll dig in another part of the property. We'll tell nobody, and we can keep to our schedule.

Geronimo will never know the difference and that will be that. Cash will keep quiet about it if he wants to keep working for me."

As Higgins moved to leave the pit, Washy put a hand on his friend's shoulder. "You got any problem if I take the bones and get rid of them myself?"

Higgins turned, a surprised look on his face. "What is it, Washy? Feeling sentimental? When his Indian friends put him in the ground he was set for eternity. Just because we disturbed his sleep by accident doesn't make us the bad guys. Let's just stick him back in the ground up the hill from here. He'll have a better view of the happy hunting ground."

"I don't know, Sparrow," Washy replied. "I'm thinking I'd like to bring the bones to Brewster and bury them there. My brothers and I used to find arrowheads near our house. There must have been a lot of Indians at one time living all up and down the Stony Brook Valley. I'm thinking that in a way, burying him there would be sort of like bringing him home to his own people. I guess what I'm saying is I don't like leaving him out here alone and forgotten."

"You're something else, Washy. You're going to make a Wellfleet Indian into a Brewster Indian just because you don't want him buried alone? Who's going to remember him anyway, wherever he gets buried? But go ahead if you want to. Means nothing to me." Higgins crushed the stub of his cigarette into the sand and climbed out of the pit.

Washy followed Higgins up the sandy incline to the steam shovel for a box to gather what was left of the Native American's remains. "I'll remember him, Sparrow. And maybe that will be good enough."

Using a flashlight, Washy carefully removed all of the bones that he could find and placed them in a box with the skull on top. He put the arrowheads in his pocket. The white quartz points were still sharp. The next morning in a light rain, Washy and Nathan dug a hole on a pine-covered rise overlooking Cobb's Pond. They positioned the Indian in the ground facing toward the east. Washy situated the arrowheads around the bones and then scattered all the ones that he and David had collected across the slope. It seemed, he thought, a much better place for them than in a forgotten box in the attic. Neither of the two men said a word as they carried out their task. As they left the new grave and walked back up to the house, a gentle wind came out of the west pushing the clouds toward Indian Neck and the Wellfleet shore.

Meadowlands Realty Trust

With no set schedule and David making only rare appearances from his home in Chatham, Nathan was now pretty much left on his own. Clara, the youngest, finished high school in 1927 and went to secretarial school in Boston. Now she lived in Quincy and worked for an insurance company, only returning to Brewster on holidays. Nathan continued with the weirs during the 1920s when prices were good enough to make it worthwhile. He'd even had a partner for a few years and they worked two traps off Saint's landing. Now it was 1930 and the national economic decline had cut the demand for fish. For the first time in as long as he could remember, Nathan hadn't set out his poles and nets. At age fifty-six, he was not a young man, but he didn't feel any constraints in his daily routine. Since Mary's death the year before, he'd kept to himself, not wishing to be greeted by the inevitable round of sympathizers dispensing advice about how he should live now that he was a widower.

On a Wednesday morning he stopped at the post office to pick up his mail. Postmaster Tom Ellis pushed a letter across the marble counter top toward him.

"Here you go, Nathan. This is the seventh letter I've given out today with the same return address on it. I think there's a few more that still need picking up. Looks like a bunch of you people down by the water have some attorney friends in Boston."

Nathan took the letter and noted the address in the upper left corner:

Lynch, McKinnon & Doyle
Attorneys at Law
55 State Street
Boston, Massachusetts

As Nathan turned to leave, several men who had been gathered around the stove followed him to the door.

"Ain't you going to open it, Nathan?"

"When I get home, boys, when I get home. I've got plenty enough time to read my mail. I'm not doing much else these days."

In truth, Nathan was as curious about the letter as everyone else. Correspondence from a Boston law office was not something that came regularly into anyone's mailbox in Brewster. It hadn't surprised Nathan that people were wondering what was in it. As he got down by the old Cobb place, he pulled his car over. He sliced open the envelope to find a typed letter on plain dove-gray paper, heavy bond with a blue embossed letterhead, the same as the one on the outside of the envelope.

October 22, 1931
To Mr. Nathan Sears et ux.

We are currently representing Meadowlands Realty Trust, a land developing company with offices in Buzzards Bay, Massachusetts. We are contacting you and a number of other property owners relative to parcels of woodland, brush land, beach upland, thatch and salt meadows and flats that are within certain boundaries of the town of Brewster, Massachusetts. It is our contention that the titles to these properties are in question based on our interpretation of the 1628 laws of proprietorship as promulgated by the Plymouth Colony. It is our intent to file suit in the state land court to determine the actual ownership of these properties.

As you may have an interest in these matters that relate to specific pieces of property, this letter will serve as notice of our intent to pursue our client's claims related to these said properties. Should you have questions about this matter, you are urged to contact our offices at the above return address or you may telephone us at Bigelow 8-R3. If you do not respond to this letter, we will assume that you will not be contesting our clients' claims to properties described in the above named petition and that any claims that you might make at some future date related to these properties, will therefore be null and void.

The letter was signed by Walter McKinnon, PC.

Nathan initially thought to crumple the letter up and throw it out the window. Similar letters had flooded the Cape during the land boom of 1925 and 1926. But there was something in this notification that made him hesitate to get rid of it. How, he wondered, could anyone think it possible to make a legitimate claim against land titles that had been recorded and passed on to generations of families for more than three centuries? It seemed ridiculous. And yet, Nathan suspected that this was a serious effort by some person or group to use an obscure colonial statute to initiate a large-scale land grab. It wasn't something that could be ignored.

Perhaps less than ten minutes after he arrived back at Sears Point, Nathan's phone started ringing. The subject of conversation was all about the notifications that had been received by almost a dozen people who owned land between the county road and the shore. By the end of the day, the recipients of the letters agreed it would be a good idea to sit down with Ralph Wilshire, an attorney in West Brewster. Wilshire had also received one of the notices. The attorney told everyone who called that he needed a day or two to do some background checking before he could be a source of any advice. Everyone who'd been addressed by Lynch, McKinnon & Doyle agreed to meet at Wilshire's house on the following Friday afternoon.

The Attorney

Nathan arrived at Ralph Wilshire's house and found a dozen worried individuals who were sitting or standing around the attorney's living room. Wilshire was originally from Brockton, where he had been a longtime partner in a small law firm. Almost seventy, it had been his intention to retire in obscurity and pursue the life of a country gentleman. Wilshire had amassed enough money to live comfortably and he looked forward to raising flowers and playing a bit of golf. His wife had immersed herself in the fundraising efforts of the East Dennis Ladies Aid Society and was a volunteer in the church swap shop. Initially, the couple avoided local politics, not even attending town meeting. But in time, Wilshire found himself being called on to provide legal services to local people who, once they knew there was a lawyer living there, "just happened by." They'd pull into his yard while he was pruning his lilacs and ask advice about wills, property transfers, even a divorce or two. There appeared to be all manner of small-town legal issues that had been hanging fire since before Wilshire's arrival.

As these interruptions to his leisure time became more frequent, Wilshire hung a sign outside to better channel the flow of potential litigants. It read: "Ralph B. Wilshire, Esq. Office hours 10 a.m. to Noon, Tuesdays and Thursdays." Somehow, either the calendars of his fellow townsmen were different from the one that he was using, or the days of the week made no difference. Wilshire found himself answering questions of the law just about every day except Sunday. Brewster residents seemed to have no legal troubles on the Sabbath.

As his reputation for fair and reasonable dealings grew, the retired attorney became a respected figure in his adopted town. The year before, he had been asked to run for town meeting moderator. After being unanimously elected, Wilshire conducted the forty-two article warrant without a flaw, all the while maintaining his authority as well as a sense of humor when faced with cod-booted fishermen who tried to second their own motions or cranberry growers who rose to points of order that made no sense. He was frequently consulted by the selectmen on matters of town policy. In point of fact, Wilshire was an unelected and unpaid town counsel. Nevertheless, he admitted to himself that he enjoyed his new role in town affairs and was pleased that his neighbors held him in such high regard. His wife took to calling him "the mayor," never in public of course, and told her old friends in Brockton that her Ralph had just about become one of Brewster's town fathers.

"I think we have all the interested parties here." Wilshire looked around the room. "I've been on the phone with several of my attorney friends in Boston. I'm told that Lynch, McKinnon & Doyle specialize in property law. They are well known as a firm that will file suit in state land court to help clients resolve unclear land titles. They are currently working with a gentleman from Rhode Island who is a title searcher of properties around New England. The name's Sebastian J. King. He's behind this Meadowlands Realty Trust Company that is mentioned in the letter we all received.

"King has spent the last few years going over records from the old Plymouth Colony. From these he's concluded that when the first parcels of land were allotted in the 1630s they were given to a group of men known as the proprietors. The earliest Cape Cod towns, Sandwich, Barnstable and Yarmouth, were started when the Plymouth court established a committee of proprietors who would have control of lands in these towns. These associations were something like common law corporations and their purpose was to secure development of settlements beyond Plymouth and to promote trade.

"The members of these corporations ran everything and decided who could settle within the town's boundaries. As people moved in and the land was divided up, the corporation members continued to hold shares in the so-called "common lands," mostly undivided shore pasture, salt meadow, and flats. For years, townspeople used these common lands to pasture animals and for haying. The land was never taxed as long as the public was allowed to use it. And it never was an issue when towns were made up of just a few hundred mostly related people.

"King claims that the rights of those early proprietors were never given up, and he's going to try and prove in court that the descendants of these associations still hold title. According to him, even when the Plymouth Colony ceased to exist, the heirs of the original proprietors never formally surrendered their interests in whatever undivided land remained in the towns. He's put together a group of people who can trace their lineage back to the original proprietors. They've agreed to sign over their shares to him as sole agent for the land court suit. Presumably, if he wins the case he'll take title to the land and pay off each of the members of the re-formed proprietary committees in proportion to how many shares they can prove they owned. I suspect they won't get much. It's a neat little scheme and it has the support of many town boards of selectmen because it would put land that is presently off the tax rolls back on them."

Listening to the attorney, it was clear to Nathan that should Sebastian J. King prevail in land court, his longtime use of the flats to set out his weirs could be in danger. Nathan's earliest ancestor was not one of the original proprietors. Richard Sears, "the Pilgrim," hadn't arrived on Cape Cod until 1643. And he hadn't been granted the status of freeman until 1652.

"Ain't there something called adverse possession – squatter's rights?" Nathan looked hopefully toward the attorney. "Some of us have families that've passed these lands down for hundreds of years. And we've got deeds to back us up."

Wilshire nodded. "I suspect that this is true, Mr. Sears. And I wouldn't doubt that you do have papers that show ownership. I'd guess, however, that they don't go back any further than 1827. That was the year that the county courthouse burned and with it went most of the land records. All land transfers after that, if they were even recorded at all, have murky titles. They have always been open to challenge because of the often vague references that were made to outline a property. King is hoping to convince a judge that none of the land could be conveyed legally to an individual without the consent of the proprietors or their heirs."

Wilshire continued. "I understand your concerns, gentlemen. Some of you have been on this ground your entire lives. You have deep roots in this land. Unlike all of you who were born here, I chose to move to Brewster and make it my home. I could have gone to a number of other places, but I decided that I'd like to finish my days here, not that I'm in a hurry to do so, mind you. I've been more content here than any other place I've ever lived in my entire life. My wife feels the same way. And now, just like you, I'm faced with dealing with someone who threatens all this. I can tell you, I don't like it any more than you do. I'm going to do my best to fight this land scheme."

His speech ended, the room erupted in applause. The assembly broke up, and Wilshire's house emptied quickly as the men headed home. Within a very short time, Brewster's self-appointed St. George, would-be slayer of dragons, and now a possible king, was alone in a deserted parlor.

The Proprietors

Over the next months, Ralph Wilshire was on the early train from Brewster to Boston several days a week. He availed himself of the Harvard Law Library where he immersed himself in the complexities of property law. He was referred by several attorney friends to a number of precedents that had similar application to the case he was preparing to argue. As a courtesy, Wilshire alerted Lynch, McKinnon & Doyle that he would be the contesting attorney in the case. They had no objection and had even offered to supply him with drafts of the colonial land agreements on which they were basing their argument. It was clear that they were confident that Wilshire wouldn't find anything that might jeopardize what they saw as an airtight case in their favor.

But the attorney was learning a great deal about the land apportionment that had been practiced in the first years of the Plymouth Colony. The early towns were not civil communities, but essentially private corporations run for the benefit of the principal stockholders, the local proprietors who had been granted land by the court. One of the things that became clear in his research was that proprietors had been resented by the growing influx of new settlers in the towns. Would-be entrepreneurs believed that the proprietors had too much power and were restricting trade and growth. They formed an alliance with people who wanted the common lands divided up and sold off. Some of the land was parceled out over the first century.

Perhaps because they saw themselves as landed gentry with their patents linked to British crown grants, many proprietors supported the British during the American Revolution. With independence, these loyalists had their land confiscated. Even some of the proprietors who had backed the Patriot cause saw their properties taken by eminent domain at the end of the war. That land, too, was divided up and sold. What remained open and undivided was meadow and pasture situated mainly along the shorefront. It was considered of little value and thus stayed in common use without taxation for almost two centuries. Over time, the proprietors' meetings ceased and their interests and whatever rights they once had were largely forgotten. By the late nineteenth century, few Cape people were sure of what they owned. But land was still conveyed and passed on to family members and individuals despite the uncertainty of its provenance. A lot of people didn't bother to register land at all, especially wood lots, because they didn't want to pay the taxes on it. It didn't matter in a time when the Cape's population was in a steady decline. It was often hard to even give land away.

During his research, Wilshire came across a land court case that was very similar to the one he was preparing. *Brown v. Sudbury* had many of the same arguments in a petition based on earlier colonial claims. The case had gone to land court, where it had been dismissed as having no merit. The judge ruled that though the plaintiff had established links to ancestral proprietors, the concession had lapsed out of disuse and transfer. To Wilshire, the Brown case was almost a mirror image of King's argument in the Meadowlands Realty Trust suit. It wasn't surprising that Lynch, McKinnon & Doyle had neglected to mention it. He suspected that they never figured a small-time lawyer would ever find the case. But in *Brown v. Sudbury*, Wilshire knew he had the key to blocking Sebastian J. King's petition for a valid land court decision. Several weeks later when he received correspondence from the court asking if he was ready for the case, he responded quickly that he was.

The Hearing

The actual petition, case number 12909, *Sebastian J. King, Trustee v. Ralph B. Wilshire* and others, was given a hearing in late March of 1932. Interest in the land suit brought reporters from several of the Cape Cod weekly newspapers, including the *Barnstable Patriot* and the *Yarmouth Register*. About twenty people from Brewster, Dennis, and Yarmouth watched from the gallery. The attorneys from Lynch, McKinnon & Doyle attempted to establish that the 1638 land grant to Anthony Thacher, Thomas Howes, and John Crowe, as the proprietors in Yarmouth, was a property arrangement made to a de facto corporation headed by these three individuals.

Because it was chartered as a British corporation, they argued that it was protected by the Treaty of 1794 and had never parted with its title to the lands in question. King's lawyers claimed that the corporation was not affected by later statutes and that only descendants of the three original proprietors could alter the terms of the parent corporation. Along with information relating to the Plymouth Court Records from 1638 to 1692, a list of descendants of Howes, Thacher, and Crowe was also submitted to Judge Charles Davis along with documents showing the assignment of their proprietary rights to Sebastian J. King.

When Wilshire's turn came, he rose slowly and looked first across at the petitioner's counsel. He then turned and acknowledged the magistrate. "Your Honor, you have just heard a most eloquent disposition presented by my learned colleagues on the other side of the aisle. Indeed it was brilliant and the result of much work and effort. But with all due respect for the earnestness of their quest to establish the validity of their client's petition, it is my contention that their claim of valid title to the lands in question is unfounded and, in fact, devoid of any legal proof."

Over the next forty-five minutes, Ralph Wilshire broke down the petitioner's argument into the simplest of terms and demolished it. He made frequent references to the *Brown* case and its dismissal several years earlier. The original land grant, he told the judge, was not to the proprietors as a corporation but rather had been made to the "first comers" as tenants in common. Wilshire argued that these tenants in common eventually became a quasi-corporation under the statute of 1686 and that they subsequently set off and divided all of their lands. He further argued that under the provisions of 1790, the corporation ceased to exist as a body politic and that no land rights were vested in their assignors. The release of rights from individuals in the Meadowlands Realty Trust group who were connected to the original proprietors was therefore invalid. "To accept the petitioner's claim that some descendants, even if they did have blood ties to the original proprietors, still have property rights to the lands in question is purely a speculative conjecture. There is certainly precedence in this case that should ease any difficulty for this court in rendering the petitioner's attempt to prove title to be null and void. I ask that the suit be dismissed."

It was a surprisingly short summation, and when Wilshire sat down, several observers in the gallery half suspected that the attorney was just pausing to catch his breath before continuing. But he remained seated. Judge Davis waited a moment to see if there were any additional arguments, and then he announced that he would take the case under advisement and render a decision in a few weeks.

In May of 1932, the ruling in the case of *Sebastian J. King, Trustee v. Ralph B. Wilshire and others*, was announced. Judge Davis mentioned the difficulty of unraveling ancient land claims and acknowledged that the subject was something better handled by tercentenary scholars. He did, however, agree that earlier cases, particularly *Brown v. Sudbury*, had influenced his decision. The petition was dismissed.

The news of Judge Davis's ruling was met with much satisfaction by those who had assumed that access to untitled land was, and always had been, theirs. Wilshire became something of a hero in his adopted town, and when he went to the post office or into the general store to get his newspaper, he was greeted by regulars as "Mayor Wilshire." Even his wife now used the term openly. In the weeks following the successful conclusion of the suit, Wilshire added "Wednesday 1 p.m. to 3 p.m." to the office hours on the sign outside his house, but people still showed up on Mondays and Fridays anyway.

Wilshire's efforts in vanquishing Sebastian J. King's land claim proved, in the long run, a hollow victory. Brewster residents continued to use the beaches and marshlands jointly for fisheries and pasturage. But over the years as the land used for these purposes steadily declined, the claim was made by some that it no longer should carry a tax exempt status. Towns began to recognize that beachfront property had value for developers.

Encouraged to add property to the tax rolls, title searchers and land brokers, many of them town hall insiders, assembled shorefront parcels and moved to secure clear title. Much of the land was taken by eminent domain and sold off. Brewster was left with just a few town landings, most of which had less than three hundred feet of beach frontage. Within several decades, just about all of the once-open land that had been used in common for centuries was forever rendered inaccessible, as non-resident property owners restricted public access.

Justine Westcott

When Prohibition ended in December of 1933, Brewster, like every Cape Cod town except Wellfleet, moved quickly to allow the sale of alcohol in package stores. At the 1934 spring town meeting, the town joined the wet category by a narrow 151 to 136 vote.

A number of bars and saloons opened up on the south side of the Cape. Young people danced at the Mill Hill Pavilion in West Yarmouth and then migrated over to Main Street in Hyannis to close out the evening. Summer weekends saw hundreds of cars lining the area from the Hyannis railroad depot all the way to the west end of the village.

On a steamy July evening in 1937, Sparrow and Washy drove over to Young's Restaurant on Main Street in Hyannis. Several of Sparrow's friends came in and noisily headed into the bar. Washy wanted to order a sandwich in the restaurant section of the eatery and said he would join them later. There was a take-out counter in the front room and when Washy finally reached the front of the line, he found himself face to face with perhaps the most attractive young woman he had ever seen in his life.

"What would you like, sir?" The woman smiled at him.

Looking at her, it took a moment for Washy to refocus on the needs of his stomach before he could reply. "I want to get something to take into the bar. Can you make me a bacon, lettuce, and tomato sandwich?"

"Wait just a minute," she replied. "It's pretty late and there may not be any bacon left. Let me check with the kitchen."

As she turned and pushed open the door to the back room, Washy couldn't help but notice that the rest of the young woman was as well-turned-out and appealing as her face.

"Cook says that he hasn't got any bacon. Would you take a slice of ham instead?"

"That'll be fine," Washy smiled back at her. "And will it come with blue eyes?"

"Blue eyes? What do you mean?"

"I mean, would you bring the sandwich out here and sit with me while I eat it?"

A blush of pink moved to the young woman's cheeks. "I'm sorry, I've got another half hour until my shift ends." Her rejection of Washy's request was not, however, unfriendly, but more like an advisory guideline that seemed to offer some hope.

"That's fine with me," Washy pushed his money across the counter. "I'll just sit over there at that table and eat real slow."

Thirty minutes later, the girl came over to where Washy was finishing up his sandwich.

"Is this seat taken?" She looked down at him. "I'm through for the night."

"I think there may be some room unless you've got a bunch of friends that plan to join us."

"No," she replied as she sat down at the small table. "All my friends are at the Idlehour watching a movie. I got stuck with the evening shift and I'm about to walk home."

He offered her a drink but she refused. "I'm not supposed to drink in here. The boss says he doesn't want his girls drinking with customers. It's policy."

"Maybe we could go somewhere else that wouldn't make the boss unhappy."

"Well there is a place up the street where we go after work. It's on my way home. The bartender knows me and can get us seats even when it's crowded. Do you mind walking?"

After ducking into the bar and letting Sparrow know that he was going to be around the corner, he rejoined the girl in the lobby.

"So you don't live in Hyannis?" She seemed surprised that he wasn't a local.

No, I'm from Brewster, over on the bay side. I come in to Hyannis once in a while to see the city."

"I don't think I've ever been to Brewster. It's pretty far down Cape, isn't it?" They were out on the sidewalk and walking together in the warm night. "What do you mean, city?" she looked at him. "Do you think Hyannis is a city?"

Washy laughed. "Well, maybe not like Brockton or New Bedford, but it's got a lot more street lights than Brewster does. In my town, nothing is open after 6 p.m."

"Well, don't strain your neck looking at all the tall buildings," she laughed.

They entered the Mayflower, a fairly new establishment near the center of the village. The bartender saw the girl and motioned the two of them to a small table in a corner.

Almost immediately a young man brought over a drink and placed it in front of the girl. "Hi, Justine." The waiter made a flourish of polishing the table in front of the girl. "What can I get your friend?"

Washy asked for a beer.

"Here's to you, Justine." Washy held up his glass and saluted. "At least now I know who I'm having a drink with. Anything else go with Justine?"

"It's Justine Westcott," she replied. "And now that you know one of my secrets, who may I say is responsible for luring me into this place?"

Washy smiled and put down his glass. "Seems to me that it was the other way around." He reached across the table and took her hand. "Washy Sears. Pleased to be in your company, Justine."

The Schoolteacher

Washy learned over the next hour that Justine Westcott was a recent graduate of Lesley College and would be teaching elementary school in Yarmouth that fall. She'd taken the waitress job to keep busy before school started. She was from Stoneham, the only child of Albert Westcott, president of the American Can Company of Woburn. With her dark bobbed hair and perky look, Washy thought she could have graced the cover of *Colliers*.

She explained that before this summer she'd never been to the Cape before.

"We always took our summer vacations at Lake Winnipesaukee in New Hampshire where we have a cottage. I'd always heard about Cape Cod and wanted to see it for myself. When I got the call that there was an opening for a teacher in Yarmouth, I took the job sight unseen. It's quite a lively place."

"What you see right now is going to be very different in just a few months," Washy told her. "They really roll up the streets on the Cape after Labor Day. Even Hyannis is pretty quiet."

"Oh, that won't bother me." She waved to the young waiter to bring her another drink. "I'll have my work and my students. That'll keep me busy enough. And I'd like to think that with you I'll have my very own real Cape Codder – a person right out of a Joe Lincoln novel, to escort me around."

"So who would I be? Mr. Pratt, or Galusha the Magnificent?"

"Oh, I don't know. You seem more like Captain Eri Hedge. Wise enough to know that you need a woman around for a number of practical purposes, but strong enough to resist any kind of permanent ties." Her eyes looked at him impishly as she stirred the drink in her hand.

Washy laughed. "Captain Hedge eventually did get hooked by Mrs. Snow the housekeeper, if I recall the book correctly."

"But not until he was good and ready. And by then, he knew it was the right decision for him. Mrs. Snow had known it all along."

It was near one in the morning. As they exited the club, a horn sounded from across the street. It was Sparrow. His car held several girls and two young men that Washy had met before.

"Come on, Washy, let's ride down to Craigville Beach. There's a good moon and the tide's high. We'll all go swimming. Bring your friend."

Justine seemed reluctant, and Washy motioned Sparrow to go on without them.

"Meet me back here in an hour or so. I'll be out front of the theater when you come by."

Sparrow didn't waste any time trying to convince his friend and was quickly off in a rush down Main Street.

"I'll walk you home." Washy took Justine's arm. The two started headed toward North Street where she had an apartment with three other women. The evening was hot and there was hardly a breeze to cool things off.

"Maybe we should have gone for that swim, Washy," she said. "I don't think a fan is going to do much against this heat."

"There'll be plenty of time for the beach in the next few weeks," he reassured her. "The summer is just starting."

She matched his stride. The moonlight guided them through the now quiet streets. Squeezing his arm, the girl looked at him. "And I think I'm going to want it to last a long time."

Summer and "Justy"

Washy spent as much time as he could with the young schoolteacher that summer but their schedules didn't make their meetings easy. He worked during the day when she was off, while she was busy several nights a week at the restaurant. Still, they managed time together. By August they were regulars among the many couples parked along the Hyannis beachfront, watching the moon late into the night as it moved across Lewis Bay. To Washy she'd become "Justy." They shared their first kiss on one of those humid nights, and Washy drove home humming a tune they had danced to earlier that night at the Mill Hill ballroom.

As Labor Day approached, Justine mentioned that her parents were coming to the Cape for the weekend. "They are going to be staying in Osterville with some family friends and want me to meet them for dinner at the Wianno Club. Would you like to go with me?"

The posh Wianno Club was a long way from Sears Point geographically and light years away socially. While Washy felt comfortable in the company of some of Justine's college friends, he wasn't so sure about the idea of sitting at a table with Mr. and Mrs. Westcott.

"I don't know, Justy. Do you think your folks will be comfortable that you keep the company of a local clam digger?"

The girl laughed and squeezed his hand. "Remember, Washy, you are my Captain Eri, a man with dignity, a possessor of homespun wisdom and local charm."

On the appointed evening, Washy drove down Seaview Avenue in Osterville to where the Wianno Club sat perched above a sparkling strand facing Nantucket Sound. He parked his old Ford far enough away from the main entrance so he wouldn't have to endure the snickers of the young men who were parking some of the more expensive automobiles. When he entered the lobby with its polished floors, Washy was directed to the main dining room. Justine, her parents, and two other couples were already seated.

Everyone rose when Washy entered and Justine's father was the first to extend his hand. Washy took it firmly and was rewarded with an equally strong clasp. Washy was gentler with Mrs. Westcott, holding her small hands lightly for just a moment.

"Mr. Sears. It's a pleasure to meet you." Mrs. Westcott gushed. Washy took a seat across from Justine. Mr. Westcott smiled at Washy. "Justine tells us that you are in the construction business, a contractor, I believe."

"Well sir, I've constructed cranberry bogs, built foundations for houses, put in water lines, and helped clear cut a lot of forest across parts of the Cape so we could get electricity down here. Several years ago, I helped bring in some heavy stone to stabilize the beach right outside this building. Without it, the way the shore was wearing away, I suspect this club would by now have become a houseboat."

There was a bit of polite laughter from the group.

"And so you supervise all of this kind of work?" The question came from one of Mr. and Mrs. Westcott's friends.

"Not exactly," Washy turned toward the man. "I drive the trucks that deliver the stone and I operate the earth moving machines that dig the foundations. I go where my boss tells me to go."

From that point, with Washy's all-too-ordinary resume on the table, the dinner took on the atmosphere of a symphony performance where a guest conductor substitutes for the real maestro and the performance doesn't match audience expectations. The conversation shifted mainly between the Westcotts and their friends, and no further inquiries were directed toward the young man in the tight-fitting suit. At one point Justine tried to bring her guest back into the mix, mentioning Washy's long Cape Cod lineage.

"The Sears family is one of the oldest on Cape Cod," she interrupted her father and his two male friends, who were vigorously discussing how President Franklin Roosevelt was ruining the country. "They just about came over on the *Mayflower*."

"Actually, one of my ancestors *was* on the *Mayflower*," one mustachioed gentleman piped up. "Even you, I'm sure, Mr. Sears, must have heard of William Bradford."

At that point, if there had been any lingering doubts that Washy didn't belong in the company of these to-the-manor-born types, they vanished. He'd earlier attempted to talk with Mrs. Westcott about the play that he and Justine had seen at the Cape Playhouse. She'd told him that she and her husband had seen it in New York, and that she hadn't liked the lead character. "He seemed to be miscast. There was something that made him just not quite right for the part. It was like he was trying to be something that he was not." She shot a look at her daughter and continued. "Sadly, that seems to happen too often these days."

As dessert was being served, Washy stood and excused himself, explaining that he had to be at a job in Barnstable early the next morning. As he shook hands with Mr. Westcott and the other two men at the table, Washy looked directly at the one who had claimed William Bradford as an ancestor.

"Oh, I just thought of something. In Hyannis there's a hardware store near the railroad depot operated by some Bradfords, probably cousins of yours. You might drop in and make your acquaintance with that branch of your family. And while you're in the store," Washy continued, "you might take a look at my family's book."

"And what possibly would that be?" There was a condescending tone in the question.

Washy ignored the slight. "Even you, I'm sure, Mr. Bradford, must have heard of the Sears & Roebuck catalog. They are some of *my* people and I believe it's more popular than anything written by William Bradford. It's certainly in more homes around the country. And if you have trouble finding a copy, you could have your footman pick one up in just about any retail store." He turned and walked out alone to his car.

A Reconciliation

Washy didn't see Justine for more than a week after the Wianno Club fiasco. And he made no attempt to call her. Just before Labor Day he drove over to Young's for dinner. When Justine saw him come in, she avoided his table. Eventually, he went over to the counter.

"Is it time to talk, Justy?"

"I'm not sure there is much to say." She looked at him. "You insulted my father's friend and left me standing alone like a fool when you left the club. Have you come to apologize?"

"Actually, I did want to tell you I was sorry about how things turned out. But we both should have known that I wasn't the sort of young man that your parents and friends would have approved of. That Bradford fellow needed to be brought down a peg and I don't regret doing it."

"I wish you might have considered the position you put me in, Washy." Her eyes met his. "Those people are friends of my parents. And that makes them my friends as well. You embarrassed me."

For that, Washy was truly sorry and he told her so. For her part, Justine acknowledged that by inviting him, she'd set up a situation that was headed for disaster. She seemed to understand that he had been hurt.

After her shift they went for a drive through Centerville. The night was dark and the crickets sounded loudly through the open car windows. At one point, Washy noticed that Justine was crying. He reached over and took her hand.

"Oh, Washy, I did want my parents to like you and I'm sorry that it didn't work." The girl looked back at him, her eyes glistening. "I so wanted it to succeed because you have become very important to me. I shouldn't have been so thoughtless. I just forgot how different our worlds are, and that was wrong of me."

Washy parked the car at a turn-out under some pine trees. "Justy, if we are going to have a relationship that amounts to anything, we're going to have to make our own world together. We can't live in someone else's." He took her in his arms and held her tenderly.

"I know that is true, darling," she looked up at him. "But how do we erase where we come from? Can we just strip it all away as if it doesn't exist?"

The same question had been on Washy's mind all that summer. "I don't know, Justy. I don't know." And in that moment, he really didn't see any way their two worlds could ever coincide. The distance was too great. He held the first girl that he had ever loved, stroking her hair until her shoulders stopped heaving and then he drove her home to her apartment.

Fall

At the start of the school year, Justine took a room on Berry Avenue in West Yarmouth near the school where she would be teaching. Two other female teachers were already boarding there, and Mrs. Althea Crocker, the owner of the place, presided over their health and virtue as a sort of unofficial housemother and chaperone. Washy was never allowed past the parlor when he called on Justine, which he did as often as they could make the time together.

During the week, both of them were unfailingly busy. Washy continued to work for the mosquito control people, digging ditches to drain the tidal marshes on both sides of the Cape. Sometimes he worked in Barnstable, but he was occasionally called to work in Harwich and Chatham. He usually had supper with Nathan. David occasionally called to invite Nathan and Washy to his home in Chatham. Washy's older brother had two children, but he was engaged in deep sea scalloping and wasn't around all that much. Washy sensed that David's wife didn't like the fact that her husband was away so often, and there was an all too obvious tension between the two of them that made Washy uncomfortable. He began to make excuses to avoid the meetings, and after a while David stopped calling.

Justine had plunged into her first teaching assignment with enthusiasm. She had about thirty third graders packed into a classroom that was shared with another class. It was clear from the outset that Justine had found her calling.

The slower pace of fall on Cape Cod, despite Washy's warnings, was a surprise to Justine. She'd assumed that he was just exaggerating. In truth, there were few places open where the couple could go for entertainment. The roads were largely deserted, and most stores closed by five o'clock.

One Saturday afternoon in early October, Washy took Justine to a large cranberry bog. The harvest was underway and the Cape Verdean migrant workers, men, women, and children, were busy scooping the red berries and dumping them into boxes. There was a rhythm to their work as they moved across the bog.

"How quaint," Justine remarked, as Washy pulled the car off the road. "It's like a scene out of Currier and Ives. I didn't think people did this sort of thing anymore. My mother will be so amused when I tell her that I saw it."

"A lot of people around here still work on the land and on the sea,"

Washy told her. "It's how most of us live. These days, work of any kind is a good thing."

He guided the girl down a worn path onto the surface of the bog out of view of the distant pickers. Lifting Justine across the drainage ditch, Washy motioned her to come out on the bog.

"Sit down and see just how thick the berries are. This year's crop is supposed to be one of the better ones in years."

Justine ran her fingers into a vine cluster, pulling up a handful of the crimson fruit.

"Can I eat one?" She held a berry up to her mouth.

"Go ahead," Washy laughed. "I think you'll be surprised, though. They're not like strawberries."

The bitter taste of the berry caused Justine to make a face. "Oh, it's so tart!" She held the small fruit at arm's length. "How could something so sweet looking and beautiful end up leaving such a bad taste? It doesn't seem fair."

Washy told her that only the addition of lots of sugar made the cranberry palatable. "My mother used to make a mock cherry pie with cranberries. I think she used about a full cup of sugar to sweeten it up. Cranberries are deceiving. They look much better than they taste. As a matter of fact, a lot of things that look good on the outside end up surprising you when you get below the surface."

"Is that a statement of philosophy, or are you commenting on the fruit?" Justine looked seriously at him. The midday sun accented the blue of her eyes. It was clear that her question hadn't been put lightly.

"I'm not one for metaphors, Justy. You know that. It was just a comment about cranberries. I could say the same thing about huckleberries or beach plums."

But on the drive home, Justine occasionally looked over at Washy, who had been silent since they'd left the bog. She wondered if his words held a lot more meaning than he was willing to own up to.

The Judas Birds

Washy celebrated his thirtieth birthday in October. Clara came down from Quincy and brought a cake. Washy picked her up at the depot in Yarmouth Port. Clara, Nathan and a couple of the aunts helped Washy usher in the beginning of the fourth decade of his life with a nice midday dinner. David was at sea, but he'd sent a card. That evening, Washy drove to Justine's place in West Yarmouth, where Mrs. Crocker, probably in gratitude for his hanging her storm windows the previous week, had baked another cake for him. He shared it with Justine and her two roommates and then the couple drove to Cotuit when they attended a minstrel show in

Freedom Hall. A harvest moon made it almost seem like daytime as the couple returned to Berry Avenue.

When Thanksgiving came a few weeks later, Justine took the train to Boston to spend the holiday break with her parents. There was no talk of Washy joining the Westcotts in Stoneham, nor did he think to ask Justine to celebrate Thanksgiving with his family.

Thanksgiving, perhaps more than any other holiday, always took on the trappings of Old Home Week, as many former Cape Codders returned to visit with relatives they might not have seen for months or even years. Sons and daughters who had moved to the cities came home to visit their parents and extended families. The New York, New Haven and Hartford Railroad added special trains to accommodate the influx of people.

It was a tradition in the Sears family that the men would rise early on Thanksgiving morning and go duck hunting. Dawn was leaking through thick clouds as Washy followed Nathan and two of his uncles, Seleck Sears and Freeman Foster, down the sandy path to a duck blind near Paine's Creek. The bay opened before them, gray and calm in the windless morning, small breakers collapsing onto the wide beach. A light snow had fallen the night before, and the icy surface crunched underfoot as the men's boots made contact with the frozen ground. Their breath crystallized in the air.

The hunters were using live decoys that were hitched to a running line that led from the blind out to an anchored buoy some hundred and fifty yards off shore. The female ducks were tethered, but the drakes, their wings clipped, swam free nearby. They had been trained to stay near the supply of corn in the blind. As the tame birds quacked to each other, their noise attracted wild ducks that were flying up and down the beach. By nine o'clock, the four men had taken a dozen birds, including mallards, canvasbacks, and blacks. They started to make their way back up to the house through the dunes.

"Washy, where's that city girl of yours spending the holiday?" Uncle Freeman turned near the ridge and looked back toward his nephew. "She back with mother and father?"

Washy nodded at the older man. "Justine is in Stoneham. I think that she probably would have found our Thanksgiving celebration a bit too quaint. She likes her condiments in cut glass dishes with special ivory-handled spoons. That's not our style."

Freeman Foster paused for a moment and put his arm around Washy. He pointed back at the distant duck blind. "See them tame ducks of ours settin' out there honkin'? They're what hunters call Judas birds. They talk the same language as the ones that we just shot. But for some reason, they never tell the wild ones that it might not be a good idea to raft in with 'em. Ever wonder about that?"

Washy was momentarily puzzled, not sure where his uncle was going with the conversation.

"I'll tell you." The older man didn't wait for an invitation to continue. "It's because, while them ducks might all look the same on the outside, they come from different roosts. It's a class thing. The tame ducks have clean straw beddin', they're warm and get all the food they want, and live pretty much a stress-free life. All they have to do is sit out there and honk once in a while lookin' pretty. The common wild ducks who are workin' to stay alive can't resist just having a little look-see at how the other side lives. When they come in to gam with their fine cousins, it's where the trouble begins."

Washy smiled at the old whaling reference, still not sure where his uncle was going.

"What I'm saying, son, is when you dip your wing and fly toward a good lookin' bird, until you're real sure about what the landing's going to be like, always keep a weather eye open and some altitude between you and the ground. Otherwise the fall could end up real painful."

Uncle Freeman winked and patted his nephew on the shoulder and then followed the crest of the dune toward the house. Washy stood there for a moment and stared back at the line of still-tethered ducks as they quacked and paddled in the ebbing tide. The sun had succeeded in pushing through the grey overcast. He thought about what his uncle had just said and wondered if he had left himself enough altitude with Justine Westcott.

In Between Holidays

The weeks between Thanksgiving and Christmas flew by. One Saturday afternoon just before Christmas, Washy brought Justine to the flooded cranberry bog at Sears Point and they spent some time before dusk gliding on the frozen surface. As much as he fancied himself a competent skater, he was no match for Justine, who had taken lessons for years at the Boston Skating Club. He watched as she carefully traced figures on the ice, and marveled at her grace and balance. In that late December afternoon, Washy imagined that he was sharing the ice with a crystal angel.

Just before dark, Nathan showed up with coffee to watch the pair as they moved across the ice in the afterglow. A full moon was rising in the east.

"You two skate well together," Nathan called to the couple as they passed. "But Justine is a yacht to your barge, Washy." He laughed, watching his son struggle to keep up with the girl. "I'd say you lack that delicate touch. Why not let me have a try?"

Washy had never seen Nathan on skates, but he watched with amazement at how well his father managed on the ice. Nathan skimmed and darted the length of the bog, at one point linking arms with Justine in a delicate tandem that silhouetted the pair against the moon.

"I never told you, Washy, but that was how I courted your mother." Nathan stopped to take a breath by the edge of the bog, with Justine leaning against him. "There used to be a Saturday night bonfire on the edge of Schoolhouse Pond. I'd meet your mother when she came with her sisters. It was about the only place where the two of us could be alone for at least a few minutes." Nathan sat down at the bog's edge and took off his skates. "I'm going in to put on some supper." Before starting back to the house, he winked at his son. "If you're as smart as I think you are, Washy, maybe you'll take advantage of the same opportunity that I had way back then."

After supper, the three sat in the parlor in front of the warm hearth. Shadows rose and fell in the fire's glow. When Justine and Washy left, they were careful not to disturb Nathan, who had fallen asleep in his chair. Before getting into the car, they took a moment to gaze up at the millions of stars sparkling in the sky above. The moon, riding now between patches of jagged clouds, washed the nearby beach with a silvery light that seemed to dance on the waves. To the north, the flash of Cape Cod Light rhythmically matched its beacon with the one at Race Point. Only the steady roar of the surf broke the night solitude.

A Surprise Phone Call

Two days after Christmas, the phone rang at Sears Point. Virginia Consodine, the local operator, announced, "I have a call for Washington Sears. Is that gentleman available to receive it?"

Laughing, Washy replied, "Ginny, what's all this formal Washington Sears stuff? Who've you got on the other end, the president of the United States?"

"Mr. Sears," she continued, her voice still very formal. "I have a young lady from the Boston area who wishes to be connected with you. She's been trying to get through for some time now. Will you take the call?"

Virginia Consodine had been two years ahead of Washy in school and had even been sweet on David for a time. She certainly knew Washy, and she also knew that the sooner she could connect the two parties, the quicker she could spread the content of the conversation across town. Continuing the charade, she asked, "Will you take the call, sir?"

Of course, Ginny," Washy laughed. "Put her on." There was some not-so-subtle clicking on the line, as several members on the Sears party line also picked up.

"Washy, can you hear me? My parents are going to be away for the next few days. They are going to Newport to spend New Year's with friends. I've still got a week before I have to be back at school and I was wondering if you might come up and visit with me in Stoneham? We can take the train back to the Cape after New Year's."

Washy paused. He knew that to casually accept the offer would have every phone line in Brewster buzzing with news of his impending affair with a mysterious woman in the city.

"Are there any good hotels or boarding houses in Stoneham?" He asked. "I'll need a place to stay."

Justine was quick to pick up on the ploy, and she replied that there were indeed excellent accommodations at a place on Shorncliffe Avenue. "It's very nice and very close to where I am," she told him. "I can meet you at the train in Boston."

Washy said good-bye after agreeing to meet Justine, and was about to place the receiver in its cradle when he heard the operator's voice. "You can catch the 1:30 out of Hyannis if you hurry, Washy." There some muffled laughter from Virginia Consodine as the call ended and the line went dead. And it was the same with the connecting phone lines in three other houses.

Quickly packing a travel bag, he left a note for Nathan and placed it on a table in the parlor. He chuckled, noticing a Christmas card sent earlier in the week from Justine to Washy and Nathan. The return address on it was 79 Shorncliffe Avenue in Stoneham.

A Trip to the City

Washy caught the afternoon train out of Hyannis. At Sandwich, one of those boarding the train was a man that Washy knew from the previous spring when the two had worked briefly for the CCC camp in West Barnstable. Calvin Gill ambled over and sat down in a seat across from Washy.

"Hi, Wash!" Gill extended his hand. "Surprised to see you headed to Boston. I thought you didn't like leaving the Cape."

"My sister lives in Quincy and I've planned to visit with her for a couple of days. How about you, Cal? What's taking you to Boston?"

Gill said that he was looking to get a job working on a state project over in Falmouth. The man showed Washy a flyer from the Walsh Construction Company of New York advertising for workers to create a new military base on the upper Cape.

"The government bought a big tract of land for a national guard training base. More than twenty thousand acres, from what I'm told. Much of it is the old Coonamessett Ranch and the Bear Hollow Farm. Over the next couple of years, the land is going to be opened up for barracks and firing ranges. A crew has already cleared a lot of brush and put in some roads. It's a good opportunity for year-round work."

Washy had heard about plans to build a major military facility on the Upper Cape. The appropriations had been pushed through the state legislature in late 1935 by Massachusetts governor James Michael Curley. The state money had been supplemented by funds from the federal Works Progress Administration.

"So who do you have to see?" Washy asked his friend.

"The Charles T. Main Company is the engineering architectural firm. They've got an office on Devonshire Street. Same building where the people who are doing the hiring are located." Gill put the flyer back into his pocket. "You have to show that you've had experience and have the appropriate licenses. They put your application in with everyone else and the jobs get drawn at random. Someone in Washington was smart enough to know that without a blind draw, every job would have gone to some Boston Irishman. You know how Boston politics works. So I'm going to deliver my application in person. I don't trust the mail. People have told me that anything that goes through the South Boston post office addressed to the Main Company gets lost."

Washy wrote the address on a piece of paper and put it in his pocket.

Justine was on the platform at South Station, and when Washy stepped down from the train she rushed into his arms.

"Not bad," she looked at him. "Just an hour late. That's got to be some kind of a record for the Cape train." She released him for a moment and then took his arm as they headed off.

"I told the engineer that I had a very important engagement in the city," Washy chuckled. "And I added that it involved a very beautiful young lady. He made a special effort to speed up the train and get me here as quick as possible. Can't keep a pretty girl waiting, you know."

The couple made train and streetcar connections to Stoneham, arriving close to 8 p.m. There were about six inches of new-fallen snow and they held on to each other to keep from slipping during the walk up Shorncliffe Avenue from the trolley. The Westcott home was an imposing Tudor-style house with a high-arching black wood shingled roof and wraparound porch. Two stone lions flanked a gated driveway that led to a three-bay garage. From the street, its three levels seemed to command the neighborhood. Undoubtedly that was how Albert Westcott had designed it.

"So this is the boarding house you mentioned on the phone?" Washy smiled, gazing up at the imposing building.

"Yes, this is it. All this for just mother, father, and me. I think my parents planned for more children but I was the only one they came up with. It does seem like quite a waste of space. Come on, let's go in. It's cold out here."

Justine fixed a light supper of leftovers, and the two sat talking in the kitchen before moving into the parlor. The house was surprisingly cozy even with its twelve-foot ceilings. The Christmas tree, a large balsam fir that had been trucked in from New Hampshire, was still in place, festooned with many ornaments and lights. Justine recounted the Christmas Eve candlelight service at the nearby Episcopal Church and how everyone had come back to the house for eggnog. "It was so beautiful. I think I love Christmas more than any other time in the year."

Washy wondered what Justine would think about his own family traditions at Christmas. He, David, and Nathan would cut a swamp cedar near Cobb's pond and then drag it up to the house to be decorated by his mother and sister with strings of cranberries and popcorn. There were no hymns and no eggnog. Most of the presents were practical things like mittens and sweaters, made by Washy's mother or his aunts. A new pair of boots was a prized gift.

The parlor clock struck eleven times, and Justine eased herself from under Washy's arm and stood up. She put out the tree lights and came back to where he sat.

"One thing I didn't tell you, Washy." She had a half-smile on her face. "We have six bedrooms, but four of them are not made up. My mother and father's room is closed while they are in Newport. There is only my room left. You could sleep with me if you like. Of course, if you prefer the couch, I can get you some blankets." She started up the stairs to her bedroom.

Washy wondered if this was the picture that Virginia Consodine and the rest of the listeners on his party line had conjured up earlier. Did they envision that he would be weighing a choice between a parlor couch with a Christmas tree for company or a warm bed filled with an even warmer Justine Westcott? Concluding that to disappoint their fantasies would be the height of neighborly irresponsibility, Washy moved quickly from the couch, picked up his travel bag, and headed up the stairs.

A Cold Winter

The winter of 1938 was one of the coldest on record. The ice covered much of Cape Cod Bay. Pipes froze and freshly washed shirts and pants pinned out on clotheslines to dry had to be hit with a mallet to get them into baskets. Because he wasn't working much because of the weather, and because there was no full-time custodian, Washy spent a lot of time at Justine's school tinkering with the balky coal heater and trying to plug holes in the window sills.

It was a day in early April, and a cold rain was pounding the side of the old school building. Washy had arrived early and was attempting to stuff some matting into the seams of the tin ceiling to keep the water out of the hallway when Justine came in. She hung her coat on a peg and called to him excitedly.

"Washy, I have the most wonderful news. I've been hired for a new job.

It's in Brockton. In the last few months I've sent applications to several cities, and my evaluations must have impressed the superintendent in Brockton because he called yesterday afternoon with an offer that has a nice increase in salary. It's an experimental school and I'll be in charge of several teachers and two grade levels."

The announcement was a complete surprise to Washy. There hadn't been any previous mention that Justine had plans to move. "Justy, you mean you will be leaving the Cape? You're not staying here after school finishes?"

"No, Washy, I have to go to Brockton in July and begin interviewing staff. I won't be spending the summer here, either."

"But what about us, Justy?" Washy looked at her. "Haven't we started to build something here? Doesn't that matter for anything?"

"Washy, it's not that we have to be apart. You can come with me. There are plenty of jobs in Brockton, certainly more than here. We would see each other just as much as we do here, perhaps even more. It would be a new start for both of us."

"I still don't understand why you want to leave the Cape," Washy responded. "I know this isn't the best situation right now, but when they move the kids to the new school in South Yarmouth, you would have your own room and the latest of everything. Wouldn't that be good enough?"

"First of all, Washy, I don't think they will ever get around to moving the children out of here. The folks in this village are too stubborn. And even if that were to happen, what kind of a future is there here for these students, or *anyone* for that matter? Cape Cod is a backwater that time has passed by. You see it. Half of your friends are in Worcester or Springfield. If I'm doing anything noble in my job, it's trying to get these children educated enough so that they can leave Cape Cod and maybe go to a city where they have a chance at something better. Here there is nothing for them, or for me, either."

"I thought *I* was enough for you, Justy."

Justine turned away from him, arms folded defensively across her chest. When she again turned to face him, her arms hadn't moved. "Oh, Washy! Of course you are special to me. But don't you see? This is a chance for me to be something, to achieve something greater than anything I could do here. If I don't do this, I'll regret it all my life. And it would be something that would always come between us. Don't condemn me for wanting something better."

"It's not that," Washy replied. "It's just that leaving Cape Cod isn't something that I've ever considered. This is really the only place I know. The Cape is where my family is. To just pick up and move to Brockton... well, the idea is just going to take a bit of thinking about."

As he looked at the first girl who had truly captured his heart, Washy already knew that no matter how much he might consider moving to Brockton, it wasn't something he could ever do. Cape Cod was as much a part of him as his own soul. It was who he was. He couldn't leave. Washy also knew that nothing he could say was going to keep Justine from taking that job. For all the things they had shared over the past eight months, it was clear that they were really two very different people with very different goals. Justine left him in the hallway and went into her classroom without saying anything else. Washy thought about Freeman Foster's remarks that previous Thanksgiving. His uncle had warned about what he'd called Judas birds. Washy wondered if indeed he'd made the mistake of flying too low around such an attractive bird.

Irreconcilable Differences

Washy and Justine continued to see each other as the school year wound down, but their meetings were strained. Sometimes Washy thought that Justine was having second thoughts about the move, but when she gave her notice to Mrs. Crocker in May, it was clear she'd made up her mind to go.

Washy made a trip to Boston, hand-delivering an application to the Charles T. Main Company for a construction job at the new military camp in Falmouth. A week after he'd submitted his request, a letter came confirming that there was a position available if he wanted it.

On a rainy morning in June after school had ended, Washy delivered Justine to the Hyannis railroad station. On the drive to the depot, Justine looked straight ahead and said very little. Two nights earlier, Washy had taken her out to dinner and tried once more to get her to stay. They could make a life together on Cape Cod, he told her, if she could give it a chance. But Justine never wavered. She again reminded him of how backward the Cape seemed to her. And she said something that he knew to be true. "Washy, you say that you love me. And I believe that you do. But I know that you love Cape Cod more than you could ever love me. I could never compete with it. Am I wrong about that?" His silence confirmed her accusation, and the evening had ended badly.

For his part, Washy couldn't understand why anyone would trade the salt air and rural freedom that was his home for any place in a city. What Justine said about the Cape was true. It was a backward place. And many people were leaving for better opportunities elsewhere. But there was a sense of community in the small Cape Cod villages, a spirit that carried people through hard times. Neighbors looked out for each other. It was a rare and beautiful thing, and he knew it wasn't something found in cities. Washy understood that just as Justine had made a decision to leave the Cape, he had made his own decision to stay. Maybe she was right. His heart was here and it wouldn't let him leave.

Just before Justine boarded the train, she took Washy's hand. "I do love you, Washy. You were my Captain Eri. But I couldn't be your Mrs. Snow. I'm sorry." She brushed a wisp of hair from her eyes. "You have the address of my new school if you ever want to visit. Perhaps if you could see what Brockton is, you might change your mind and we could start over. Promise you will write to me."

Justine squeezed his hand and stepped up into the coach. The conductor moved to help her. Washy watched as the train began to move. Justine was at a window and their eyes met momentarily, and then she turned away. What had she expected of him? Tears? Maybe anger? He felt nothing at all. Unlike a Joe Lincoln novel, Washy had known for some time that this story wasn't going to have a happy ending. As he walked back to his car, he'd already accepted the fact that he would never see Justine Westcott again.

A New Job

The western part of Cape Cod rises up from Buzzards Bay to confront the glacial moraine that nature laid down thousands of years ago. Like a table with shorter legs on one side, the land slopes gradually eastward toward the Atlantic Ocean. From West Falmouth and into Sandwich, there is a broad belt of hills backed by extensive pine barrens, interspersed with deep hollows and scattered ponds. For years this section of the Cape was sparsely populated, and while it encompassed parts of four towns, no village center had ever developed there. Because so much of it was open and unpopulated, it wasn't surprising that state officials looked favorably on establishing a military facility there.

When Washy arrived at construction headquarters at the beginning of the summer of 1938, activity was already underway. Clouds of dust rose from convoys of trucks hauling sand and gravel on newly carved roads. The sound of hammers and saws echoed from rows of wooden barracks that were being hastily assembled. The facility, newly named Camp Edwards after Major General Clarence R. Edwards, who had commanded the Twenty-sixth Yankee Division in World War I, was the largest WPA project in the entire state, perhaps in the entire northeast. After parking near the main entrance, Washy entered a building still smelling of new wood. Behind a large counter, several men were gathered around a table covered with maps and engineering plans. An overhead fan was unsuccessfully attempting to move the air in a room that even in the early morning was heavy with humidity.

"What can I do for you?" A man in a sweat-stained shirt rose from the table and walked over to where Washy was standing.

"I'm here to start work," Washy answered, introducing himself and presenting his papers to the man, who took a quick glance at them and then extended his hand.

"Avery Taggart," the greeting was friendly. "I'm the supervisor here. We've been waiting for you to arrive, Sears. We've got an oversupply of nail bangers and truck drivers, but there aren't many men here who can handle heavy equipment. I suspect that's why the engineers at the Main Company were so eager to get you signed up. Paperwork usually doesn't move that fast around here. Come on, I'll show you what we've got going."

As superintendent Taggart drove him around, Washy learned that literally thousands of men were already at work finishing twelve hundred buildings, miles of interior roads, and a long runway designed to handle large aircraft. A big sewer plant was already half completed and several 150-foot water towers were being connected to a vast network of water mains. A new rail spur linked the base to the Woods Hole branch railroad line and tons of construction materials were moved each day into the developing site.

"When's all this supposed to be completed?" Washy asked his guide.

"We've got orders to get the place ready for next summer so the Massachusetts National Guard can begin using it. They've already conducted maneuvers in the northern end of the property over the last few summers, but they want a permanent setting for the troops in place by next year. It's going to be a year-round training facility."

"Well, Avery, if we've got all this work to do, I guess you should be dropping me at the equipment center so I can get started. We're probably wasting some time here. I can see the rest of the place on my own."

The supervisor laughed and slapped Washy on the back. "By God, Sears, with all of the people that have been showing up here just looking for a paycheck, it's good to find a man who is actually interested in working. Let's go."

Over the next few weeks, Washy found a family in Hatchville with a small room for rent at four dollars a week. He returned to Sears Point on weekends except when he was required to work an overtime shift. It was his first experience living and working on the Upper Cape, and he used the freedom of his summer evenings to drive along the Buzzards Bay shore from Monument Beach to West Falmouth, impressed by the rolling landscape with its fine summer homes and many small harbors. Thoughts of Justine would occasionally enter his mind, but they intruded less and less as the summer wore on. On a weekend visit at Sears Point, Nathan handed him two letters with Brockton postmarks. Washy took them to his room and put them on a bureau, where they remained unopened. They were still there when he returned to Camp Edwards.

The pace of work and his enjoyment of what he was doing eased the still-raw edge of losing Justine. Washy grew comfortable with the company of the men on his construction team and Avery Taggart proved to be a good boss, a fair man possessed of a good sense of humor. Several nights after work, Washy and his crew closed places like Jake's in East Falmouth and the more infamous Blue Parrot Club in Cataumet. In that brotherhood of workers, Washy's heart gradually began to heal. By September, Justine Westcott had become a shadowy memory in what now seemed a long-ago part of another life.

The Storm

On Wednesday, September 21, 1938, the dawn sky had a yellowish tinge to it and there were hints of a thunderstorm. A light rain fell and there were indications that more was coming. By noon, the barometer had dropped precipitously and the humid air had a dead feeling. Just after lunch, Avery Taggart stopped by the work site and announced that radio stations in Boston were talking about a big tropical storm that had come ashore earlier that day in New Jersey, causing major damage to Cape May.

"Better get the equipment under cover. We could be in for some high winds this afternoon. The weather people say that it's blowing and raining hard in New York City. It looks like it's coming our way."

By late afternoon, gusting winds drove people to shelter wherever they could find it. Anything not tied down began to blow away. Boards, windows, pieces of metal pipe, and electrical wires were lifted and tossed across the newly cleared open areas at the base, to end up snarled crazily in the trees.

The south-facing beach areas of Cape Cod suffered the worst of the damage. High winds coupled with an afternoon high tide produced a storm surge that carried whole villages of summer cottages inland. At Woods Hole, houses floated off their foundations. Sixteen people died as the storm moved up Buzzards Bay. In Onset more than three hundred people were made homeless as wind-driven water smashed into the village.

Fortunately, the point of the storm's actual landfall was west of the Cape, and the worst damage occurred from Providence, Rhode Island, west toward the Connecticut River Valley. At Sears Point, Nathan felt the impact of the storm, and he could see the large pines near the house bend ominously as the winds increased. The shallow-rooted poplars and willows toppled quickly in the higher gusts. Nathan closed the shutters on the south side of the house but the rain still found a way under window sills and began to streak the plaster inside.

The electricity went out shortly after four o'clock in the afternoon. The phone was dead. When the hurricane's eye passed, the wind shifted from northeast to southwest. As he passed between the house and the barn to get some kerosene for the lamps, Nathan heard the howl of a dog coming from the direction of Cobb's Pond. The animal was clearly in some kind of distress. Putting on a rain slicker, Nathan began searching for the source of the cries. Halfway down the path to the pond, he saw the dog, a Lab mix, its collar entangled with a large branch that had pinned the terrified animal so it could hardly move. The dog's back showed blood and as it unsuccessfully tried to free itself, it cried out piteously in pain.

Easing himself under a downed tree, Nathan spoke calmly to the animal, trying to reassure the panicked creature. Undoing the collar, he attempted to coax the dog to take shelter under his slicker. Suddenly freed from its tether, it bolted wildly from the thicket, knocking Nathan over. Just as he struggled to regain his footing, a strong gust snapped one of the large old pines behind him. The sound of the break was like a gunshot. The tree crushed Nathan at almost the same spot where years ago he and Washy had buried the remains of the Wellfleet Indian. His abbreviated cry was lost in the wind and roar from the nearby ocean.

David found his father the next day. With the power out and no telephone, he hadn't been able to check on Nathan during the storm. It was difficult negotiating the roads back into Brewster from Barnstable Harbor where he'd spent the previous night trying to keep boats from being blown ashore onto Sandy Neck. Downed trees were the biggest problem, and fallen telephone lines and electric wires were everywhere.

When he finally arrived at Sears Point just before dark, David found the back door to the house open, and no sign of his father. He found him lying face up under the tree that had killed him. It appeared Nathan had died instantly. Because of the communications outage, Washy and Clara didn't learn of their father's death until several days later. On Sunday, with train service out, Washy drove to Plymouth and met Clara, who had taken a bus from Quincy. They needed a pass at the Sagamore Bridge to be allowed back onto the Cape, as only residents could continue below Sandwich.

A few days later, Nathan's three surviving children accompanied his remains on the familiar road up to the Red Top cemetery where his body was placed in the ground next to his parents and alongside his wife, Mary. It was a sobering moment. Nathan's death had been sudden, and even though he was in his mid-sixties, he'd been healthy. It didn't seem possible that he could be gone. All three knew that with Nathan's death, Sears Point would never be the same.

Family Changes

In the weeks and months after the storm, Washy worked with his crew to clear the many downed trees on the base. It was well into December before the pace of construction at Camp Edwards reached anything like it had been the previous summer.

In the spring, Clara married a young attorney. Not the most attractive woman, Washy had often wondered if his sister would ever find a man for herself. Her husband, John Newcomb, had roots on the Cape but had gone away to boarding school as a teenager, eventually taking his law degree at Boston University. The wedding was held on a beautiful June day at the Unitarian Church. What was left of the family, a few aunts and uncles and some cousins, gathered after the ceremony at the Consodine House.

Sparrow Higgins came with his wife. He'd given up his construction business and had a steady job with the Nickerson Lumber Company, where he'd been appointed yard foreman at the Orleans branch. The two friends spent much of the afternoon reliving the days they'd worked together and the lively nights spent at the Owl Inn. Washy judged that Sparrow was very content in his role as husband and provider, and Sparrow's wife seemed a warm and charming woman.

David Sears missed his sister's wedding. He had signed on in April as a crewmember aboard Arctic explorer Donald MacMillan's schooner *Bowdoin* for a summer expedition to Labrador, Baffin Island, and Greenland.

Before returning to Hatchville, Washy drove up to the Red Top Cemetery and walked among the silent graves. There was the familiar presence that he always felt when visiting the small burial enclosure atop the wooded hill overlooking the bay. As he paused near the silent stones bearing his mother and father's names, he knew that nothing could ever separate him from this place.

War Clouds

In the summer of 1939, Taggart chose Washy as his assistant superintendent, supervising two dozen men and setting the daily base maintenance schedule. Just cutting the grass in the huge military complex occupied a half-dozen men working seven days a week. The expansion of firing ranges at the northern end of the reservation required long days of earth moving and more road building. The aircraft runway had been lengthened to accept large transport planes. As the year ended, Camp Edwards became, in effect, Cape Cod's sixteenth town.

Washy rarely returned to Sears Point. For much of the year the place was shut up and unoccupied. Estranged from his wife, David stayed there occasionally when he wasn't at sea. In May of 1940, he made a second voyage with Admiral MacMillan, this time as the *Bowdoin*'s first mate. At Thanksgiving, Washy, Clara, and David had a rare reunion at the old homestead. Clara had a new baby girl, born just two months earlier. The glow of motherhood gave her an attractiveness that she hadn't seemed to possess before. David recounted his adventures with Admiral MacMillan aboard the *Bowdoin*, tracking across the northern latitudes in uncharted regions. For his part, Washy talked about his work at the base and how he thought that with the war expanding in Europe, America wouldn't be spared involvement.

David surprised his brother and sister by revealing that he had signed up with the U.S. Navy. "When I got back home in September I didn't have any real job prospects. I couldn't see going back to dragging for sea clams and I've pretty much cut my ties in Chatham. The navy is organizing a fleet of high-speed torpedo boats and they are looking for experienced skippers. When I told them I was thirty-six years old, they didn't bat an eye. Time at sea is what they were looking for, and I have plenty of that. They've offered me a commission. I'm supposed to report to Melville, Rhode Island, for training in January. Until I get my reporting date, I'll stay here at the house and get a few things done around the property."

David's news about his impending naval service was unexpected. David and Washy were both beyond the age of men who would likely be drafted into active service. Washy found himself wondering if what his brother had done might be something he'd eventually consider himself.

Washy now had a solid job and a chance to better his status in life. There was a good future for him at the base. That Washy had been Taggart's choice as his assistant was a tribute to the confidence his boss placed in him. And Washy knew he'd earned that trust. Creating the massive military reservation out of nothing had been a job for strong men. If the country was going to go to war, Camp Edwards would play an important role in how the nation would fare. Keeping the base operating was just as important as putting on a uniform. If David wanted to put himself in harm's way, that was his business. For a time, the matter receded in importance and Washy turned to the immediate task at hand, making sure that everything was in order for the arrival of the Twenty-sixth Yankee Division.

A Last Peaceful Summer

In January of 1941, the Twenty-sixth Yankee Division was mobilized for a year of active service. It was no longer unusual to see military uniforms, not just at Camp Edwards but in other parts of Cape Cod as well. Troop convoys were a regular presence on the roadways, and several beaches were temporarily closed for artillery training. Powerful searchlights crisscrossed the night sky as anti-aircraft crews practiced picking out aerial targets from mobile batteries.

When the troops were paid on Fridays, there was a spike in automobile accidents and disorderly behavior. Police were called to break up fights in places like The Barclay in West Falmouth and the Domino Club in

Buzzards Bay. The year also brought a record number of weddings, as soldiers married sweethearts with the full awareness that a honeymoon could well be interrupted by a full national mobilization. The twenty-eight thousand members of the Twenty-sixth Division approached Labor Day with the knowledge that for a lot of them, training would continue into the fall in North Carolina and Texas.

In September, after about six months of training in Rhode Island, David received orders to report to the U.S. Naval station at Almeida, California. Just before he left, Washy and Clara joined David at Sears Point for a farewell party. Clara was pregnant again and the trip to Brewster had tired her out to the point where she spent much of the afternoon napping. The brothers walked out on the sun-washed flats enjoying the clean air that was autumn's signature.

"I want you to do something for me, Washy. I'm not sure how this is all going to turn out. The higher-ups haven't told us anything about where we're going. But since we're heading west, I'm guessing that we're not looking to fight the Germans. I figure that the navy is going to make some sort of show of force against Japan. I could end up in the Philippines.

"I've put a little money away in the last six months and I'd like you to take care of it while I'm away," David continued. "Anything happens to me, I'd like it to go to my boys. I haven't been much of a father, and the least I can do is try to leave them with something. I wish it could be more than what it is."

The two brothers continued walking through the remains of a long abandoned weir, the stubs of the old poles just above the sand still forming a rough circle across a wide bar.

"Listen, David." Washy put his arm on his older brother's shoulder. "First of all, you'll probably spend the next year in sunny California. If the climate and lifestyle doesn't make you a permanent resident, you'll be back here with a lot of stories to tell about life out there. You won't need that insurance policy. Everything I see points toward us helping Britain against the Nazis. You're headed the other way. You'll be fine."

"I'm not so sure." David looked seriously at his brother. "Our boats are designed to attack large capital ships with torpedoes. The Germans don't have a big fleet but the Japs do. We didn't do all that training for nothing. Just tell me you'll look after my boys if something happens."

Washy saw David off that day on the evening train out of Hyannis. The last look he had of David, his brother was lighting a cigarette in the smoking car as he waved a goodbye through the window. Two weeks later a telegram arrived from California that read: "Arrived Safely. Don't Expect to Be Here Long. David." The message left Washy wondering what, indeed, the navy had in mind for Ensign David Sears.

Action at Camp Edwards

Washy learned about the Pearl Harbor attack on December 7 at about the same time it was being conveyed to the soldiers at Camp Edwards. He was half way through a tuna sandwich at Sheehan's Grill in Falmouth when a man ran into the restaurant and announced the attack. A woman at a table near Washy cried out and had to be comforted by her husband. Her son had recently enlisted in the Marine Corps. In a very short time, Main Street was deserted as people ran to the nearest radio for news of what had happened. Across the country, all Americans were tuned in the following day when President Franklin D. Roosevelt made his famous radio broadcast and war declaration.

In the first hours after the attack, estimates of damage and casualties in Hawaii went from negligible to devastating and back again. It was pretty clear that nobody really knew anything yet. Thoughts rushed through Washy's mind after he heard the news. Foremost was the uncertainty as to where his brother was. David's telegram had been pretty clear that California was not going to be his final destination. Was he somewhere at sea, perhaps bound for the Philippines, maybe aboard some troop ship? And what about Camp Edwards? What changes would come to the base in light of the attack? Washy paid his bill and drove straight to Avery Taggart's house, figuring that his boss would have a better picture of what was happening.

Taggart's wife came out of the house when she saw Washy's car. "If you're looking for Avery, he's already gone over to the base. He told me not to wait supper for him."

Normally there would be two sentries at the main entrance to Camp Edwards. Now, at mid-afternoon on this seventh day of December, there were no less than a dozen heavily armed soldiers arrayed across the roadway. Passes were checked and Washy had to wait in line to be waved through. One of the guards told him that soldiers had already been sent to guard all three bridges over the Cape Cod Canal.

Taggart's Dodge was in its parking spot at engineering headquarters. Inside, phones were ringing and several men were busily arranging schedules on clipboards. The small Christmas tree, decorated the day before, had been tossed unceremoniously into a corner to make room for a series of large area maps that were in place on a makeshift table in the center of the room. Taggart was tracing lines across one of the charts.

"Washy! I'm glad you came in. I'm putting together four crew sections that'll be needed to handle the load of commitments that will be coming. I've already had several calls from the base commander, who wants us to start clearing a perimeter around the entire reservation to keep out anyone who doesn't have official business here. Take Doug Parsons with you and see about the status of all of our vehicles."

As Washy left the building with Parsons, Taggart shouted after them. "Don't plan on going home any time soon, either of you. The base is essentially on lockdown. We're all bunking right here for the moment. This is going to take a bit of time to sort out."

For the next several days, Camp Edwards buzzed with rumors. Someone claimed that a relative had called his wife from the west coast, reporting that Japanese battleships were off Santa Barbara. A Chinese laundry in Wareham center was burned by some teenagers who thought the aged proprietor might be a Japanese spy. Members of the Twenty-sixth expected momentarily to be loaded on troop trains bound for the west coast.

Finally, when it became clear that the Japanese Navy was not steaming up Buzzards Bay and coming ashore at Barlow's Landing, things began to calm down. The idea of bulldozing a perimeter around the base was shelved and troops started getting weekend passes again. Most of the division spent Christmas at home.

Clara called Washy in early February to say she'd received a telegram from David, sent from Hawaii where he'd arrived safely. At least they knew where their brother was, or where he had been in the last weeks of January. Clara had given birth to her second child, another daughter. Just after Christmas she wrote Washy that her husband had accepted a commission from the Army Judge Advocate General's Office and was already at his new assignment in Washington, D.C. She and the children were going to follow him as soon as they could locate housing in the increasingly crowded capital. Overnight, that usually sleepy city had become a boomtown bursting with politicians, bureaucrats, military personnel, and anyone who could extract a dollar from all three.

One Sunday in March, Washy drove back to Brewster to check on the house at Sears Point. No one had been there since the autumn, and the building carried an abandoned look that disturbed him. Every time he'd been there in the past there had been some kind of human presence. Now it was unnaturally quiet, dark and filled with the smell of mothballs.

After shutting up the house, Washy stopped at W.W. Knowles's store, now run by Henry Crocker. As always, the place remained a gathering place for the idle and the unemployed, and a number of men sat warming themselves around the stove in the back. Several recognized Washy.

"Washy! Ain't seen you around much recently. You still working up at Camp Edwards?"

Washy nodded, and after shaking a few hands, he related what he'd been doing since the war had begun. While he was renewing acquaintances, he saw Earl Eldridge, an old friend of his father, who motioned that he wanted a word. Eldridge held out a chair and pulled another up for himself.

"You know that Brewster has a quota of men whose names have to be sent to the draft board in Hyannis. It's the same for all the towns. There's a committee been formed to screen men who might be called to serve. Technically you're in the pool, Washy. But because we knew that you were working at the base, we've so far left you off the list. Your brother's already in the service, and we're trying to do the best we can to spread the obligations around so that one family doesn't get hit more than others. You're on the upper end of draft age anyway, and so far there've been plenty enough volunteers to cover what they're asking for."

Washy stopped the older man before he'd finished. "Listen, Earl. One thing I want clear is that I'm not looking for any special treatment just because David's in the navy. If the town runs short of volunteers, I want my name sent in to the board just like the rest of the eligible men. If you need a body, I'll go."

"Actually, that isn't what I wanted to talk to you about, Washy. We weren't doing you any favors. And I know that you don't want any. What I wanted to ask you about is the status of the house at Sears Point. You aren't living in it and I've heard that Clara is headed to Washington to join her husband. We had a request from the army's Eastern Defense Command to come up with a building near the shore that could be used by soldiers who will be patrolling the beaches. The army's worried about saboteurs. Our committee was wondering if you would authorize the use of the house. It'll probably be a temporary thing. They say they will pay for it. If you do, we'll call the command and make the offer."

"Seems like an easy decision for me, Earl. I can't get back here on any kind of a regular basis. Gas is hard to come by, and probably will be more so in the next few months. I don't see why the army can't have it for a while. Better the place is lived in than just sit empty. There's enough room for probably eight to ten men. If they use dogs, they can bed them in the shed out back."

There was a look of relief on Eldridge's face. "Thanks Washy, I figured you'd see it that way. You're your father's son, that's for sure. It's a generous offer that I know won't be forgotten around here."

"By that I hope you aren't meaning that you're going to lose my name when the draft quota needs to be filled. Promise me you won't do that, Earl."

The older man smiled, pumping Washy's hand. "You can be sure of that. Don't you worry."

Washy took his leave from the men around the stove. It was pretty clear that his friends were waiting for the shoe to drop, some kind of push that would move them to act. Outside the sky in the west held storm clouds. Washy threw the Ford in gear and was back in Hatchville just before dark.

The Seabee

"Look down there toward Washburn's Island." Avery Taggart pointed south across Waquoit Bay. "The army wants us to open up some roads so they can start amphibious training in June. Washy, you and two of the crews will move into some temporary quarters next week and start cutting trees."

It was the first of April but the weather was more like January. A cold wind came off Nantucket Sound and cut sharply through the knot of engineers that had accompanied Taggart and Washy to East Falmouth that morning. "There are a couple of summer houses close by that you can stage out of. We've got permission from the owners. I talked to Olin Kelley who runs the Waquoit Shellfish Company, and we can use his barn to keep the equipment in. He's not doing a whole lot of business these days anyway."

Washy surveyed the wide beach in front of them. Washburn's Island was no different from the usual coastal environment found on Cape Cod. The dunes were home to sandpipers and piping plovers and featured clumps of goldenrod, bayberry, and beach plum bushes. But unlike Brewster, it did not have the extended tidal flats that Washy was used to on the bay side. The island ran due south until it jogged east for about a mile and was separated from the mainland on its western side by a small river. A bridge would have to be constructed so that support equipment could be moved to the beach landing area, a job that could take several months.

On the drive back to Camp Edwards, Washy was mostly silent as Taggart talked about the work that was going to be done along the south coast of the Cape. "The army's interested in doing something over in Cotuit, too. They're looking at Sampson's Island and the area over on Dead Neck as another training site for amphibious landings. It's similar to what we've got here, a barrier beach with no land access. At least there are some roads already built over from Osterville. And the river is not as deep. We can stage out of Chester Crosby's boatyard when we get to that project."

As they pulled into Taggart's parking space near the office, Washy stopped his boss from getting out of the car. "Avery, I'm giving a serious look to joining up with the Naval Construction Battalion that is being put together over in Rhode Island. I spoke with a recruiter in Providence and I'm more than qualified to get into the outfit. They're calling themselves 'Seabees' and will work under the navy's Civil Engineer Corps. They've already started building a base at Davisville."

Taggart was clearly taken by surprise. Pausing to light a cigarette, he let out a long sigh. "Washy, I was hoping that you wouldn't do something like this. I've come to depend on you to get things done. With all we've got to do, I can't afford to lose you. Most of the good young men are already in the service, or will be soon, and if you leave, I'm going to have to train someone from scratch. I'd ask you to reconsider what you're thinking. Why do this?"

"I know what you say is true, Avery." Washy looked at his boss. "And it bothers me that I'd be leaving you in the lurch. But I can't see letting my brother be the only one to carry the family's end of the war. I feel that I can't let this thing play out without being part of it."

"But Washy, you *are* already part of it." Taggart finished his cigarette and tossed the stub out of the window. "There are a lot of good people who are doing civilian war work that is just as important as being on the front lines. Who do you think are building the ships and planes? Who's staying behind to grow the food that the troops will need? Who's driving the locomotives and the trucks transporting everything for the war effort?"

Washy was sorry that he had revealed his thoughts to his boss. Taggart was correct in everything that he'd said. And even factoring in the man's interest in trying to talk Washy out of enlisting, there wasn't much in Taggart's words that Washy could argue against.

Taggart made it a bit more personal. "Washy, I'm in my mid-fifties. I've got about five more years in me before I look at retiring. I'll have a pension and I can sit on my porch and watch the birds coming to my feeder. You're my assistant and you would be in line for my job. You'd be a supervisor before you are forty years old. Not many people have the opportunity that you're about to throw away. And if you leave now and join the navy, that is what you are going to do, throw it away."

"Look, Avery. I'm not looking ten or twenty years down the road. I've never been that kind of a planner. You've been a good man to work for and I'm not saying that we don't have an important role here at Camp Edwards. I just feel that I need to do this. Maybe I'm trying to find out something about myself."

Taggart was out of the car. Before walking toward the office he turned and looked back. "Maybe if I were twenty-five years younger, I'd be thinking like you are, Washy. But I'm not. I just know I don't want to see you leave, and it's as much about me as it is about you, I'll admit that. I know I can't change things by talking. Just let me know as soon as you make a decision so I can start thinking about your replacement."

Washy sat a while in Taggart's car before getting out and heading to the equipment area. Maybe Taggart was right. He should be thinking long-term. Why was he about to throw away a career opportunity that he'd worked so hard to create? There were plenty of younger men who could fill the ranks and fight this war. The military didn't need him. But one thing kept coming back in Washy's mind, something that had been part of every one of his days and nights since his last visit to Brewster. It was the smiling face and the firm handshake of Earl Eldridge and the man's assurance that the town's quota committee wasn't doing any special favors by leaving Washy's name off the monthly lists going to the Hyannis draft board. That was hard for Washy to believe, and he knew that others didn't believe it either.

He remembered the faces of the men sitting around the stove in Brewster that day, uncertain about what they were going to do, and painfully uncomfortable in Washy's presence. He knew he didn't want to look in the mirror and see that same uncertainty in his own face. The next morning he drove to Rhode Island, and enlisted in the Seabees.

Davisville, Rhode Island

The navy recruiter told Washy that he'd be getting orders to report to the Davisville Advanced Base Depot, south of Warwick. Unlike regular navy enlistees, there was no standard boot camp for men entering the Seabees. There would instead be a three-week orientation at Camp Allen in Virginia to introduce volunteers to basic military regulations and discipline. Chosen largely from people in the civilian construction trades, the average age of recruits for the Seabees was around thirty-seven. They were experienced carpenters, electricians, plumbers, and heavy equipment operators.

While none were expected to directly engage in frontline fighting, their proximity to the battle zones did require some basic training in military weaponry. Many of the men were familiar with guns and, like Washy, had grown up hunting with their uncles and fathers. Their job was to modify the battle area favorably to make it easier for the military to operate. Roads, airfields, hospitals, docks, defensive ramparts, and utility buildings had to be built, and the Seabees were the ones tasked to do it.

Because he wasn't scheduled to report to Davisville until quite late in the spring, Washy continued working at Camp Edwards. The army had taken over the house at Sears Point, so he stayed in Hatchville. His decision to join the Seabees had clearly not pleased Taggart, and as his reporting date drew closer their relationship cooled. Taggart spent a lot of time training a new man from Pocasset as Washy's replacement. The sudden new distance between the supervisor and his former assistant was a source of discomfort for Washy. He was surprised, then, when on the eve of his departure for Davisville, he got a phone call from Taggart, asking him to meet for dinner at the Blue Parrot in Cataumet.

Washy wondered if the meeting would be awkward. Taggart had clearly taken Washy's enlistment in the navy personally. As he entered the club, Washy wasn't sure what was in store for him. Before his eyes could adjust to the darkened room, he heard shouts, and a dozen men, including Taggart, emerged and grabbed the surprised soon-to-be Seabee, parading him enthusiastically to the bar.

Taggart pushed his way to the front of the crowd. Waving for silence, he put an arm around Washy. "Men, we've come together tonight to celebrate the departure of one of our best people. He's been with me for almost three full years and I've never worried about whether any job I assigned him would be done. It always was. Most of you know that I'm not happy that Washy has decided to join the navy and leave us. I tried to talk him out of it. But I have to feel fortunate that I've had his advice and good sense for as long as I have. In some ways, I feel like I'm losing a son but I'm proud and happy that the navy is going to be getting a first-rate sailor. On behalf of all of the men who have been privileged to work with you, Washy, here's wishing you fair winds and following seas."

Never at ease in this kind of a circumstance, Washy paused a bit before opening his mouth. "Thanks, Avery, and thank you guys for putting together this party. I've enjoyed working with all of you over the past couple of years. It probably seems strange that I've decided to join the navy. As Avery has said, I could have stayed here. And it's true that all of us are playing an important role in keeping Camp Edwards in good shape for the troops that are training there. I've never had doubts about that. Maybe it's just because I've seen so many young men come and go through Edwards on their way to war that I decided to join them. If I can make it any easier for our men to succeed and come home, I'll feel that it was worth it." Washy made eye contact with each man in the room. On this last evening, he wanted to remember their faces. "I'll miss you all and I won't forget the good times that we had here. Don't forget me."

Over the next hour as the men left, only Taggart and Washy were left, at a table near the bar.

"Washy, I admire what you're doing. I really do. Even though I hate losing you." Taggart looked across the table at his friend through the lingering cigarette smoke. "When the last war started, I was in my early thirties. Like you, I felt I should join the army and do my part. But as an only son, I was supporting my mother. I couldn't leave her. A lot of my friends did go overseas and a couple of them didn't make it back. I've always carried some guilt about it. At least you won't have that around your neck as you get older. I still wish you weren't leaving, but I understand, more than you know."

Washy was surprised by Taggart's admission of guilt. He knew that his own motivation for joining the navy stemmed at least in part from the same reason. It had nothing to do with David's decision to volunteer. It was more the idea that so many others were leaving to fight, and Washy felt he had no right to stay comfortable at home while they were sacrificing. He didn't want to be sitting someday in a smoky club trying to explain to a younger man why he'd stayed home while others fought and died. As much as the man across the table from him was a friend, he knew he didn't want to end up like Taggart.

"Avery, it was you that told me once that a man's got to do what he's got to do. Taking care of your mother was no small responsibility and there were a lot of other men who were in a better position to go off to war. You can't beat yourself up about that."

The waitresses were wiping down the tables. The two men exited the club together and headed slowly out to the now quiet parking lot. Taggart got into his Dodge and rolled down the window. "Wash, you make sure you come back in one piece. And when you do, I want you to come back to Camp Edwards and work for me. Will you promise me you'll do that?"

"Avery, you'll be the first person I visit when I get home. After all," Washy winked, "you still owe me twenty-five dollars from the last time we played cards at your house. By the time I'm back, the interest alone should double it. I'm going to be looking for that money."

Taggart smiled, and with a wave, he was gone. Washy took a moment before starting his car. The bell from the darkened Cleveland Ledge lighthouse in Buzzards Bay struck eight times. It occurred to him that this might be the last evening he'd ever spend on Cape Cod. He breathed in the cool spring air and was glad that he'd shared it with a friend like Avery Taggart.

A Promotion

During June of 1942 Washy completed three weeks of training at Camp Allen, learning how to integrate construction objectives within a combat environment. The equipment that the navy was using was no different than what he'd operated at Camp Edwards. A bulldozer was a bulldozer no matter the location. Every Seabee was expected not only to know how to operate the equipment, but how to fix it as well. What Washy did gain was the experience of military leadership, and he impressed his company officers as someone who could get others to follow and complete a task.

On an August morning, Washy was told to report to battalion headquarters at Camp Endicott. He entered the room of the commanding officer and stood at attention. Lieutenant Commander John Williams, a reserve officer, was a road engineer in civilian life. He'd recently been mobilized for active duty. Williams was nursing a cup of coffee, and he didn't rise when Washy walked in.

"Stand at ease, Sears." Williams looked up from his crowded desk. "I'm told that you've demonstrated some good leadership during recent training. Lieutenant Sobers and Lieutenant Bohannan report that you know the equipment better than anyone else and that the rest of the men look up to you. I'm going to recommend that you be given an administrative promotion to petty officer first class. If things work out, you could make chief within a year."

Washy hadn't expected anything of the sort, and the announcement came as a complete surprise. "Thank you, sir." He shifted awkwardly in front of Williams's desk. "I've hardly been in the navy three months. Do you think a promotion like this might be a bit premature?"

"Are you saying that you don't want it, Sears?"

"No, sir. I'm just wondering why the navy would put three stripes on my arm before I've actually done anything. It just seems pretty quick, that's all."

"We do things fast around here, Sears. We're fighting a war on two fronts and haven't had a lot to show for it so far. Now we're trying to block the Jap invasion of the Solomons. Civilization has pretty much skipped over the whole area. It's nothing like Europe. Airfields, harbors, roads, water supplies, decent buildings to operate out of, all of it will need to be built from scratch. That is our job. I looked at your service record and see that you have a brother already in the service. I'm sure that you'd want to do anything you could to make his job easier. I've got orders for you to accompany a group to the west coast for eventual deployment to the southwest Pacific. We need to start shaping the battlefield for troops that will be conducting the island campaign."

Williams dismissed his new petty officer and watched as he walked toward the enlisted barracks. He turned the now cold coffee mug in his hands and thought about some of the other men that he'd picked for key roles. Sears was like so many of them. Products of small towns, each mature, capable, and sure enough of their abilities to successfully carry out the war strategy against Japan. None were professional soldiers. They had no designs on making the service a career. They were, in fact, ordinary men with more than ordinary skills. America had always produced people like Sears, and Lieutenant Commander Williams had no doubt that they would make a difference in how the war turned out. He leaned comfortably back in his chair. The day had gone well and the officer was smiling when his yeoman entered the room with a fresh cup of coffee.

West Coast War

Instead of getting immediate orders to one of the forward areas in the Pacific, Washy's battalion ended up at Port Hueneme in California. They ran heavy equipment on the base, operated cranes, and loaded ships bound for Hawaii. It wasn't unlike the work Washy had been doing at Camp Edwards, and he found himself wondering whether his decision to join the active navy had made any sense. Los Angeles was a short drive down the coast, and with weekends off, his routine was pretty much like the thousands of other military personnel and civilian workers who nightly crowded the bars and movie houses in the San Fernando Valley. The commanding officer of his battalion kept saying that they'd be getting orders to move at any time. But as the end of 1942 approached, Washy didn't believe it. Christmas day saw temperatures in the eighties, and the small plastic Santa and sleigh that someone had put in the window of the barracks seemed strangely out of place.

Along with occasional letters from Clara, Harriet Ellis, one of Washy's former teachers, had also taken it upon herself to write to him. Her letters were filled with local news. Mrs. John Brier had been re-elected to the presidency of the Brewster Woman's Alliance. A fire in the woods near Nate Black's house had blackened several acres of woodland. People were turning in old keys and padlocks for the scrap metal drive. John Gage and Herbie Peterson had just been drafted and were at Fort Devens to begin training. People in town were worried that the government was going to close the East Brewster Post Office. Milton Gray, Jr. had won a twenty-five dollar war bond for his 4H victory garden. Tommy Hooper had just become engaged to Pauline Newcomb, the daughter of Percie Newcomb, the town clerk. Mrs. Ellis reported that the army coastal patrols had settled into the house at Sears Point. "We take pies and other desserts out to the men at least once a week," she wrote. "They seem rather bored with what they are doing."

The pace of activity at Port Hueneme increased in January of 1943. There was heightened anticipation that the battalion would finally leave their stateside assignment and join the campaign of island hopping that was the grand strategy of the Pacific war.

Washy had just finished work for the day and was headed for his barracks and a shower when he was hailed by one of the communications yeomen outside headquarters. "Washy, there was a call for you just a little while ago from the east coast. The caller left a number. She said it was important. You can use the phone in my office if you want. The CO said it would be OK."

A call from back east! It had to be from Clara. Washy wondered why she would call the base during working hours. Why hadn't she waited until evening? Thanking the yeoman, Washy headed to the CO's office. He sat waiting for the connection, which the operator said would take about ten minutes. The yeoman who had offered the use of the phone brought in a fresh cup of coffee and left it on the table and then excused himself, closing the door quietly behind him as he exited the room.

The phone rang and Washy picked it up. It was Clara. She told him that her husband had learned that David was missing and presumed lost in action in the Pacific. "John left work right away and came home and told me. The cablegram from the Navy Department said that David's entire crew was apparently lost in action somewhere near Guadalcanal."

It was as if his sister's words were coming across the wires in slow motion. There had to be some mistake. Washy held the phone receiver away, momentarily unsure of what to say, too stunned to reply until he heard Clara's tearful voice asking if he was still on the line.

"Yes, I'm still here. I can't believe it. David gone? Is John there with you?" Clara assured him that her husband was with her and trying as best he could to be a comfort.

"I love you, Clara," Washy managed. "And I'm glad you've got John. He'll be a comfort. There's not much else to do but pray that David didn't suffer. He shifted the phone to his other hand. "I still can't believe he's gone."

After asking Clara to send him the address for David's sons, Washy said goodbye. He sat alone for a few minutes. The clerks in the outer office were looking his way as he left, and they nodded in obvious sympathy. They'd known all along why he'd come in to use the phone. Washy felt a hand on his shoulder, and the yeoman escorted him to the door. Still in a daze, Washy began the long walk to his barracks in the fading sunset. The western sky over the Pacific was particularly brilliant that afternoon, but the scene was lost on Washy. He couldn't see it through the tears that came with the awful truth that he'd never see his brother again.

Destination: Southwest Pacific

In February of 1943, Washy's battalion finally received orders for the southwestern Pacific. They boarded the *USS Almaack*, an old pre-war transport ship. Everyone had a theory on where they were headed. "We're going to New Guinea," a grizzled boatswain's mate offered. Another was sure it would be Midway. "They need re-building after last year's battle."

A veteran sailor thought the battalion might be going to support an amphibious operation in the Marianas. "It makes sense," he said, as younger sailors crowded around him listening. "Guadalcanal proved that taking islands spreads the Japs too thin to defend their whole empire. I think we are headed for Guam to liberate it before summer."

In fact, the *Almaack* had been directed to Australia, and after twenty-two days at sea, she arrived at Melbourne in early March. Washy and his Seabee battalion were off-loaded and moved to the grounds of the Melbourne Cricket Club to wait for the orders that they expected would take them into the combat area. After several days Washy's unit was instead transported by train to a small town outside the city, where they went into makeshift quarters.

Harriet Ellis's letters continued to follow Washy halfway across the world. She wrote with news about other Brewster men who were in the service. Hollis Theall and Washington Chase were at Camp Devens, training as aviation ground crewmembers. John Latham had been accepted into the Army Aviation Corps. Ernie Gage Jr. was stationed in Portsmouth, New Hampshire, with the Coast Guard. It had been a hard winter with much more snow than usual. A house had burned in West Brewster near the Dennis line and a family was homeless. The Cape Playhouse was not going to open this summer. Most people were staying close to home. Washy read the letters, then put them in his footlocker. They were all he had by way of a connection home.

In the fall of 1943 there was a major move into New Guinea by both the army and navy. The First Marine Division landed in December at Cape Gloucester in New Britain. To assist the marines, the navy ordered Washy's Seabee battalion to follow and provide logistical support. The battalion cleared one hundred acres for an airstrip, built miles of coral gravel roads, and buried more miles of pipelines. At one point, Washy came under sniper fire while making repairs to a coral jetty. As soon as he realized he had become a target, he raised the blade of his bulldozer to deflect the bullets. Some nearby marines soon located the enemy soldier and killed him.

Curious, Washy maneuvered past one of the exultant marines to get a better look at the dead man. The body lying on the ground had a shock of dark hair and looked to be about five feet tall. The Japanese soldier's legs were wrapped in khaki puttees and his blouse and trousers were stuffed with rice. The face was unmarked and smooth, almost girlish. Just a kid, really. The only thing that confirmed his gender was the short, black stubble of hair across his upper lip. Now what remained of the foe was a pathetic lump of flesh grotesquely propped up against a palm tree, bleeding out into the jungle carpet. Someone had stuck a cigarette between the dead soldier's lips. There was some laughter among the onlookers as a large fly landed on the dead man's face and crawled across the still open left eye.

After New Britain, the Seabee battalion was rotated back to Australia. A few months later in June of 1944, the battalion returned to action at Saipan in the southern Marianas. The Second and Fourth Marine Divisions overcame a strong Japanese defense and captured Aslito airfield within the first week. Washy and the rest of his Seabee battalion were close behind the marines and they quickly had the field operational. The Japanese continued to occasionally bomb the airfield, and repairing bomb craters became an art. A large crater could be filled and the surface re-matted in less than a half hour.

Washy had just finished such a patch when he saw some men running away from one of the craters. "What's going on?" He flagged down one fleeing man. "Where's everyone going?

"It's an unexploded bomb. Looks like about a five-hundred-pounder and it's half buried in the runway." The man didn't stay to give more details.

Washy got down from his bulldozer, and with two other men carefully approached the crater where the live bomb lay. A closer look revealed that the explosive was sitting in the hole at about a thirty-degree angle. Part of one of its stabilizing fins was still on the weapon and there was a large dent along the exposed side.

"Think you can get a cable on the stabilizer?" Washy looked at the sailor who was peering into the hole.

"Probably can," the man replied. "But pressure on it might make it pull away from the bomb casing, and if it's allowed to drop back into the hole, it might go off. It's risky."

"We've got some planes coming in here soon that are going to need this runway. They'll be low on gas and there isn't much room around here for a safe ditch." Washy pointed in the direction of the low hills where the American planes would make their approach. "I've got a cable on my bulldozer. Let's give it a go."

Washy backed his bulldozer close to the live bomb crater and one of the men gingerly lowered himself into the hole.

"Get at least one twist around it," Washy shouted down to him. "I'm going to go over and bring back a crane. We've got to lift the bomb straight up. It's the only way. We can't haul it sideways with the bulldozer. I'm going to need something with leverage."

By the time Washy returned with a piece of equipment with a crane arm, his two companions had secured the bomb with the cable. "Now, you two! Get out of here, over to the blast bunkers and keep your heads down. Go, go, go!" The two did not need to be further encouraged.

When he was sure they were safe in the bunker, Washy slowly put upward pressure on the crane arm. At first nothing happened. Then the cable tightened and the bomb moved. Ever so slowly, it started out of the pit. When it was about three feet above ground level, Washy reversed the tracked vehicle and backed slowly away from the crater. He took the bomb across the runway and lowered it carefully into one of the sandbagged aircraft hard stands just off the adjacent taxiway. There was a tense moment when the bomb contacted the ground and the cable came loose. The explosive rolled a couple of feet and Washy worried that he'd set it down too hard. The bomb lay on its side like some deadly sleeping being, its destructive energy just waiting for something, or someone, to wake it up. Not wanting to be the alarm clock, Washy dismounted from the crane and slowly walked back in the direction he'd come. Finally away from the immediate danger, he sank to his knees and threw up. He was in the chow line later getting supper when a runner came by and pulled him out of line.

"Skipper wants to see you, Washy. Get over to headquarters on the double."

"On the double better mean after I've had supper," Washy replied.

And he sat for a while with other men who were just as tired and hungry before making his way over to the headquarters building, a green Quonset hut with a hastily built wooden porch. An officer in khaki was shuffling through a stack of paperwork that was piled on a desk. He had no visible insignia and with his sweat-stained shirt, it was hard to tell what rank he held.

"Can I help you, petty officer?" The officer's tone was not unfriendly. There was an informality in the man's greeting that put Washy at ease.

"Petty officer Sears, reporting as requested, sir."

"Sears? Oh, Sears. Yes, Sears. Have a seat." The officer pushed a chair to Washy.

"That was quite a thing that you and the other two men did this afternoon. It was one of the bravest acts I've seen since I've been on this island."

"You were there?" Washy looked over at the officer.

"Well, like everyone else, I was down in one of the bunkers. But I could see all three of you wrestling with that bomb. Jesus, it was a hell of a thing. You all could have been blown to hell."

"Well, we weren't, sir. I guess it was our day to catch a break."

The two men sat talking about what had taken place, and the officer said that he was going to put all three men in for special commendations. "Hell, you all should be getting the Silver Star for what you did. And I'm going to make it happen. You'll be on the cover of *Stars and Stripes* by the end of the month. They'll have you home for bond drives."

It was dark by the time Washy excused himself from the meeting. He fell asleep on his cot almost immediately, and when he awoke the next morning, it was as if the previous day had never happened. There were more craters to fill and roads to grade. There was no holiday routine on Saipan, just another day of war. There was no further mention of what Washy and the other two men had done that day, and the exploit never made it to *Stars and Stripes*. It was actually a very small event in a war filled with thousands of similar acts of heroism. But it was special for those who had been there to see it, and the story of the lone Seabee crane operator moving a live bomb suspended on a wire across a bomb-cratered airfield was told and retold in Legion halls and VFW posts for years after.

Peleliu

By the time Washy's group arrived on the island of Peleliu in November of 1944, it had been mostly secured. A few Japanese soldiers were holding out in the many caves that coursed through the island hills, but the Marines were using flamethrowers to seek them out. The Seabees began work on the airfield at the south end of the island so it could take aircraft in support of General MacArthur's return to the Philippines.

Washy had been promoted to chief petty officer a month earlier. But other than a somewhat better situation in living quarters and a small increase in pay, life didn't change all that much. Harriet Ellis's letters still reached Washy, although not with their earlier regularity. Sometimes they caught up with him in twos and threes. He learned that Charlie Delano, Henry Whittemore, and Irving Eldridge had each been wounded in Europe. Staff Sergeant Bob Sanders, an aerial gunner aboard a B-17, was reported missing and presumed dead after his bomber was shot down over Austria. Mabel Morse had been promoted to the rank of lieutenant in the Army Nurse Corps and was stationed in Panama. Lieutenant Constance Bragg was home on furlough after serving in North Africa for the past year as an army nurse. Machinist Mate Leslie Chase was at sea with the navy. One of the most amazing things that Mrs. Ellis revealed in her letters was that Sheldon Brier, a sergeant in the Marine Corps, had been wounded on Saipan during the same time that Washy had been there. The two Brewster men had been fighting on the same Pacific island, neither aware of the other's presence.

Perhaps the items that affected Washy the most were the ordinary things that Mrs. Ellis passed on in her letters. In a world that now seemed remote to him, people back home were leading a normal existence. Frederick MacMulkin had been called to jury duty. Cigarettes had finally been taken off the rationing list. The cranberry crop was reported to be the worst in years, off by as much as seventy-five percent. Charlie Briggs had died at age sixty-seven. The Brewster Grange, down to only thirteen members, had voted to disband after a thirty-seven-year existence. Camp Monomoy in East Brewster had been full during the summer, as had the girls' Camp Wono. A September hurricane had been devastating but with the help of German prisoners of war at Camp Edwards, most of the downed trees had been cleared. In the November presidential election, Brewster had cast three hundred votes for New York governor Thomas Dewey, and only ninety-seven for President Roosevelt.

Near the end of one of the letters, Washy learned that Serena Clark's husband, Harris had been killed at Normandy the previous June, and the widow was left with an infant girl that Harris had never seen. Washy remembered Serena. She was the youngest sister of his classmate Albion Rogers Jr. and was perhaps in her early thirties. Her late husband had been a bit older and was an apprentice plumber to Lloyd Ellis before being drafted in 1943. Without any real reason, Washy decided to write to Serena and express his sympathy over the loss of her husband. He was surprised when in mid-December he received an answer to his letter.

Iwo Jima

After Peleliu, Washy's Seabee battalion was assigned to Task Force 54 and transported to Ulithi where the Iwo Jima invasion group was assembling. As he read Serena Clark's unexpected letter, he sensed her vulnerability. He could identify with her loss just as he remembered his own brother's fate. Serena thanked him for his note about her husband and wrote how the town had rallied around her. She added more information about what the townspeople were up to, and told Washy that she was very sad about David's death. "We've all lost things in this war that we'll never have again," she wrote. "We have to bear it and move on. I'm doing the best I can."

In the weeks that followed, Washy found himself re-reading Serena Clark's letter. Each time he did so, he was intrigued to learn something more about this woman who lived in the place that had once been home to him. As more letters passed between the two, the desire for a deeper attachment grew.

On February 19, 1945, thirty thousand Marines attacked Iwo Jima. There were two airfields on the eight-mile-long island. The Marines quickly captured the first and a Seabee group began making improvements just two days later. Washy's battalion went ashore on February 22 and moved across the island to the second airfield. The Japanese contested every inch of ground, and construction work commenced under live fire.

At midday on February 25, four bulldozers were boxed together next to a blasted pillbox. Washy and a half-dozen men were hunkered down in their shelter taking a break, smoking and sharing water from their canteens. One of the men peered through a space between the machines.

"Hey, would you look at that! Look, chief, up on the mountain."

Washy moved over to look. Still in a defensive crouch, he could see a small group of soldiers on top of Mount Suribachi steadying a pole with an American flag on it. The rest of the men crowded together for a look.

"Maybe it means that the Japs have given up," said one of them.

"Not likely," Washy told him. "The Japs don't give up. They'll fight to the last man. Especially now that we're in their back yard. We've seen it before. Keep your heads down."

And indeed, of the twenty thousand defenders on Iwo Jima, less than a thousand were taken prisoner. The rest perished in caves, incinerated in their strongholds. It was almost as bad for the Americans. Of the thirty thousand U.S. Marines involved in the operation, over six thousand were killed and thousands more wounded. The Seabees lost several hundred men from their force of seventy-five hundred, some of them Washy's close friends. John Gifford, from Falmouth, had worked at Wood Lumber before entering the service. He was wounded on the second day of the battle. Washy wrote Serena that he'd visited Gifford in the aid station, where the two Cape men talked about home and what they were going to do after the war. "He was laughing and seemed to be fine," Washy told her. "He was looking to be evacuated shortly and asked me for a cigarette. I'd just lit it for him and he died right there."

For years afterward, there were debates as to whether the terrible casualty toll suffered by marines on Iwo Jima had really been worth the cost. For his part, Washy had no opinion. He was just glad to have survived.

Letters to Iwo Jima

The war effectively ended for Washy on Iwo Jima. His battalion was not assigned to the Okinawa invasion that took place in April of 1945. Everyone listened to the reports of the bloody struggle for that island as it raged into May. No one was sorry they'd been left behind on Iwo Jima.

On May 8 came the announcement that Germany had surrendered. The European war was over. Everyone on Iwo Jima was certain that an invasion of Japan was next. Serena Clark's letters came regularly now and Washy sensed that she was using her correspondence as a way of dealing with the loss of her husband. He wrote back, aware that he was filling her need, but he also knew he was putting himself at risk. For all the years since Justine, Washy had avoided serious relationships. Now, in the loneliness of a distant place, he relaxed his guard, seizing on the chance to share his feelings with Serena. Across the thousands of miles that separated the pair, Washy began to think that perhaps he could eventually love again.

In August the United States dropped two atomic bombs on the Japanese cities of Hiroshima and Nagasaki. While the future would entertain discussions about the morality of the bombing, there were no doubts among the men who had lived through the hell of Guadalcanal, Saipan, Tarawa, Iwo Jima and Okinawa. To a man they believed it had been the right thing to do. Future debates about the use of atomic bombs against Japan would be left to the philosophers who had never seen combat.

When Japan surrendered unconditionally on August 15, 1945, there was jubilation among the troops on Iwo Jima and throughout the rest of the Pacific. There would be no invasion of Japan, and the soldiers, airmen, and marines assumed that they would be rotated home quickly. But many found themselves at the mercy of the overwhelming logistical problem of getting everyone back to the United States. The War Department point system for determining who got home the quickest was also a problem. The GIs in the European and Mediterranean theaters would go home first. Some already had. Even though Washy's battalion had been in the Pacific combat area since the early months of 1943, their return to the United States would be delayed until at least November. It was a bitter pill to swallow, and many of the Seabees were angry. Washy, too, was disappointed. Harriet Ellis's letters mentioned that many of Brewster's soldiers and airmen who had been in Europe were already home. Ted Ellis had been discharged from the Air Corps after less than two years in Italy. Joe Latham, Jr. was back in Brewster and Larry Crocker had re-enrolled at Tufts University for the fall semester. In his letters to Serena, Washy attempted to hide his frustration, but she could sense his impatience.

"You will be coming home soon enough, Washy," she wrote back. "Don't begrudge the men who have already returned. I'm just glad that you are safe, and like many in town, I wait for you. But I can't forget those like David and Harris who will never return. Be patient and thank God that you are alive."

She'd put it far better than he could have, and Washy repeated that message of restraint to anyone who came by his tent with complaints about how long it was taking to get home. They took it as the wisdom of a chief petty officer exercising good leadership. But in reality, the sentiments Washy offered had come from the heart of a young Cape Cod widow.

San Francisco Bound

The trip back to the states aboard the transport ship *Latona* was nothing like the deployment two years earlier that had taken the Seabees out to the war zone. The ship's lights blazed at night and the course set by the navigator was a straight line to Hawaii. There was a good deal of card playing, sunbathing on deck, movies at night, and by the time the ship reached Pearl Harbor, the men were long over their seasickness and ready for liberty in an American port. Washy was able to cable Clara that he was finally on his way home.

Perhaps for the first time in a long time, Washy began to think about his future. He faced the uncertainties that all the returning soldiers, sailors, and airmen would have to deal with. Where would he live? Did he have a job waiting? Could he readjust to a life that required far fewer rules than he had been used to in the military? He was pretty sure that Clara wouldn't be returning to the Cape. She mentioned in a letter that John was being tabbed for duty in Europe as a serving counsel for the German War Crimes Tribunal scheduled for Nuremberg later that year. She and the two girls would be staying in the Washington, D.C., area where they had army friends.

The house at Sears Point was also not an option. Mrs. Ellis had written that when the soldiers abandoned the place more than a year before, they hadn't taken many pains to leave it in good order. Before Washy could settle in, a lot of work needed to be done and the cold months weren't the best of times to do it. And then there was the situation with Serena Clark. Washy knew he'd opened himself up more than any cautious man might have done, confiding feelings that now in hindsight, he wondered if he should have so freely offered. How would Serena factor in his return home? Was it just the war that had connected them? All of these things swirled in his mind as the *Latona* plowed its way toward California.

On November 19, 1945, the *Latona* steamed under the Golden Gate Bridge to the wild cheers of the almost eight hundred men on board. Hats flew in the air, men danced with each other, and more than a few joyful tears were shed as the ship took on a pilot who would guide her to a berth at Hunters Point Naval Shipyard. By late afternoon, she was moored securely at Pier 6 near the dry docks. In less than a day, silent and devoid of any human activity, the *Latona* was a ghost ship.

Washy spent several days in San Francisco, mostly ensconced at the bar in the Mark Hopkins Hotel. It was his first time in the city but he had no real interest in venturing out into its unfamiliar streets. He checked in at the personnel office at Mare Island and was told that he could take his discharge on the west coast immediately. But in doing that, he'd forfeit a paid trip back home. A few men, eager to be released from the service, took that option and had their papers in just a few days. Some intended on staying in California. Others just wanted to be free. There were promises of getting together at some future date, but few who were leaving really believed that would ever happen. Once outside the gate they were swallowed up by the bustle and noise of the city. Since he didn't have any reason to be discharged in California, Washy moved into the Chief's Quarters at the base and waited for his transfer orders and a train ticket home.

A few days later, while having lunch in the Chief's Club he was approached by a waiter "Are you Chief Sears?" The waiter looked at Washy.

"That's me," Washy acknowledged.

"There's a phone call for you, chief. It's from the east coast. They've routed it from the main base switchboard to the club. You can take it in the office."

When he picked up the phone, Washy was greeted by a voice he didn't recognize.

"Washy, I've had the worst time tracking you down. It's four o'clock in the afternoon here in Brewster. It's snowing and I've just come back from the post office with one of your letters. Everyone in town wants to know when you are coming home." Serena Clark's voice came through the wire so clearly, she sounded like she was in the next room.

It struck Washy that with all of the letters that had passed between the two of them, he was actually hearing this woman's voice for the first time. Until now, she had just been words on a page. And yet their correspondence over all those months had buoyed him against his loneliness and the loss of his brother. Washy had needed her in those months in the Pacific, and he knew that he needed her just as much now. He was smiling when he spoke into the receiver.

"Serena! Is this really you? I can't believe it!"

The voice at the other end hinted of tears. "I tried several times to get a call through but it was impossible," she told him. "I'm so glad you got my letters."

"I'm just waiting for my orders to come through," he replied. "There's a good chance I could be back home by Christmas."

Serena couldn't stay on for more than a few minutes. But in the short time they spoke, Washy knew that she wanted him home as soon as he could get there. As he hung up the phone and returned to the dining room, he thought to himself that there was indeed a very good reason to expedite his travel plans.

The Homecoming

The afternoon fog that spiraled like clockwork over the low hills fronting Golden Gate Park did nothing to dampen the spirits of Chief Washington Sears as he walked back from the Mare Island personnel support detachment. His orders had come. The following day, Washy checked out of his quarters and took a cab to the train station in San Francisco. He was able to get a ticket to St. Louis. From there, his route would take him to Chicago and then east to Boston via Cleveland, Buffalo, and Albany. As he settled into the worn seat of the smoky Pullman car, Washy reflected on what the past three-and-a-half years had done to him. Like all the other veterans aboard that train, he was expected to somehow make the transition from a world of fire and death to a life that was ordinary and predictable. He wondered if that was possible. Could anyone even remotely understand what they had been through? There were more questions than answers, and as tired as he was, Washy didn't want to think further. He adjusted a pillow behind his head in an attempt to get comfortable. A club car attendant came through and asked if anyone wanted coffee or a soft drink. Washy ordered a cup but was asleep before the train had crossed the Bay Bridge to Oakland.

The six-day trip across the country was uncomfortable. The view out of the dirt-streaked windows revealed scenery that was exceedingly drab in the shortened days of winter. Many of the small towns along the route still carried a wartime look and there was virtually no automobile traffic. The train passed small farms, stubbled land, and beaten houses. The barns had worn siding and their tarpaper roofs flapped forlornly, sprained doors hanging open on rusty hinges. Despite the fact that it was December, inside the train it was intolerably hot, smoky, and filled with the smell of unwashed men. They were delayed almost fourteen hours in St. Louis and another half-day just outside of Chicago. At Buffalo, Washy felt confident enough to make a call to an aunt's house in Brewster to ask that someone meet him at the train station in Hyannis. His arrival was tentatively scheduled for December 19. Could someone be there to pick him up? His aunt assured him that someone would be there. There were just two daily trains running from Boston to Hyannis. If he wasn't on the early one, he told her, he'd arrive on the afternoon one. That was how it was left.

There had been no further delays from Buffalo and Washy was able to make the afternoon Cape train at South Station. The rolling stock, two half-filled passenger cars and a baggage car, was in no better shape than what he had endured across the country. The seats were worn and the windows needed washing. As the cars swayed across the Wareham narrows, Washy saw some of the devastation still left from a hurricane that had hit the area the previous year. The Cape had been cut off from train service for almost a month before a new bridge over the narrows had been put in place. There were still shells of houses littering the nearby right-of-way and the cleanup was still in progress. Down through Sandwich and Barnstable, acres of trees had gone down, and many still lay where they'd fallen over a year ago, waiting to be salvaged by woodcutters.

When the train pulled into Hyannis, a small number of people milled around on the station platform. Half were railway workers getting ready to pull sacks of mail and express packages from the baggage car. Washy hefted his sea bag over his shoulder and gave the ticket for his foot locker to one of the men who headed off to find it amid the jumble of other railway freight. The air was crisp and there was a hint of snow in the dull gray sky.

A figure swathed in a heavy coat and fur scarf emerged from the building and moved toward him. As the person came closer, the scarf slipped down and Washy could see she was a small, dark-haired woman.

"Is that you, Washy?" she moved toward him. "Is it really you? It's me, Serena."

That Serena Clark would be at the station to meet him had never entered Washy's mind. He'd figured on Uncle Sileck or maybe Earl Ryder or Dick Rogers, and he was flummoxed enough by her unexpected appearance that he didn't react immediately. Serena, on the other hand, had no compunctions about how Washy should be welcomed home. She flung her arms around him, and through tears she nestled her head in the crook of his shoulder.

"Thank God you are safe, Washy. And thank God you are finally home. Put your foot locker on a cart and let's get it out to my car. It's too cold to be standing out here." She looked up at the ominous sky. "And I'm not too good at driving in snow."

Washy followed Serena through the station house and into the parking lot where an older Ford Model A was waiting.

"I borrowed my father's car. When we heard that you were coming in today, there were a number of people who volunteered to come and get you. But I told them all that I wanted to do it. I was here this morning when the early train came, but you weren't on it. I stayed around. I hope you don't mind. It was just that we'd been writing for so long, I wanted to be the first person to welcome you back home."

Once in the car, he eyed her, this woman that he knew only through letters, as she manhandled the gear shift and bucked the car down the Main Street of Hyannis. She was much smaller than he'd imagined she would be.

"Where'd you leave the baby?" he asked as they passed through a set of street lights and headed north on Willow Street.

"Oh, she's with my mother," Serena told him. "I've been living with my folks for about a year now. Harris and I were renting a small place on Mill Stone Road near the Cowens before he went overseas. But it was lonely out there with him gone, and they suggested I come and live with them. It's been good. The baby's got a regular routine. She sleeps a good bit of the day and then spends the rest of the time keeping my father occupied. He fusses more about that child than I do. Actually, both of them do, but I think the baby has got a special eye for my father. She's all smiles and giggles when he's around. When I come in, she cries."

"You know, Serena, I don't think I ever asked what the baby's name was." Washy was embarrassed to have to admit that he didn't know it.

"It's Mary. She was named after my grandmother, Mary Augusta Bangs. I think I remember that Mary was your mother's name. Isn't that so?

He nodded. The mention of his mother made Washy aware that he was really going to be quite alone in the town where he'd grown up. His parents were gone. David had been killed in the war and Clara was in Washington, D.C. Other than a few aunts and uncles and several distant cousins, Washy's family tree looked like a swamp willow in winter. Serena, on the other hand, seemed to be related to just about everyone in Brewster. Beside the Bangs family on her mother's side, and the Rogers, she had Fosters, Bakers, Doanes, Eldridges, Newcombs, Robbins, and even a few Sears in her lineage. Most of the latter were from Dennis, she told him.

"Well, I hope we're not cousins," Washy remarked with a chuckle, continuing to admire Serena's skill in negotiating the many curves in the road that disappeared ahead in the twilight.

"We probably are," She took her eyes off the road for a minute and looked over at him. "But I don't think anyone is going to make much of it. Just about the whole town is related in one way or another. A couple of years ago, Stanley Briggs married his cousin Alice Briggs. The only problem they've had is when he ran for town meeting moderator. He would have been elected unanimously but for one write-in vote for Walter Briggs, Alice's brother. When Stanley found out that Alice had cast a vote for her brother and not him, he didn't speak to her for a month. But they're fine now." She laughed and her face crinkled up as if the memory had tickled something deep inside her.

"I'm to drop you at Uncle Sileck's," Serena told him as they rounded Betty's Curve. "He said you could stay with him and Alma for as long as you want. They've got plenty of room. My mother and father's house is on Old North Street. When you've had a chance to get settled, I'll call you. Imagine! I won't have to sit down and write a letter."

Serena helped Washy unload his sea bag and foot locker when they arrived at Sileck Sears's house on Main Street. His uncle clasped his hand firmly. "Good to see you, Washy. Train must have been on time for a change." Sileck looked at the two young people standing by the car. "Get in the house quick, Washy. Alma's got dinner on. Serena, you get on home. They say we're going to get a storm." He went inside, stomping his boots on the porch as he opened the door. Serena was a head shorter than Washy and as she looked up at him, snowflakes were starting to drift through the bare branches of the surrounding elm trees. They lit on her eyelashes and caught strands of hair that had escaped her scarf. The porch light did little to break the lengthening shadows but it struck Washy that Serena's eyes emitted a light of their own.

Serena moved closer and kissed Washy lightly on the cheek. Then she got into the car and drove away toward the town center. Her departure left Washy with just as many questions as when he'd boarded the train in San Francisco. He stood for a few moments looking down the road at Serena's departing car. Inside the house, Alma Sears smiled to herself as she set the table for dinner. She knew the answers, even if Washy didn't.

Digging Out

A hushed feather-soft snow fell for the next day-and-a-half, covering Brewster with at least a foot on that twentieth day of December, 1945. Roads were impassable and phone lines were down. With the power out, old kerosene lamps came out of closets to supplement the candles placed in strategic places around the house. The woodstove in Uncle Sileck's living room kept the space cozy, and three quilts made sure Washy was warm enough at night, even when the temperatures dropped to close to freezing in the unheated upstairs bedroom.

By the time Washy had Uncle Sileck's car shoveled out two days later, the sun was out and a single path, wide enough for maybe one car, had been plowed down Main Street. He and Sileck drove past the center to a small coffee shop owned by Peter Dillingham. Someone had commandeered a surplus military electric generator. It was warm inside and plenty of hot coffee was being dispensed. When the two entered the building, every counter stool was occupied. Several of the occupants turned in their direction, boots shuffling as the door clanged shut.

"Hi, Sileck. Good to see that you got out. Who's that fellow you got there with you?"

When Sileck told them who it was, several men came off their stools and approached, smiling with their hands extended.

"Washy Sears! Well I'll be damned. Didn't know that you'd gotten back. Didn't recognize you there. When'd you get in?" A knot of men started to come over from the tables and stools.

Accepting the offered hands and enthusiastic claps on the back, Washy told them of his train trip across the country and how he'd gotten back to Brewster on the eve of the snowstorm.

"I've been in town for a couple of days. But this is the first time I've been able to get out of the house. Aunt Alma has been trying to feed me just about every hour. I don't know how Sileck does it. I needed a break from all that food!"

Over the next hour, Washy reacquainted himself with his old friends. Some were recently back from the war just as he was. There was a lively exchange of experiences about people and places, where some of them had been and what they'd seen in their war service. There was no telling where truth ended and exaggeration began, but the tales ran the gamut from Berlin to Bougainville, and the stories might well have continued without a break had it not been for the arrival of several state trucks looking for workers to clear snow off Routes 137 and 124. A jumble of men poured out into the sun-bright day, climbed into a collection of vintage cars and followed the state trucks down the road. It was suddenly quiet in the small building. Outside, the snow was melting, trickling into downspouts and rolling down the windows of the coffee shop. Washy told Sileck to go ahead and drive home without him. He wanted to take a walk and get some air. It was warm enough that Washy removed his hat, and that was why Serena Clark had no trouble recognizing him when he walked up Old North Street.

A Peacetime Christmas 1945

Washy attended Christmas Eve services at the Baptist church with Serena and her parents. Little Mary Clark was seated between the couple and Mr. and Mrs. Rogers. The child amused herself during the service, twisting her braids and playing with Washy's hat while the choir and the congregation sang the familiar carols. At the conclusion, Harriet Ellis came by and gave Washy a welcoming hug. He thanked her for her letters. There was a life-size manger scene in front of the church, and it was all Serena could do to keep Mary from climbing up into it and removing the statue of the baby Jesus from the crib. There was a muffled laugh from Serena's parents when the girl suddenly looked up at Washy and called him "Daddy."

"Be careful, Washy," Albion Rogers put his arm on Washy's shoulder.

"That child has a way of getting whatever she wants. I can tell you that. Sounds like she's looking for a father for Christmas." The older man laughed again. Serena, standing nearby, turned bright red and hustled the child off to look at some of the lights in front of the church. Her mother followed.

"Seriously, son, you could do a lot worse," Serena's father cocked his head and winked, turning to look in Serena's direction. "I know you just got back in town, Washy. And you've got a lot of things to take care of and catch up with. But Kay and I would have no objections to you calling on Serena. In fact, we'd be pleased if you did. She's a damn fine young woman."

These words of encouragement didn't exactly take Washy by surprise. But Albion Rogers's approach had been a bit bolder and more direct than expected. "Thank you, sir. You're right that I'm going to need a bit of time to get settled. And I appreciate your kind words. Any idea how Serena might feel about my coming over to see her?"

"I think it's a good bet that she'd be very pleased," the older man smiled. "When you came up the road to the house the other day just after the storm, I couldn't tell which was lit up more, Serena or our Christmas tree. Anyway, think about it Washy. A successful man's got to have a good woman in this life. I'm living proof of that. And if you don't mind my saying this, my daughter could certainly use a good man."

Washy drove the Rogers family home. Serena sat next to him with the baby, now fast asleep, bundled on her lap. When they got to the house, Serena's parents went inside, carrying the child with them. Serena lingered a moment in the car. She put her hand on Washy's arm.

"I'm sorry that you were put in a bit of an awkward position tonight, Washy. Sometimes parents can be just as much of an embarrassment as children. Lord knows mine can be. Father meant well and I hope you didn't mind terribly. He's been worried sick about what is going to happen to me, especially what is going to happen to his granddaughter. I know he doesn't want me to have to move away. I'd be lying if I told you that you were the first man that he's shopped me to."

Washy liked this small woman who sat looking over at him. There was nothing artificial about Serena Clark. What passed between them seemed natural and good. Much like her letters, he thought. He got out of the car and went around to the passenger side to let her out.

"No need to make any apologies, Serena. Your father's a good man. If I had a daughter, I'd be doing my best to smooth things out for her, especially if she'd gone through something like you have. He wasn't out of line."

Washy held the door open and Serena stepped out. She reached up, and placing a hand behind Washy's neck and drawing his face down, she gave him a kiss on the cheek. She went into the house leaving him standing alone in the driveway. Perhaps it was his imagination, but Washy had the feeling that her lips had lingered just a bit longer than the kiss she'd given him outside of Uncle Sileck's house. As he got back into the car, he thought about how nice it would be if Serena's next kiss found his lips instead of his cheek. The thought warmed him all the way back home.

The Homestead

After Christmas, Washy drove to Rhode Island where he was mustered out of the navy. When he got back to Sileck's house, Washy took off his uniform and put it away in a dry cleaning bag with some moth balls.

He took a day and drove over to see Avery Taggart at Camp Edwards. Taggart was just a few months from retirement, and his job would be filled by the man who had taken Washy's place when he'd left for the war. There would be no assistant. That job and many others were being eliminated as the base went into its expected post-war draw-down.

"Not much opportunity here, Washy," Taggart counseled him over coffee. "We're headed for caretaker status. The air force is making some noises about retaining the use of the runway and keeping some planes here but that's about it."

Washy hadn't really counted on getting his old position back, but the reality of the job situation was a bit sobering. He couldn't see himself driving a truck part-time, not after the experiences he'd had. Thanking his old boss, Washy promised that they'd get together later in the spring. Exiting the main gate, he passed by some civilian guards who were paying more attention to several deer crossing Route 28 than they were to who was entering or leaving the base.

It wasn't until a few days into January that Washy was finally able to take a close look at the house at Sears Point. It was clear there was a lot of work to be done before he could even think of moving back in. Putting a board over a broken window, he exited the house and walked with some difficulty through what remained of the pre-Christmas snow up to the top of the sand dune in the back. The water in the bay was a cold blue with just a few white clouds in an otherwise empty sky. Large chunks of ice floated on the high tide, and he could hear them scraping against each other as waves pushed them toward shore.

Thoughts of his mother and father, David and Clara, even a brief memory of Freeman, filtered through Washy's mind as he contemplated where he fit into it all. Perhaps it was time to put the homestead up for sale and let whatever employment he might find determine where he should live. It was a big country. He'd seen that. But, as he returned to the front of the house and got into Uncle Sileck's car, there was something that kept going through his mind – a deeply implanted sentiment that he couldn't shake.

There would always be Sears in this place. And they would be connected through history and time – one and all, the first and the last, by the land that surrounded them.

Taking Stock

The Brewster that Washy had come back to was not all that different from the one he had left. As it had been in the decades before the war, the town's population totaled less than a thousand people. The official number in the 1945 annual town report was 757. Occupations still included farmers, caretakers, carpenters, painters, cranberry growers, and some retirees. What government existed was effectively administered by a three-man elected board of selectmen. George "Fobe" Foster, Chester Williams, and Harold Swift held occasional office hours in the town hall on Main Street and the trio seemed to have things well in hand.

The railroad still ran through town, but only once or twice a week, hauling freight to the Lower Cape. Passenger service had ended years ago. There was not a single traffic light in town. There was no bank, no drugstore and just three gas stations, four if you counted Ivan Dugan's place in West Brewster, open only when the spirit moved him or when he wasn't on some other venture. The town was still a place where if you got a divorce, it made the local paper. There were four small grocery stores and two post offices. No formal police force existed, and the fire department consisted of two trucks and about twenty-five volunteers. When the whistle blew, the "cellar savers," as they were called, came running. In 1945, fifteen children were born, twenty-two couples got married, and twenty people finished their allotted days on earth. The youngest to die was Nathan Crowell at age forty-five. Alice Newcomb passed away at the age of one hundred, after living a full century of life in the same town – indeed, in the very same house where she was born. No one seemed to think that was unusual.

There were few year-round jobs, and the tourist industry, despite the efforts of the Brewster Board of Trade, still lagged far behind places like Falmouth, Yarmouth, Chatham, and Provincetown. Most local men worked in some capacity for the town, clearing snow in the winter months or as volunteer firemen or temporary road workers. The town report still listed weighers of hay, grain, and coal, fence viewers, field drivers, and an inspector of slaughtering. Always, it seemed, that job went to Hudson Ellis. Each of these longstanding positions was a reminder of the town's still functioning, if clearly declining, agricultural heritage.

After his visit with Avery Taggart, Washy decided that finding work on the Upper Cape was probably not likely. Nickerson State Park in East Brewster offered some seasonal employment, and supervisors Robbie and

Freddy Hooper encouraged Washy to see if he could "get on the state." There was a buzz about extending a new highway from Sandwich to Orleans, but so far it was just talk, and many believed that the strong railroad lobby in the state legislature would kill any such plan. A lot of the business owners in the old village centers were also not keen on the idea that a new highway might bypass them. Washy gave some thought to becoming a private contractor, using his heavy equipment skills, but he didn't have the money to purchase the necessary machines, and local banks, despite the government veterans' benefits bill, were not all that generous with loans for ex-servicemen who were unemployed with little collateral. He caught up with Sparrow Higgins who was still with Nickerson Lumber. Over lunch at Reno's Diner in Orleans, Washy asked about employment there. Sparrow didn't see anything opening up soon.

"Oscar Nickerson promised all of the boys who went into the service that they'd have their old jobs back when they came out. He's been true to his word. If things get going in the building trades, we might be hiring a couple of yard men in the fall, but probably nothing before then." Sparrow could see some disappointment in his friend. "It's going to be tough for a while, Washy, especially in the winters. I did hear that Frank Sargent, Willis Gould, and Freddie Macfarlane are going to open up a fishing and hunting supply business out on Nauset Beach Road. They're all veterans and they might be able to give you something."

"I don't know, Sparrow," Washy looked across the table. "I can't see myself behind a counter trying to explain to some city fellow how to set the proper choke on a 12-gauge shotgun. And I don't know fish. That was my father's specialty. But thanks. I'm hoping I can get something that keeps me outdoors working with equipment. That's where I belong." He shook his friend's hand. "Let's keep in touch."

On the personal front, Washy was still trying to sort out where the relationship with Serena Clark was going. She seemed to understand his need to approach things at a pace that made him comfortable. Washy appreciated that. He knew he was going to have to find some kind of a job before too long or face the prospect of going to Brockton or Worcester, something that held little appeal for him. Fortunately, he had some money saved, and planned to use it to get the Sears Point house habitable again. But the funds weren't going to last forever.

Town Meeting

On an unseasonably warm Tuesday morning in March, Washy attended Brewster's annual town meeting. Serena and her parents were there in the crowd of about two hundred people, but he didn't sit with them. The session was called to order at ten o'clock by moderator Winthrop Crocker, and the assembly began the business of raising and appropriating monies for various town projects. Fifteen hundred dollars was voted to construct a drain from Cobbs Pond to the Breakwater town landing. A proposed survey that would make Paine's Creek into a harbor was tabled after long discussion. One hundred dollars was approved for planting a community Christmas tree in front of town hall. The annual payment of a thousand dollars to Cape Cod Hospital for the establishment and maintenance of a free bed for needy residents was also approved without discussion. Monies to suppress moths and propagate clams were passed. The more than $21,000 school budget passed unanimously. Some minor town positions were filled by voice vote. At noon, Moderator Crocker signaled that it was time for a break and the voters headed down to the first floor of the building where a light lunch was provided by the ladies of the Brewster Alliance.

As Washy worked his way down the serving line he noticed that Serena had left her parents and was engaged in conversation with Frank Ellis. The two were laughing about something, and at one point Ellis put his arm around Serena and gave her a squeeze. Washy continued to watch the pair as they chatted. The two were clearly enjoying themselves, and Washy had to stop himself from going over and interrupting their merriment. By the time he finished his lunch and was back upstairs, Ellis was nowhere to be seen, and Serena was back sitting with her parents. Washy had no idea what had transpired between Serena and Frank Ellis. And what business was it of his, anyway? He had no claim on Serena, she was perfectly free to talk with anyone she wanted. Still, he wondered what he'd missed during the break and he sat there thinking about it until the moderator announced the resumption of the meeting.

The afternoon session saw some of the more important articles coming before the assembly. Arthur Coakley spoke to an article about creating an airport in town. There was considerable interest in the idea, and Coakley, along with Art Daniels, Harold Swift, George Foster, and Chet Williams were instructed to form a committee to study the matter. Catherine Crocker asked the town to investigate building a gymnasium and community auditorium, and another study group was formed. Two hundred dollars was voted for maintaining the town dumping ground off Run Hill Road. When the matter of appropriating six thousand dollars for a new road grader came up, Dennis Dugan raised his hand to be recognized.

"Mr. Moderator. Before we decide on this new machine, we need to vote on the position of highway surveyor. I've been told that Lloyd Ellis don't want the job anymore. We need to know who'll be in charge of the roads before we spend money on machines."

There was a nod of agreement among the voters.

"This is the first I've heard that Lloyd didn't want his name proposed for the job," Crocker interposed. "He's had it for a number of years now. Do you know why he's removed himself from consideration?"

"No sir, I don't. But that's the talk in the coffee shop and at HT's."

A hand went up to be recognized. It was Albion Rogers, Sr.

"Mr. Moderator. Lloyd is out of town visiting his sister. He called me before he left and said that he hoped to eventually become fire chief when Michael Cummings steps down. Lloyd's got a plumbing business going and wants to concentrate on that. So he's not going to run for surveyor this year."

There was a murmur in the hall.

"Well we've got a problem, then," Crocker commented. "We are looking at a large expenditure of money for a road grader, but we have no idea who's going to supervise its use. The chair is open for suggestions."

Rogers was on his feet again. "Mr. Moderator, if I may. Lloyd gave me a name of someone that he felt would be a good fit for the job." At these words, Dugan and Roland Tabor perked up. It was an open secret that they had an interest in the surveyor's job. Rogers continued, "This might come as a bit of a surprise, but Lloyd suggested Washy Sears."

The eyes of every voter in the hall turned in Washy's direction as Rogers continued. "Washy knows highway equipment. He did it for years before the war and worked with the Seabees supervising men and machines all across the Pacific. He's the right man for the job and I'm placing his name in nomination." Almost immediately from the other side of the hall, a second voice called out, "I second the nomination." It was Frank Ellis.

Washy was no less surprised than the rest of the voters at his sudden elevation from obscurity. Taking over the job of Brewster's highway surveyor was the last thing he'd envisioned when he decided to attend the meeting. It took him a moment to focus. In that time, Crocker turned to look in his direction.

"Mr. Sears, you've been nominated and seconded for the position of town highway surveyor. It's a one-year term. Do you consent to serve if so voted?"

Washy stood up slowly, still not sure of what had just happened. "Mr. Moderator. It wasn't my intention to seek any kind of office or job at this meeting. I'm flattered that Mr. Rogers sees me as a person up to the responsibility that goes with the position of highway surveyor. I'm not known as one who makes hasty decisions, but yes, if the voters think I'm the best candidate, I'd be proud to take it on for a year." He sat down. Looking disappointed, Dugan and Tabor found something of interest to examine on the floor.

In short order, Washy was confirmed by voice vote as the town's highway surveyor. There was no discussion or debate. Only later did he find out that the total pay amounted to about twelve hundred dollars annually, a pretty good sum for the times. The position also included the title of fence viewer and field driver. The six thousand dollars for the new road grader passed easily, and at three o'clock, after setting the tax rate at $22.85, a three-dollar increase over the previous year, the town concluded its annual business. Quite a number of people made it a point to amble over and shake Washy's hand as they were leaving the hall. A few smiled and told him how much they had liked his father and mother. Several remembered David. It was still a very small town.

Walking out to his car, Washy spotted Albion Rogers talking with Frank Ellis. He wondered if the conversation concerned Ellis's apparent interest in Serena. As the two men parted, Washy caught Rogers's attention.

"Mr. Rogers, I'll have to say that you took me by surprise back there. I didn't even know that Lloyd Ellis still remembered me."

"Washy, I'm not sure that he does." There was a hint of a smile on the older man's face.

Washy's puzzled look caused Rogers' face to break out in a full grin.

"To be truthful, Washy, I haven't talked with Lloyd Ellis for more than a year. He never seemed to get around to plowing Old North Street in the winter and I let him know that I thought he was a lousy highway surveyor. He didn't like my criticism. I made the whole thing up about the phone call. You see, son, I wanted to give you a reason to stay in town. You need a job."

Washy stood there, hardly sure that he was hearing Serena's father correctly. "You made it all up? I don't believe it. Where does Frank Ellis fit in all this?" he asked.

"That was Serena's idea. She put Frank up to it. He was the one who started the rumor around town that Lloyd didn't want the job any more. People believed it because Frank is Lloyd's cousin. Serena wants you to stay around just as much as I do; actually, I think more."

Rogers was almost to his car as Washy continued to stand in the parking lot, a stunned look on his face.

"And by the way, Washy. I expect I'm going to have no trouble getting my street plowed next winter." Rogers slid into the front seat and the noise of the slamming door did little to hide the laughter that clearly could be heard coming from inside.

"There'll be enough to do in April."

The following day, Washy drove out behind the town hall to survey his new domain as town highway surveyor. On a patch of cleared dirt at the edge of a sand pit stood a ramshackle two-bay wood frame barn that had clearly seen better days. Both front doors were closed, so Washy entered the building by an unlocked side entrance. A 1934 Ford dump truck occupied one side, while the second bay housed a tar pot on wheels and an assortment of rakes, shovels, scythes, and brooms. In the side lean-to there was a small office with a single window. A desk and well-worn chair filled the space and a single bulb with a copper shade hung from a cobweb-encased ceiling joist, its long wire reaching to just above the desk. A 1946 calendar from a local auto parts store still showed February. A picture of a pretty girl holding a wrench and wearing a mechanic's outfit smiled out from the calendar. Washy lifted the plastic to change the month and noticed that the girl's clothing lifted with it, revealing both of her breasts. With March properly in place, she resumed her chaste appearance.

John Linnell and Lester Crowell were the two full-time regulars in the department, and they'd been there since coming home from military service in 1944. Both men were younger than Washy, but he'd known them before the war. Linnell had never seen combat beyond Troy, New York, where he'd been stationed for almost two years as a supply sergeant. "Let" Crowell had joined the navy before his senior year of high school, serving as a crewman aboard the destroyer *USS Samuel B. Roberts* in the Pacific. He'd been discharged and sent home when his brother Wilbert was killed in France in August of 1944. As the only surviving child, Crowell was given a hardship discharge in order to take care of his ill mother. Lloyd Ellis had made a space for him on the highway department knowing that Let needed to work close to home. Some said that Crowell's drinking came from the loss of his brother. Others thought his obsession with the bottle stemmed from guilt at being home safe when many of his former shipmates had died after the *Roberts* was sunk during the Battle off Samar in 1944. When he was sober, Let was as good a worker as there could be. But too often he failed to show up, offering excuses that were as lame as the leg that he favored when it appeared the day was going to be especially hot. Both men were single, and on this early March morning there was no sign of either one.

Opening one of the front doors in the barn to let in more light, Washy bent to examine the front left tire of the dump truck, which appeared low, when he heard a voice.

"Washy, over here!! The voice sounded from across the town hall parking lot. A window was open on the second floor and from it a hand waved.

"Washy, come on up! Me and Let are up here!"

Filling most of the tall window, which was half open, was the wide body of John Linnell. He was holding a pool cue and waving with his free hand for Washy to use the east side fire escape and join him. "Climb up this way, Washy, the door's unlocked."

Reaching the second floor, Washy entered the hall where the day before he'd been elected highway surveyor. A head appeared at the center of the stage where the curtains met. It was John Linnell.

"Back here, Washy. We got a game going."

In the stage area behind the curtain there was a pool table. Around it stood Let Crowell, Leland Eldridge, and Warren Burgess.

"Come on in and join us, Washy. Let's runnin' the table and we'll see if he can keep it up."

With just a slight acknowledgement of his new boss, Let Crowell concentrated on the task at hand, expertly sinking the next four shots before missing an easy one. With an oath, he surrendered the table to Burgess. Crowell stepped away and took a drag from a cigarette that he had temporarily balanced on the windowsill. Hitching up his pants, he walked over to Washy with his hand extended.

"Glad to have you aboard, Skipper." Crowell's nautical expression showed that he was still in partial blue water mode. "Heard you got surprised into the job yesterday." There was a chuckle from the other men. Off to one side, Eldridge puffed a healthy cloud of cigar smoke toward Burgess. Washy sized up the man standing in front of him. Crowell was small and wiry, with a touch of red in his face. His hair was thin with a tonsure that gave him the look of a monk. The man's handshake was firm enough but there was a noticeable tremor in it. Linnell also ambled over from his space by the window and put out his hand. "Welcome home, Washy. It's been quite a while."

Accepting the greeting, Washy looked at the two men who were supposedly in his charge. "What are you two doing up here? Aren't you supposed to be in the barn doing something?"

Linnell stepped back and carefully placed his pool cue, which was about half his height, against the table. Had there been a bright sun that day, Linnell's huge shadow would have put Washy completely in the dark. Unlike his mate Crowell, Linnell had a full head of hair that was as black as a crow's wings. It wasn't surprising that as a teenager he'd picked up the nickname "Tiny." He spread his arms out, making himself seem even bigger. "Ain't much to do today, Washy. This bein' early March and all. It's too cold to patch roads, and the snow's gone, so no plowin'. Trees along the roads ain't ready for brushin' yet. And anyways, the truck's got a bad tire. When we showed up this morning, Warren and Leland came by and wanted to shoot some pool. The hickory poles for their weirs were supposed to be delivered yesterday but they ain't come yet. We figured it was as good a use of time as anything else. Lloyd never minded when we came up here on rainy days like this. There'll be enough to do in April."

Figuring that it would be better to ease into his supervisory role by letting his two men finish their game, Washy told them that he'd be out back in the office and asked them to join him when the game was over. "I need you both to help me find some of the equipment that I thought we had."

Crowell looked back toward the green covered table. It was Linnell's turn to play. "Tide's low in about two hours." The big man picked up his cue and gestured toward Burgess and Eldridge. "By then Warren and Leland can get out to the flats and lay out where the traps are goin' to be. We'll see you back in the barn around lunch time."

Exiting out the fire escape door, Washy wondered what he had gotten himself into. He was head of a department with two Mutt-and-Jeff-like characters and no real equipment. Clearly there were some department needs that hadn't been met by the town. He thought maybe Lloyd Ellis really had a good reason for keeping his hat out of the ring for the job.

Washy sat in his office, trying to sort out a jumble of paperwork from an old file cabinet. The noon whistle sounded from the roof of the small three-bay building next to the Brewster Garage that served as the fire station. Linnell and Crowell entered the barn just before the last neighborhood dogs finished echoing the signal.

"It's lunchtime, Washy." Linnell smiled and opened a big black metal pail, pulling out an enormous sandwich. "Want some of mine?"

Springtime 1946

Over the remainder of the spring, Washy got answers to a few of his questions. Besides the old truck with the bad front tire, there wasn't a lot of equipment to supervise, and Washy wasn't all that sure what he was expected to accomplish. Much of what he had expected to be part of the highway department inventory really didn't exist. Or it had existed at one time and had migrated out of the barn to one place or another. The interconnectedness of Brewster families made for a rather loose arrangement of accountability. If you were related to someone who held office, it wasn't that hard to ask a favor, and it was a practice of past town surveyors to lend out machinery to local contractors who were doing private jobs, on a kind of honor system. They were supposed to pay the town for the use, but rarely did that happen. Some of the equipment never returned, and what did make its way back was often damaged and unusable. Much of that was piled as junk out back of the highway barn.

John Linnell and Let Crowell proved to be dependable workers, even if they were occasionally hard to find. If Washy sent them out to put some cold patch in a pothole or remove sand from a catch basin, he knew it would be done. He also learned quickly that "visibility" was an important part of his job. There were about 40 miles of road in Brewster. Fixing the problems in areas where the most people lived was the best approach. If you wanted to stay in the good graces of the voters and keep your job, you had to be out where they could see you doing something.

It was taking a while for the town to acquire the road grader from Dyar Sales and Machinery, and the Taunton dealer wasn't sure when the machine would actually arrive. This was mixed news for Washy. With spring, a lot of the town's dirt roads needed to be scraped. The grader was important. At the same time, Washy wasn't sure where the machine would be stored. It was about twice the length of the second empty bay in the town barn. It appeared that no one had given this a thought when they contracted to buy it.

When several calls to Dyar proved futile, Washy decided to get in touch with Avery Taggart at Camp Edwards. His old boss hadn't heard of Washy's new position and offered his congratulations. Taggart was just a few weeks from retiring, but when Washy asked if any of the equipment being auctioned off by the base included a road grader, he was pleasantly surprised to learn that there were two machines available.

"Come up when you can, Washy, and I'll give you the pick of the best one. I can't vouch for their condition but there ought to be one that's salvageable. But remember, I'm out of here in just a few weeks and after that, I can't help you."

Not wasting any time, Washy put Crowell and Linnell in the used pickup truck that he had purchased from Chase Chevrolet in Chatham, and the three drove to Bourne the next day. Linnell rode the entire way to Camp Edwards sprawled out in the back of the truck, filling the bed like a huge and lumpy bale of cotton. At the base, they found what had been a former motor pool now filled with a variety of worn-out jeeps and trucks. The men surveyed the two surplus road graders. The best one needed two tires and the cab's windows were broken out. Someone had substituted a swivel stool, probably from an old diner, for the long-gone original seat. But after some priming, the machine started and ran with a steady, if ear splitting, roar. The muffler had clearly gone the way of the missing seat.

"That looks like the one." Washy turned toward his two assistants. "We can grab two tires off the other grader and put them on the one we're going to take."

Linnell scratched his head and looked at Brewster's newest acquisition. "How we goin' to get this thing home?" The same puzzled look was reflected on Crowell's face.

"Simple enough." Washy put his hand on Linnell's shoulder. "You and Let are going to drive it back to Brewster. Start changing those two tires. I'm going up to see Taggart."

There wasn't a lot of hard bargaining done in Taggart's office. The retiring supervisor made his pitch. "I'd say five hundred dollars ought to satisfy the government."

"Make it three hundred and we've got a deal," Washy countered, figuring the original number was just a starting point.

"Well, I don't know, Washy. I've heard that Falmouth is interested in picking up a road grader," Taggart smiled at this former assistant. "But then again, I'd say I owe you for old times, and for your war service. Three hundred dollars it is. The government isn't going to miss the difference."

Taggart told him that he could take the grader home any time it was ready. "You got tags for it?" Taggart asked.

"Not a problem, Avery. We'll get them later and I'll tell my boys to stick to the back roads. Just put together a letter on base stationery so that if any police spot them they won't think it's been stolen."

Carrying the receipt back to where his two men were struggling with the second tire, Washy handed it, along with a twenty-dollar bill, to Linnell. "Get back to town as soon as you can. The money should let you fuel up and leave a bit left over for lunch. Stick to the back roads."

"But chief," Crowell looked up at his boss, addressing Washy by his old navy rank. "Me and Tiny have never been up here in Bourne. We don't know what roads to take to get home."

"Just remember the old Boy Scout rule, Let. The sun rises in the east and sets in the west. And all rivers eventually flow to the sea." Washy chuckled to himself as he got back into his truck. As he drove away, Tiny and Let were beside the second big tire, covered with sweat and still scratching their heads.

When Washy told Percy Newcomb the deal that he'd made with Taggart, the longtime town clerk was surprised and a bit concerned. "We've never done anything quite like this before, Washy. I don't know how the selectmen are going to react. Town meeting did appropriate the six thousand dollars for the new grader, and I don't know if we can get out of the contract with Dyar."

Washy had known Newcomb for most of his life. The official's daughter, Pauline, had been in school with Clara, and Washy was friends with her husband, Tommy Hooper. "Percy, when you tell the selectmen that they're going to get a serviceable road grader for three hundred dollars instead of having to shell out six thousand, I think they will come around pretty fast. As for Dyar, they've hemmed and hawed about delivering a machine for two months. Seems to me you can claim they haven't fulfilled their end of the contract and it's no longer valid."

Newcomb, who hadn't left his desk when Washy entered, sat with his fingers arched and touching in front of his stomach. He opened and closed them several times before replying. "You say the grader is already headed here with Linnell and Crowell?"

"That's right," Washy nodded.

"Well then, I'd say the deed is pretty much done. I'll cut a check for the government and we'll put the surplus back into the general fund. Could even drop the tax rate a bit. The selectmen aren't going to have any problem about that."

The rest of the day went by with no sign of Linnell and Crowell. Washy was still in his office at 7 p.m. Even though he was a bit worried, he hesitated to call authorities in Mashpee or Barnstable, fearing that they might impound the grader because it had no tags. And because both Let and Tiny were single, there were no calls inquiring about the two men. He closed the barn at 9 p.m. and went home. In the late afternoon of the next day, Washy was startled to hear the loud, unmuffled roar of a large machine entering the town hall parking lot. It was the grader with Tiny at the controls. Let stood behind him holding on to the cab housing. Several vines and branches were tangled in the upper part of the structure. About three feet short of the building, the machine bounced to a stop. The two occupants climbed down and stood there for a minute, shaking the road dust off their clothes.

"Where'd you guys go?" Washy asked them. "I figured you would make it in one day."

Let was the first to respond. "Chief, we remembered you tellin' us about the sun risin' in the east and all. That warn't the problem. We got to a river and figured it flowed to the ocean like you said, so we followed it. Turned out to be the Santuit River and we ended up at some godforsaken beach in Mashpee. Had to wait for the sun to come up this mornin' to figure out which way to go from there. We slept under the grader and stopped for breakfast in Marstons Mills. If it hadn't been for some Cape and Vineyard electric workers heading this way, we'd probably still be out there."

It was all Washy could do to keep from laughing out loud. "Well, boys, I'd say you did a good job. Don't plan on coming in early tomorrow. I think you deserve a good long sleep in your own beds. I'm going to see if I can get Arthur Chase to come by and listen to her. He's good at fixing just about any kind of engine. If she needs some tweaking, I'll get him to do it."

Facing his crew, Washy looked them up and down and suddenly snapped a salute which was immediately returned by his two subordinates. "Road grader detachment dismissed!" The lights were put out, the barn doors closed and locked, and the Brewster Highway Department, all three members strong, drove home in the gathering twilight.

Settling with Serena

With spring, Washy was able to do a lot of work on the house at Sears Point. He had Joe Latham and his son John do the plumbing upgrades. A new well was driven and the old cistern filled in. The center chimney was re-pointed and an oil burner and radiators were installed on the ground floor. The Glenwood stove in the kitchen was cleaned up and the walls and ceiling were re-plastered. Slowly the old place started to come back to life.

Washy was already spending nights there by the first week of May. One night after supper, he sat outside listening to the Pinky winks serenading each other in the nearby bog. Across Cobb's Pond through the trees, he could see lights in the house once occupied by Harrison Calderwood. After Calderwood left, the property was sold to Howard Gibbs, another artist who, with his wife Peggy and young daughter, had joined a number of writers and painters that had discovered Brewster. They included "Whitey" and Susie Lutz, who bought Ed Sylver's place near the Old Mill on Stony Brook Road; Eugene Fitsch, a set designer at the Cape Playhouse; and portrait artist Chester Slack, who built a new house and studio up the hill from the mill in High Brewster on Airline Road. The writer Conrad Aiken and his wife, Mary Hoover Aiken, were also living on Stony Brook Road along with Thomas Bouchard, a noted New York photographer. Brooklyn-born novelist Harry Sylvester of *Dearly Beloved* fame also lived in town.

Originally, all of them had vacationed on the Cape in the summertime, but now they were looking at Brewster as a more permanent place of residence. Some local people saw this colony of creative nonconformists as a bit strange. And in many of their affectations and mannerisms, they probably were more than a little different. Subscriptions to the New York Times were up at H.T. Crocker's store, which was now run by Donald Doane, another of Washy's schoolmates. The newcomers, in their turn, evaluated Brewster's long-settled stock as equally peculiar, joking among themselves that the town's limited gene pool had run pretty dry over the past couple of centuries. But in a small town, it was impossible for either side to completely isolate from one another, and as the calendar moved toward mid-century, the citizens of both camps were able to live side by side in something more than just an uneasy peace.

As he stood taking in the smell of early lilacs and watching the sunset across Quivet Neck, Washy heard a car coming up from Lower Road. The automobile approached the house and he recognized the person driving. It was Serena. She'd come by frequently in the past two months to see how Washy was coming along on the house. Often she had little Mary with her and the three would take a break and walk on the beach in front of Sears Point. Sometimes Serena brought food and they enjoyed a picnic lunch. Washy had a lot still inside connected to the war and he felt comfortable talking about it with Serena. As with her letters, she proved just as good a listener in person. With warmer temperatures, the two often sat together savoring the lengthening days of spring. The time together proved a continuing healing process for both of them. On this evening, Serena was alone. She eased her father's car into a space next to the fence encircling the bog. Smiling at Washy, she got out and walked up to where he stood.

"Well, chief," she laughed, mimicking Let Crowell's customary title for the boss of Brewster's highways. "What can you show me today? Do the lights work yet?"

Washy had finally gotten the electric company to service the line out to the house, and he took Serena's arm and walked her to the side entrance where he reached inside and flicked a wall switch. Several lights came on immediately, brightening the room and chasing the shadows that had come with the onset of evening.

"See? I told you I'd have everything I needed. It's all here right in front of you." He led Serena into the living room, where she sat down in a heavy stuffed chair lately of Eldridge's used furniture store in Chatham.

"You have indeed been quite a busy man, Washy," she smiled. "Now you need to finalize things with a woman's touch. You're not supposed to live with cobwebs in every ceiling corner."

She pointed toward the kitchen. "Why don't you let me come in tomorrow and give everything a thorough cleaning."

Washy looked at the woman sitting so naturally in the chair across from him and it struck him that she belonged right there just as she was, relaxed and comfortable in the front room of a house that had never been meant for just one person. "Serena, I wasn't completely truthful a few minutes ago when I told you that I had everything that I needed. You were right when you said that the house needed a woman's touch. It's pretty clear that's true. But I don't mind saying that I need a woman's touch just as much as the house does." He fumbled for a moment before continuing. "I'm wondering if you might consider moving in here with me, with Mary, of course."

Serena looked at him, the beginnings of a smile on her face. "Washy Sears! You aren't planning to make me a kept woman, are you? Unlawful cohabitation? What would people say?"

"Serena, you know what I'm asking. I want us to get married. I've got a house and a job that looks like it could amount to something. I'd like maybe to bring the cranberry bog back and work it. Ever since you wrote me that first letter during the war, I've thought about you and me being together. I don't do much of anything in a hurry and maybe that's my trouble. You've been far more patient than I've had a right to expect. Anyway, I'd like to think you're kind of interested in me, more than just a friend, I mean."

Serena rose from the chair and moved to the window as the last hint of daylight faded in the western sky. She seemed to hesitate for a moment before turning to face him. "Washy, I didn't come out here tonight with any idea that you planned to ask me to marry you. And I didn't hear any rumors around town that you were about to do it, although my father I'm sure may have wanted to plant some. I'm flattered that you'd consider me as someone that you would want to share your life with. I'm not one to make hasty decisions either, Washy, but if you think I'd be the best candidate for the job, yes, I'd be proud to take it on."

With that, she was across the room and into his arms. The two held each other for some time, and in between laughter and some tears, the seed that had been planted in a wartime letter of sympathy to a young widow blossomed into something that somehow had always seemed destined to be. After a while, Washy drove Serena home in her car and the two announced to Serena's parents their plans to wed. Neither showed much in the way of surprise at the news, although Kay Rogers did a fair amount of crying. Later, after a round of celebratory drinks, Albion Rogers drove Washy back to Sears Point. It was close to ten o'clock when they reached the house. Fog had rolled in and only the sound of the surf hitting the beach behind the bluff could be heard. Rogers didn't get out of the car but as Washy exited, the older man reached across the front seat and grabbed his arm.

"Washy, you goddamned took enough time to finally get around to proposin' to Serena. I thought you'd never get to it. I think it will be a good match for both of you. She's getting a good man and you're getting a good woman, and Mary is going to have a real father. I just hope, for God's sakes, it don't take you as long to get to plowing my road next winter as it did for you to finally do what everyone in town was expecting you to do all along. Now go get a good night's sleep. I know I'm finally going to get one."

Rogers had the car in gear and on the way back toward Lower Road before Washy even had a chance to say goodnight.

The First Year

The wedding was scheduled for a Saturday in late June. Serena remained true to her Baptist roots and opted for the ceremony to take place in the church just down from the Ladies' Library. It was all the same to Washy, and he made no objection. The Rev. Charles Griffin performed the marriage and Mary served as flower girl. Puella Snow played the organ. It was a glorious, cloudless day, warm enough inside so that fans were in use. The couple had enough friends between them that the church was nearly full. Serena's extended family took up more than half of the pews. Clara came up from Washington with her two girls. John was still in Europe finishing up the last of the Nazi war crimes trials. Washy was surprised and pleased to see Avery Taggart at the wedding. "I do occasionally get down to the lower Cape," he laughed when Washy went over to him. "But only when it is a very special event. And this is certainly one of them." Milton Gray, Jr. was there, newly released from the marines, to offer his congratulations. Sparrow Higgins came with his wife and toasted the bride and groom, citing his long friendship with Washy and his fond hope that the newly married couple would experience a future of love and happiness.

The reception continued on until late in the afternoon. Afterward, Clara took her two girls back to Sears Point where they were going to spend a few days enjoying the beach. Albion and Kay Rogers were the last to leave. A sleeping Mary was deposited on the back seat of their car.

"We'll take care of her for a few days. She's used to us and there'll be no problem," Serena's mother assured the couple. "I don't know if you will be able to get the Boston train out of Hyannis with the railroad strike and all. But there's always the Ferguson Hotel if you get stuck."

Washy had a few not-so-wonderful memories of the Ferguson from back before the war and decided, without telling his new mother-in-law, that if he and Serena couldn't get out of Hyannis on the train, he was going to drive up to Plymouth and the two would stay there.

Albion Rogers pushed the couple toward Washy's truck. "Don't worry about anything here. Let told me that he and Tiny would take care of things at the highway barn, and I'll check in on Clara at the house tomorrow to see if she and the girls need anything. Have a great honeymoon."

The train didn't arrive as scheduled, and no one was sure when one would be coming. The rail strike had paralyzed much of the country, and the Cape wasn't spared. Washy and Serena drove the forty-some-odd miles to Plymouth, where they stayed for three nights at the Pilgrim Hotel. After the beautiful day they had experienced for their wedding, the next two days were rainy, with high wind gusts. The couple had little need or reason to stray from their room, preferring instead to have room service bring up their meals.

On the third morning, they awoke to bright sunshine, and retraced their route back to the Cape. Albion and Kay were at Sears Point when they arrived, and Mary bounded happily across the yard to embrace Washy and Serena. The bright early summer day gave the house a warm look, almost as if it realized that at last, after so many years, it would be home to a real family again.

Washy was gradually able to retrieve some of the equipment that had been parceled out to local contractors. Perhaps most important was a front end loader in pretty good shape. A cranberry grower had been using it for the past year, housing it in his barn. During the summer, Washy hired on some high school boys to supplement his permanent work force, cutting the grass in cemeteries, brushing side roads, filling potholes, and making sure that the dump was pushed back occasionally.

Several town roads were improved with a sand and oil mix, something that needed to be done every few years. The oil came in trucks from Pawtucket, Rhode Island, and mixed with sand from a pit off Harwich Road. The surplus grader proved to have a strong heart, and with Tiny at the controls, all of Brewster's dirt roads were scraped and smoothed to the satisfaction of the townspeople. Washy was able to get the selectmen to put the purchase of a new dump truck on the proposed warrant for the coming year. Things were rounding out quite nicely as autumn turned the leaves to a rainbow of colors.

The winter was milder than in several previous years. At Sears Point, Serena and Washy closed off the upstairs part of the house and moved their bedroom next to the kitchen to conserve heat. Mary slept in the same room. A January snow isolated them for two days, but Washy made sure that Old North Street was the first priority for plowing. The rest of the winter saw more rain than snow, and there was a lot of pool playing on the second floor of town hall.

When the first week of March brought the annual town meeting, Washy felt pretty confident that his efforts during the past year would be appreciated enough by the residents that he'd be confirmed as highway surveyor for another one-year term.

An Election Challenge

The business for the 1947 annual town meeting was fairly routine. Fifteen hundred dollars was voted to give the town hall a coat of paint. Harry Alexander, Gene Ellis, and Warren Burgess were elected clam wardens, and trawl lines were banned on the flats during July and August after the exposed hooks were deemed a hazard to bathers.

There was an attempt to establish public control of the beachfront, but town clerk Percie Newcomb pointed out that there were a number of private deeded claims to shore properties that would likely end up costing the town a good sum to clear up. Many old families like the Consodines, Bakers, and Cahoons paid a yearly rent for bathhouses and were worried they might lose their privileges. The measure died. Citing the creeping tax rate, opponents of raising the hourly wage of town laborers from eighty to ninety cents an hour were successful in blocking the article. Likewise there was little interest in a proposal to establish a town water system. It went down to defeat with a loud "No!"

A spirited debate centered on a proposal to create a planning board. Opponents claimed that too many regulations would hurt development. "How you goin' to tell a returning veteran that he'll have to abide by a costly set of rules to build his house on his own property? They just got finished fighting overseas to prevent that sort of thing over here. They ain't got a plannin' board in Orleans and that's a bigger town then Brewster. It just ain't American." Despite such pleas, the planning board measure was approved by a narrow seventy-three to fifty-one vote.

When the election of highway surveyor came before the voters, Washy was surprised when Earl Eldridge, Jr. and Roland Gallant had their names placed in nomination. His own name was proposed by Charlie Freeman and seconded by Lloyd Coggeshall.

"We have three candidates for the position of highway surveyor," moderator Crocker announced to the assembly. "Is there discussion on the floor?"

Washy listened as Eldridge and Gallant each made a pitch for the position. Both had experience working for private contractors and several supporters spoke positively about their characters. To some degree, Washy was taken aback and even a little angry that he was going to have to fight for his job after what he considered a very good first year. He wondered if people knew that he'd saved the town considerable money on the road grader and that he'd brought order to a department that had sorely lacked it. Had he somehow forgotten to plow Gallant's or Eldridge's road? It was hard to figure. He had his hand up and was ready to rise and make his case for re-appointment when Crocker pointed in his direction. But instead of acknowledging Washy, the moderator said, "The Chair recognizes Kay Rogers."

Serena's mother was a quiet woman, generally happy to take a back seat to her often outspoken husband. No one could remember that she had ever done much more than knit calmly during past town meetings. It was for certain she'd never spoken on a warrant article. Kay Rogers was as round as she was tall, and had some difficulty getting to her feet to speak. Washy was sitting next to his mother-in-law and she had her hand on his shoulder when she began speaking.

"Mr. Moderator. I really hadn't planned to say anything tonight. Perhaps I'm even out of order for talking about this job because it is presently held by my son-in-law, Washy Sears. But I'm going to speak on it anyway." Voters nodded approvingly, apparently unconcerned that there could be a conflict of interest in what Kay Rogers might say. Crocker had no objections. She looked around and somewhat nervously continued.

"Earl Eldridge and Rollie Gallant are two very good men who could certainly do the job of highway surveyor as well as anyone. That I don't doubt for a minute. But with Washy Sears, we have a man who has done a fine job for the town this past year. He's respected by everyone in town and deserves re-appointment." There was a smattering of applause in the hall.

Kay Rogers continued. "Washy Sears has made a home for my daughter and granddaughter. There was nothing that said he had to do this. He could have left town and made more money in the city. A year ago he wasn't looking to be highway surveyor. But he took the job because you wanted him to and did it well, just at the same time he became a fine husband and father."

There was more applause. Kay paused for a moment, glanced briefly at Washy, and proceeded to deliver her final statement, looking right at Serena, and pausing for effect. "Now, with a new baby on the way, I think it's most important that we continue Washy Sears in his job as our highway surveyor. I ask, as a mother, grandmother, and very proud mother-in-law, that you vote for his re-appointment." And with that, she sat down. Applause, mingled with gales of laughter, rattled the windows in the hall.

Washy had been following the speech up to the point where Kay mentioned a new baby. He wasn't sure he'd heard that last part correctly. After Albion Rogers's calculated maneuver the previous year, Washy figured that this was just another ploy on the part of his in-laws to get him re-elected. He was about to rise and admit the whole thing was the creation of an over-eager relative when he felt a hand on his free arm. Sitting to Washy's left, Serena looked at him and nodded, whispering, "It's true, darling. I told mother this morning. I never for a minute thought she'd announce it to the whole town before I got a chance to tell you."

Crocker had all he could do to put the meeting back in order. Banging his gavel to quiet the assembly, he announced, "There are three candidates for the office of highway surveyor. We'll settle it by a show of hands. Tellers prepare to take a count." When the vote was tallied, Washy was re-elected with one hundred sixty-eight votes. Eldridge finished with thirty-two, and Gallant got fourteen. Right after the final tally, Eldridge rose to a point of order. "Mr. Moderator, if it would meet with Rollie's approval, and yours, of course, I'd like to move that our votes be delivered over to Washy Sears to make the count unanimous." A lot of the voters began clapping again. Across the hall, Gallant nodded his assent. The measure was quickly seconded and there was no further debate. Washy Sears got a second year as Brewster highway surveyor.

In the balcony, Tiny Linnell clapped Let Crowell on the back so that the smaller man almost went over the railing. "See, there was nothin' to worry about. I told you he'd get back in."

Let wasn't smiling, and Tiny asked if he'd rather work for Gallant or maybe Eldridge.

"It ain't that, Tiny, the chief's a good boss. I'm just disappointed that we didn't get that raise to ninety cents an hour!"

The remaining few articles were tabled and the meeting was adjourned.

Washy hadn't moved from his seat, still stunned at the sudden news that he was going to be a father. No one in the hall was any more astonished about the news than the male contributor to the accomplishment. People began to mill around Serena, offering congratulations. For her part, Serena seemed to take everyone's best wishes in stride and there were hugs and kisses from her many friends. Kay Rogers was next to Serena, basking in the reflected glow of her daughter's newly revealed condition, and only after most of the people had left did she walk back to where Washy was still sitting.

"Washy, I hope you didn't mind that I let the cat out of the bag the way I did. It just came out. Serena told me this morning and said she was going to tell you later today. I thought that you already knew! Anyway, when it looked like you had some competition for the job, I had to say something. Please don't be mad at me."

Finally getting to his feet, Washy put his arm around his mother-in-law. "Kay, even if you don't open your mouth at a town meeting ever again, people in Brewster are never going to forget the speech you made today. I'd say you were a first-rate politician. My opponents never had a chance. One thing seems pretty clear. I guess there is truth in the old saying that the husband is the last to know."

Kay laughed, and Washy made his way to Serena to escort her out of the hall. Albion Rogers was still shaking hands with people when they left. Once out to the truck, Washy looked across at the woman who had changed his life. "So when were you going to tell me?"

"Washy, I just found out myself yesterday. I called my mother and told her. I was going to wait until supper to tell you. I never meant for it to come out like it did."

Looking at the small figure sitting next to him, Washy couldn't stifle a laugh. Serena relaxed a bit and smiled back.

"So your mother decides to let the whole town know that we're going to have a baby. Just like that, at the annual town meeting, no less." Both of them were laughing now. "And that to save my job!"

He took Serena's face in his hands. "You know, sweetheart," he chuckled. "It just might have made the difference. Rollie and Earl are two pretty good fellows. Either of them could do my job."

Serena took Washy's hands from her face. "Your job, darling, has always been to love me. And no election would have changed that. You were chosen to care for me and Mary, and now we've got another little one to think about. The baby's going to arrive sometime in October." She moved over and kissed him.

The Antiques Dealer

The summer of 1947 was delayed by an unusually wet spring. It was cold and damp right through early June. Washy drove up Run Hill Road one morning to the town dump. Some teenagers had set the dump on fire the night before after a round of rat shooting, and Washy wanted to make sure that there were no remaining hot spots. As he drove up the dirt road leading to the dump's deep gully, he noticed a newer sedan with New Jersey plates parked near the edge. A faux captain's hat, white with plastic crossed anchors in front, lay upside down on the hood. There wasn't anyone in sight and Washy was puzzled until he heard noises coming from somewhere below the dump edge. Someone was down in the collection of rubbish, cursing a blue streak. Getting out of his truck, Washy walked to the edge and was surprised to see a tall, well-dressed man grappling with a large wooden piece of furniture. The fellow was so engrossed in what he was doing that he hadn't noticed Washy.

"Hey! What are you doing down there?" Washy shouted at him. "Be careful. It's a pretty dangerous spot you're in."

The man looked up, momentarily startled. He appeared to be in his thirties with dark hair and was wearing nicely pressed slacks and a clean white shirt. His shoes were as shiny as the hubcaps on the new DeSoto.

"Oh – you gave me a start." The man backed away from the cast-off wardrobe and looked up. "I didn't hear you drive up. Say, do you think you could give me a hand down here? This old armoire is turning out to be more difficult to move than I'd first thought."

Easing his way carefully down to where the stranger was precariously balanced on a discarded water heater, Washy was about two feet away when the man took out a handkerchief and swiped it across his forehead. Smiling broadly, he put out his hand after wiping it with the handkerchief. "Windsor Burkhart. I'm new in town. My partner and I just bought the old Captain Bragg house. We're in the antiques business. I came up to dump off some trash and happened to see this nice mahogany wardrobe. It's got a bad leg and some scratches but I can fix it up and sell it if I can just get it out of here. These things are in demand right now. Thanks for giving me a hand."

It was soon clear that even with the two of them pushing the wardrobe, it was going to be virtually impossible to move it up the mountain of trash.

"Listen Mr. Burkhart, I've got some rope. I'll go up and attach it to my truck and we'll put a loop around the wardrobe to free it." Washy turned and carefully retraced his steps up the incline through empty cardboard boxes of breakfast cereal, tied-up newspapers, and broken appliances.

Slowly, the two men eased the wardrobe out of the mire. Burkhart followed it up until it stood at the dump's edge, freed from its temporary entombment.

"See, it's not in such bad shape." Burkhart seemed delighted as he walked around his newly liberated treasure, running his hand over the wood. "A little touch-up here and there and a replacement leg and we've got something."

"How are you going to get it back to your house?" Washy's question produced a puzzled look on Burkhart's face. "It's not going to fit in your car."

Burkhart walked around the wardrobe, his hand rubbing his neck. "Perhaps I can get someone at the Brewster Garage to help me. They've got a truck. I'll leave the wardrobe here and go ask."

"If you leave it, Mr. Burkhart, I can tell you that when you come back, it won't be here. Harry and Kenny Alexander check the dump a couple of times a day. If they see it, it's going to be gone. They don't miss much up here that has any value. Why don't we put it in my truck and I'll drive it to your place."

"Say, that's really nice of you." Burkhart brightened. "And by the way, call me Win. I don't think I got your name."

"It's Washy Sears. I'm the town highway surveyor. Part of my job is to make sure the dump is cleaned up. That's why I came up here this morning."

"Well, I'd have to say that was a bit of luck on my part." Burkhart tipped the wardrobe forward. "Let's get it aboard."

Washy followed Burkhart to the former Captain Bragg house. It was a big old place on Brier Road, one of a number of once grand dwelling places for Brewster's legendary crop of nineteenth-century sea captains. Abandoned several years earlier, the house had fallen on hard times and real estate agent Marge Wrigley had been trying to sell it for about two years. But when Washy drove past the overgrown hedge that guarded the property, he could see a cleanup was in progress. The grass had been recently cut and several ladders stood against the side of the house, an indication that some local handyman or house painter had staked a claim to the job. A newly painted sign leaned against the barn. It said, "Sea-Wind Antiques."

At the sound of the cars coming in the driveway, an older man came out of the house to greet them. Like Windsor Burkhart, he was impeccably dressed. Washy couldn't help but think that it was only mid-morning on a weekday, and Burkhart's partner looked like he was ready to attend the theater.

"Hello, Windsor. Who's that you've brought with you?"

"Robbie, you won't believe the incredible luck I had this morning at the dump." Burkhart proceeded to tell his partner about spotting the wardrobe and his good fortune when Washy dropped by. "Washy Sears here happened to arrive just when I needed help with the wardrobe. He had a truck. It was Kismet if I don't mind saying so."

After shaking Washy's hand, Robbie Seabury pointed to the antiques sign. "We thought we'd combine our names for the business. Sea-Wind seemed to have a nautical flavor. I'm quite proud of it myself. Do you like it?"

Washy nodded and replied that indeed the name had a ring to it. "When you get that sign up, I'm sure it will be the talk of the town."

Seabury beamed at the comment and excused himself to go back into the house. "Thank you again for helping Windsor, Mr. Sears," He called back over his shoulder. "And don't be a stranger around here."

Burkhart again thanked Washy for assisting in delivering the wardrobe. "We've been in town just a few weeks and everyone has been so friendly. I think we've found a home." He waved as Washy got into his truck.

Pulling out of the yard, Washy wondered about these two peculiar newcomers and their antiques business. They were certainly different, even more so than the town's new literati. And he was quite certain that once people in Brewster had some exposure to these two men, it wouldn't be just the antiques sign that they would be talking about.

Cyrus Joshua Sears

Serena bore up well under the heat of the summer. Dr. Curtis advised her to stay close to home and slow down a bit as the last few days of September fell away from the calendar. By Serena's calculations the baby was late by more than a week when, on October 13, she woke Washy just before sunrise to tell him that it was time to take her to the hospital in Hyannis.

Washy called Kay to come and take care of Mary and he readied the truck with extra pillows and a blanket for the ride to the hospital. He and Serena left Sears Point at just about 7 a.m. for the forty-five minute ride to Hyannis where Serena was admitted to a birthing room. After Washy had waited for several hours, pacing in the waiting area, a nurse came to tell Washy that he was the father of a healthy boy.

The child, ironically, arrived on Washy's birthday. It was almost as if the baby had made up its mind to delay and come into the world on the same day. At forty, Washy was just a year older than Nathan had been when Washy'd been born. But Nathan had already experienced the birth of three other children. This was something completely new for Washy and he was a bit wobbly thinking about his new status. His world had changed. That was certain. About a half hour later, he was ushered in to see his wife.

Serena looked tired, but she perked up when Washy entered the hospital room and took her hand. He sat on the edge of the bed, careful not to disturb the covers.

"It was a bit easier than Mary," Serena replied. "But I'm still pretty exhausted. The baby is fine. The doctor said he had a strong cry. I was so doped up, I didn't hear it. They are supposed to bring him to me any time now. Can you stay?"

"Of course, silly. Where would I be going when I have a new son to greet?" Washy squeezed her hand again.

"Darling, we talked about what we'd call the baby, and I remember you said that you wanted to use your grandfather's name if it was a boy. Do you still want that?"

Washy smiled at her. "Well, I do like the traditional names, and I've been thinking that it might be a good idea to name him after your mother's father instead. How does Cyrus sound for a first name? I think Kay would like it. And we could use my grandfather's name for his middle name, Joshua."

A nurse came into the room with a small bundle that she placed against Serena's breast. The baby was red-faced from some extended crying, but when nestled against the warmth of his mother, he calmed almost immediately. Washy looked at the baby beside Serena, filled with wonder at how every feature of the child's face was so perfectly formed. The boy was Washy in miniature, with a sharp nose and a pair of ears that he'd unmistakably inherited from his father.

"He's beautiful, Serena. I've never seen anything so perfect." Washy put his hand on the warm little body that was now busily engaged in feeding. "There you are, Cyrus Joshua. The world has been waiting for you – your father and mother and your sister. We've all wondered when you'd finally get here. And you came on my birthday. I'd say that is the most amazing present I've ever had."

After sitting with Serena and the baby for a while, Washy left so his wife could get some sleep. As he moved to leave the room, he walked back for another look at his new son. The baby was fast asleep in the bed next to his mother. "Good-bye, Cyrus Joshua. I'll be back to see you tomorrow." He blew a kiss to his now-sleeping wife and drove home to Sears Point.

A Tell-Tale Snub

Cyrus Joshua Sears came home with his mother a few days later. Young Mary immediately took over as the baby's protector and guardian. Kay Rogers beamed with grandmotherly pride while Alpheus Rogers handed out dozens of cigars to the hangers-on at Donald Doane's store.

Washy was in Ken's Market one afternoon when he heard two local men talking about the new television set they had seen at the Orleans Inn. "Pretty small fuzzy picture, I'd say," said one of them. "I can't see it will do much to replace radio. Don't think many people will go for it." As they left the market, owner Ken Jorgensen told Washy that he'd heard of several people in Brewster who had already ordered television sets from Ellis Electric. "I think it's the coming thing," Jorgensen said to Washy as he went out the door. "I might get one for myself."

Clara and her husband were finally together again after John's lengthy stint in Europe with the War Crimes Tribunals. Discharged from the army and settled in Newton, John had gained partnership in the Boston law firm Spaulding, Foster, and Hague. The practice was doing very well. The couple had purchased a summer cottage in East Brewster. They were on the Cape with their girls during weekends getting their new place ready and Washy and Serena saw a lot of them.

Windsor Burkhart was rapidly becoming a man in demand around town. Cutting a dashing figure and sporting a sophisticated charm that hadn't been seen around Brewster for as long as anyone could remember, Burkhart ran the weekly whist parties at town hall. He enthralled the ladies with funny stories and was a favorite invitee at social gatherings. His partner, Robert Seabury, was no less engaging but seemed content to let Burkhart be the star, remaining in the background almost like a proud parent. Clearly the two men had some money between them and weren't dependent on the sale of antiques. Burkhart ran for school committee and was gracious in defeat when he lost by just a few dozen votes. He headed up the Red Cross blood drive and joined the Unitarian Church, becoming a mainstay in the choir. He was on the search committee that brought the Rev. Charles De Vries to town to serve as the new minister when Pastor Westwood resigned to take a new position in Illinois.

Washy had found a friend in Win Burkhart and enjoyed his frequent unannounced visits to Sears Point. "It's Uncle Win!" was Mary's shout when she would see his DeSoto coming up the road. Burkhart always had a present or some kind of trinket for her. He reserved his greatest hugs for Serena. It was Burkhart who shortened Cyrus Joshua's name to CJ. "No child should have to grow up carrying such a serious moniker," he told Washy and Serena. And CJ it became from that day on.

Burkhart told Washy that during the war he had developed an almost fatal case of malaria during service in the Air Force in India, and when he was healthy enough to be rotated stateside in 1945, he'd met Bob Seabury at Fitzimmons Army Hospital in Denver, Colorado. "Robbie took care of me. My family is a pretty staid bunch from Wilmington, Delaware, friends of the DuPonts and all, and they disapproved of my staying in Colorado with Robbie. My mother died just before the war and Father hasn't spoken a word to me since I told him I wanted a life of my own. I have a sister but she wants nothing to do with me. Robbie and I decided, after living together for a while in New Jersey, to come out to the Cape and see if we could make a go of it here."

As unorthodox as Burkhart's living arrangement with Seabury was, it made little difference to Washy. Burkhart was charming and courteous, and he had a way of telling a story that made everyone laugh. Washy assumed that just about everyone in town felt the same way about the handsome transplant. But it eventually became clear that some of Brewster's residents weren't as tolerant when it came to the idea of two men living together.

Up until 1948, Brewster's veterans had been meeting in Orleans with the VFW affiliate in that town. That May, they formed their own organization, Brewster United Veterans, soliciting members from qualified ex-servicemen and women. Washy had never been much of a joiner, but he was interested in being part of the new group and having a chance to share his war experiences with fellow townsmen. He picked up an application from Arthur Coakley at the East Brewster Post Office, filled it in and sent it off. Several days later he received a letter informing him of his acceptance into the group.

As Washy left the highway barn one afternoon, he saw Windsor Burkhart coming out of the town clerk's office. "Hey Win!" he rolled down the truck window. "Finally come to pay your back taxes?"

Burkhart walked over to the truck and leaned against the door. "No, Washy. As a matter of fact I came in to register our dog. I just paid Percie Newcomb the two dollars for the privilege of having a five-month-old spayed female cocker spaniel legally running around on our hacienda. I should have done it earlier in the year but I forgot. I got a stern lecture from Mr. Newcomb about my lack of civic responsibility."

Washy laughed, knowing how that scene played repeatedly with all tardy registrations. "Say, are you going to the veterans' meeting on Saturday? I think it starts at one o'clock."

The antiques dealer shook his head. "I didn't know about any meeting. I'm still waiting for a letter back from the membership committee. I sent my application in more than a week ago and haven't heard anything yet."

"Well, it'll probably come in the mail tomorrow. You know where and when the meeting is now because I told you. I'll see you there Saturday."

"Sounds good, Wash, see you then." Burkhart went back to his own car and waved as he drove away. The cocker spaniel had its head out the window, both ears flapping in the wind as the car sped toward Brier Lane.

On Saturday, Washy went to town hall where the new veterans group was getting ready to meet. A lot of his friends were there and it was a nice reunion. He stood for a while talking to Frannie Gallant, Joe Crowley, and Charlie Linnell. Later, he saw Tiny and Let and joined them at the coffee table. When the hall was just about full, the newly elected post commander called the meeting to order. Washy looked for Windsor Burkhart in the crowd of about sixty men and a handful of women, to no avail. When the meeting was adjourned, he still hadn't shown up. Washy saw Roland Foster, one of the new organization's officials and went over to him. "Rollie, I was looking for Windsor Burkhart at the meeting today and didn't see him. Did the membership committee get his application? He told me he'd sent it in."

Foster suddenly looked uncomfortable. In a lowered voice he answered Washy. "Yes, we got Burkhart's application but there were a couple of guys on the screening committee that decided they didn't want him."

Washy looked at Foster. "What do you mean, didn't want him? He's a veteran isn't he?"

"It wasn't that." Foster kept shifting his feet, looking away. "It was just that some of us, er, some of them, I mean, felt that Burkhart is sort of queer, living with that older guy Seabury. Something just ain't right there. He's an odd duck. All that fancy talk and all. We think he's queer as a three-dollar bill, Seabury too, and we, ah, the committee, didn't want him in our group. So we voted to reject his application."

"Did anyone tell Burkhart that?" Washy asked.

"Of course not, Washy," Foster answered. "We didn't want to insult the guy directly. We just threw his application away and didn't reply to it. We never said anything to the rest of the membership."

Washy let Foster go without pursuing anything further about Burkhart's application. As the man walked away, Washy couldn't get over what he'd just heard. Of course, Burkhart and Seabury's arrangement was a bit unusual. But queer? Burkhart certainly seemed well enough at ease in the company of either sex, maybe even more so among the ladies. The thought that Burkhart and Seabury were anything more than just eccentric partners sharing a house seemed over the top. That an assumption like this, with no proof of any kind beyond hearsay and innuendo, could deprive a man of membership in an organization like the Brewster United Veterans seemed beyond belief. Washy wondered if he should tell his friend about what he'd learned, but he had a feeling, after thinking about it for a while, that Burkhart already knew what had happened to his application. In the weeks that followed, it was never spoken about by either man, and Washy made the first meeting of the Brewster United Veterans his last.

Revival at Red Top

While other towns on Cape Cod saw considerable population growth in the post-war period, Brewster continued to slumber in peaceful obscurity. It seemed that for every new person that took up permanent residency, another person left town or died. The birth rate was just enough to sustain a small elementary school with grades one through eight. The high school had been dissolved in the late 1930s and students in the upper grades generally went off to Orleans to complete their schooling. A few enrolled in the vocational school in Barnstable. In 1949, Lawrence Doyle replaced long-serving Harold I. Swift on the board of selectmen. Percie Newcomb was re-elected as town clerk for the thirty-third time. There was a polio scare with twelve cases reported in Massachusetts. None were on Cape Cod.

The state instituted a program of reclaiming some of the ponds in town, putting the poison rotenone in the water to kill the less than desirable fish, later re-stocking the ponds with trout. The new miracle insect killer DDT was sprayed liberally across the Cape from noisy helicopters that were almost as much a curiosity as were the shiny new jet fighter planes from Otis Air Force Base, silvery specks high in the sky that left their sound far behind them. The New York, New Haven & Hartford Railroad continued to fight a losing battle with the growing number of automobiles bringing people to Cape Cod, and bids were let for the first phase of a new highway that would eventually put the rail passenger line out of business.

Young Jimmy Gage, an outstanding high school baseball player, got a tryout with the Chicago White Sox, and thirty-six deer were taken in town during the 1950 fall hunting season. Despite Barnstable County Sheriff Donald Tulloch's personal appearance at town meeting to encourage the establishment of a town police force, Brewster voters rejected a formal constabulary, preferring to keep Fred Nash as constable for an annual payment of seventy-five dollars. A theater group from Middlebury College took over the stage in town hall during July and August, enriching the cultural scene for summer visitors. Red-headed John McAnnistan, a local boy and the pride of Anna and Herb McAnnistan, was given a small part in one of the plays, and it was almost impossible to get a ticket because of the demand by Brewster residents to see one of their own perform.

Little CJ grew into a healthy and active boy, and Mary entered the first grade. Whenever Washy made a trip to Orleans or Harwich Center, they were with him. Both children learned the wonders of exploring Brewster's woodlands and ponds with their father. The shore was like a second home for them. The two walked regularly with Washy along the deserted off-season beaches to pick up driftwood for the fireplace.

Washy had just returned from one of those excursions and was unloading the children at the house, when he saw Ethel Crocker's Cadillac come up the road. Serena was in the front seat. The two women had returned from setting up the annual rummage sale at the Brewster Baptist Church.

Serena didn't get out of the car immediately and Washy saw that both women were engaged in a highly animated conversation. He walked over to the Cadillac and Serena rolled down the window.

"Hi Washy," she smiled at him from inside the car. Ethel greeted him warmly from the driver's side. "We were just finishing up. Did you know that someone is doing something up at the old Red Top church? Some of the ladies at church said that a new minister was coming to town and that he was going to open it back up."

Leaning against the car, Washy admitted that he hadn't heard anything about changes up at Red Top. "Can't see why anyone would try and bring that old place back. It hasn't been used as a church for about as long as I can remember. It would need a lot of work. Any idea who's behind it?"

Ethel Crocker said that she'd heard that one of the ministers who had been at the Yarmouth tent revival the previous summer was connected to what was going on. "My friend Ginny Wilkens said that a young preacher had stayed in the village after the revival and expressed interest in opening a ministry on the Cape. Someone told him about the Red Top church being vacant and apparently he's the one behind it. Why he would pick that God-forsaken place I don't know."

"We were wondering who would end up going there if it did open." Serena continued. "I was telling Ethel that I think we would lose a lot of our young people to a new church, especially since we are waiting for the new Baptist minister to come in, but she doesn't agree."

"It'll be some kind of holy roller church," Ethel cut in. "I can't see much interest in that sort of thing. That new minister will end up preaching to the raccoons and squirrels. Maybe he'll get Nate Black. He's about the only one who lives near there." Ethel was chuckling when Serena got out of the car. "If you hear any howling coming down the Stony Brook Valley in the next few weeks, it'll be that new preacher calling for converts among the Punkhorn heathens." Ethel Crocker was still laughing as she drove away.

Out of curiosity and not by accident, Washy drove up to the Red Top cemetery that afternoon. In the lot next to the old church, he saw several parked cars and heard hammering coming from inside the old building. As he got out of his truck, Washy noticed that the boards had been removed from the church windows, revealing lots of cobwebs and a few broken panes.

Inside, a half dozen young men were scraping the walls and applying plaster to the ceiling. The dust swirled in the sunlight, touching walls that had known only darkness for decades. One of the men inside came out to where Washy was standing.

"Hello there! Anything I can do for you?" The man was covered with plaster chips and appeared to be in his early twenties. Washy had never seen him before.

"Well, not really," Washy replied. "I was just passing by the cemetery and saw the activity in the building and thought I'd stop in to see what was happening."

The young man motioned him to come inside. "Let me introduce you to Pastor Peterson. He's in charge of our new mission here and I'm sure he'd like to meet you."

It was difficult to see features clearly in the dim light. Piles of fallen plaster made it difficult to navigate the room. Gaps in the walls showed the exposed lathing. At the foot of a stepladder, Washy's guide stopped and shouted up to a blond-haired man who was scraping paint from the edge of the narrow balcony. "Pastor Martin, there is someone here to see you."

Descending the ladder, the man came over smiling. "Hello there. I'm Martin Peterson, the new pastor. Are you a town inspector?"

Washy laughed, and introduced himself. "No! Members of my family are buried in the cemetery and I was making a visit and wondered what was going on. You've got quite a project on your hands here. This place hasn't been used for years."

"Well, I'll tell you, Mr. Sears, if I'd known what the building was like inside, I might have had some second thoughts. But God doesn't always give us easy choices."

Despite the dust and the heat, it was clear that progress was being made. Peterson led Washy up a narrow set of stairs to the belfry, pushing aside cobwebs as he went.

"Look at this, Mr. Sears. There's even an old bell up here. I never expected to find that. When the church is ready, it will call God's people to worship. The spirit of the Lord will ring across the land." The pastor swept his arms across the horizon. "And we are going to revive that old custom of ringing the years of the local departed on that day of personal judgment, even if they are not members of our church!"

Thanking Peterson for the tour of the old building, Washy left the men to their work, pausing to walk by the family graves before driving home. He wondered about this enthusiastic group of church people. Why had they chosen Brewster? Were there enough souls to be saved in this town that would make rebuilding an old dilapidated church building worth the effort? And what about Pastor Martin Peterson? He seemed a man of strong religious convictions. Would that enthusiasm translate to something good, or would it perhaps become a source of division in the town? As he approached Sears Point, Washy wondered whether the arrival of this new minister would have any impact on his own family.

Tensions at Home and Abroad

The summer of 1950 started well enough. Cottage owners reported few vacancies and the weather cooperated. Newspaper headlines carried ominous reports of a growing conflict in Korea. Several young men in town were drafted and a few reservists like school committee chairman Bob Ellis were recalled to active duty. And there were volunteers. Tommy Gage and Karl Clark, Jr. entered the air force. Ralph Eldridge and Bill Sydenstricker ended up in the army. Charlie Gregson was in the navy and Al Robbins served with the marines. Some of the men who had stayed in the army after World War II, like Tommy Hooper and Kenny Hall, had new assignments. Katherine Gage left her job at the telephone office and joined the air force, as did Ray Rogers's daughter, Joyce. Major Connie Bragg was back in the service and awaiting an overseas assignment. All told, over thirty men and women from Brewster ended up in military service during the Korean War.

Up at the Red Top church, Pastor Martin Peterson was attracting quite a number of worshippers, most of them summer people, but there were a few locals who were curious enough to attend. One of them was Serena. After a Sunday morning gathering, she came back to the house with her friend Virginia Moffett and Washy listened as the two women spoke enthusiastically about the service.

After Virginia left, Serena related how the old church had been nicely repainted and how there was a small choir of young people dressed in blue robes with red trim. "There must have been fifty or sixty people there, Washy. Quite a number of young people, too. There's a nursery for the children. A few people I knew from Brewster, but a lot were from Dennis and South Dennis. Someone donated a small piano and we sang a lot of the old hymns."

Serena mentioned that Pastor Peterson was a graduate of Princeton University and had been ordained as a Presbyterian minister just after the war. "He was on the Cape last summer and wanted to start a ministry here. He has his family with him so it looks like he's planning to stay a while. A woman in East Brewster has given him a place to live, a vacant wing of her house, and they've moved in."

"Where did he serve in the war?" Washy asked. "Was he in the army?"

"Oh no," Serena replied. "He was in divinity school studying for the ministry. He was following a higher calling."

Washy got up and poured himself some tea, a drink that he didn't normally take if coffee was available. He put the cup down. "What do you mean, a higher calling? Wouldn't you say that defending the country was a pretty high calling?"

"That's not what I meant, Washy. It's just that Pastor Peterson is a man of God. It would only be natural that he'd put an emphasis on spiritual things rather than things like war."

"We had men of God with us out there in the Pacific." Washy looked over at her. "They were called chaplains. And we needed them to be with us. Couldn't Peterson have done that?"

Washy could tell that Serena didn't like the direction of the conversation. She stood up to bring the cups and saucers into the kitchen. Before she left the room she turned back and looked at him. "We saw what war did to the world. And what it did to people like Bob Sanders, Harris and David, and even you, Washy. Maybe we needed some people to stay at home and study God's word instead of learning how to kill each other. Pastor Peterson doesn't have to apologize for anything." She left Washy sitting alone in the living room. From his seat he could hear some very determined dishwashing being done in the kitchen. He decided that it was best to let the talk about Pastor Peterson drop for the moment.

The Preacher

As the fall leaves began to turn, quite a bit of background information on Pastor Martin Peterson came to light. The new preacher was the son of the Rev. Elwood Peterson, a renowned graduate of Moody Bible Institute in Chicago. The senior Peterson had established one of the larger

Pentecostal churches in that city in the 1920s. He'd been a spiritual advisor to a number of national personalities including President Calvin Coolidge and was a much-sought-after speaker on the Mid-West Chautauqua circuit. The family lineage included an impressive list of religious luminaries going well back into the nineteenth century.

In the God business, the Peterson family had things pretty much covered. Martin Peterson had been afforded an expensive private education at St. Paul's Academy in Chicago and only with some trepidation had his father finally assented to his attending college at Princeton. "Better to be tempted by the forces of darkness early in life than to die old and in sin," his father had told Martin as he left for the Ivy League school in 1938. "It will be God's test to see if you can survive." In talking with others about those years, the younger Peterson was quick to admit that the forces of darkness had indeed challenged his soul at Princeton, and he acknowledged that too often he had succumbed to the temptations flung at him by the Devil. Peterson was fond of using vivid examples of his personal failings in his sermons, and he repeatedly told his growing congregation that in the end he'd been hardened by the flames of wickedness to be reborn as a better Christian.

Serena had never made religion an issue in the first years of their marriage, preferring to leave Washy alone on Sundays. She had always taken the two children with her to services at the Brewster Baptist Church where her parents attended. But now she started urging Washy to go with her to Red Top to hear Pastor Peterson.

"We should be going to church as a family," she told him one night at dinner. "It's not a good example for you to be staying home while I take the children on Sunday mornings. Pastor Peterson says that it's wrong for a Christian household to be split."

Washy's religious experience had always been decidedly lukewarm and his Unitarian background made him wary of narrow interpretations of the divine mind. He tried to use whatever excuses he could to forestall a visit to the new church. But he knew that Serena would get her way. He eventually agreed to attend the Thanksgiving service, and that concession eased at least some of the tension that had swirled around Sears Point.

That November holiday dawned bright and crisp. After scraping a skim of ice off the windshield, Washy packed the children into the truck and with Serena drove up Stony Brook Road, pausing momentarily at the Dillingham Road intersection to watch three deer nonchalantly cross in front of the car. They would be moving a bit faster, Washy thought, when deer season opened. At the Red Top church, cars filled the parking lot lining the dirt road past the cemetery. After dropping the children off in the nursery, Washy looked around and was impressed to see just how much work had been done to restore the building. New lighting erased the former interior gloom and the recently sanded wooden floor gleamed underfoot. Windows had been re-glazed, broken panes replaced, and fresh flowers brightened the altar.

Pastor Peterson welcomed the congregation and began to speak about sin and forgiveness. He stood with arms wide, eyes closed, and head occasionally thrown heavenward. As the sermon grew in intensity, there were a few emphatic "amens" from seated individuals. Peterson was a natural preacher and clearly a man in love with his own words. "Glory" rolled off his lips more like "glowry" and each exultation elicited more loud "amens" from the assembly. There were apparently a lot of sinners in need of redemption that Thanksgiving morning at Red Top.

Following the hour-long service, people gathered briefly in what Pastor Peterson called a "fellowship circle." They embraced each other and then broke for the cider and donuts that appeared as if by magic at the rear of the church. There was mingling and laughter as the children were released from the nursery.

Pastor Peterson, flanked by his wife and two daughters, stationed himself by the door as people left, making sure to personally greet everyone who had attended the service. The preacher was clearly in his element, smiling and reaching out to shake the hands of those in line. It wasn't lost on Washy that many of the women in the congregation seemed to get special attention from the handsome minister. Washy also observed that Peterson's wife, a rather plain looking woman, appeared to be uncomfortable with the ritual. Her smiles were forced and it was clear that her heart wasn't in it. When Washy and Serena reached the door, Pastor Peterson clasped Washy's hand firmly. "I see you've gotten him to come. Praise Jesus!" He smiled at Serena. Turning to Washy, he nodded. "Ah, Mr. Sears, it's good to see you. I'm thinking that you must have finally heard our bell. I told you it would ring out God's call to the faithful."

Before heading back to Sears Point, Washy stopped at Francis O'Day's store at Betty's Curve to pick up a newspaper. Once back in the truck, he looked over at Serena. "You know what I think? The Peterson household is not a happy one. Did you see how Mrs. Peterson seemed to be playacting her role? I'm telling you, there's trouble in paradise. You must have noticed it."

Serena refused to acknowledge Washy's comment, only noting briefly that being a minister's wife had to be difficult. Once back at Sears Point, the smell of the turkey that had been slow roasting since they departed for church took Washy's mind off things theological and he busied himself outside splitting kindling for the fireplace. Albion and Kay Rogers were due shortly, along with a few of the aunts. In the distance, the Red Top church bell sounded resolutely down Stony Brook Valley. Washy wondered what sinner had been convinced by Pastor Peterson to stay after the service to pull the rope.

Road Work

In addition to the extension of the long-awaited modern highway from Sandwich to Barnstable, Brewster had its own road projects underway. Some of the curves in Long Pond Road near the Harwich line were taken out and the state unveiled a new layout of Stony Brook Road that, despite protests by Brad Clark and Mary Aiken, ended up straightening out sections of that rural track. No one was sure that it was an improvement. A new town truck had been purchased the previous year, and Tiny and Let were busy hauling sand and tree debris away from each work site. Extra workers in July and August, mostly local teenagers, kept the back roads from getting overgrown. Beach landings were scraped and hardening added. Roads needed seal coating.

There was a new doctor in town. Rene Murad, a Czechoslovak-born physician, had come from Mt. Kisco, New York, and opened a practice in East Brewster in the old Chillingsworth Foster homestead. He shared the position of school physician with Doctor Curtis and was immediately popular. When a measles epidemic raged through the lower Cape, Dr. Murad calmed and reassured worried parents. When CJ got into some poison ivy near the cranberry bog, the physician came to Sears Point with his black bag and gave the boy something to relieve the itching.

Schools all over the Cape were bursting with the products of the post-war baby boom. Mary was one of the lucky students to first occupy the three bright classrooms in the new addition at the school. Her quarterly report cards, bearing the neat handwriting of her third grade teacher, Lucy Keefe, reflected excellent achievement and she eagerly boarded the school bus in the mornings. CJ didn't like staying home when his sister left for school, and Serena enrolled him in Little Bo-Peep nursery school run by Charlie Owen's wife, and that seemed to satisfy him, at least for the moment.

There were a lot of military convoys heading through town for Camp Wellfleet and the artillery range. The half-tracks and heavy trucks, with their constant pounding, punished the state highway, and Washy's men were often asked to supplement state crews in patching cracks in the pavement. The convoys seemed to have little regard for local traffic laws, and a number of mishaps with civilian cars were reported. The Office of Price Administration was back in business fixing food prices again. People didn't like that, either. A lot of the anger and frustration related to the changing world situation was vented daily over breakfast at Mary and Andy's, the little coffee shop that had succeeded Peter Dillingham's place.

"Did you see this story in the *Standard Times*?" Art Daniels buttonholed Washy one morning, waving the daily paper. "We're supposed to dig holes in the ground if the Russians bomb us. If we get a warning, we should try to evacuate the Cape and head inland to God knows where. Is that what our local civil defense committee recommends? It makes no sense."

The winter of 1952 was one of the worst on record. In February, snow fell for several days. Electricity was out for more than a week and Washy had to use an old pair of snowshoes to walk from Sears Point to the highway barn. It wasn't until a large tracked vehicle from Camp Wellfleet broke through the six-foot-high drifts on Main Street that Let was able to get the grader out to smooth the major streets in town. It was impossible to dig sand for the roads. The Orleans High School boys and girls basketball teams were marooned on Nantucket for five days before a boat could make it from Woods Hole to take them home, and at the height of the storm, the Snow Library in Orleans burned to the ground when the fire department was unable to get through the snowdrifts.

But spring came as it always did, and the trials of the winter were forgotten. Pastor Peterson's church bell was kept busy ringing out the years of the departed. In a three-month period, three venerable members of the Eldridge family made their earthly departure. Carrie died at eighty-two in February, followed in April by her sister Sarah Jane, who was ninety. A month later, another cousin, Rebecca, also died at ninety. Little Eddie Richardson got only twelve peals of the bell when he left the earth much too soon.

One of the contentious topics that occupied the annual town meeting was the oft-discussed issue of creating some sort of planning guide for the town. The Board of Trade backed a zoning measure, but the majority of voters continued to feel that private property was sacrosanct. "A man's home is his castle" was the prevailing sentiment, and what was offered as a mild zoning proposal went down to defeat. Howard MacGlashing took over the position of constable for the same seventy-five-dollar annual salary that had been paid to Fred Nash. With Serena one night at Crowley's restaurant, Washy saw MacGlashing and his wife, Vivian, having dinner at a nearby table and asked the new constable if he owned a gun. "Sure I've got one, Washy. But I don't plan on ever firing it, because with the little money the town pays me to keep law and order, I can't afford to replace the bullets!"

Ungodly Rumors

Serena was out one or two nights a week for Bible study and was a volunteer in the Red Top church nursery on Sunday. Some nights the prayer study didn't get over until nearly midnight. Washy occasionally attended services to keep peace in the house, but he was usually so sour afterward that Serena decided it was far better if he stayed home. He took to reserving Sunday mornings for working on the cranberry bog. There was a bit of a dust-up when Washy found out that Serena was donating some of the family money to Peterson's ministry, but she argued that "God's work" had a price. "We are starting a building fund to make the church bigger because of the number of people that are coming on Sundays."

The issue of financial support for Pastor Peterson's new church was being aired strongly one morning when Washy entered Mary and Andy's for coffee. Frank Ellis was sitting with George Dunsford and the two of them were involved in an animated discussion.

"You say that Richard Clark came home from Korea and found that his wife had given most of the money he'd been sending home for family support to Peterson's church?"

"That's right. Clark told me that he found his wife and two children living with no heat and hardly any food because Peterson had convinced her that she needed to contribute more money to his church. She claimed that Peterson told her that only by giving money could his prayers convince God to protect Richard in Korea. Clark was wild. He threatened to go right up there and confront Peterson. Said he might kill him. His wife cried and carried on and finally convinced him to stay home. But he's still mighty angry."

Washy listened quietly as the two men continued talking about the minister.

"You know, that ain't all that's making at least some people wonder about that preacher man. Two fellows I know claim that Peterson has an eye for the ladies."

"What do you mean by that?" Others in the coffee shop were now keyed into the discussion.

"Charlie Rutherford told me that the good reverend makes a lot of what he calls 'prayer visits' to some of the young women in the area. Rutherford says he's seen Peterson's car at several houses in Dennis late at night. A bit late to be paying a pastoral call, I'd say." Heads nodded at that.

"Maybe he's working on the laying on of hands," Dunsford chuckled, as he got up to refill his coffee cup. "Seems like I once read that to be saved you have to know three things: what to believe, what to desire, and what to do. Looks like Peterson's got the last two requirements down pretty good." There was some laughter.

Two days later, as Washy was finishing up work, he heard a car drive up to the highway barn. Albion Rogers huffed into the office and sat down. He had a concerned look on his face.

"Washy, what's going on up there at Red Top? What is this Peterson fellow up to?"

"What do you mean, Albion?"

"What I mean is, why is Peterson trying to spread a lot of doubts about religion around town? Serena was at our house yesterday and had Kay in tears after telling her that our church wasn't following the spirit of God. Serena said that we needed to accept Jesus and be re-baptized in Peterson's church. I talked to Reverend Bentley, our minister, and he said that it wasn't the first time he'd heard that kind of talk from people who'd left for the Red Top church. They're convinced that anyone not following Peterson is going to be damned to hell."

Washy shifted in his seat. "Albion, you know that I don't have much truck with religion. Maybe it's the way I was raised, but I've always felt that too much religion is a lot like a man who has too much liquor to drink. It feels good to begin with but ends up making him a little crazy. With Serena, I've tried to stay out of what she wants to believe. And she's been pretty good about leaving me alone in that area. If I thought it was really going to be a problem in my house, I'd put my foot down."

Rogers looked across the desk at his son-in-law. "Well you know, Washy, maybe that time is coming. Serena told Kay that Pastor Peterson is urging his flock to get away from what he calls the 'un-Godly.' He says that just being around what he calls unbelievers is an occasion of sin. As Peterson and the rest of his followers see it, Washy, that means us! You, me, and Kay!"

As he drove home in the dusk, Washy told himself that the situation with Peterson had to be just a phase. Serena was a level-headed woman. But there were nagging doubts in his own mind. His wife was indeed acting strangely and it was pretty clear that it was connected at least in some way to her involvement in Peterson's church. Despite his reassurance to his father-in-law, Washy was very worried.

Fighting Change

Washy sat in the back of the new school auditorium with Win Burkhart as Roland Hall, acting chairman of the recently formed Brewster planning board, banged the gavel in an attempt to maintain order. There were about eighty people who'd come to hear about the board's new proposed subdivision rules. Most of the crowd wasn't happy with the planned restrictions on private property and had been very vocal in opposing anything that might limit what they could do with their land. Osborne Bearse and George Foster had given strong testimony as to why the board should do away with any plans regarding lot size and road frontage requirements. Both men also questioned the right of the board to enact regulations without town meeting approval. "We thought your role was strictly advisory," they said. "You are pushing something favored just by rich people."

Roger Bassett said he opposed any sort of zoning because he felt there were enough laws regulating his life already. "Why put rules where they don't need to be? Ain't nothing up on Slough Road but a bumblebee on a shingle!" But it was Washington Chase who sparked the furor that Hall was trying to control. "I understand Hitler used to take land like this," the

East Brewster man said as he stood and addressed the assembly. Pointing at Hall, he said, "I wonder if he's here in disguise." The words were like a match to dry leaves. Proponents and opponents jawed loudly at each other. There were shouts about doing away with the planning board altogether, and maybe recalling the board of selectmen for good measure. Recognizing that there was no point in continuing, Hall adjourned the meeting.

As the crowd exited the auditorium, Burkhart nudged Washy. "You've been here all of your life, Washy. What do you think of all this?"

Washy paused a moment before replying. "Win, I see both sides of this issue. People like Washy Chase, Roger Bassett, and Ozzy Bearse who were born in Brewster want it to remain the place they've always known. Those men have probably lived as freely as any people have in history. And that includes freedom to do just about anything they want with their own property. For most people, and I'll include myself in this, the feeling is the fewer rules the better. But I also see what's happening in other places on the Cape, and I'm worried that we might face the same thing in Brewster if we don't have some regulations in place to prevent it. We are changing, Win. And a lot of people don't want to face it. We've had twenty-four new houses built in town just this year. Most of them are summer people. We need some kind of a protective bylaw to keep us from looking like Dennisport. So yes, I support what Hall and his board are trying to do."

"Would you be willing to say that at town meeting?" Burkhart asked.

"If it comes to a need for it, yes, I would," Washy replied.

"I'll be calling you in February," Burkhart patted Washy on the arm just before walking to his car. "It's going to take a lot of convincing to make people see things the way you and I do."

When the annual meeting did come, Washy was busy with articles related to his department. There was considerable discussion about approving funds to lay out Freeman's Way, a wooded track traditionally known as South Orleans Road. Selectman George "Fobe" Foster pushed the creation of the roadway, noting that the new Mid-Cape Highway, when completed, would be cutting off a section of Brewster. "We need that road to have access to that part of the town. If we get a woods fire going up there, there'll be no way to get to it." Others who wanted the road talked of future development off Route 137 and pointed to the long-term benefits of a connection over toward Pleasant Bay. In a strong voice vote, the layout was approved.

Voters once again rejected the planning board's request for a zoning bylaw despite a number of speakers who spoke in favor of it. Washy was one of them, and he reminded voters that Brewster would soon be one of the only towns on the Cape without at least some minimal controls on building. But the opponents couldn't be moved. They also rejected a town building code and tabled the request for an appointed town legal counsel.

"This ain't Brockton, New Bedford, or even Hyannis," said one voter who spoke for the majority. "This is Brewster. We can handle things ourselves." Howard MacGlashing was re-elected to his post of constable, once again without a raise.

CJ entered elementary school that year and joined a dozen first grade classmates in Katherine Livesey's room. From the day he started school, he looked forward to it. But like most boys, he had a mischievous streak in him, and periodically Serena had to have a conference with Osborne Bearse, the school principal, about CJ's behavior.

"Don't worry, Serena," the veteran educator reassured her. "CJ will be fine. I've got one of my own and I know what I'm talking about." Mary, on the other hand, was already in the fifth grade and Lillian Callahan, her teacher, couldn't say enough good things about the girl. "She's definitely cut out for college, Serena. She's one of the best students I've ever taught."

That summer, along with the usual mix of local boys, Washy hired Ben Eldridge for the expanded road crew. Eldridge was twenty-two and had done some time in the House of Correction for some petty larceny. He'd not finished high school and was married and the father of two small girls. The couple had a "cellar house" framed out of cinder blocks on a piece of family property up near Slough Pond. It didn't look like he was in any hurry to complete the structure beyond how it stood. Eldridge's youngest child, a girl not much more than a year old, suffered from chronic breathing problems and had been in and out of the hospital for much of the year. The young man needed work, and because of his stint in jail, few in town were willing to take a chance on him. When he approached Washy in April, Eldridge asked only that he have a chance to prove himself. Washy had agreed to take him on. There was a bit of grumbling, especially from Tiny, who kept making references to "that jailbird," but Eldridge never rose to the bait and showed up on time, giving a good day's work.

When Serena heard about the hiring, she was pleased. Eldridge's teenage wife, Verna, was a member of the Red Top Church. By the end of the summer, Washy had started to rely on Eldridge to keep the high school boys in line and to cover for Let on days when the older man wasn't able to do his job. The alcoholism that had plagued Crowell for years was starting to affect his reliability and there were times when Washy didn't hear from his worker for days. Dropping by Let's small house to check on him, Washy often found him passed out in a drunken fog, surrounded by liquor bottles. Even worse were the times that Washy found Let shivering in his bed with the DTs. "I'll be alright tomorrow, chief," he would tearfully tell Washy. But more and more, tomorrow didn't come for several days.

Washy asked Ben Eldridge to stay on when Labor Day came. Tiny had pretty much accepted the younger man, and with Let showing up less and less frequently, he understood why Washy had kept Eldridge working.

There were no more remarks about "that jailbird."

A couple of the selectmen, though, weren't so sympathetic. "You got to let Crowell go, Washy," Larry Doyle told Washy one afternoon when he stopped by the highway barn. "We can't have three permanent men besides you on the highway payroll."

Washy had been expecting the visit and was ready with his reply. "I'm not going to do that, Larry. Crowell's problem started in the war. He's still fighting the demons that he picked up in the Pacific. He's had a rough go of it. Are you going to just throw a guy out in the street? He'd have nothing."

"But the town's got a budget to think about," Doyle said. "The tax rate is going up and me and Fobe don't want to have to stand in front of the voters and try to justify another worker when we don't need one. If you keep Eldridge, Crowell has to go."

"I'll tell you this, Larry," Washy rose out of his seat, nose to nose with the official. "If you move to get rid of Let Crowell, I'll fight it on the floor of town meeting. And I'll point out that Let is a veteran who is presently down on his luck. Cutting him off the payroll would essentially kill the man. There are a lot of veterans in Brewster and it wouldn't play well among them. The few hours that Let works beyond Linnell and Eldridge ain't going to break the budget and you know it."

Doyle left the office muttering some angry words about highway department welfare and criminal rehabilitation programs, but it was the last Washy heard about sacking Let Crowell.

A Mystifying Departure

The sound of blasting could be heard daily over toward Dennis as tons of rocks were torn out of the north side moraine to build jetties along the bay beaches. In the summer of 1954, Sesuit Harbor was being improved. Big trucks hauled the rocks to cranes that hefted the pieces of granite into place. Gradually, the shoreline in front of Sears Point was changing. One of the things that Washy noticed during occasional walks on the flats was the diminished amount of eel grass. Where it had once covered most of the exposed sandbars, there was now little or none. The papers cited a scientist from Woods Hole who said that an imported blight was killing the grass. There were also fewer clams, and some were speculating that the absence of grass was related to the decline in the once abundant shellfish beds. Clint Eldredge and his cousin Leland continued with their weir off Robbins Hill, and Washy could see the two of them driving out on the flats at low tide to harvest the catch, which wasn't much. Even the fish numbers were down.

The town had finally approved the formation of a police department.

Despite objections by the selectmen that such a force wasn't necessary and was altogether too expensive, Howard MacGlashing became the town's first true police chief. Voters, however, didn't see the value in providing him with a police car, and he patrolled all of Brewster in his own vehicle at eight cents a mile. More tourists were finding Brewster an attractive place to spend the summer, and car accidents, traffic problems, and loud parties kept MacGlashing and his small cadre of reserve officers busy. Hurricane Carol caused enough damage that Chief Mac had all he could do to come up with additional deputies to keep essential services moving. On the south side of the Cape, especially in West Yarmouth and Dennisport, the National Guard was called in to prevent looting. Just a few weeks later, another hurricane, called Edna, made a half-hearted slap at the Cape, ending the season on a sour note.

One night as they were finishing supper, Serena mentioned that Pastor Peterson's secretary, Sandy Hardwick, had resigned. "It was all so sudden," she told Washy. "She'd been up at Red Top since the very first days that Pastor Peterson opened the ministry. No one had any idea that she was going to leave her job. And apparently she's left town as well."

"Does this woman have a family?" Washy asked.

"Not around here," Serena continued. "Her husband died, and they didn't have any children. What relatives she has live in Springfield."

"Maybe she went home to take care of her elderly parents." Washy helped himself to some pie and took a paper airplane away from CJ.

"That's not likely," said Serena. "Sandy is only in her mid-30s. Her parents are probably younger than mine are. And why leave so quickly? That's the strangest part of it."

The subject of Sandy Hardwick's sudden departure didn't resurface in subsequent days. There seemed no shortage of young women in the Red Top congregation with an interest in the secretarial job, and the position was filled quickly. Not a single church bulletin was missed, the monthly newsletter came out on time, and the bells for the departed kept ringing. In fact, the church seemed to be prospering, attracting new members weekly. An architect had been retained to design a new wing on the old building.

Win Burkhart stopped by the house one afternoon and announced that he was heading up a committee to research the lives of some of Brewster's prominent nineteenth-century sea captains. "You must have a lot of ship masters in your family tree, Washy. Do you have anything in the way of old records, pictures, or letters? We want to do an exhibit at the Ladies' Library."

"My father used to talk a lot about Luther Sears," said Washy. "He was an uncle to my grandfather and a packet captain back in the 1830s. He had a small sloop named the *Patriot*, about twenty-five tons, and he kept it down near Point of Rocks, loading his cargo at low tide with a horse and team. That was before they built the breakwater. From what my father said, Luther made about fifty trips a year from Brewster to Boston and back. I think he also occasionally ran cargo down as far as the Delaware River. Before the railroad, that was about the only way people could travel. Seems to me there might be something about him in the attic."

Tucked away under the eaves were two old wooden chests that had been there for as long as Washy could remember. Pushing away the cobwebs, Washy lifted the lid on the top chest.

"Looks like some charts, mostly of the East Coast down toward New York. There are a couple of account books and some old newspapers. I never bothered to look at this stuff myself. I'm surprised it's still up here."

The two spent a good part of the afternoon going through both chests, and when Burkhart left Sears Point, he had a box full of documents and charts, along with some old photographs and glass plate negatives.

"I think we've got some really important material for the exhibit," exclaimed Burkhart. "And you know, Washy, all this might go beyond just a library exhibit. Some of us are thinking about starting a historical society."

"Well, Win, I'm guessing that Captain Luther was probably just an ordinary coasting sailor, nothing special. I doubt he ever made much money, unlike some of my more distant relatives like Joseph and Elisha Sears who were clipper ship captains. Luther was more connected to our side of the family. I suspect that's why he never had a big house up on Main Street like the more important Sears captains did. And it's probably why Luther ended up in a plot at Red Top instead of on Lower Road. The clipper ship captains made the money and got the glory. Everyone else, it seems, just sailed in their wake."

"Doesn't matter for our exhibit." Burkhart stowed the box on the floor behind the driver's seat. "They all had an important role to play in building America's maritime fortunes. And when we get this exhibit up and running, a lot of people are going to be surprised at the part Brewster played in that history. I'm on my way to see Frank Crocker. His grandfather was a member of the Boston Marine Society, and Frank's going to loan the painting of the clipper ship *Expounder* that he has over his fireplace."

As Washy watched his friend drive away, it struck him that it took newcomers like Burkhart to put some focus on Brewster's history, polishing it up for everyone to see. All of the old families in town seemed pretty much to take their history for granted. And Washy had to admit that he'd been like all the rest of them. What seemed so ordinary to the old families was truly extraordinary to the newer people arriving in town. He was glad that Windsor Burkhart was doing something about making some of it known.

A Season of Doubt

As Brewster emerged from another very cold winter, townspeople had all the usual things to talk about, and more. The school budget for 1955 went over fifty thousand dollars for the first time and the building was bursting with almost 140 students. Richard Laporte had to teach music lessons in a closet off the auditorium, and the new addition hardly took the pressure off the building. Scouting activities were popular, and CJ was a Cub Scout member of Den 3. Betty Story, his den mother, had all she could handle with almost a dozen boys under ten years of age. All the children in the first few grades got polio shots. Winter afternoons were spent skating at Schoolhouse Pond when the ice was thick. When Serena found out that CJ and some of his friends had been spying on the "goat lady" up on Tubman Road, she gave him a good spanking. "Don't you and your friends give that poor lady a hard time," his mother told him. "There are lots of people in this world who choose to live their own way. They don't bother anybody and just ask to be left alone."

Mary continued in her Girl Scout troop and was making plans for a week's summer camp in Bourne. Both children joined John Hay's Cape Cod Junior Museum, a natural history group that met on Saturdays at the town hall. The Mid-Cape Highway was inching its way down from the West Barnstable rotary and had reached the north-south road in Dennis. The Stabins family, a group of refugees from Latvia, came to town under the sponsorship of the Baptist Church and took up residence in a house on Harwich Road.

Several people in town were startled one morning when it appeared that a low-flying plane was about to crash on the flats down by Paine's Creek. But it was Alan Taber in his Ercoupe landing at Ivan Dugan's dirt airstrip, a thousand-foot stretch of level ground behind Dugan's West Brewster garage. Dugan flew his own Taylorcraft daily from the field, and once people got used to seeing planes come and go, there were no more calls to Chief MacGlashing about possible plane crashes.

Voters at the annual town meeting tackled the issue of a new town hall to replace the old 1881 structure and estimates were that it could be completed for about forty thousand dollars. A study group was put together to find some land and an acceptable design. After efforts to convince Stephen Hopkins to sell a thousand feet of shore front in East Brewster for a town beach fell through, voters couldn't muster a two-thirds vote in favor of taking the property by eminent domain. The matter was tabled.

Following the finance committee's recommendation, voters also refused to allot twenty-five hundred dollars to the highway department to carry an extra worker through the winter, and Washy had to lay off Ben Eldridge, bringing him in only on days when Let didn't show up.

Voters did agree that the surveyor's job should be a three-year term and Washy got a bit of security when that measure passed and he was re-elected.

To Washy's surprise and relief, Serena seemed to be backing off a bit from her religious fervor, and began skipping services at Pastor Peterson's church to attend the Baptist church with Kay. She didn't say much about how things were going at Red Top, but one night when they were driving to Orleans to attend a minstrel show, she let slip that Reverend Peterson's wife had taken her children for a visit to her parents in Michigan and hadn't been around for several weeks.

"I'm not sure what's happened," she said. "They went out for Palm Sunday and didn't come back for Easter. Usually the whole family is at sunrise service, but Pastor Peterson was there by himself."

"Anything else going on up there that's being talked about?" Washy asked her.

"I don't know," her eyes avoided his. "We had a guest preacher two weeks ago, a friend of Pastor Peterson's from Connecticut. He said some things that bothered me."

"Like what?"

"Well, he said we needed to strengthen our faith by following the example of the early Christians. He said that we would only be dragged down by non-believers. We should only associate with the true followers of Christ. He has a large farm in Connecticut that he wants to make into a Christian renewal center. And he wants members of the church to think about moving there."

Washy's greatest fear was now out in the open. It was the thing that had worried him from the outset. "So what are you going to do?" He pulled the truck over and made her look at him.

"Washy, I could never leave you." Serena was on the verge of tears. "And I couldn't take the children away. It makes no sense to me. And others in the congregation, they aren't comfortable with an idea like that, either. But there are some that are going to go. And I think Pastor Peterson is going to go with them. It's dividing people so much. Some are saying that it's what caused Alice Peterson to leave. Apparently she told some of the women in our fellowship group that her husband wasn't satisfied with just a small church. She said he wants something that will give him a much bigger stage."

"Might there be any other reason why Peterson's wife hasn't come back?" Washy got back on the road.

She didn't respond right away. But Washy could see that Serena had considered some of the possible options and wasn't about to go there.

"I don't think she's left him," she finally answered. "She may just feel she needs some time to sort things out."

Before shutting down the truck and going into Odd Fellows Hall, Washy took his wife's hand. "Perhaps, Serena, you need to do the same thing."

The End of a Ministry

The morning mist had just started to lift when Graham Bates drove up to Sears Point to make his regular Pine Ridge Dairy milk delivery. Washy had already been up for an hour and was outside near the bog when Bates left his truck to place the cream-topped milk bottles by the door. For the first time since Washy could remember, the sounds of Olle Lund's cows weren't part of the dawn. After buying the remaining cows from Jim Leach's Nauset Moors Farm in Eastham, Lund had combined them with his own herd and moved his milking operations from the Welcome House farm on Main Street to Millstone Road in East Brewster. The thirty or so cows that had occasionally stopped traffic on their way to pasture on Lower Road now grazed contentedly just outside of Nickerson Park on some acreage Lund had bought from Lydia Hopkins.

"Morning, Graham," Washy waved to the short, stocky delivery man. "How's it going?"

Bates was fairly new in town, having just moved down from Hingham. He'd risen to deputy chief in the fire department and was very much involved in scouting. Despite his milk delivery schedule he never missed a chance to stop and talk when the opportunity arose. And on this morning, he had a story that just couldn't wait. "Hi, Washy. You hear about Reverend Peterson?"

The mention of that name brought Washy over to the truck. "Can't say's I've heard anything lately. What you got?"

"Well," said Bates, "Reverend Bullock, the new minister at the Baptist Church, was counseling a couple that had come from Peterson's church. It came out that apparently there's a good chunk of money missing from the building account. Several people in Peterson's flock believe that it was funneled off to Connecticut to help build that Christian farm that's been talked about. Peterson denies it, but it's rumored that he would get a position there where he could concentrate on taking his ministry nationwide when the farm gets its own radio station."

"How'd you find out about all this?"

"You know what a small town this is, Washy. People talk. And I listen. Everybody's got a party line. Reverend Bullock wasn't the only person that they told."

"So what are they going to do about it?"

Bates had started up his truck. "Nobody's sure. Peterson keeps claiming that he's doing God's work. And most of the people up there at the church don't want to take him on. Frankly, I think he's got 'em all scared that if they make trouble, he'll call down the Almighty on 'em."

As Bates drove away to complete his rounds, Washy wondered what would be the next chapter in the Red Top story. He didn't have long to wait.

About nine o'clock that evening, the telephone rang. Serena answered it and called Washy. "It's Chief Mac. He says it's important."

"I'd like you to come down to the dispatch office right away, Washy," said the chief. "I need to talk to you. Just meet me there as soon as you can." MacGlashing hung up.

Serena sensed that something was wrong. "What do you think he wants at this hour?"

"I don't know." Washy put the receiver back on the hook. "But I suspect that whatever it is, he didn't want it all over town by telling me over the phone. I'll be glad when we get that dial system they are supposed to put in next year. Word travels too fast around here. Especially if it's gossip. I'm just hoping it isn't about Let."

Chief Mac was waiting for him. Brewster's full time law officer rarely wore a uniform, and he wasn't wearing one now.

"Washy, I've got a situation and I need your help. Get in."

Pushing the chief's boxer dog into the back seat, Washy got in.

"Is this about Let?' Washy knew that his troubled worker had been picked up several times in the past two weeks for being drunk and disorderly.

"No, Washy, but it is about one of your men, and that's why I called you. It's Ben Eldridge."

MacGlashing told Washy that Verna Eldridge had driven to his house in the last half hour to say that Ben had gone off in a rage and she thought he was headed up to Red Top to find Pastor Peterson. "Verna told me he said he was going to kill Peterson if he found him. From what I could gather, it was something that Peterson said that caused a rift between the couple. She said she tried to stop him, but Ben pushed her out of the way and left."

"But why did you call me, chief? What about Lawren Cowen or Sabin Lord? They are your special officers."

"Washy, I don't want either of them right now. They're good men but if I get them involved, it will become a police matter. If Ben Eldridge kills Martin Peterson, and frankly I don't think a lot of people in this town would consider that a crime, *then* it will be a police matter. But I'm hoping the two of us can prevent that from happening. Ben's got a record and it wouldn't go down well if he assaulted Peterson. I think Ben knows that you were the one who gave him a chance when no one else would. He trusts you. If we can get there before things get out of hand, we'll keep that boy out of prison. I'm going to let you talk to him."

When they got to Red Top, Eldridge's old car was outside of the church. Peterson's Ford was the only other vehicle in the lot.

"Looks like Ben's found Peterson," said the chief. "Let's hope we're in time."

The two men entered the church, and just below the altar, they saw Ben standing over a badly beaten Martin Peterson. Overturned chairs made it clear that there had been a struggle. Peterson's bloodied face was a clear indicator that he'd come off second best. The bell rope that came down through a hole in the ceiling was looped around Peterson's neck and his hands were tied behind his back.

"Ben, what the hell are you doing?" It was Washy who spoke first. Chief Mac stayed slightly behind in the shadows.

"I'm going to hang this son-of-a-bitch from his own church bells. That's what I'm going to do. And I don't want you getting in the way, Washy."

Washy moved toward the two men. Peterson, although a big man himself, was cowering at Eldridge's feet. Blood seeped from a corner of his mouth and one of his eyes was partially closed and swollen.

"Ben, ease up." Washy hoped that he could reason with the young man. "What's this all about?"

Keeping a knee positioned in the center of Peterson's back, Eldridge looked at his boss. "The Reverend Peterson here has persuaded my wife to leave me. He told her that it was my sin that caused our daughter to be so sick. Something about my idolatry, whatever that is. The bastard has convinced Verna to take my two girls and join up with that commune in Connecticut."

"You don't want to do this, Ben." Washy was within a few feet of both men. "You've already been in some trouble and if you hurt this man, you'll be put in jail for a long time. You won't see your girls or Verna. Whether he's got it coming or not, let him go. He's not worth it."

"Peterson's got it coming," Eldridge said. "He's ruined a lot of families in the time he's been here. He's put husbands against wives, children against parents, and made my Verna want to leave me. I can't let him get away with that."

At that moment, Chief Mac came out of the shadows. "Ben, you know who I am and I'm telling you to get away from Peterson. Don't make this any worse than it already is."

To many in Brewster, Howard MacGlashing had often been the brunt of jokes. In a town where crime was virtually non-existent, the population could afford to laugh at the man who represented law and order. And all too often they had done that. He seemed too much like a cartoon character with his mustache and the ever-present boxer that some referred to as the chief's deputy.

But on this night, the steady voice of the old lawman carried the kind of sharp authority that made Benjamin Eldridge momentarily think about what he was doing. He loosened his grip on Martin Peterson and slowly backed away as instructed. Washy immediately put himself between Peterson and his antagonist. He eased the noose from around the minister's neck and the color gradually returned to his face.

Chief Mac pointed again at Eldridge. "You get on out of here right now and go straight home. I'll deal with you later."

Peterson was now standing with Washy, who was keeping the pastor upright. In a hoarse voice the minister croaked, "What do you mean, deal with him later? Arrest that man right now, chief. He was going to kill me!"

MacGlashing instead grabbed Peterson and held him against the wall.

"I'll do no such thing. As far as I'm concerned, there's been no crime committed here and I think my friend Washy will agree with me."

Peterson was visibly shaking with anger. "I'll call the state police and I'll have you fired for incompetence. This is outrageous!" He started toward his office.

"I don't think you want to do that, Reverend," The chief blocked Peterson's advance. "I've been in contact with Sandy Hardwick. You remember her, the secretary that you knocked up? She told me everything and said that if she had to, she'd come back to town and tell her story. And she'll bring your baby with her. There are several other women who have some stories to tell about your late night prayer visits. At the very least, you'll never preach anywhere around here again."

Peterson had stopped outside his office. Whatever color had come back to his face after his recent ordeal had vanished. He was white as a sheet.

"You wouldn't do that." Peterson's once haughty demeanor had deflated. His hands were shaking.

Chief Mac continued to lay out the situation. "If you say anything about what happened here tonight, Reverend, even to a single soul, I guarantee that I'll bring Sandy Hardwick back to town. Now, Washy and I are going to leave, and I suggest you straighten out this place. And at the same time, you might do some serious thinking about your future as a man of the cloth in this town."

Washy stayed silent as the two left the church. Eldridge's car was already gone.

"Chief, are you going to leave things just like that?" Washy was still stunned at how quickly the situation had been resolved. "Suppose Peterson calls the state police."

"Right now, Washy, there are only four people who know what happened in that church tonight. Each of us has a good reason to keep it that way. When Peterson thinks about his situation, I'm pretty sure he's going to keep quiet. And I think we won't hear anything from Ben Eldridge either."

They were already past the Old Mill. The moon had risen and night shadows covered the valley. "But what about Sandy Hardwick? What are you going to tell her?" Washy looked across at the chief.

"Sandy Hardwick?" The chief reached back over the seat and rubbed the boxer's ears. "I never talked to her. Fact is, I don't know as I would have known where to get in touch with her if I'd had to. I was just playing a hunch. And I think I was right from the way Peterson reacted." There was a slight smile on the chief's face.

It was close to midnight when Washy got into the house. Serena had waited up for him. "So what was that all about?" she asked.

"It was Let again." Washy sat on the couch next to her. "The poor guy had gotten himself thrown out of Lee's after a fight. Mac wanted me to help calm him down so he wouldn't have to go to the lockup. We took him home and I stayed long enough to see that he was all right."

"I'm glad that the chief thought to call you, Washy." Serena said. "Poor Let. His demons seem to be getting worse."

Before the end of the next day, word had spread that Pastor Martin Peterson had cleared out of his rented apartment and departed the town. He hadn't left a note, nor was there a forwarding address. The charismatic preacher disappeared just as quickly as he'd arrived. Only a few people were sorry to see him go, and they pretty much kept that to themselves.

A month later, on another moonlit night, the church at Red Top burned completely to the ground. There was no chance of saving the building. As the volunteer fire department gathered by the cemetery to make sure the fire didn't spread, the old steeple gave a groan and crashed to the ground. The bell, which had rung its message of redemption and marked the passing of both saints and sinners, was the only thing that wasn't totally consumed by the flames. It was later towed away for scrap.

Transformative Times

Like the rest of the country, Brewster at mid-twentieth-century was in transition. The deprivation of the war years was put aside with great enthusiasm, and Americans set about improving their lives. There was a rush out to the suburbs. The country was moving from an agrarian model to one based on manufacturing, and there were lots of jobs. There was also more mobility than ever before, and a sense that everyone could enjoy the good life. More people owned their own homes. Many of the childhood illnesses that had plagued Washy's generation were eliminated. The scourge of polio appeared to be over with the Salk and Sabin vaccines. The rush of modernity was reflected across Cape Cod as young families moved in from the Boston and Worcester suburbs and started businesses. Town populations rose steadily, and by 1956 there were almost 1,300 people living in Brewster.

When Charles Campbell wanted to build a gas station at the corner of Tubman Road and Route 124, the request was turned down by the board of selectmen. The site had been approved by the fire chief for public safety.

Campbell chose not to appeal the decision, but it was clear to many that the selectmen had acted improperly in rejecting the application since their only licensing authority was whether proposed structures represented a threat to public safety. A growing number of residents recognized that others might come along with projects that couldn't be legally stopped in the absence of a zoning statute.

John Sydenstricker submitted a thirty-two-lot subdivision on Paine Creek Road. Ralph Guida followed shortly after with a seventy-seven-lot plan. A fifty-lot trailer park on Griffith's Pond was also up for consideration. They were the first of a number of multi-lot developments that came before the planning board, and without a zoning code, the board had little choice but to approve them. Gordon Brooks organized a group that pushed to adopt a zoning code and brought the measure before a special town meeting, but there still wasn't enough sentiment to enact it.

A new cinder block highway barn was constructed behind town hall, and Washy argued successfully for a new dump truck with a snowplow attachment. The selectmen wanted to put all Chapter 90 road work out to bid, but Washy was able to convince them that in doing so, he wouldn't have enough year-round work for his own small crew to keep busy, and they backed off. He got a phone call one day from Freddie Lawrence, an old Falmouth acquaintance from his Camp Edwards days. Lawrence asked Washy if he might like to come to work for his company in extending the new Mid-Cape Highway. Already, the trees had been cleared as far as Route 137, and Lawrence said he was hard pressed to find enough qualified people to run the machines that were grading the new road bed. Tiny and Let were already working part-time on the new highway construction. Washy thought about it but decided that he'd keep the highway surveyor's job. He was making almost four thousand dollars and it seemed enough. It was almost as much as the school principal was making.

When he was not supervising the roads, Washy spent time reclaiming the cranberry bog. With the exception of the war years, when demand for berries drove the price higher, most of the 1940s and 1950s saw prices averaging about ten dollars a barrel. It wasn't something to get rich on. Still, the extra money from the annual harvest helped the family budget, and Washy derived satisfaction from his hours of hand weeding and ditch clearing. And sometimes it just seemed good to be alone for a while.

The town finally got dial telephones, and with the closure of the old telephone building on Main Street, a staple of rural life ended. Thirty-year veteran operator Alice Freeman made the last connection from the old magneto switchboard before the cable was disconnected and rewired to the new white brick building just up the road toward the elementary school. The new Brewster telephone exchange was given the rather unimaginative name of Twin Oaks. The continuation of party lines, however, guaranteed that quite a few people in town were still able to keep track of their neighbors' business. Voters rejected building a new town hall but couldn't decide how much to spend on repairing the old building. Meanwhile, the roof leaked and the plaster continued to fall off the walls.

There was a lot of excitement when Brewster entered a team in the Cape Cod Baseball League with Bob Hall as the manager. A good number of talented ballplayers had been part of the Orleans high school championship team, and with the addition of some of the older men who had been playing for other towns, Brewster fielded a very respectable nine for several years. The field in front of the school wasn't always in the best of shape, and a special rule was instituted declaring balls hit into Osborne Bearse's right field vegetable garden as automatic doubles. CJ took to riding his bicycle to the field after supper to shag balls for the players during spring practice and he was a regular at the home games. Unlike Washy, CJ was a natural athlete. Hall told Washy that if CJ was just a few years older, he'd suit him up. "That boy's got talent, Wash. You ought to get him into the Little League over in Yarmouth next summer."

It wasn't just the game of baseball where CJ excelled. He caddied during the summer at the Brewster Golf Club and started playing the game himself, taking advantage of course owner Orrin Smith's offer to let the caddies play for free after four o'clock in the afternoon. When he didn't come in for supper, Serena knew that her son was either at the golf course or watching a baseball game at school. After supper, Serena, Washy, and Mary often piled into the truck and drove over to the elementary school to park behind the backstop with other fans, cheering the Gages, Clarks and Bearses and blowing the horn loudly when Red Watson put one off the roof of Bob Williams' Mobil Station. By the second season CJ, at eleven, became the team's batboy and rode with the players to away games.

Washy bought a television from Al Holler, a black and white set that occasionally got some Boston channels when weather conditions were just right. On those occasions, the family watched the Milton Berle and Jack Benny shows. The children favored Walt Disney's Mickey Mouse Club. In 1956, when television impresario Ed Sullivan introduced Elvis Presley to the nation, Serena made both children leave the room.

On one October night in 1957, the Sears family stayed up late. They sat wrapped in blankets on the dune behind the house and stared heavenward to watch a small Soviet satellite, just a pinpoint of moving light, track across the dark, star studded sky. No one viewing the sight was really sure what it meant.

Serena got a job in the school cafeteria working with Althea Hall and Hilda Cash. Mary attended high school in Yarmouth and continued to excel academically. Brewster had studied joining Orleans, Wellfleet, and Eastham in a regional school arrangement. The town had also been wooed by Dennis and Yarmouth. But without the conclusion of a formal agreement, students had the option to go on a tuition basis to any of the surrounding high schools. For the most part, teenagers in the east part of town went to Orleans, while those in West Brewster were bussed over to Yarmouth.

It was in these years that Kay and Albion Rogers began to fail. Serena spent a lot of time looking in on them, but gradually it became clear that they couldn't stay in their old house. When Albion died in the spring of 1958, Kay became a resident at Bud Kerrigan's Brewster Rest Home. She hung on there, never too happy about the loss of her independence, until she followed her husband two years later across the eternal threshold. They were both buried in the old cemetery at the end of Cathedral Road.

By the time he was a teenager, CJ had developed into a tall and lean boy. As Bob Hall had predicted, CJ became a star in the Yarmouth Little League. He also showed promise as a basketball player in the Saturday morning league at the Ezra Baker School in Dennis. His activities centered on sports, school, and scouts. As a member of Troop 73, he spent parts of each summer at Camp Greenough in Yarmouth Port and shared many nights under the stars with other boys in the troop at Nickerson State Park. He played the drums in the school band and sang in the chorus. Perhaps because of his height, but just as much because of his outgoing personality, other boys just naturally liked CJ and looked to him as a leader. Girls assessed him as a handsome, if maybe a bit clumsy, dance partner. He was the popular choice as president of his graduating class at Brewster Elementary School.

The growing problem of Let Crowell's alcoholism finally resolved itself when a hunter came upon his dead body off Slough Road one October morning. Let's car was nearby, the driver's side door open. He'd fallen into a cranberry bog drainage ditch and apparently drowned in the foot-deep water. Several whiskey bottles were in the car, and it was pretty clear that alcohol had caused his misstep and death. "Probably lost his balance and hit his head when he got out to take a leak," was Chief Mac's conclusion. The state medical examiner concurred, and there was no further investigation.

When Washy went in to Crowell's small house to try and put things in order, it struck him that the man he'd supervised for more than ten years was really a stranger to him. Amid all of the accumulated debris naturally expected of a single man, Washy found a neatly catalogued collection of moths and butterflies. The collection filled half of the spare room off the kitchen and had been lovingly kept. The insects were carefully nestled in several old shirt boxes filled with cotton batting and covered with pieces of Plexiglas. Washy gave the collection to John Hay for the natural history museum, to be exhibited with Let's name.

There were boxes of unopened letters with postmarks from different places around the country, evidence that some of Crowell's surviving shipmates had attempted to contact him over the years. Why they hadn't been opened was a mystery. An old cat that belonged to Let went home with Washy. Because Crowell had no close living relatives, Washy handled the funeral service, which was attended by less than a dozen people. Lester Crowell returned to the earth in the town where he'd been born thirty-seven years earlier. He'd been away from it for only three years during the war. If the war hadn't come along, Let probably would never have seen anything beyond Cape Cod. And as it had for so many other men, the experiences of war had forever changed and defined his short and often unhappy life. By order of the selectmen, a flag flew at half-mast for a week in front of town hall.

The Cranberry Scare of 1959

Early one October morning Washy had just entered Donald Doane's store when he caught a glimpse of the headline story in the *Boston Globe*. It read, "Tainted Cranberries Pulled from Market." A government bureaucrat in Washington had declared that cranberries should be avoided because some had been found with high levels of weed killer in them. The official said that there was a possibility that the berries could cause cancer. The news could not have come at a worse time. Washy had just harvested his own bog in the previous weeks, trucking about a hundred barrels of berries to the processing plant in North Harwich. Other area growers had also finished their picking and done the same. He folded the paper and handed a coin to Doane.

"Doesn't look so good for this year's crop from what I'm hearing," Doane said, as he put the dime in the cash register. "John Freeman said he was going to call the co-op this morning to see what the impact on the market would be once the news got around. He left here about twenty minutes ago."

Hurrying out of the store, Washy drove to the highway barn, where he got on the phone to see what he could learn.

John Freeman answered on the first ring. "I just talked with Irving DeMoranville at the cranberry experimentation center in Wareham. It seems that some west coast growers used too much Aminotriazole and the Secretary of Agriculture has issued a warning about potential contamination of the entire U.S. crop. It makes no sense. We don't use that stuff here."

"Sounds though like we're being tarred by the same brush," Washy said. "Any idea what we are going to do?" Freeman tried to be reassuring, telling Washy that DeMoranville had said the cooperative would challenge the government's finding. But both men knew that bad publicity would kill the chances for a decent price for berries that year. Thanksgiving was just a few weeks away. "I'm not too confident that we'll change things, Washy," Freeman said.

Washy took the town truck and drove around to different bogs in Brewster. There was substantial acreage in the town, especially in the southern section near the Harwich line and in parts of West Brewster. All had been recently harvested and growers had put everything to bed for the winter. As he viewed the autumn colors and the neat bogs with their old screen houses, Washy knew that a lot of people were going to be hurt by the scare. Thanksgiving was the biggest cranberry holiday of the year. A cranberry farmer either made money or lost it in November.

The announcement that cranberries might be tainted had immediate effects. Schools stopped serving cranberry products and restaurants dropped cranberries from their menu. Thousands of barrels of berries had to be destroyed. The federal government, in an attempt to ease the burden on growers, instituted an indemnification program of ten million dollars for compensation. But with federal red tape, most of the money never got to the bog owners, and small farmers went out of business when they couldn't pay back their creditors. Washy would have suffered the same fate had he not had other income. As it was, he was unable to sell his crop profitably for several years. He'd never used Aminotriazole on his bog nor had anyone else on the Cape, but that didn't matter. Bogs became overgrown swamps, fit only for frogs, muskrats, and the occasional furtive deer.

More Changes

As the 1960s began, Brewster continued to fight a stubborn rear guard action against change. Nothing made that more plain than when, at a special town meeting in the spring of 1962, voters had trouble mustering enough votes to take some beachfront land at the west end of Long Pond. Washy was sitting with Windsor Burkett as the debate heated up. The three selectmen were fully against purchasing the land from the Kazanjian family. There were three small parcels, and the sellers wanted twelve hundred dollars for each. In total, the package would have added three hundred feet on the pond for possible use as a public beach. The planning board and the finance committee had both signed off on the purchase but, because one of the lots was smaller than the other, the selectmen balked at paying the same for all three.

Win Burkett was one of a number of people who spoke in favor of the article. "We are seeing some of our access to beaches getting closed off as land gets developed," he pointed out. "Here we have a good opportunity to purchase and preserve a piece of waterfront that will be used by future generations. We should approve it." But several speakers objected to buying the parcels. "It's too far out of the town center," said one. "The only ones who will benefit from it will be people from Harwich." Another objected to the loss of tax revenue if the town purchased it. But when the vote came, the measure surprisingly passed.

No one alive in November of 1963 ever forgot where they were or what they'd been doing when the news came that President John F. Kennedy had been shot and killed in Dallas, Texas. It was just after two in the afternoon on November 22 when Washy got a call from Serena. She'd just returned home from the elementary school and had the television on. Serena was short of breath as she relayed news of the president's death. "Dear God, how could such a thing have happened?"

Washy was just as stunned. As he looked out the window toward the front of town hall, he could see the flag already being lowered to half-staff. "Mac" Sencabaugh, the police and fire dispatcher, had already done this at the small office behind the fire station. It was a warm day for the eleventh month of the year and the afternoon was punctuated with the smell of burning leaves. A strange quiet descended over the town and roads were absent of traffic.

As Washy got into his truck, his thoughts went back to a November day just three years earlier. The day after the 1960 election, he'd been at the Hyannis Armory on South Street to see the young president-elect and his lovely wife. He'd driven over with Alton "Plum" Hall, the Harwich highway surveyor. On that day, despite the cold, there was an air of optimism and excitement as people milled around waiting for Kennedy to make his acceptance speech. Despite the fact that the new president had lost Cape Cod to Richard Nixon, even local Republicans took a quiet measure of pride that the thirty-seventh President had a strong connection to the Cape. Washy hadn't been a fan of President Kennedy and, in fact, hadn't voted for him. But Washy had nonetheless respected the connection that Kennedy had with his brother David as PT boat skippers in the Pacific during the war. It was hard not to admire the man for a number of reasons.

The Athlete

Walking through the halls of the high school in South Yarmouth, Washy marveled at the bright rooms and the polished corridors. The towns of Dennis and Yarmouth had put together a first-rate learning center in 1957 and the care and pride of both communities was reflected in the special touches inside the building. Even after almost ten years, the place still looked like new. Pausing for a drink at a water fountain,

Washy noticed the tiles with the famous Shiverick clipper ships on them. One portrayed the *Ellen Sears*, a vessel that had been owned by one of his distant ancestors. CJ had opted to attend the regional school in Yarmouth, following in the footsteps of his sister, Mary.

Washy had come to watch CJ play basketball against rival Harwich. It was hard to get a seat for the game despite the fact that the gym held about eight hundred people. Matches were fiercely contested and television had few offerings that could match their excitement. CJ had left two tickets for his parents, but Serena hadn't felt well so Washy offered the extra ticket to a Portuguese man who was waiting patiently outside the gymnasium in hopes that he might be able to get in at half-time when a lot of the crowd came out for a smoke.

"I'll tell you right up front, I'm a Harwich fan," the man said to Washy when he was offered the ticket. "I see by your colors you root for the Dolphins."

"That's right. I have a son who plays on the team, CJ Sears."

"I know him," the man replied. "Pretty good baseball player. Beat us last year in the finals with a double. My boy's playing tonight too. Greg Medeiros."

"Seems I recognize you." Washy put the ticket in the outstretched hand. "Don't you drive a truck for Buddy Julan?

"You got it. And when I'm not working for him or Bobby Our, I'm at the salvage yard on Route 124, Jimmy Marceline's place. Name's Bob Medeiros."

The two men quickly realized they were acquainted through some of the work done over the past several years rebuilding Harwich Road. Several of the contractors from Harwich had been hired to haul sand from the project and Medeiros was one of the regular drivers. "How long you think that job's going to last, Washy? I get a lot of hours working up there."

"I'm figuring at least a couple more summers before we've finished the final grade and straightened out the roadbed," Washy told him. "I think you'll have a job for a while anyway. That's as long as the state continues to fund it."

"Thanks for the ticket, Washy. Say, I hope you don't mind if I go over and watch the game with the Harwich fans, do you?"

Washy laughed. "If you sat with me, I'd have to put my hand on your head to keep you from jumping up at the wrong time. Better get on over there." They shook hands and parted.

The varsity contest was close and the lead changed hands several times. CJ played well but ended up fouling out with about two minutes to go. Meanwhile, the game was dominated from start to finish by Greg Medeiros. The Harwich player scored twenty-three points and his jump shot at the buzzer gave the Rough Riders the victory. Washy saw Bob

Medeiros grinning broadly across the floor as he waved to his son. Despite the loss, Washy couldn't help but smile. It had been an exciting contest.

That night when CJ got home he was frustrated about how the game had ended. "I can't believe that they called that last foul on me. The Harwich player drove into me while I was standing still! I should have been out there to finish the game."

"I don't know, son. The refs do the best they can. Sometimes they get it right and sometimes they don't. It was hard for me to call it either way, and John McGinn has been doing games for years."

"Well, I just wish I'd been in there to block that last-second shot by Medeiros. Halunen had no chance." CJ slumped on the couch.

Washy poured a glass of milk and looked over at his son. "I'm not sure anyone could have blocked that shot. That kid Medeiros might be the best player I've seen since I started going to the games. You'll get another chance at him in the Principal's Tournament."

"I hope we do Dad. Losing tonight dropped us out of the final four. Unless we beat Falmouth next Friday, we're done."

D-Y did beat Falmouth and qualified for the tournament. But when they were matched against Harwich in the finals, it was Greg Medeiros who once again dominated play. CJ was hardly a factor as Harwich clinched the title with an easy 81 to 68 victory. After the game Bob Medeiros saw Washy leaving the gymnasium. "Too bad about the outcome," he said as he caught up to him. "Everything seemed to click for Harwich tonight." The powerfully built Medeiros gave Washy a playful clap on the back.

"There'll be more games in the future," Washy countered. "Baseball season is just around the corner. Maybe I'll be the one smiling then."

"When it comes right down to it, Washy, I think we'll both be smiling watching these kids play the way they do. It's really too bad that either team has to lose. They are all good kids." Medeiros chuckled loudly. "But if one does have to down go, I'm hoping that it will be your team." And he was off to find his son.

Thoughts – And Doubts – About War

With over one hundred building permits being pulled every year, Brewster was growing rapidly. There were more than fifteen hundred people in town. New roads were being laid out, especially in South Brewster. Police Chief Sabin Lord, who succeeded Chief Mac who died suddenly in 1964, reported that break-ins in non-occupied homes were up considerably, nineteen in 1965 and thirty-four in 1966.

A study was underway to see if the town should look into a municipal water system. Another group was formed to investigate relocating the town dump out toward Freeman's Way. After dithering for years,

Brewster joined the Nauset Regional School District.

In an administrative shuffle, management of the dump, park department, and cemetery care came under the newly created Department of Public Works. Washy was appointed head and got a raise of four hundred dollars. In an expansive mood, town meeting voters approved sixteen hundred dollars to put a heating system in the highway garage. But it was only designed to heat the east side. "Don't want them boys to get too comfortable," the chairman of the finance committee said when asked why the entire building wouldn't be heated. "We'd never get 'em out of there." February 5 was officially designated Founder's Day in commemoration of the town's break from Harwich in 1803. Windsor Burkett was chosen to put together a proper celebration. Longtime Town Clerk Percy Newcomb died in October of 1966, and Donald Consodine was tapped to replace him. In a sign of things to come, Jean Condit became the first woman to run for the board of selectman, gathering thirty-nine votes.

CJ finished high school that year. On the national scene, the United States was intensifying its military efforts in Vietnam. But America was sharply divided over the war and there were those, especially the young men who were expected to bear the brunt of the conflict, who wanted no part of it. Mary was at Boston University, a school where there were a number of radical groups protesting American involvement in the conflict. She was a quick convert to the cause and participated in demonstrations around the city, getting herself arrested more than once. At times it seemed that she spent more time at sit-ins and peace rallies than attending classes.

Washy had his own doubts about the war, and wondered about America's increasing willingness to get involved in faraway conflicts, many of which seemed to have no real bearing on national security. He wasn't the only veteran that felt that way. He could understand and even sympathize to some extent with Mary's anger. Serena, though, was irritated at Mary's protest activities. Her strong Baptist background had always favored God, flag, and country and her daughter's rebellion seemed directed at all three. Mary's visits back to Sears Point were usually filled with tension. After a while, Mary stopped coming home at all.

As CJ neared the end of high school, Washy worried that his son might be caught up in the war. The local draft board wasn't granting many exceptions.

"What should I do, Dad?" CJ asked his father one day when they were working on the bog. "Some of my friends are talking about going into the service. They want to fight. Maybe I should, too." And then he added, "You did."

That CJ was even thinking about military service came as a surprise. Washy looked away for a moment and carefully considered his response.

"War isn't like what we see in the movies, CJ. It's true that I fought in World War II. And it's true that I volunteered. But that was different. There was no doubt then about the threat to the country. That wasn't true in Korea and from what I can see, it certainly isn't true with Vietnam."

"But what if I get drafted?"

"You're not going to be drafted. First of all you've got several offers to go to college on a baseball scholarship. Your mother and I are hoping that you'll take advantage of that. As long as you stay in school, you'll be fine."

"If I go to college, Dad, do you think people will call me a draft dodger or a slacker?"

"Maybe some will think that, CJ. But what does it matter? There are a lot of people looking for a way out of this war. And frankly, I can't blame them. The draft is unfair. It's always been so. The poor, the uneducated and the people with no pull are always the ones who get grabbed. The wealthy rarely serve. The sons of the people who make the policies never go. You've been accepted at college and you've got an out because you're smart and can hit a baseball. There is no reason why you should give up your opportunity just because the current president thinks you need to go off to war."

"You do sound a lot like Mary, Dad." The boy chuckled.

Washy had to smile at the comparison. "Well, I can't say that I'm in love with her methods, but she's taken a stand and I do admire that. And I think opinion about Vietnam is shifting in her direction." Later that night, while watching the television news showing what looked to be unending columns of young soldiers loading aboard airplanes in California for the flight to Vietnam, Washy felt certain he'd given his son the right advice.

It was shortly after this when, on one of her infrequent visits home, Mary announced that she was going to study for a master's degree in social work when she finished at Boston University. She planned to move out west and enroll at the University of Oregon. Two weeks after graduation, she was gone.

The Scholarship

Win Burkhart telephoned Washy one day to ask whether he had any more old documents such as deeds, maps, photographs, account books or anything else that connected to Brewster's history. "What I'd like to do is collect some of these pieces of history and establish an archive for the historical society," Burkhart said. "Gordon Brooks got the idea and I think it's a good one. A lot of stuff is being thrown away by people who are cleaning out their attics, and I just think they are important parts of Brewster's history."

Burkhart had become president of the historical society, and with a small but dedicated group of volunteers he was looking to set up a revolving display of artifacts at town hall. People had responded with more material than he'd expected, and now he was intent on asking new town clerk Donald Consodine for some vault storage space in Millie Reed's office.

"It's a shame how much has been lost or damaged," Burkhart commented. "Since the county courthouse burned in the 1820s, some of these duplicate documents are about the only thing we have that shows who lived here. I don't want to see the information forgotten or destroyed."

Washy gathered up what he could find, and presented Burkhart with a boxful of folded pieces of weathered paper and several ancient account books that the mice had missed. Burkhart drove away a very happy man.

The phone rang as Burkhart left, and Washy went in to answer it. "Mr. Sears?" A man's voice was on the other end of the line. "This is John Monahan. I'm assistant to Eddie Pellagrini at Boston College. You know, the baseball coach. I was down there in Brewster not too long ago."

Washy remembered meeting Monahan when he'd come by Sears Point a few weeks earlier asking that CJ look at some brochures from the Jesuit school. "We'd like you to think about coming to school at BC," Monahan had told CJ. "And we'd like you to play baseball for us." Apparently several coaches on the Cape with ties to the school had alerted Pellagrini to CJ's diamond skills. CJ had been non-committal at the time, and Washy hadn't pushed him.

Monahan asked if CJ was around. "He's out somewhere with my truck," Washy told him. "I'm not sure when he'll be back in. I can have him call you tomorrow if you like."

"That would be fine, Mr. Sears. And while I have you, I just want you to know that we are prepared to offer your son a full athletic scholarship, everything included. It's quite an opportunity. And we're hoping that CJ will consider it."

Thanking Monahan, Washy hung up the phone. He turned on the television and caught the last segment of the evening news. Pictures of anti-war protesters filled the screen. In various cities across the country, students had mobilized in anger against the military draft. Washy wondered for a moment if there might be a clip from Eugene, Oregon. In one of the few letters they had received from Mary, she'd written that tensions were high at the university campus and class interruptions were a regular occurrence. Wouldn't it be strange, he thought, to see his daughter on national television, face filled with rage, shaking her fist at the camera? As the news program ended, the anchorman announced that the Johnson Administration was planning to increase the troop level in Vietnam to at least 350,000 men. In the upper corner of the screen was a sort of score card listing how many North and South Vietnamese soldiers had been killed in the past week. A third category showed how many American soldiers had died in Vietnam during the same seven-day period. CJ's high school graduating class could have fit twice into the number.

Washy waited up for his son to come in that night, and then the two sat in the living room and had a long talk about the future. The next day, CJ called Monahan's office and accepted the scholarship to Boston College.

A Disillusioning College Experience

CJ's experience at Boston College didn't start well. Despite being a scholarship athlete, his application for on-campus housing had gotten lost and he ended up assigned to a dingy six-story apartment house on Orkney Road just above Cleveland Circle in Brookline. Some school official, no doubt on a very sunny day, had enthusiastically labeled the place "Greenleaf Hall."

Not only was the building in poor condition and overcrowded, but it was a mile-and-a-half from the campus, and the college didn't provide any regular bus service. Six students were assigned to each small apartment. They were expected to take their meals in the on-campus dining hall. The difficulty was in getting to and from the campus, especially in bad weather. A number of meals and classes were missed. When a group went to the college administration with their grievances, they were assured that the problems would be addressed. Nothing changed. Washy was aware that something wasn't right at school, because more and more, CJ was spending the weekends at home. On several occasions he indicated to Washy that he'd been thinking about leaving school but Washy cautioned him about that. "Give it another semester. When the baseball season starts, things will get better." The real and unspoken reason that Washy didn't want CJ out of school had nothing to do with academics, or even baseball. Once out of school, he knew the boy would very likely be drafted into the army.

So CJ returned to Boston College after the Christmas break and for at least a time, it seemed that his father's advice had been the right decision. As spring came, the athletic department called the candidates for the baseball team together and each player was given a conditioning check list. CJ spent a good deal of after class time working out at the Roberts Center gymnasium. But during one pick-up basketball game, CJ suffered a bad ankle sprain. He ended up on crutches and wasn't able to follow his teammates outside for live practice when sun finally vanquished the April showers. He was still hobbling around when the first games of the season were played. Frustrated with how things were going, CJ started going home again to Sears Point on weekends. By the time his rehabilitation was completed, the baseball team had played more than half of its season. With the lineup set, CJ never really got a chance to show coach Pellegrini what he could do. The team failed to make the NCAA tournament that year and following final exams, CJ packed up his stuff and headed home. It was the end of a very frustrating first year of college.

That summer, Washy put CJ to work on the highway crew. The two rode into work together each morning. On one of those mornings in early August, CJ announced that he'd decided not to return to school in the fall. When September arrived, CJ remained with the highway crew.

It was one of those comfortable early fall evenings that marks Indian summer on Cape Cod. CJ had just come into the house after doing an errand in Orleans. Washy was sitting in the living room watching the evening news. Serena was in the kitchen. Washy was surprised when CJ passed in front of him and turned the television off.

"Dad, I've got something to tell you," CJ said, as he stood with one hand still resting on the television. "I've made a decision to enlist in the Marine Corps."

Serena, while washing dishes in the kitchen, had been listening. She came in and sat down next to Washy. "Why are you doing this, CJ?" she asked him. "There are plenty of people who can go off to fight. They don't need you."

"I know that, Ma. But if I don't join up, I'm going to be drafted. I'd rather at least have some say in what was going to happen to me."

Washy had initially been too stunned by CJ's announcement to say anything. After Serena's question, he voiced one of his own. "Why the marines, CJ? Did you talk to anyone else, the air force, the navy? What about getting into another school for the spring semester?"

"This is what I want to do, Dad. College just isn't for me, at least right now. Charlie Monroe and George Challies are going in with me. You remember them from school. The marine recruiter said we could stay together through boot camp. It will be better than going in alone. It's not something that I haven't been thinking a lot about, just about every day. Ever since I decided not to go back to school, I've been trying to figure out what to do. There aren't a lot of choices out there and I don't want to get drafted. If I get lucky, maybe I'll get assigned to a marine detachment aboard a navy ship, maybe get sent to Korea, or even Europe. It doesn't have to be Vietnam. And in two years I'll be done and I can come back home to start my life."

There was an awkward silence in the room. Somewhere in his mind, Washy remembered Avery Taggart trying to dissuade him from joining the Seabees so many years ago. Nothing Taggart said then had changed Washy's mind. Why should it be any different now? He got up from his chair and walked to where his son was standing. "CJ, I can't say I'm really happy about what you are going to do. I'm not going to lie about that. But the decision is yours, you are right about that. It's not something that I would choose, especially this war. But if this is what you feel you must do, I'm not going to stand in your way. You're almost twenty years old. We'll make the best of it, all of us. Your mother will come around. It's how your sister Mary is going to react that I'm worried about."

CJ relaxed and laughed. "I guess you are right about that, Dad. She won't be happy if she finds out." They walked outside to watch the sun go down across Quivet Neck. As the two stood looking at the descending fireball in the western sky, Washy remembered the old sailors' adage, "Red sky at night, sailor's delight. Red sky at morning, sailors take warning." He pointed at the deep crimson afterglow visible on the horizon. "CJ, I think you're going to be fine."

Flower Child

After spending the better part of a year at the University of Oregon, Mary moved to San Francisco. About six months after arriving there, she met and became involved with a young man from lake Oswego, Oregon. Jeff Ballas was an army deserter who had walked away from his unit at Fort Lewis, Washington, ending up in the Bay area where he'd been given shelter by some anti-war protestors. Ballas convinced Mary that the two of them would be better off heading up to a commune that he had heard about near Mendocino, California. In a patched-up old Dodge van, they made their way up the coast to Rainbow Farm, where they joined a group that typified the counter culture of the period.

The commune proved to be a fluid community in the sense that people arrived for a time and then left. Some weren't able to find internal peace at Rainbow Farm. Others couldn't get used to the lack of indoor plumbing. Not a lot of work got done, and Mary soon found that the few women at the commune were the ones expected to do the daily chores.

Mary had long ceased contact with Washy and Serena. Occasionally, she thought of calling Sears Point but she knew that any conversation would lead to a lecture from her mother. It wasn't something she wanted to deal with. She wondered about CJ and what he might be up to. He was old enough to be in college. Where was he going to school? She considered writing to him but never did.

With almost a year at the farm, Mary could see that there wasn't much of a future there. Jeff Ballas kept saying that he wanted to move to Canada rather than face the possibility of jail time for desertion. He asked her to go with him, but she couldn't bring herself to do it. One morning, she woke up to find that he'd left in the middle of the night. A note on the table revealed that he was headed for Vancouver. He left nothing else behind. With no reason to remain, Mary left Rainbow Farm and returned to San Francisco where she obtained her California certification as a social worker. She landed a position at the Clayton Street Psychiatric Hospital after a single interview.

Red Sky at Morning

After a rigorous twelve-week boot camp at Parris Island, South Carolina, CJ was given a short period of leave while awaiting orders to the School of Infantry at Camp Geiger, North Carolina. Back in Brewster, father and son celebrated their October birthdays together. After completing the six weeks of training at Camp Geiger, CJ was home again, this time with orders for Vietnam.

Early on a November morning, Washy went into CJ's room to get him up. It was still dark but his son was already awake. "Let's go. Your mother's making breakfast. We've got a bit of a drive ahead of us."

CJ was scheduled to catch a plane that would take him to California, where he would connect to the cross-Pacific flight to Vietnam. The orders weren't all that much of a surprise. The war was ramping up, and a lot of marines were headed that way in the late fall of 1967. Almost ten thousand Americans had been added to the horrific total of soldiers that had been killed in Vietnam in that year alone. The Johnson Administration was determined to replace them. Following breakfast and after a tearful goodby with Serena, father and son got into the car and left Sears Point. The drive to Boston was quiet and there wasn't much talk. Frost on the trees reflected the early morning sun off their icy casings.

At Logan Airport there were lots of other young men in uniform with duffel bags. They were accompanied by mothers, fathers, wives or girlfriends. Some talked quietly, a few embraced loved ones. Sharply dressed MP's walked up and down through the terminal. Outside, a fog hung like a shroud over the tarmac.

CJ got his ticket, checked his bag, and got into line. Washy stood with him. The few civilians in line appeared uncomfortable in the mix of military men. They had a pretty good idea where the soldiers were going.

"You OK, son?" Washy put his arm on CJ's.

"I'll be fine, Dad. Don't worry. The time will go by fast, and when I get back, we'll go out and hunt some ducks. Take care of Mom."

Washy hesitated a minute and then clasped CJ tightly. "Come home safe, son." He stepped away and looked at the grown man standing in front of him, and for a moment he imagined he was standing with his brother David. And then CJ was gone, out the terminal door into the cold air and down to the waiting aircraft. Washy got to his car and took the tunnel back into Boston. The rush hour traffic slowed things to a crawl. It struck Washy how people could be going about normal business while his son was going off to war. While he was still in the harbor tunnel, CJ and the rest of the passengers aboard his flight lifted off from the runway and the big Boeing jet climbed away from the rising sun. As Washy edged onto the Southeast Expressway, the radio was talking about a major protest march on the Pentagon in Washington. The Celtics had won a pre-season game with the Hawks. Washy looked across Boston Harbor and noticed that the eastern sky had a reddish hue to it. "Red sky at morning, sailors take warning." Despite the heater's effort, it seemed suddenly colder in the car. He turned off the radio and continued driving south toward the Cape.

Leaving the World

Arriving on the West Coast, CJ joined other marines on a bus that took them to Marine Corps Air Station El Toro. From there, he flew aboard a chartered airline to Hawaii where the plane stopped briefly for refueling. It occurred to CJ that twenty-five years earlier, both his father and his uncle David had passed this way on their way to war. Now he was following their footsteps to another conflict. The next stop was Okinawa. After a two-day layover, during which CJ and the rest of the Marines "volunteered" to give blood, they were flown to the coastal city of Da Nang, Republic of Vietnam.

The first thing CJ noticed when the aircraft doors opened was the smell of rotten garbage and burning charcoal. It literally took his breath away. The same plane that had brought him to Vietnam would be taking marines that had finished their year in the war zone back to "the World." The plane was aptly nicknamed the "Freedom Bird" by those who would leave on it. As CJ's group walked down the ramp away from the jet, one of the new arrivals asked, "What are those bags stacked over there?"

"Body bags," he was told by one of the aircraft crewmen. "Their tour of duty was up early."

Even though it was located in the northern sector of the country, Da Nang was relatively secure. But in the weeks just prior to CJ's arrival the base had suffered sporadic rocket attacks. Heavily armed soldiers wearing camouflage bandannas and round-brimmed boonie hats walked past the replacements. A couple of wrecked buildings gave testimony to the fact that the port city was no longer a rear area. Reporting to a staging area, a sort of tent city surrounded by sand bags, CJ was issued an M-16 rifle, a helmet and a flak jacket and ended up joining some other marines aboard a truck. They were all bound for the same place: Company A of the First Battalion, First Marine Division, presently situated on the edge of what some of the veterans they spoke with referred wryly to as "Indian country."

The land here rose dramatically, and west of Da Nang a mountain chain featured spurs running horizontally down to the South China Sea. It was cool in the foothills where Company A was spread out near a village named Hoi An. Solid gray clouds hinted of rain and a steady wind came out of the northeast. The dirt track they followed wound through rice paddies and crossed a few small rivers. When the truck arrived at the outpost, CJ was taken to the command center, a "hootch" surrounded by some tents. An earthen berm had been bulldozed around the small compound, giving some protection from sniper fire. It did nothing, however, for the frequent enemy mortar attacks.

After about a month in Vietnam, CJ was assigned to a rifle squad that was headed for a patrol outside the wire. A typical search and destroy mission in Vietnam lasted about two weeks, some as long as thirty days. CJ became more familiar with the bush than with his primitive digs back at the compound. The squad did a lot of walking. They crossed rice paddies wearing eighty-pound packs, forded rivers, and stepped over the carcasses of dead water buffalos. They tried, not always successfully, to avoid booby traps and mines.

Heat exhaustion, dehydration, diarrhea, and plagues of bugs the size of small birds pestered the marines. The halogen-treated water they drank made everyone sick. Their jungle fatigues faded, old sweat stains ringed in white, newer ones dark green. At night the squad would establish a defensive perimeter on some high ground behind rolls of razor wire and hunker down in fighting holes. CJ was often assigned to a listening post about three hundred yards outside the perimeter. He proved good at it. He had a sixth sense that alerted him to anything out of the ordinary. Several times he detected enemy sappers moving near his position and was able to direct fire at them. He developed more and more self-confidence as the weeks went on.

His letters home always said how he missed the Cape, and how he believed the experience of Vietnam was doing him some good. He mentioned running into Joe Straughn near Nah Trang. Straughn had brought him up to date on two other Brewster boys who were in Vietnam, Harold Clark and Ed Walsh. Never mentioned in CJ's letters was how men cried in combat and sometimes wet themselves when under enemy fire. He also didn't write anything about what it was like to take another human being's life or how it felt to wipe a buddy's still-warm brains off one's boots after a firefight. In a strange way, going into battle with other men with the intent to kill something produced a rush unlike anything else a person could imagine. More than some would ever admit, a lot of soldiers secretly liked it.

After a short R & R break at China Beach near Da Nang, the battalion got orders to a new defense line near Dong Ha. The location was close enough to the DMZ to get regular rocket fire from the North Vietnamese. Casualties mounted. The marines that were posted there began to refer to the area as a special DMZ – Dead Marine Zone.

Sailor Take Warning

The weather near the DMZ was much different than it was where CJ's unit had operated before. The monsoon season had started and there was constant rain and drizzle. The nights were cold. On January 31, 1968, the North Vietnamese, in concert with their Viet Cong allies, launched a countrywide attack all across South Vietnam. It began just before dark.

CJ's squad readied to meet the advancing North Vietnamese, who were silhouetted about fifty yards out front of the wire. Green and white tracers were coming up along the right side of the perimeter. CJ heard the screams of men and the shrill sound of whistles as the North Vietnamese officers directed their men in the attack.

As the enemy began to roll up the outer defense perimeter, several marines were cut off and isolated. The North Vietnamese had the advantage of knowing the terrain and they also knew where the marines were. They shot several of them and then withdrew. One of the marines was still alive and began crying for help. He was in the grass about fifty yards out and in the open, a clear target. As he lay there, the rest of the company hugged the ground, aware that the enemy was intentionally not trying to finish the wounded marine. They were waiting for someone to run out to get him.

It's never clear why some men do things that others will avoid. Sometimes it's a conscious choice. More often it is a reflex action that can't be explained in any rational way. "I'm going out there," CJ told the gunny. And before the sergeant could stop him, CJ sprinted to where the fallen marine lay. A barrage of gunfire rang out from the enemy positions. Bullets sprayed around him as he ran. Behind him the company returned covering fire. CJ reached the fallen marine and looped his arm under the man's shoulder and lifted, at the same time pivoting in the direction of his comrades' fire.

When the incoming mortar round hit, CJ was just about to get the wounded marine on his back to carry back to the perimeter. The force of the blast separated the two and hurled CJ about ten feet in the air. When he landed on his back, one of his legs didn't land with him. It hung suspended in a tree about thirty feet away, bootless. The artery in his severed leg was pumping dark blood into the sand and when CJ tried to call out, no sound came from his mouth. For a hot day, it was suddenly cold. His eyes dimmed, and the last thing CJ saw was the gunny standing over him shouting, "Corpsman, Corpsman!" But CJ could only see the gunny's lips moving. It was strange. The gunny looked as if he were going to cry.

“Your Son Was a Good Marine, Sir.”

Agatha Gervais was the first to spot the black Ford as it drove into the parking lot behind the fire station. “Gabby,” as she was known around town, missed very little of what happened in Brewster. Everybody had a story about the aged spinster. She dressed like a man and ran the station like a captain on the quarterdeck. As the person who pumped gas at the Brewster Garage, she was famous for dispensing equal amounts of gossip along with the fuel to the locals who stopped there.

“Did you see that car going out back?” she leaned in the window of Larry Baker’s Plymouth. “That’s a government car. I wonder what they want around here?”

Baker shrugged, “Probably just something about a state inspection or some sort. They are down here all the time now.”

Just then the Ford came back out from the dispatch office, drove across Main Street to the town hall and went into the back lot.

“Did you see?” Gervais pointed. “Both men in the car were wearing uniforms – navy, I think. I’m going next door to see what they were up to.”

She left Baker in front of the station with the gas hose still sticking in his car and hurried across to the dispatch office where Mac Sencabaugh was up front looking through the garage windows toward town hall.

“What’s that all about, Mac? What are those two military people doing here?”

“They wanted to know where Washy Sears was,” Sencabaugh replied. “I told them that if he’s not out on the road, he’s probably in his office over at the highway barn. They left without saying anything. From the way they looked, I’m thinking they didn’t come here to bring any good news.”

In his office, Washy was reviewing some drawings of the proposed town water system. A representative of Whitman & Howard, the engineers who had conducted the town water survey, had dropped them off the previous day. For years the issue of town water had come up, only to be voted down by town meeting. But it was clear that town water would eventually come to Brewster, and Washy knew that it would be his responsibility to budget for equipment to assist the engineers installing the pipes throughout town. There was an article on the warrant again this year. If it passed, he’d be the one to put words into action.

Easing out of their car, both naval officers in their dark blue uniforms and white hats went into the highway barn. Washy had seen them coming and was standing by his desk when they entered the small office.

“Are you Mr. Washington Sears, sir?” The taller of the two officers, a lieutenant commander, came directly into the room and stood in front of Washy’s desk. The second, a lieutenant, stayed back a bit, almost as if he felt he didn’t belong in there.

“Yes I am,” Washy looked up. “What can I do for you two gentlemen?”

The other officer came further into the room and was standing just behind his compatriot.

"Mr. Sears, we regret to inform you that we have just received word that your son, Marine Private First Class Cyrus J. Sears, has been killed in action in Vietnam."

With that abrupt announcement, the air seemed to go out of the room. Washy, who had been standing, sat back down in his chair as if his legs had been cut from under him.

The tall officer had experienced this moment far too many times in his role as a casualty assistance calls officer. This was the third face-to-face personal notification he'd had to make this week. It was the other officer's first CACO assignment. Every visit produced the same reaction, a moment of stunned silence, followed by the understandable and natural urge to disbelieve the message. "There must be some mistake!" And then always, the shoulder-slumping acceptance of reality that seemed to turn the recipient of the news into jelly.

"I'm very sorry to have to bring you this news, Mr. Sears. The navy believes that it's far more preferable that we personally inform family members when any of our personnel have been killed in action. We are very sorry for your loss. If there is anything we can do in the way of funeral arrangements or ceremony, here is my card. I'm attached to the First Naval District headquarters in Boston, and I can be available on short notice. Your son was a good marine, sir. He contributed greatly to the accomplishment of his company's mission and upheld the highest traditions of the Marine Corps and of the United States Naval service."

The officer handed the card over. Following several more expressions of sadness, both officers exited the building and were in their car and out of the lot.

Washy sat there in his chair, empty of all feeling. He hadn't said a word from the time he'd acknowledged who he was to the two officers. The unfolding scene had taken about ten minutes. Ten minutes to announce the end of a life. He looked out of the window. A few daffodils were already in bloom on the sunny side of the building. It struck Washy that his son would never again see their beauty.

After some time, he left a note in the window telling the crew to close up the shop. He'd be gone for the rest of the afternoon. Strangely, as he drove home, even though he tried, Washy had trouble conjuring up CJ's face. Instead, a long-buried vision of a boy with sightless eyes lying under a tree on a forgotten South Pacific island came into his mind. Pulling into the road that led out to Sears Point, the image of that dead young Japanese soldier on New Britain wouldn't leave him. He'd been about CJ's age. Washy wondered how his family had learned of his fate. Did anyone personally inform the dead soldier's mother and father? Ahead, the homestead loomed. There was no escaping what had to be done or who had to do it. Washy parked and went into the house to break the awful news to Serena.

Across the street from Town Hall in the Brewster Garage, Agatha Gervais just shook her head as she watched Washy's car pull out of the parking lot. She'd taken it all in and had correctly figured out what was going on. She'd seen the officers go in and come out quickly. Agatha Gervais was no fool. This was perhaps the biggest piece of news that Brewster had seen for decades. And other than Washy, she was the only one who knew it. But as other customers came in for gas the rest of that afternoon, Gabby said nothing. At closing time, she said good night to Stanley Ryder, and walked the short distance up Long Pond Road to the house she shared with her sister. She paused for a moment in the doorway and looked toward the setting sun. The clouds were purple and pink. Never married and now in her seventies, Gervais had watched generations of the town's children grow up and had taken a vicarious pride in how they had all done. In a way that only she understood, she thought of them as her own children, Brewster's promise to the world. Now her own government had sent strangers to announce that one of them had been killed in a war that no one understood. It didn't seem right to talk about it. She went into the house and after removing the phone receiver from the hook, Agatha Gervais poured herself a very stiff drink. She took off her shoes and sat alone by her fireplace surrounded by all of her memories.

CJ's Homecoming

The rain that had been falling all the previous night ended with the dawn. CJ's body had arrived back in the United States several days earlier and was then brought to the Hallett Funeral Home in Yarmouth. Norman Hallett had called Washy to let him know that the transfer had taken place. Lieutenant Commander Jerry Fennell, the senior officer who had brought news of C.J's death to Washy three weeks earlier, had followed through in setting up the marine honor guard that carefully accompanied the coffin from Hallett's to the Brewster Baptist Church.

The honor guard arrived at Sears Point at mid-morning. They were to escort Washy and Serena to the church where CJ's coffin was in place in front of the altar. Seeing the four uniformed marines step out of the car, Serena needed the support of Washy's arm to remain standing.

Windsor Burkhart had been a constant presence at Sears Point ever since the news of CJ's death had become known. It had been Burkhart who had kept the outside world at bay as Washy and Serena tried to cope with CJ's death. Today, he was the one who would drive them to the church and later to the burial at Red Top of Serena and Washy's only son.

"Thanks, Win," Washy looked appreciatively at his longtime friend as he got into the back seat next to Serena. "I don't think I would have been such a good driver today if I'd had to do this myself." Burkhart squeezed Washy's shoulder. He got behind the wheel and the two cars, the second with the military officers, slowly made their way down the familiar narrow lane to Lower Road.

The Brewster Baptist Church had been built in 1824. Other than a modest addition added in the 1950s, it was little changed from the simple structure it had always been. The interior of the church reflected the unembellished expression of the denomination's faith. There was a constancy here that went deep in the town's history. The simple coffin, covered fully with an American flag, was set on a platform in front of the altar, surrounded by a number of individual floral arrangements. CJ's high school graduation picture faced toward the pews. By eleven o'clock, the church was full.

Poised behind the raised dais, Reverend Edward Ellmore spoke directly to the pain that was so evident on the faces of those sitting in the pews below. Afterwards the funeral cortege made its way slowly west on Main Street to Stony Brook Road. The route took CJ's body past familiar places, the Ladies' Library, Ken's Market, the Brewster Garage and town hall. It passed Schoolhouse Pond where CJ had spent hours as a youngster fishing for hornpout and sunfish and catching turtles. And then it was up the long hill past Donald Howes' antiques shop, Tubman Road and the Tip Top House. Groups of people clustered along the side of the road. At the intersection of Route 6A and Stony Brook Road, a crowd, including a fair number of schoolchildren who had been released from classes, gathered to watch the procession. Many waved small American flags as the cortege passed. At the Stony Brook Mill, the procession made the final leg past the new Catholic church to the Red Top Cemetery. The closer to the burial ground, the more people seemed to gather, scores of neighbors and friends standing quietly to witness CJ's final ride. It was as if the entire town had come to a standstill on this April day.

The sun had erased the lingering morning clouds, and it was almost hot on the old hill where the granite and rail enclosure had for so long provided a quiet sanctuary for the dead. The coffin was lifted from the hearse and carried by the honor guard to the edge of the grave. A temporary green-colored canopy shielded Washy and Serena as the guard fired the ceremonial volley, precisely smart and absolutely correct in their rehearsed movements. The haunting strains of Taps were accompanied by a few nearby crows that were angered about something back in the woods along Red Top Road. The flag that had covered CJ's coffin was carefully folded and the triangular package presented to Serena by one of the marines. And then CJ went into the earth, one more member of the Sears family embraced for eternity in the sandy soil of Cape Cod. Out on the distant flats, the sound of a gull carried on the wind.

The Clayton Street Psychiatric Hospital

It took three long flights of stairs to reach the windowless office that had Mary's name on it. The door was stenciled: "Mary Clark: Resident Social Worker." She'd started using her birth father's name since returning to San Francisco. The opaque half-glass panel in the door didn't let anyone see in or out. As small as it was, the room had been tastefully decorated. Table lamps gave the effect of a family den and black and white prints of Yosemite by Alfred Eisenstaedt were on the walls. A cabinet of medical files crammed full of session notes occupied one side of the room. A small desk in one corner and two chairs in front of it allowed for more than one person, perhaps a married couple, to take advantage of the counseling that was available at Clayton.

Along with eleven other counselors, Mary also served as a social worker to clients that had been referred through the hospital. Even though she had been at Clayton for more than a year, Mary knew just a few of her co-workers. The arrangement of the rooms with their hallway of closed doors acted as an impediment to any kind of social interaction. There was a staff psychologist at least nominally in charge of the counseling program but he was seldom in the building. Like the elevator that never worked, what went on in the third floor offices of Clayton didn't seem to catch the attention of anyone in the city bureaucracy. The facility carried out its daily routine of caring for the more troubled of the city's population pretty much in anonymity.

Initially Mary was given a modest caseload of clients with whom she had to meet at least twice a week. Her job was to mediate between these people and a host of doctors, counselors, landlords and lawyers, bill collectors, bureaucrats, disappointed parents, and disappointed children. At some point she began picking up a number of Vietnam veterans who had come home from the war with some form of post-traumatic stress. The experience of combat had literally broken them in both mind and body. Many were drug and alcohol dependent. Some were psychotic, homeless and living on the streets.

One morning a young man came in and asked to see a counselor. He introduced himself as Bill Noonan and said that he'd been referred by Doctor Blustein. "I was in the clinic for a while," he told Mary. "Once I got dried out, the Doc told me that I had two choices. I could leave the hospital and go back to the street or come up here to get some help. It didn't seem all that hard to choose coming up here."

Instead of remaining behind her desk, Mary came out and took the spare chair. "I'm not a psychologist," she told him. "My job is to try and make sure that you are getting all of the services you require to put your life back on track. Have you connected with the Veterans Administration?"

"They've got more vets than they can take care of at the moment," Noonan said. "The police picked me up about a month ago and took me to Clayton. They told me it was too crowded at the VA facility. I'd been homeless for about six months. I spent time in a lockdown here for a while until I dried out. I want to be able to go back to living normally on my own."

Noonan said that he'd grown up in a small town in Idaho. He'd joined the marines right out of high school and had been sent to Vietnam in early 1968. He'd served his obligatory one-year tour there and was then rotated to Okinawa where he had completed his enlistment. He'd been discharged and sent home in December of 1969.

"After my experiences in 'Nam, everything changed," he told Mary. "We did a lot of drugs over there and I started drinking heavily. When I got home, I continued. I wanted to erase some of the things that I saw and did during my time overseas. Sometimes it worked. But never for long. I had some disciplinary trouble in Okinawa and spent time in the brig. By the time my enlistment was up, I was lucky to get an honorable discharge."

"Did you go home to Idaho?" she asked.

"I did," Noonan replied. "But it wasn't the same. People treated me well enough. It was just that I couldn't hold a job for very long. I was still drinking and looking for drugs. I went to court a few times. I think initially they gave me just a slap on the wrist because I was a Vietnam vet. After a while, though, I think the town gave up on me. I know my parents did. I can't say that I blame them. I left and eventually drifted over here to San Francisco."

Mary didn't write anything down while she listened to the young ex-marine. The story wasn't much different than so many others she had transcribed over the past year. She could have taken out any file and plugged Bill Noonan's name into the narrative and it would reflect a common experience. She let him talk on for nearly two hours. When the session finished, she handed him some brochures.

"I think we've made a start, Bill. We can work together." She stood and shook his hand "You have my card. I want you to call me next week and we'll set up a series of sessions that can hopefully help you deal with some of your problems."

Noonan nodded that he would do that and stood up to leave. As Mary heard his footsteps retreating down the stairs, she realized that she'd never asked him where he was living, or if he even had a place to stay. As she settled back behind her desk, she decided it didn't really matter. She was pretty sure she would never hear from Bill Noonan again.

The Car Dealer

In the weeks and months following CJ's death, Washy and Serena did the best they could to come to grips with the loss of their only son. Serena threw herself into her church activities, relying on the spiritual comfort that she got from attending frequent Bible classes during the week. Sometimes Washy would pass CJ's old room and see her sitting quietly on the bed, her Bible open, looking at the boy's school jacket that still hung in the closet. The room was just as CJ had left it. In her mind, Serena clearly believed that Washy at least in some way had contributed to what had happened to her son. She blamed him for letting CJ join the marines.

For his part, Washy never stopped thinking about how things might have been different. Should he have more vigorously discouraged CJ from signing up? Had he not been supportive enough when Mary began to display attitudes that bothered Serena? Could he perhaps have met Serena at least half-way in the matter of religion? But what was done was done. He had to live with it.

Sometimes when walking alone out on the flats, Washy was confronted with the reality that he was no longer a young man. George Foster, Ray Tubman, Allie Ellis, Roger Bassett, Donald Doane, Hudson Eldridge, and Henry Crocker, all were gone. The stabilizing pillars that for much of Washy's lifetime had held Brewster together were disappearing one by one. The year before he'd attended Sparrow Higgins's funeral. Time had just about erased his father's generation. Washy was now a senior member of the community.

Thoughts of retirement occasionally crossed his mind but he really couldn't see himself without a job of some sort. He'd handled the road construction and maintenance requirements of the town for more than twenty years, and Brewster's needs were constantly growing. The population was approaching two thousand year-round residents. The state had condemned the town dump in 1967 and a new site was being considered off the newly paved Freeman's Way. The elementary school was bulging at the seams and portable classrooms housed the overflow. There was talk of a new building. In 1968, Jean Olmstead became the first woman elected to the board of selectmen. The town hired its first permanent legal counsel in 1970. In his annual report that year, Police Chief Sabin Lord noted that arrests for drug use were up, almost exclusively among summer people, he made sure to note. And Lord asked for additions to his three permanent patrolman force to provide twenty-four hour police coverage for the town. The fire department had already added four women to its volunteer ranks.

The annual town budget that in 1969 was about $425,000, rose to $640,000 in 1970. It would reach a million dollars in 1971. The year before, voters finally approved spending three million dollars for the long-debated town water system. This project required the oversight of an experienced person who knew both the road system and the town. The engineers from Whitman and Calderwood would need to rely on that person. Washy was urged by the selectman to stay on the job at least until the water project was completed. It wasn't a difficult decision for Washy to make, as he knew that he needed to stay busy lest CJ's death plunge him into the same depression that was afflicting Serena. He accepted the town's appointment for another three-year term.

Through all of this, his closest friend continued to be Windsor Burkhart. The man that Washy had first encountered years ago salvaging an old bureau at the Brewster dump had become a sounding board for thoughts and feelings that Washy needed to voice. Burkhart's counsel was always carefully considered. Not that far apart in age, the two spent long hours comparing notes about life and the paths they had taken. There were other things that bound them. Burkhart loved the history of his adopted town and never tired of asking Washy about his ancestors. Searching through old documents and pictures, the two friends worked to piece together Brewster's historical record. For his part, Washy enjoyed kidding Burkhart good naturedly about his antiques business and how he thought it must take a lot of time sanding off the "Made in Japan" markers on the underside of some of the items in Burkhart's shop. They laughed often and looked forward to their times spent together.

One Saturday in June as the noon hour approached, Washy was out weeding a section of the cranberry bog. A new blue and white Buick came up the narrow track toward Sears Point. The car, with its large fins and tinted windows, made no noise as it approached, and Washy, his back to the road and occupied with his thoughts, never heard it. When the operator leaned on the horn, the piercing noise so startled him that he tipped over the small pail of garden tools he was working with and fell clumsily on his back.

The passenger side window of the Buick rolled down automatically and a loud voice boomed out, "Hey over there! You Washy Sears?"

Regaining his feet, Washy walked the short distance to the ditch that separated the road from the bog. He stood looking at the stranger's car. Slightly below the level of the road, he couldn't see who was inside. "Yes, I'm Washy Sears. What can I do for you?"

The Buick's engine shut off and a solid looking man got out, an unlit cigar clenched firmly in his mouth. He had a slicked-down shock of thick black hair mounted over a round face, set off by two black and bushy eyebrows. The man's nose somehow found space in the middle.

"Nice place you got here, Sears. A little hard to get to, narrow road and all, but I guess it will work." The man didn't make any move to leave the side of his car.

Washy negotiated the narrow drainage ditch and approached the stranger, who put out his hand. "Good to meet you, Sears. I'm glad I caught you at home. I just came down for the weekend to look at my property. I'm guessing it's right over there." The man pointed to the upland on the west side of Sears Point. "It's about seven acres with a couple hundred feet of beach front. Hell of a price I got. So good, in fact, I bought it sight unseen. You couldn't touch a piece of property like this anywhere on the Connecticut shore for what I paid."

All this talk from the stranger wasn't making a lot of sense to Washy, who hadn't heard that any of the surrounding land between Sears Point and the Brewster Park settlement was for sale. "Who did you buy the land from?" he asked.

"I saw a notice almost a year ago in the *Hartford Courant* advertising some beachfront in Brewster," the man replied. "My wife and I had vacationed down here a few times, so we knew the area. The piece was part of something called the Young estate, held by some kind of land trust. I put in a bid. I guess my offer was the highest."

"Are you sure you have the right location?" Washy looked at the man. "I think I would have known about any sale of property around here, and I haven't heard anything."

The man reached into the front seat of the car and pulled out a rolled up plot plan. "Here is the perimeter layout. I finally got the parcel surveyed about a month ago by Nickerson & Berger. Things don't move too quickly down here. Had to call 'em a bunch of times. Funny thing, when I bid on it, the advertisement said it was about six acres more or less. The deed wasn't all that clear. Turns out it was a bit more than less!"

Still confused, Washy shook his head. "The plan looks good enough, but I still can't believe that the land next to me went on the market without my knowing about it."

The stranger smiled and put the rolled plan back in the car. "I'll tell you, Sears. I think someone in town hall did a little research and found out that the taxes on this property were in arrears. From what I heard, the owners died some time ago. There was apparently a quiet tax auction maybe a year and a half ago, never advertised. I'm guessing it was posted on the back of the men's room door in town hall. Probably just a few people were there. Someone bought it, set up the real estate trust and put it up for a quick sale. Probably didn't want anyone local to know, and that's why it was advertised in an out-of-town paper and sold through a Boston broker. I'm guessing a lot of this kind of thing goes on around here. Compared to waterfront prices back home, this land was just about given away."

The man paused to re-light his cigar, tossing the still flaming match down on the ground and stepping on it. He leaned back on the Buick's fender and looked toward the bay, blowing out another large puff of smoke. "Real nice piece of property. Yes, sir. I think me and the wife are going to like it a lot here in the summers. When the kids get married they can build places of their own." Belching out more cigar smoke, he reached into his shirt pocket and took out a business card. It read, "Vincent Martone, Buick & Oldsmobile Dealer, Norwalk, Connecticut. Offering Deals You Can't Refuse Since 1952!"

"Should've given you this when I first got out of the car," Martone handed the card to the still bewildered Washy. "Nice meeting you, Sears. And just call me Vinnie. We're going to be neighbors."

"Plant Some Forsythia Bushes!"

Since it was Saturday, Washy knew that he wouldn't get anyone in town hall who could provide answers about this surprising turn of events. He got into his car and drove up Long Pond Road to Larry Doyle's house. Doyle had just been re-elected to the board of selectmen, part of an on-and-off pattern of office holding that had been the man's political record since the war and would be until his death. If there was anyone who had his finger on what went on in town, it was Larry Doyle.

Doyle's wife, Lee, greeted Washy at the door. "Hi Washy. If you are here to try and convince Larry to get behind that new highway barn, I don't think you are going to have much luck. The selectmen aren't going to recommend it this year."

Ushering himself toward the living room, Washy laughed and assured her that he never did town business on a Saturday. "We public servants get a couple of days of rest, Lee, and Larry, too. I just had something I wanted to check with him about. Personal stuff. No town business today."

Doyle was sitting in the living room watching television when Washy went in. "Hi, Wash. Saw your car coming in. What brings you around here?"

Washy took a seat. "I was hoping to find out how that land next to me got sold without me even knowing it was going on the market."

Doyle looked away from the television for the first time since Washy had come into the room. "You mean the Young property?"

"That's exactly what I mean," said Washy. And wanting to make sure he got Doyle's full attention, he got up and switched off the TV. "Why didn't I know about it?"

Getting up from his chair, Doyle lit a cigarette and went over by the window. "Washy, a couple of years ago the board of selectmen started looking at pieces of land in town that were either owners unknown or properties that hadn't had taxes paid for years. The town needed to raise some money, and it was felt that selling off these parcels would do that and put them back on the tax rolls. I wasn't on the board then but I heard about it. It was done openly and the bidding was fair."

"But I was told that the land was put up for sale only in off-Cape papers," Washy told Doyle.

"That may be true, Washy, but the tax auction was posted in the *Cape Cod Standard Times* and the *Cape Codder*. After the auction, the buyer was free to advertise the property any way he wanted. Apparently, that is what happened and that's why no one saw it around here."

"So who bought it at the auction?" Washy asked.

"On that parcel, it was Murray Wiseman," Doyle replied. "There were several bidders, but Wiseman got it. Didn't pay a whole lot for it either, I was told." Doyle turned and stepped away from the window. "I think you didn't get the word about the auction because it happened just about the time that CJ was killed and you had a lot on your plate. None of us figured it would matter much because the land had no access other than the road out to your house. There's a bit of wetland and bog in there. Anyone who bought it couldn't develop it because, even with the easement that went with the deed, the road couldn't meet the zoning code. At best, only a single house could ever be put on the property. Frankly, I don't know if the eventual buyer knew that. And Wiseman, I'm sure, never told him."

"Well, I think he's going to know pretty soon, Larry." Washy said. "I just met the guy. He's some car dealer from Connecticut, and he's planning to start building out there. He may not like the fact that he's only going to get maybe one house on seven acres."

Doyle smiled for the first time. "Well there isn't much the guy can do about it. Unless, of course, you agree to let him fill, widen, and pave the road so he has more frontage. I'm figuring that you aren't going to agree to that. Right now the property is only good for one house. The planning board won't give him a variance. One house is going to be it."

"That may be true." Washy stood up and put his hat back on. "But it's *where* that one house is going to go that has me most concerned. There's only so much upland in there. And he's going to want to be near the beach."

Doyle followed Washy out into the kitchen. "Really, Washy, even if he puts up a little cottage near you, it will only be occupied maybe two months of the year. That's not much to worry about. Hell, I can see my neighbors across the street." Doyle swept his arm toward the window where the old railroad depot had been. "You get used to it. Just plant some forsythia bushes."

Bob Seabury

The rest of the year went by with no sign of Vincent Martone. In the meantime, Washy took a look at the zoning bylaw that governed building in Brewster. Other than frontage and setback requirements, the code allowed a good bit of latitude for any builder. Lot sizes were small, the idea being to encourage people to consider Brewster as a place to put up a reasonably-priced home. There were no special provisions regarding construction along the beach nor was there a wetlands restriction in place. A couple of old cranberry bogs in town had recently been filled for house lots. It was pretty clear that Martone could put his new house just about anywhere on his property. Washy checked regularly with the planning board to see if any building plans for the seven-acre parcel had been submitted, but there were none.

All this concern over what Vincent Martone might have in mind was at least temporarily shelved as Washy and his now eight-man crew did a lot of the work related to installing the town water system. Much of the construction was contracted out by the Whitman and Calderwood Engineering Company but there was still enough work to keep the DPW busy. And complaints about chopped-up roads came to Washy's office, not the prime contractors. He was either in the office or out on the road during the week. With the continuing tension with Serena, it was just as well.

Windsor Burkhart stopped in the DPW barn occasionally when he had nothing to do. He would joke that he was checking in to see how many shovels were being leaned on by Washy's crew or how the card games were going in the back room. But one morning the antiques dealer arrived and took a seat in the vacant chair in front of Washy's desk. There was no opening line of wisecrack. Burkhart was clearly subdued.

"You're looking kind of down today, Win," Washy greeted his friend. "Some sharp-eyed tourist find out that those antique lamps you were selling came from Spag's?"

Burkhart didn't laugh. "It's Robbie, Washy," Burkhart replied in a low voice. "He's not been well for a while now, and I took him to the doctor a couple of weeks ago. We were referred to a specialist in Boston. He's got cancer."

The news that Burkhart's longtime partner was seriously ill was a shock. While Burkhart was the more outgoing of the duo, Bob Seabury had always been part of any project or endeavor where Burkhart was involved. The two men complemented each other and it was unusual to see one at a social function without the other. Over the years, both men had been great benefactors for their adopted town, raising money for just about every cause that came along. In the twenty-plus years the partners had lived in Brewster, the two had become an accepted part of the fabric of local life.

After an awkward silence, Washy walked around to where Burkhart had been sitting. He put his hand on his friend's arm. "I don't know what to say, Win, except that you know that people in this town will be very concerned for Bob, and for you as well. And you can count on Serena and me to be there when you need us."

Burkhart hadn't taken his eyes away from the window since he'd sat down. It was almost as if he were reluctant to look at Washy. Now he turned to his friend and there were tears in his eyes. "Washy, Robbie and I have been together for more than half of my life. I don't know what I will do without him. The doctors say that he's only got a few months to live."

"Win, it's not going to be an easy thing to deal with. It's terrible news. But we'll go through it together, I promise you. You won't be alone in this."

Composing himself somewhat, Burkhart stood up and walked to the door. "I've told no one else Washy," he said. "Neither Robbie nor I want a lot of pity. This is a small town and people will find out soon enough. I'd just as soon you didn't mention this to anyone else."

"Just Serena, Win," Washy replied. "She loves you and Robbie just as much as I do. She needs to know."

"Of course, Serena," said Burkhart. "And thanks for being someone I could talk to. I didn't want to burden you with this. But I had to speak about it with someone."

As Burkhart opened the door to leave, Washy followed him. "Win, remember that when things get hard, there are always people who care. I think you reminded me of that not that long ago. That's what friends are for."

Burkhart smiled for the first time. "I know that, Washy. Maybe that's why I came here this morning, certainly it wasn't to see anyone working!" As he headed out to his car he turned and looked over his shoulder. "And don't you start any rumors that my antique lamps come from Spag's. Anyone who knows anything knows they come from Harry Snow's in Orleans!"

Later that day, Washy told Serena about Burkhart's news. Serena was visibly shaken. "I can't believe it. Only a few months to live? That's horrible. I feel so badly for Win. What will he ever do without Robbie?"

"It's going to be very hard for Win," Washy said. "I told him that we'd be there for both of them, but there really isn't all that much we can do. It's a sad situation."

Serena stood and looked at her husband. Her gaze was firm but not hard. "You told him that we would be there, Washy. And as God is my judge, we will be." She turned and went into the kitchen and picked up the phone.

"What are you doing? Washy asked. "You aren't calling Win now, are you?"

"Don't be silly Washy," Serena replied as she continued dialing. "I'm calling some of the ladies in my church group. We'll organize meals and regular house cleaning for them. And we'll do it as long as it takes. We look after people in Brewster. We always have." She was already in conversation with someone when she put her hand over the receiver and gestured at her husband. "Washy, don't just stand around. Get on over to Windsor's place and get a list of what they need."

Finding Something That Was Lost

Serena's efforts in helping Win Burkhart and Bob Seabury seemed to energize her. Once she got her church group on a daily schedule, meals appeared for the two men like clockwork. Laundry was done, rooms dusted and cleaned, and errands done. All of this effort was a virtual godsend for Burkhart, as it gave him more time to devote to his companion. Dr. Ralph Moyer, new in town after Dr. Murad had retired and moved to Vermont, made daily visits to the Brier Lane house, administering pain killers that kept Seabury moderately comfortable.

But the cancer was moving quickly. Despite Dr. Moyer's efforts, the time came when Seabury had to be transferred to Hyannis for round-the-clock care. Even then, Serena managed to get herself to the nursing facility on a regular basis, bringing whatever she thought Seabury needed. It wasn't unusual for Burkhart to drive Serena to Hyannis for a visit and then drive her back to Sears Point several times a week. She and Washy made their way to Hyannis together on other days.

It was on one of those trips back from Hyannis that Serena reflected on what had come between the two of them. "I thought my heart would break when we got the news about CJ," she told Washy. "Maybe it did. But I was wrong to shut you out, Washy, and I know it. It was God's will what happened and neither of us could have changed it. Mary was my responsibility and I drove her away. You had nothing to do with that. I think maybe it took Bob Seabury's illness to show me that I shouldn't be living just for myself. I was being selfish. He and Win needed me just as I've come to realize that you do, too. I love you and I hope you'll forgive me."

The days and weeks that followed prove to be something of a renewal for Washy and Serena. Whatever had been temporarily lost since CJ's death seemed to come back even stronger. Serena continued her busy schedule of trying to make things easier for Win Burkhart, who was spending his nights alone in the big house on Brier Lane. She invited him to eat at Sears Point several times a week, and in the interim made sure he was taken care of by her church ladies' group. When Bob Seabury died, the town turned out to give him a proper send-off. And following a ceremony at the First Parish Church, a small party of Burkhart and Seabury's closest friends witnessed Seabury's ashes released on an outgoing tide at Paine's Creek.

One day not long after this, when he'd come home from work early, Washy went upstairs and passed by CJ's room. Serena was out. He was surprised to see that everything in the room had changed. The boy's possessions were gone and the bed was re-positioned with a new spread on it. The clothes that had hung in the closet were also missing. New curtains hung on the windows and there were different pictures on the wall. Only CJ's high school graduation picture, positioned on a small desk next to the bed, gave any indication that their son had ever lived in that room.

A Shocking Revelation

The second floor of the two-family apartment building on Grant Street seemed to groan under the weight of several dozen partygoers. Frank Sinatra sang *Summer Wind* from the tinny speakers of a tape player perched precariously on a pile of magazines against a wall. Grease-stained pizza boxes were scattered around a faux fireplace. A lurid red party light blinked on and off. The small window air conditioner did little to cool the room.

Mary sat on a worn sofa sipping a mixed drink. Bill Noonan came up behind her and squeezed her shoulders. "Cigarette?" He asked.

She nodded and took one, holding it to her lips as he lit it for her.

After Noonan's initial visit to Mary's office, she hadn't expected to see him again. But Noonan had returned the following week and had started counseling sessions. And he was faithful about showing up on a regular basis. As the weeks went by, the relationship between the two grew beyond professional boundaries.

Mary allowed Noonan to move in with her. She told herself that it was to keep him off the street. But it was more than that. Alone in the city, she had tried to find some kind of a group that she could identify with, some kind of personal shared pathway. It couldn't happen at Clayton Hospital. The old Taylor Street neighborhood had been taken over by a new and more violent group of anti-establishment types. Gangs were a growing threat, and the bar scene had produced lots of men who proclaimed endless love and devotion with the barely disguised motive of getting her into bed.

Noonan seemed different. To be sure, he was a wounded spirit, haunted by his experience in Vietnam. Mary saw him as vulnerable in the world that he'd come back to. Mary justified her connection to Noonan, rationalizing to herself that without her, he would end up like so many other veterans, strung out and living a life of despair on the street. But underneath, she realized the truth – she was just like Noonan, without direction and haunted by memories that wouldn't die.

At one point during the evening, Mary's eyes were drawn to a man sitting on a nearby couch. The man had tattoos on both arms. One of them read "U.S.M.C." across an anchor and shield. He was telling his female companion about his experiences in Vietnam. Noonan, who had just come out of the apartment kitchen carrying a beer, stopped abruptly when he passed the couple. "Did I hear you say you spent some time in 'Nam?'"

The tattooed man looked up at Noonan. "Yeah, I was in I Corps with the First Marine Division in '68' and part of '69,' north of Quang Tri near the DMZ."

"I never got up that far north," Noonan told the man. "I was with the army, Ninth Division, Riverine Force down in the Delta. About the same time."

"Didn't really matter," the man responded. "'Nam sucked wherever you were. I never heard anyone who served there ever say a good thing about the fuckin' place."

Mary had remained on the sofa, listening. Now, carrying her drink with her, she moved over to them and sat down on the couch. As she slid over next to Noonan, he gestured to the man he was talking with.

"Mary, this guy and I were in Vietnam about the same time." Noonan pointed to the former marine.

"Hi, the name's Jerry Sawzyn," the man replied. "I live a couple of streets over from here. Herb Overton has this apartment. He and I operate a drywall business together."

Mary mentioned her work at Clayton Hospital and Sawzyn nodded that he was familiar with the place. "A couple of my marine buddies got good treatment there," he said.

During the conversation Mary mentioned that she was from the East Coast. When Sawzyn heard her say "Cape Cod," he perked up. "Hey, there was a guy from Cape Cod in another marine unit that operated a bit north of where we were. Quite a story. I knew him from Parris Island and I ran into him one more time after about six months in 'Nam when I had an overnight resupply trip to Con Thien. We had a couple of beers together in the enlisted club. Maybe a month later, the kid bought it when he ended up on the wrong end of a mortar round while trying to bring a wounded buddy back to the perimeter. I heard he got a medal. A lot of good it did him. The last name was Sears. Had an old fashioned first name, something like Caleb, Cain, Cyrus, I think it was Cyrus. Yeah, that was it, Cyrus Sears. Everybody just called him 'CJ.'"

Mary gasped, and for a moment she couldn't breathe. The room began to spin. Standing next to her, Noonan moved to keep her from collapsing. Holding her stomach, Mary pushed him away, and with some effort stood up. The bathroom was just off the hallway. A strong odor of perfume mixed with marijuana hit Mary as she opened the door. It wasn't the smell that caused her to vomit before she reached the toilet.

The Summer Cottage

The phone rang in the highway barn. It was Serena. "Washy, you've got to come home. There's a great big truck just beyond our driveway and it's dumping a load of clay and stone. I think he may be stuck. You didn't order anything like that, did you?"

Washy assured her that he hadn't done any such thing. "Can you see any name on the cab of the truck?" he asked her.

"No it's just a big blue truck and there are two men in it."

As Washy drove up the narrow track that led to his house, he could see where the truck had knocked off pieces of trees and bushes as it progressed toward the bay. When he saw the truck, it was in the process of discharging a load of clay.

"What's going on here?" Washy shouted to the man who was directing the truck driver.

The man waved to his partner to lower the dumper and came over to Washy. He explained that he and his companion had been hired to put down some hardening to make a road surface over the sand for other trucks that were going to bring in building materials. "They're going to build a house over there," He pointed toward the bluff just to the west of Sears Point.

"Who are 'they'?" Washy asked.

"It's a construction company from Rhode Island," the man replied. "Torrissi and Nunes. They specialize in modular housing. A car dealer from Connecticut has hired them to put a house up on this lot. Pretty nice view, I'd say. But it's a hell of a small road to get everything out here." Indicating that they had a schedule to keep, the two men went back to working. Very shortly, the noise of several other trucks could be heard coming up the narrow road.

"I can't believe that Martone is just going to start building," Washy said to Serena. "Doesn't he know about building permits and other requirements?"

Washy called Neal Nevin, the building inspector. "Neal. A couple of guys are clearing land right next to my property. They tell me they're getting ready to put up a house. Know anything about it?"

"You must mean that guy from Connecticut? We just got his application for a building permit yesterday. There were no architect drawings with it. We've called and told him he's going to need them when he comes before the planning board. He was under the impression that he could come in right away and get his permit. I told him that we had over 300 applications last year for new construction, and it's looking like even more than that this year. He didn't like it when I said that it might be six months before he got a hearing. And of course, conservation will want to have a say on what he's going to do as well."

"Well, it looks like he's going ahead right now." Washy looked out the window of the kitchen. "He's got a truck up here dumping hardening. Some others are coming up the road. Looks like they're putting in the base for the driveway."

"If he's just improving the site to get access to where he wants to put up his building, I think he's OK," Nevin replied. "No rules against that. He can't start construction, though, until we approve his plans. I'll come up later this afternoon and look at what's going on."

Washy looked to where the truck was dumping its load of clay. If the sideline stakes were accurate, the new road layout looked like it was going to end up just at the edge of a dune about 100 yards west of Sears Point.

In the time it took for Neal Nevin to get over to the site, several more big trucks had rumbled up and offloaded their clay. A bulldozer was brought in on a big flatbed to smooth out the piles, and the machine crunched through the bayberry and beach plum bushes, spreading the hardening twenty-five feet wide and about a foot deep. A man drove up in a white pickup truck. He had a set of plans under his arm, and after consulting it a number of times, he hammered four orange-colored stakes into the dune just back from the beach. It was clear that the stakes marked the four corners of the intended new house.

Win Burkhart dropped by just as Nevin arrived. The two followed the building inspector over to where the new road branched off the old track. "Can someone put up a house right on the edge of this dune?" Burkhart asked Nevin.

"Well, given what happens in the winter around here, it wouldn't be my choice, but yes, he could do it." Nevin crushed a cigarette out on the freshly spread clay. "But then again, I'm guessing that the person who is building this place isn't going to be spending winters out here. It'll probably just be a seasonal cottage." The three men walked around the four foundation stakes. Nevin took out a measuring tape. "Actually, these stakes indicate that it's going to be a pretty big cottage. Our present zoning doesn't restrict how big a place can be, square footage-wise. He'll probably have to have a well out here. John Latham will advise him where he'll have to put it. It's got to be at least a hundred feet away from his septic system. But as long as it meets setback requirements, I guess he could build his cottage as big as he wants. I see from the plot plan he's got about seven acres."

"How high up could the building go?" Washy looked across the dune toward the beach.

"Wouldn't make a whole lot of sense to go up more than one-and-a-half, maybe two stories at most. The site is high enough already to get a good view of the bay. And the fire department only has ladders that can go as high as thirty feet. It wouldn't be smart to go higher than that. I wouldn't worry."

But a few months later at the planning board hearing, Washy learned that there was indeed a lot to worry about. It was an unseasonably hot June night in the Brewster school auditorium, and ten applicants were waiting before the planning board. Without air conditioning, everyone in the room was sweating, none more so than Vincent Martone. He had arrived just before 7 p.m. with his attorney and his architect, expecting that it would be a quick in-and-out. Instead, Rosamond Gage told him that his would be the last hearing of the evening.

He sat down heavily in a seat toward the rear of the hall, glowering at the board members. At around 9:45 p.m. when the plans for Martone's proposed new structure were finally unveiled, they showed a very large house with several balconies on the beach side. A central atrium with a vaulted ceiling was highlighted by a huge Palladian window that gave expansive views of the bay. The main room was flanked to the side by no less than seven bedrooms and eight baths. An outside pool was tucked into the western corner of the plan. A three-car garage with living space above was connected to the house on the eastern side. The drawing showed abundant bushes that the architect said were designed to mute the house's impact on the land. But there was no doubt that with its height, an estimated thirty-eight feet above grade, the "cottage" would dominate everything around it.

When Windsor Burkhart asked the board whether it was legal to build on what was essentially a barrier dune, they admitted that while they had tried to impose restrictions on this kind of thing, there were no laws presently prohibiting it. "We've brought this up a number of times, but haven't found enough support at town meeting to put it in the code," Gordon Sylver said. "The restriction may well be coming down soon from the state. I hope so. But that hasn't happened yet. All we can do is to respectfully ask that applicants hold destruction of the dunes to a minimum during construction."

Martone's lawyer, who'd been silent, stood and asked permission to address the board. "So with the plans we've submitted, is there an objection to my client's application for a building permit? We believe we've satisfied all requirements that the town has. And we'd like a decision tonight, if at all possible. My client would like to get started with the project."

There was some back-and-forth between the members of the planning board but in the end, unable to do much else, they voted to approve Martone's plan. Without acknowledging Washy and Serena, Martone got up to leave. With no more business to deal with, the meeting was adjourned.

As Washy and Serena left the meeting with Windsor Burkhart, Washy glanced at his watch. Tonight's hearing would have a major impact on his and Serena's world. There wasn't any doubt about that. They had sat through almost three hours of testimony by groups of hopeful applicants, yet the only part of the evening that had any meaning for them had taken less than twenty minutes.

A Growing Delusion

The first time that Bill Noonan physically assaulted Mary it produced more shock than it did actual pain. Thinking later about what had happened, she knew that she should have seen it coming. Since the night he'd learned that Mary had a brother who had died in Vietnam, Noonan had started to exhibit an increasing pattern of mood swings.

"Why didn't you tell me you had a brother in Vietnam?" he shouted at her. "Did you think somehow his service was better than mine? And how was he your brother? His name was Sears. Yours is Clark."

She explained about using her real father's name as a way of forging a new start in San Francisco, and that she'd not had contact with her family for several years. She didn't even know that her brother was in the marines.

But the explanations weren't enough. Noonan became increasingly paranoid and suspicious about everything Mary did or said. One day when Noonan was out of the apartment, Mary discovered some vials of white powder and amphetamines hidden in a jar in the kitchen. Noonan had been mixing coke with steroids. For how long, Mary didn't know. When she confronted him, Noonan went into a rage and slapped her. Her nose bled. When he saw the blood running down her face, however, he was immediately contrite. He cried and begged her to forgive him. But less than two days later Mary came home to find Noonan once again juiced and infuriated about some little thing that she had done. Nothing she said could calm him down. That time, when he hit her, she didn't wake up for almost an hour.

Often he would leave the apartment and not come back for several days, never indicating where he had been. When he did return, Noonan brought the same pattern of anger and apology with him. The anger showed itself in the beatings he meted out to Mary. Tearful apologies always followed the mayhem. He constantly told her that she couldn't leave him. Mary knew it was more than an emotional request. It was clearly a threat. She began to look for a way to get away from Bill Noonan.

A Mansion Grows – and Grows

Less than a week after the planning board hearing, builders showed up at Sears Point and began to erect the summer home on Martone's property. The foundation was poured over several days, and large trucks brought in a number of prefabricated modules that were fitted together with a large crane. A veritable army of plumbers, electricians, stone masons, and floor and tile people followed in their wake. None of them were local. As the summer waned, it wasn't unusual for Washy to wait a considerable time for a construction vehicle to exit the narrow road before he could get to his own house. The dust created by the trucks coated the trees and bushes and seeped into Serena's kitchen. It settled like brown snow on the cranberry bog.

Martone came to the site several times over the summer to inspect the work. Sometimes his wife accompanied him. She was a bottle blond, heavily made up and considerably younger than her husband. While there was some obvious wear and tear, it could be said that Mrs. Martone had held up reasonably well. In the car trade, she would have been described as a high mileage, high maintenance model but still very capable of delivering a comfortable ride. Martone's accountant was fond of describing his boss's wife as having a "favorable balance sheet." He was careful never to make that comment in Martone's presence.

The construction was clearly a rush job. Martone entertained the hope that he might be able to spend some fall weekends at his new house, and quality was clearly being sacrificed for speed. In the evenings when the workers were gone, Washy walked through the partially framed structure and noted that a lot of corners were being cut. The most impressive feature of the house was the floor-to-ceiling Palladian window in the living room. As Washy stood there in the half-finished building, he looked across the beach to the bay and marveled at the vista that spread out before him. The immense height of the building, sitting as it did to the west of Washy's house, obscured his own view of Wing's Island. For the first time in his life, Washy couldn't see Quivet Neck from his west-facing porch.

Martone and his wife were able to spend Thanksgiving in their newly completed waterfront getaway. For the holiday, Martone's extended Connecticut family joined them, a veritable legion of relatives and friends who arrived in separate cars. Vehicles spilled out onto the road and Washy had to ask for a couple of them to be moved so he could drive out.

Clara and her husband had come down to join Washy and Serena for the holiday, and were staying the night. Their two girls were both married and Clara was a grandmother of four. As it was with most holidays, the girls were spending Thanksgiving with their own families, one in Albany, New York, and the other in Richmond, Virginia. That arrangement seemed the new norm in this age of mobility.

Serena invited Windsor Burkhart for dinner and he joined them just after noon. With the meal finished, Washy, Burkhart and John Newcomb took a walk on the beach. Later that evening the five were watching television when they heard what sounded like explosions coming from next door. Rushing out to the porch facing Martone's mansion, they saw fireworks arching up into the sky from one of the decks. The night was clear and cold. Martone's guests stood on the dune above the bay, muffled like Eskimos, applauding each shower of crimson, blue, and white. Following the fireworks, the entourage retreated back into the house where a band played dance music. Even with the windows closed, the heavy base caused Washy's house to vibrate. The party went on long into the night.

As quickly as the Martone party had arrived the previous Wednesday, they all packed up and departed at the same time on Sunday afternoon. A convoy of vehicles resembling a long black snake with tinted windows headed down the track back to Lower Road. Martone and his wife were the last to leave. They didn't wave as they drove away.

The Old Guard Passes

In the life of a town there is rarely any single event that later can be cited as a pivotal point of change. Communities gradually transform themselves over time in a kind of subtle drift that is almost imperceptible to the people living through it. But the year 1973 saw a clear shift in both the fortunes and the character of Brewster. In an upset, Boston-born retired civil engineer Freddy Krapohl defeated longtime selectman Don Smith. Krapohl had been a director of a summer camp in East Brewster but had only been a permanent resident for about five years. Don Smith had been a fixture in town hall since his election in1964 and a lot of people were caught by surprise when he lost.

Finishing a close third behind Smith in the March election was a newcomer, Bob Sawtelle. A former U.S. Treasury intelligence law enforcement special agent, Sawtelle had moved to Brewster only a year earlier. When a special election was held later in June to fill the spot vacated by Selectman Steve Chilton's resignation, Sawtelle won a convincing victory, defeating Don Smith by a considerable margin. He drew his support mainly from the many new residents in town. For the first time the majority of the Brewster board of selectmen did not feature a person who either had been born in Brewster or had deep roots in the town. Only Jean Olmsted remained. And it was no secret that Sawtelle and Krapohl held no sentimental attachment to anyone who had been part of the town administration for more than a few years. As Sawtelle put it in his victory statement, he saw his election as "the beginning of a quiet revolution in Brewster."

Windsor Burkhart and Washy were sitting on the porch at Sears Point a few weeks after the election. It was high tide and the water in the bay was a vivid blue. Down on the beach, gulls carried clams into the air and dropped them on rocks. The two men had chosen the eastern side of Washy's house to escape the noise that was coming from Martone's cottage. It was a low humidity day and with no need for air conditioning, Martone's windows were open, and loud music interspersed with raucous laughter filled the air. Cars came and went with great regularity.

"It's pretty bad, isn't it." Burkhart nodded toward Martone's property.

"The weekends are the worst," Washy replied. "Monday through Friday it's not too bad. The days when Serena and I had this place all to ourselves, though, are gone. I never knew how much I valued peace and quiet until this year."

"You know, Washy, it seems that a lot of what we once took for granted is on the way to disappearing. The Millstone Road area is booming with new houses. Same with Freeman's Way. Lots of families are moving into town. There's going to have to be a new elementary school in the next year or so. You've seen the plans for what they want to do at the west end of Sheep Pond. Since the town turned down the La Salette property, Freddie Walters and Marty Rich have taken an option on it. The golf course is part of it. They want to make Brewster a prime resort destination. You've seen the start of construction over there behind the old Sea Pines school. It's scheduled for about a hundred and seventy-five condo units and will add maybe three hundred people to the town. Developments have reduced public access along the beaches, and fences and signs are going up to keep people out. Some property owners over near Point of Rocks gave Lester Gillespie a hard time when he went out recently to get some quahogs. Said he had no right to trespass on their flats."

"I heard that," Washy said. "And Lester's been quahogging out there for probably sixty years. You could probably get a good clam chowder by wringing out his hat."

The two men were silent for a while.

Washy stood up to stretch his legs. "It's not just the old familiar landscape that is disappearing, Win. The new majority in town hall has made it pretty clear that they want some new blood running things. Frankly, I think Sawtelle's talk about a quiet revolution includes me."

Burkhart appeared surprised by Washy's statement. "You think they might not reappoint you as public works superintendent? I don't believe it."

"That's exactly what I think, Win, and there's been enough undercurrent coming out of town hall to let me know that there is no certainty that I'll be kept on. They'd like me to retire. Jean Olmstead told me as much. She came by the barn the other day and said that she wasn't going to run for another term."

"Maybe we can get Larry Doyle to run again." Burkhart looked up at his friend.

Washy laughed. "You know, Win, I think he's still got a nose for it, but his news delivery business is keeping him pretty busy. In some ways I think that even Larry's time is over. You saw what happened to Don Smith. If you went into the Brewster Store today and asked people who Larry is, probably half of them wouldn't know. And the same thing would happen if you asked who's running the DPW. The only time my name has come up in the past year or so is when the roads were torn up for the new water pipes. Everyone was mad as hell. And I really didn't have anything to do with that. I've been doing some serious thinking that it might be a better move to retire now rather than be embarrassed by not being reappointed."

"But you've been doing this job for such a long time," Burkhart said.

Washy looked down toward the nearly filled parking lot at Breakwater Beach. "Maybe that's it, Win. Maybe I've been doing the job for too long. Twenty-seven years now. It's for sure someone else could do it. Perhaps even do it better. I don't doubt that for a minute. And you know, Krapohl and Sawtelle could be right. Brewster might really need some new blood."

Burkhart got up and walked over to the porch railing. "Whatever you decide, Washy, have some kind of a plan as to what you will do once you leave the job. A lot of men retire and have nothing to make them get out of bed in the morning. They don't last long. Maybe you and Serena could do some traveling, see what's out there. It's a big country."

Washy smiled at his friend. "You know, Win, seeing something new might be good for both of us. Serena's never been to Falmouth. And I've heard that Martha's Vineyard can be real nice in the fall."

A Decision to Retire

On one of the last days of June, Washy parked the car in his usual spot behind town hall. But instead of going directly into the highway barn, he went into the administrative building. After greeting Millie Reed, he continued down the corridor to the town clerk's office.

"Good morning, Ruth." Washy stood in front of the recently appointed clerk's desk. Ruth Eddy had been given an interim appointment following the death of Don Consodine. As a former member of the finance committee and Consodine's temporary assistant for more than a year, she was comfortable with the job. The transition had been seamless. "I wanted to leave something off for the selectmen."

Eddy smiled up at him. She'd known Washy for most of her life. He was fourteen years older, but Ruth and her sister Mary Louise had grown up on the flats with the rest of the Sears family. While they were still considered "summer people" by some of the old-timers in town, their grandfather was Augustus Thorndike and his farm had backed up to Sears Point. Thorndike's wife, Cora Nickerson, was a cousin of Washy's father, and like so many offspring of old Brewster families, Ruth and Washy were undoubtedly related somewhere on the extended family tree.

Washy took out an envelope and handed it to Eddy. "Here it is. Would you make sure that they get it?"

"Something I should know about, Washy?" With a cocked eyebrow, Eddy took the envelope and put it in the selectmen's box.

Washy smiled and said, "Serena and I have decided that it's time for the two of us to do a bit of traveling. The new fiscal year begins on July 1 and I wanted to give the board some time to name a new DPW superintendent. I've indicated that I'll stay on until they find a replacement."

"Anybody else know about this?" Eddy asked.

"No, I suspect you are the first, Ruth. But I'm guessing that word will get around soon enough. It's still a small town." He winked and turned to leave.

Eddy stopped him for a moment. "Just so you know, Washy. Bill Doyle was in here just a short time ago. He told me he was thinking about resigning from the finance committee. After fourteen years, he's not happy with the direction of the new regime either. You aren't the only one."

Outside, Washy paused beside Millie Reed's turquoise and white Ford. It was done. Twenty-seven years of taking care of Brewster's roads, shepherding the goings-on at the dump, and plowing snow and clearing sidewalks was officially over. Washy had seen the department grow from a single truck and a road grader to several trucks and up-to-date equipment befitting a modern municipality. There were six permanent men in the department. Plans had been approved to tear down Addie Hazzard's old house across from Latham's and build a modern police and fire station. DPW operations were scheduled to shift into the old quarters next to the Brewster Garage. Voters had also finally approved a major restoration of town hall. Brewster was entering a new age, and as he stood there, Washy knew that he was more of the town's past than its future. Just in the past year, new construction in town topped five-and-a-half million dollars. There were eighteen new subdivisions approved. Olle Lund's farm on Millstone Road was gone, the property now being used by Lloyd and Betty Avery as a riding stable. Like the railroad, the cows of Pine Ridge Dairy had passed into history.

At the first selectmen's meeting following Washy's letter of resignation, the board named John Featherstone to the newly vacated post. The position that Washy had occupied was split in two. Dennis Hanson, a young civil engineer recently out of Lowell Institute of Technology, was named superintendent-engineer. Both men seemed to have their own vision of what the job entailed. And they didn't expect any hand-holding from Washy. Phil Whitely was named as water superintendent. Washy had just about enough time to clean out his desk before the new men were in place.

A Late-night Phone Call

That fall Washy busied himself getting the bog ready for harvest. Serena continued with her volunteer projects. She liked Donald Mills, the new minister at the Baptist Church, and looked forward to meetings of the Golden Links group. Washy and Serena usually ate supper together and afterwards watched the evening news. If they were up past nine o'clock it was unusual.

So it was a jolt when, one night late in November, the phone rang. The caller was from the Marin County sheriff's office in San Francisco.

"Is this the Sears family?" The man on the phone apologized for the late hour and came to the point of his call. "Mr. Sears, we have a young woman here who was found earlier today in her apartment quite badly beaten. Right now she is in grave but stable condition at St. John's Memorial Hospital in the city. We had a hard time establishing whether she had any next of kin. She was unconscious when transferred to the hospital so we couldn't talk to her. Looking through her apartment we found out that her name was Mary Clark. An address book listed you, and we didn't make the connection until we saw the name Mary Sears and a telephone number written in the inside cover. We think she may be related to you."

Washy was stunned, and the look on his face brought Serena to the phone. She told the man in San Francisco that yes, Mary Clark was their daughter. Serena explained that both she and Washy hadn't had any contact with Mary for several years, and had no idea where she was living.

"Mrs. Sears, I can't tell you what to do, but your daughter's situation is touch-and-go at the moment. We haven't been able to interview her, and the doctors aren't sure whether she is going to make it. It could go either way. If there is any possible way you could do it, you should think about getting out here as soon as you can."

Serena thanked the officer and assured him that they would do whatever needed to be done. "We'll be on our way out there tomorrow," she told him.

Washy and Serena didn't return to bed that night. Serena packed enough clothes for the two of them. Washy called Windsor Burkhart just before first light to tell him what had happened. Burkhart offered to drive them to Boston but Washy said that he and Serena would be taking the bus out of Hyannis. Burkhart insisted that he at least take them to the bus terminal.

And so just after dawn, Serena and Washy were headed to Logan Airport. They were going to the side of a daughter that they hadn't seen or talked to in over five years. Whether she would be alive or dead when they got to San Francisco, they didn't know. At 9:30 in the morning the two were in the air headed three thousand miles across the country. Neither of them had ever flown in an airplane.

A Wounded Child

St. John's Memorial Hospital was in the Lower Nob Hill section of San Francisco. An older building with a modern façade, the hospital was known as a place where the indigent and poor got free care. Because of the neighborhood, the staff was no stranger to severe trauma cases, including gunshot wounds. Washy and Serena had arrived the night before and stayed for just a few hours in a motel near the airport before renting a car and driving to St. John's. The San Francisco police department had alerted the hospital that they would be arriving and they were met by an administrator who escorted them to a small room off the main lobby.

"I know this is very difficult for you." The hospital spokeswoman settled herself behind her desk. "But I'm very glad that you were able to come out. Your daughter has been here over a week and it wasn't until three days ago that the police were able to identify her. Mary was found in her apartment by a neighbor who saw her newspapers and magazines piling up. It appears she had been lying on the floor for perhaps as long as three days. She'd been badly beaten and was unconscious. When the police arrived they thought at first she was dead. Once she was brought in, the doctors were able to get her stabilized, but she's remained in a coma since her arrival. Several times we thought we had lost her, but I can tell you she's still alive. Her prognosis is extremely guarded."

"Does anyone have an idea who might have done this? Or why this happened?" Serena asked.

"The police aren't telling us much," the woman said. "They believe that Mary was sharing her apartment with a man. He's the prime suspect right now and they are looking for him. But I don't know any more than that."

The administrator stood up and walked around to Serena and Washy. "I have to tell you that you are probably not going to recognize your daughter. Her face took quite a beating and is still very swollen. She's got a broken arm, some cracked ribs, and we think there's some internal damage. She's got a lot of tubes in her and she's completely immobile."

"I want to see her now," Serena said.

"Of course. I'll let the nurses know that you are coming up. She's in the ICU." The woman made a phone call and Washy and Serena were escorted to the elevator. The hospital administrator did not go up with them. Not a word was said as the elevator doors closed.

Mary's room was on the fourth floor. When Washy and Serena got off the elevator they were taken to the nurse's station where a nurse who identified herself as Althea briefed them on what they were about to see. Althea scanned a clipboard before giving her summary of Mary's condition. "We've got your daughter in a private room and we're checking on her regularly. Her signs have been steady over the last forty-eight hours, blood pressure, heart rate, and pulse. She'll open her eyes now and then, but doesn't respond to verbal commands. There may be some brain damage. Whoever did this to her did it with a vengeance. You need to be ready for a pretty devastating sight."

Outside the room, Washy hung back a bit as Serena went in with Althea. When he did enter, he saw Serena by the bed holding the exposed hand of something that resembled a person. Mary was bandaged from head to toe and lying on her back. Her face was swollen and purple and she was breathing through a ventilator. Her eyes were closed. An IV dripped fluid and wires ran under the blanket connecting to three different monitors. They showed green lines crossing the screen at regular intervals. Washy moved to Serena and squeezed her arm. "My God, Serena! Who could have done something like this to her?"

To his surprise, there were no tears. Instead, Serena held and stroked the exposed hand of her lost daughter and began speaking softly, assuring Mary that she and Washy were there and would take care of her.

"We love you Mary. You aren't alone. Washy and I are going to be here with you." There was no response from the figure lying in the hospital bed.

For the rest of that day Serena didn't move from Mary's bedside. She continued speaking softly and squeezing Mary's hand. Washy gave mother and daughter time alone together. He brought drinks and food and gave his wife an occasional short break. At the end of the day, he wasn't surprised that Serena had talked the nurses into putting a cot in the room so that she could stay the night next to Mary. Washy took a room at a nearby hotel. Just before he left, Serena asked that before he came the next day, he find a bookstore and buy a copy of *Wind in the Willows*. "It was Mary's favorite book as a child," she told him. "I'm going to reach back and bring Mary back to us. And I'm going to start at the beginning. Wherever her mind might be right now, I think I can find the window that will let her back in."

It seemed a strange request but Washy didn't ask any questions. Serena was a very determined woman. The next morning he was there with the book and Serena began her program of reclaiming her lost child.

Therapy and Recovery

It was almost two weeks to the day after Washy and Serena's arrival at the hospital that Mary said her first words. Progress had been frustratingly slow. Serena hadn't left Mary's bedside for more than just a few minutes each day. For hours she read to Mary with no apparent reaction, until the eighth day, when in response to a question, Mary squeezed Serena's hand. It was then that Serena's tears finally came, tears of joy and thanksgiving for her daughter's deliverance from whatever dark place her mind had been in.

In the weeks that followed, Mary made slow progress. It was almost a month before she was able to take a few halting steps. She eventually was able to feed herself and sit in a chair for short periods of time. All the while, Serena was nearby, holding her daughter when it was necessary and offering words of encouragement during Mary's physical therapy sessions.

Recognizing that Mary's rehabilitation was going to take considerable time, Washy and Serena took a monthly room rental in an apartment building near the hospital. Washy called Windsor Burkhart and asked him to look after things at Sears Point. Though Serena felt comfortable leaving the hospital at night, she spent her days sitting for hours in the solarium with her daughter. Gradually, Mary began to reveal details of her life over the past six years. She told Serena about the Mendocino commune and how she had tired of it and returned to San Francisco to do social work. She admitted to many mistakes in judgment and wondered ruefully how she had been foolish enough to pursue a relationship with someone like Bill Noonan.

Serena raised no judgments about her daughter's choices, and at one point she told Mary about her own doubts in her early marriage to Harris Clark. "We were both very young and had no real idea about what married life would be like. The war was on and I think we felt that we should grab what we could before he had to go off to fight. My parents were against it. We didn't know each other all that well." Serena paused and looked out of the window. "And I'm not sure that we would have stayed together had he come home alive. War changes a man. Looking back on it, what we did in getting married was really selfish. But I've thanked God every day that we had you."

"I always think of Washy as my real father," Mary remarked one day. "He was always there, looking after CJ and me." At the mention of her stepbrother, she began to cry. "And I didn't even know that CJ had been killed in Vietnam. I can never forgive myself for not being with you when you needed me most. I don't know how you can even look at me."

Serena hugged Mary. "Some things we can't undo. But we have to move on. You are my daughter and I love you very much. And you *have* a real father. It's always been Washy. Someone else's blood might run in your veins, but you've always had Washy's heart. He loved us and made us a home. And with CJ we were a family. Even with CJ gone, we're still a family. Nothing can change that."

When it came time for Mary's discharge from the hospital, she decided to return to Brewster with Washy and Serena. The decision had been Mary's, not influenced by any coaxing by Serena. Mary, Serena, and Washy boarded an American Airlines flight for Logan Airport. When Washy called him, Windsor Burkhart wouldn't hear of them taking the bus back to Hyannis. He was waiting in Boston when they arrived.

Two months later, San Francisco police called and notified the family that Bill Noonan's body had washed up on the shores of Marina Bay, an apparent suicide.

A Very Different Place

As Windsor Burkhart drove Mary, Serena and Washy back to Brewster from Logan Airport, it was light enough for Mary to see the familiar marsh and bay landscape as they entered the town along Route 6A. The Jolly Whaler cottages, still closed up tight for the winter, loomed on the right at Betty's Curve. There was a single light on in Doris Ellis's house on Paine's Creek Road. Other than the neon sign from the corner package store that blinked two colors against the lengthening shadows, there was no other sign of life.

"I can't believe I'm here," Mary remarked from the back seat of Burkhart's car where she sat with Serena. "It just doesn't seem real yet."

Washy looked back from the front passenger's seat. "Perhaps what you might find unreal are all the changes that have happened since you've been gone. It's a very different town."

Burkhart chimed in. "Your old elementary school is about to close up. It's overcrowded and the roof's leaking. They're planning to build a new one on Underpass Road. The high school kids now all go to Nauset Regional. Grade seven and eight are now in Orleans. The underpass is no more, either. They're talking about putting in a bicycle trail where the railroad used to go. The town's over three thousand people now. Donald Doane died a couple of years ago, and a new family – you remember the Dibbles from Brewster Park? They now run the old store. And all that stuff Donald had in his upstairs museum? It's all gone, auctioned away after he died. His mother, Beulah, is still around, though. In her nineties now. Oh, and Harry Alexander died earlier this year."

"Hey, slow down, Win," Washy laughed. "You'll get Mary to thinking that instead of Brewster, she's coming home to somewhere else."

Burkhart looked over at Washy. "Perhaps she is, Washy, perhaps she is."

As they pulled off Lower Road and made their way out to Sears Point in the twilight, there remained just enough of a sunset to silhouette the old homestead above the bay. Suddenly Mary exclaimed. "What is that?"

"That's our new neighbor," Washy answered her. "A bit over a year ago a fellow from Connecticut built it as a summer place for his family."

"My God, it's a monstrosity!!" Mary said. "How could anything like that be allowed out here?"

"There were no regulations to stop it," Serena said. "And we aren't the only ones who are seeing this kind of thing. Go on the other side of Sesuit Harbor and there are probably a dozen or so just as big as this one. It's going on all over the Cape. Everyone wants to be right on the water. And money seems to be no object."

"But the natural view, the beauty of the land? Doesn't that matter?"

"It's their view now, just as much as it's always been ours," Washy said. "That's just the way it is."

Entering the old house, Mary looked around to the familiar walls and rooms. "You haven't changed all that much in here since I've been gone," she said to Serena. "Same wallpaper in the living room. Even the same old kitchen counter."

Serena put her arm around Mary. "We try to keep things the same. There're so many changes happening outside of this house that preserving what we're used to seems the right thing to do. Washy and I have never had a lot of needs and we're comfortable here."

Mary followed her mother up the stairs. Passing CJ's room, she paused a moment and looked in. "He never really had a chance to live," Mary looked at Serena, who was already half way down the hall. "It's so sad."

"His life was short. That's true. And yes, it is very sad. But CJ lived. He put a lot into his twenty-one years. Your brother died a brave man and he's not forgotten. There isn't a day that I don't think of him." Serena gently took Mary's arm and accompanied her further down the hall. "Here's your old room. It's yours for as long as you want it. When you feel you're ready you can make your own plans about where you want to live."

Sitting on her bed later that evening, Mary looked out one of the west-facing windows. The moon was low in the sky but already the shadow of the large building on the other side of the cranberry bog lay almost fully across the yard. As the moon rose, the shadow shortened but never completely freed Sears Point from its grasp. It was, Mary thought, as if the new house had taken possession of the land. Its immense size seemed to swallow up everything around it. She walked over and closed the curtains, hoping that in the morning it would be gone. When she woke up, it was still there.

King's Grant

What Mary observed in the days following her return home may have surprised her. But for people living in Brewster in the 1970s, change had become the norm. The entire Cape was growing rapidly with demands for services that couldn't have been imagined just a decade earlier. Retirees were turning former vacation homes into permanent residences. Hyannis sported a new mall, reflecting a new retail marketing pattern that was sweeping the country. The town still lacked a single bank or pharmacy, but it did have a hardware store. There was no longer a doctor in town. Two locally owned small markets still took care of the grocery needs of townspeople. Local newspapers had more pages devoted to real estate than actual news items. If a person could hammer a nail straight, it wasn't difficult to find a decent paying job. Families flocked to the town.

All of this growth put a lot of pressure on the school system. Brewster's school budget went over a half million dollars in 1974 and the new elementary school was finally approved. The town agreed to take by eminent domain twenty-eight acres adjacent to the dump to enlarge that facility. A new half-million dollar police and fire station was occupied the fall of 1974. As the nation readied for its two-hundredth birthday in 1976, Brewster formed its own bicentennial committee with Windsor Burkhart as its chairman. Richard Lazarus joined Sawtelle and Krapohl on the board of selectmen. The Ladies Library proposed and completed a major expansion. With the Arab oil embargo, woodstoves made a comeback and there was a momentary demand for small cars. Gas at sixty cents a gallon impacted family budgets and it was getting more and more expensive for young families to own their own homes. As a partial response to that, an affordable housing complex with subsidized rents went up on Underpass Road.

Mary continued to have problems with a damaged kidney, and just a few months after returning to Brewster she had it removed at Brigham and Woman's Hospital in Boston. Her recovery from the surgery extended into the spring and during that time she continued living with Washy and Serena.

One April morning, Washy and Windsor Burkhart started out from Sears Point on their usual walk along the beach. They took the familiar path across the dune near Martone's house. As they came out on the beach, they saw two men putting up a fence starting at the edge of the dune toward the tide mark.

"What are you doing?" Washy went over to one of the men.

Hardly looking up from his task, the worker replied with obvious sarcasm, "Putting up a fence! What does it look like?"

"That wasn't what I asked," Washy told him. "I want to know what you are doing putting up this fence? Who gave you the authority to do it? And I'm not looking for a smart answer."

His attention now focused on Washy, the fence installer stood up and pointed up toward Martone's house. "Look mister, I'm doing a job for the property owner up there. He wants a fence to keep people off his beach. And that's what we're doing. If you've got any questions, get in touch with Vincent Martone. He's the guy that hired us."

With that, the fence builder rejoined his partner and started rolling out a section of snow fencing.

"That's a hell of a note," Burkhart said. "How can Martone think he's got the right to cut off access to the beach. We've had the common use of the shoreline along here for as long as I can remember."

Washy nodded, but then hesitated. "Seems I remember my father getting involved in some beach dispute back in the 1930s. Someone using some old deeds was trying to claim title to a lot of waterfront property in Brewster and Yarmouth. I wasn't living at home then, but he told me that under state law, the common use of the beach wasn't something guaranteed. There've been court cases about it and the rulings have been pretty consistent. Property owners can establish rights over the shoreline and prohibit access to it. It's from some colonial law. I think my father called it 'King's Grant.'"

Later that day, Washy and Burkhart were in the office of Larry Spaulding, Brewster's town counsel. Describing what they had seen that morning, they asked him if Martone had the right to fence off the beach in front of his property.

"You're not the first to come in here asking this question," Spaulding told them. "We had a couple of similar situations over at Point of Rocks last year, and it forced me to call the attorney general's office to get some background on who actually owns the shorefront. The long and the short of it is that it's perfectly legal for Martone to close off his beach. That right comes from a colonial ordinance that dates back into the seventeenth century when the Massachusetts Bay Colony, in an attempt to encourage dock building, gave waterfront landowners title to the flats adjacent to their properties. And the title extended to the low water mark. Over time, the ordinance acquired the force of common law in all of Massachusetts. As long as Martone's deed states his waterside boundary to be 'by the sea' without exclusionary language, it grants him the rights to the flats to the low water mark. My guess is he's had his lawyer check the wordage and that is why the fence is going up."

"What about all of the weirs that were out there for centuries?" Washy asked. "My father and grandfather had several. The flats go out for almost a mile. You can still see the stumps where they were."

"Technically, until about the Civil War they were probably illegal under the colonial ordinance," Spaulding replied. "But nobody pressed it then. In fact, there was little interest in owning shorefront property at all. It's only in the past few years that these issues have come up because of the desirability of building on the shorefront."

"So you are saying that we can no longer walk along the beach in front of Martone's house?"

"That's not exactly what I'm saying. Actually, there are several exemptions to the closing off of beach access," Spaulding answered. "Chapter 91 of state law says you can cross Martone's beach if engaged in fishing, fowling and navigation. But if you don't carry a fishing pole or a shotgun, Martone is within his rights to call the police and have you thrown off. And from what I've seen and heard of the guy, I'm guessing he'd do it."

"That's about the damnedest thing I've ever heard," Burkhart said, looking at Washy. "You've got a neighbor at Sears Point who spends maybe two months in his summer house, but he has the right to keep us off the beach the entire year?"

"Look at it this way," Spaulding said. "Property on the beach is very expensive. Owners pay a lot in taxes to be there. They naturally expect that for what they've invested they'll have a lot of privacy. I'm not saying that I completely agree with it, but that's their argument."

"Thanks, Larry," Burkhart was the first to get up and move toward leaving the office. "C'mon Washy, we've got to go over to Snow's and buy us a couple of fishing poles."

A New Concern

The situation with Martone's property didn't improve when summer returned. The police were called out on a regular basis to kick people off his beach. When he wasn't there, private security people enforced the prohibition on trespassing. In September, Martone had television cameras installed on the roof of the house to monitor the beach. Rather than risk a confrontation, Washy started taking his walks down toward Breakwater Beach. But even heading east, there were enough private beach signs to discourage a continuous walk for much more than a half mile.

Mary recovered and moved to an apartment in Hyannis where she took a job with a local social service agency. She joined several activist groups including the Association for the Preservation of Cape Cod and the Women's International League for Peace and Freedom. She also became a lightning rod spokesperson against the overdevelopment that was plaguing the Cape.

Occasionally Mary took one of those beach walks with Washy. On one of their early morning excursions, Mary walked to one of the no trespassing signs and started pulling it down. "Don't do that!" Washy told her. "No sense in adding us to Chief Ehrhart's list of trespassers."

"But this should be a crime, Washy. How can these people keep others from freely passing by their property? The beaches should be open to the public like they are on the west coast."

Washy explained how the law gave exclusive rights to beachfront owners. "The state legislature has tried several times to scrap the old colonial grants, but the issue of financial compensation sinks any possibility of change. Massachusetts can't afford to pay owners for what would be a land taking by eminent domain. The bills always die in committee because of the cost."

"But it's just wrong," Mary said. "The owners really aren't paying full property taxes for the land between the high and low water marks. If they want to claim it, the town should fully tax it."

"I don't disagree," Washy replied. "But the effort to collect any taxes beyond what are already being paid would be a huge legal undertaking for the town. Like the state, Brewster can't afford to do it, either."

As they continued their walk, Washy thought about something else that he wasn't about to share with Mary. He hadn't even brought it up with Serena. Under the recently announced "Sudbury Decision," towns in Massachusetts were being directed to assess property at its highest and best use. No longer could towns use arbitrary assessing systems that varied from community to community. This "full and fair" valuation had the potential to affect Sears Point. On paper, the location of Washy's property on the bay was worth considerably more than its current tax level. With Washy on a fixed pension, there was the real possibility that he and Serena might have to sell out and move.

Mary's voice broke through his train of thought. "If I were in charge, I'd have all of these new waterfront houses removed. The land along the beach should go back to its natural state, like it is on Wing's Island. If the legislature can't take the required action, someone else will surely do it."

"Don't say that too loudly," Washy laughed. He was more than just half joking. "The property owners have the law and the courts on their side."

"Maybe, but a lot of things can happen out here in the off-season, especially late at night." Mary looked back toward Sears Point and shifted her glance to a new house being built on the bluff above. "Yes, someone else will surely do it," she said quietly. But Washy heard what she said, and realized that he might have some new concerns about his daughter.

More Changes

The rest of the 1970s flashed by. The Cape worried about the possibility of offshore oil leases. The Russian fishing fleet seemed to be permanently anchored in plain sight off the Cape's Atlantic shore until the two hundred-mile limit was imposed. "Red Tide" closed down shellfish beds from Provincetown to Yarmouth.

Following the 1975 May town meeting, Washy sought out Bob Franklin, who was chairman of the conservation commission. The rising property taxes on the seven acres at Sears Point had finally reached a point that Washy felt he had to do something. Everyone was feeling the pinch as assessments rose. Ironically, the "full and fair" evaluation of open land was adding to the Cape building boom as old families who found themselves land rich but cash poor began to sell off large acreage holdings. Washy didn't want to subdivide or sell his property, but he needed some kind of relief.

Washy stopped Franklin as he was getting into his car. "Bob, I'd like to know more about the tax abatement that comes with putting land in conservation."

"Hi, Wash. Yes, that's something available to property owners that can reduce the property tax. We've already had a number of people take advantage of it. You can do a term restriction or a permanent one. Because it reduces the potential for development, the assessment is considerably lower. You still keep title but you waive your right to build on it. We support it because it preserves some open space. I've got a brochure here in the car."

Washy thanked Franklin and took the information home. After discussing it with Serena, he went to town hall and signed the paperwork. Sears Point, at least Washy's section of it, now had a permanent conservation restriction.

Larry Doyle re-entered town politics in 1976, running against Freddie Krapohl for selectman. He lost by just a handful of votes. Doyle was more successful a year later when he defeated incumbent Richard Lazarus for a three-year term. Gordon Sylver succeeded his uncle as fire chief and Barbara Vaughn became town clerk when Ruth Eddy retired. Continuing the resurgence of old family political power in Brewster, longtime school committee chairman Stephen Hopkins defeated selectman Bob Sawtelle by a wide margin in 1978. Town hall operations moved to the old elementary school on Route 6A. Brewster's population edged up toward four thousand people and for the first time, Democrats outnumbered Republicans, as reflected in the vote totals for the 1976 presidential primaries. Incidents of drug use became a regular part of the police department's annual crime report. The town debated building a public golf course off Freeman's Way. Arguing against the proposal, one person said that no one would ever play golf in such a "desolate place." The measure was defeated. In an angry meeting that was delayed by a bomb scare, voters banned hunting on town land, citing the increasing lack of open space for the sport. Just as divisive was a proposal to include just about all of Brewster in the proposed Old Kings Highway Historical District. Eventually it passed with the support of many of the new residents in town.

Washy continued his regular walks along the beach, venturing far out on the exposed flats at low tide. He noticed how different the flats had become over the years. He looked at old photos of his father's weir and could see that the flats had once been covered with eelgrass. It was now mostly gone. The sand appeared almost sterile, bleached out and lifeless. Bloodworms seemed to be the only thing thriving there. Clams were increasingly hard to find. When the state allowed the use of hydraulic pumping by draggers in less than twenty feet of water, the sea clams disappeared. The shoreline too, had changed. The jetties that had been built in the 1950s created a scouring effect that left some beach areas almost without sand. Some beachfront homes were threatened and there was a push to add more stone to the eroding bluffs.

After the 1976 Bicentennial, Win Burkhart announced that he was cutting back on his activities. He'd poured himself into the year-long celebration and was clearly exhausted. Washy could see his friend slowing down physically, and their walks together were less frequent. Burkhart even missed Washy's 70th birthday in October, a clear sign that something wasn't right. But whenever Washy brought it up, Burkhart insisted that he was just tired from all the activities of the past two years. "I just need some rest, Washy. I'll be as good as new by next summer." But Washy wasn't convinced.

"I just wish Win would go see his doctor and find out what's ailing him," Serena told Washy after Burkhart had left the house after a Sunday dinner. "He's lost weight and doesn't look good."

Washy nodded in agreement and wondered to himself whether Burkhart had already seen his doctor and perhaps knew something that he didn't want to talk about.

The Fire

The January wind rattled the windows in the new police and fire station. The snow had been falling since late afternoon, and as dispatcher Don Savoy looked out into the parking lot he could see in the glare of the streetlight that at least five inches had come down in the last hour. In the gusting wind it was already starting to pile up in drifts. Savoy had been sitting alone in the office watching a small black and white television that faded in and out with each gust. The Celtics were leading the Knicks in the third quarter. The wall-mounted VHF radio on the other side of the room suddenly crackled. It was Charlie May, one of the snowplow drivers who was out that night trying to keep Brewster's roads open in the storm.

"Hey, Don! Me and Wally Matthews are down here in the parking lot at Breakwater Beach. We can see a house on fire over on Sears Point. It's going pretty good."

Savoy was out of his seat. "There are two houses out there, Charlie. Can you tell which one it is?"

"It's the new house, the one the Connecticut guy owns. The flames are already coming out through that big window on the bay side. Wind's pretty bad and we can't get closer."

May told Savoy that the wind direction was from the east, which meant that Washy's house was not in immediate danger. "Blowing like a bastard out here," he repeated to the dispatcher.

"OK, Charlie, I'll get the crew up. See if you can plow a track out to

Sears Point and we'll try and get some equipment out there."

Savoy put the receiver down and walked back to the desk. He lit a cigarette and sat down heavily in his chair. He dialed Washy's number. There was no answer, a good sign. Washy and Serena were apparently not home. The third quarter of the game had about four minutes to go. The Knicks were putting on a rally, cutting the Celtics' lead to just four. With the quarter's end Savoy got up and went into the bathroom. Finishing his cigarette, he flicked the spent butt into the toilet and flushed, watching as the swirling water carried the stub away. Savoy then walked back into the office, picked up the phone and called Gordon Sylver.

By the time the fire department was able to get out to Sears Point, the Martone house was fully involved. Just as the 1941 Buffalo pumper navigated the narrow track into Martone's driveway, the center of the building collapsed and the wind carried a huge plume of sparks toward Paine's Creek. Without any nearby hydrants, a pumper truck had to be used. But other than wetting down what was left of the ruined structure, there wasn't anything that could be done.

On his arrival, Chief Sylver immediately sent someone over to Washy's house but there was no car in the driveway, and it was clear right away that no one was home. Henry Sears arrived and confirmed that Washy and Serena had gone to Newton to see Washy's sister. "They left yesterday, chief. Washy mentioned to Lionel Ferris about going when he ran into him on the flats on Tuesday."

Sylver looked eastward. "Damn good thing the wind was pushing the flames away from there," he pointed toward Washy's house. "A wind out of the west might have carried sparks right over to Washy's place. An old wooden building like that would have gone up fast. There's not a lot of distance between the two houses."

Sears looked at the smoldering ruin of Martone's summer house. "There is now, chief. Maybe someone felt that the neighborhood was getting too crowded."

Surprise in the Ashes

After getting a call the next day at Clara's house about the fire, Washy and Serena drove back to Sears Point. There were several vehicles parked in Martone's driveway, including Chief Sylver's truck. There was a heavy smell of burned material in the air. The snow had turned into sleet after midnight. Now even in the weak January sun there were just a few patches of the white stuff left. Gordon Sylver was standing near the ruined house talking with Deputy Fire Chief Freddie Hooper.

Before Washy could get out of his car, Sylver waved and walked over. "Washy, do you know if anyone was staying at Martone's last night? We tried calling him in Connecticut but no one picked up the phone."

"Not to my knowledge, chief," Washy spoke through the rolled-down car window. "There hasn't been anyone around the place since Thanksgiving. The house has basically been shut up for the winter. I just see a caretaker now and then."

"Well somebody sure was up here yesterday," Sylver replied. "Fires don't just start from nothing. Know anyone who might want to put the torch to Martone's house?"

Washy had all he could do to keep from bursting out laughing. "Chief, my guess is that Martone has made his share of enemies over the years. And not just back where he comes from. He doesn't have too many friends around here, either."

Sylver realized right away that the question he'd posed had far too many answers. Smiling, he thumped his hand on the roof of the car. "I left myself open for that one, Washy. I guess you're right. Martone's not a guy that grows on you. And it couldn't have been either of you two, as you were up in the city."

He brought his face down to the window and spoke quietly. "Washy, Chief Ehrhart and I are pretty sure that this fire was set. You can smell the strong odor of some type of accelerant, probably gasoline. Ehrhart asked me to ask you where your daughter Mary was last night."

"My God, Gordy! You don't think that Mary would do something like this."

"I don't, Washy. But she's been pretty outspoken about hating these big beachfront houses. Several people have heard her say that she'd like them all gone. Can you be sure that she, or someone connected to her, didn't have something to do with this?"

"Come on, Gordy, this is ridiculous. Let's go into the house and call her."

Mary answered her phone right away. When Serena told her about the suspicious fire at Martone's house, there was a pause at the end of the line. "Are you calling me because you think I had something to do with it?"

"Of course not, Mary. But people are going to want to know where you were when the fire started. It's routine. They just want to cover all bases. If we hadn't been at Clara's they'd be asking us the same thing. They are just trying to find out what happened."

"I was right here in my apartment last night. I'm not the kind to go out of the house in a heavy snowstorm. I went to bed about ten o'clock. Actually, I am sorry that I wasn't the one to set fire to Martone's monstrosity. I would have liked to take credit for it."

When Serena related Mary's story to Sylver, he didn't look happy. "Chief Ehrhart will probably ask Mary to come in to the station. Unfortunately, she's going to be a suspect until we find someone else."

Just then, there was a knock at the door. Before Washy could move to open it, Roy Jones pushed it open and entered. "Sorry to rush in like this. But we've been poking through the wreckage and we've discovered a body. It's pretty badly burned, but we're pretty sure it's Windsor Burkhart."

A Letter of Explanation

The body in Martone's house was indeed Windsor Burkhart. His car was found parked behind a summer cottage in Brewster Park. It appeared that at the height of the storm, Burkhart had left it there and walked through the woods to the Martone property, where he had broken in and set the fire. What was even more of a surprise was that after setting the fire, Burkhart had apparently made no effort to get away from the conflagration. His body was found sitting in a chair in what Martone had used as a mini-movie theater. The door by which he had entered was still wide open. Because the storm had knocked the power out, the intruder alarm connected to the police department never sounded.

Certainly there were a lot of people who didn't like Martone. Any number of them could have destroyed his home. But Windsor Burkhart? Washy just couldn't figure why his friend had taken the action that he did, especially without leaving himself any room for escape.

Two days after the fire, a letter came to Washy. When he opened the envelope, the note inside was from Windsor Burkhart.

Washy,

When you read this, I'll be dead. And if I've done my job right, Martone's little "cottage" will be gone too. No loss there. About two months ago, I saw my doctor and he told me that I had advanced liver cancer. He didn't give me a long time to live. I said nothing to anyone because I didn't want a big fuss made over me. And I knew that you and Serena would do that, being the kind of people you are. I have a good relationship with my doctor and he gave me a prescription for some Seconal. Just to help me sleep, we agreed. Both of us knew what the pills were for. I planned to wait as long as I could before taking them but when the snow storm came in, something told me that I could make my final act just a bit more meaningful. It was an opportunity that I wasn't going to let pass. So I'm heading out tonight with a couple of cans of gasoline from the garage. If all goes well and my matches stay dry, I'll be going out in a blaze of glory. I only wish that bastard Martone was spending the night at Sears Point.

Washy, you were my first friend in Brewster. I remember that day at the dump when you helped me with that old piece of furniture. I know it was a lifetime ago but through all these years, you've remained my best and closest friend. You never judged me when others certainly did. I've loved you for that, just as I love Serena. When Robbie and I came to Brewster after the war, it was like we had at last found the place where we were meant to live. It was truly our home. Brewster was a town like no other – especially then.

I don't have any family – at least any that I'm connected to, so I'm asking that you sell off all my assets and give the money to the historical society and the expansion fund for the library. I've given you written authority to do that in the form of a letter I left with attorney William Earnest Crowell in Dennis. Promise me, Washy, you will accept what I've done as the act of a rational man. I'm not crazy. I know what I'm doing. Think of me next summer when it's once again quiet at Sears Point. And give Serena a special kiss for me. You are a very lucky man, my friend.

PS: Those "antique" lamps I sold to the tourists really were from Harry Snow's.

Win

Washy sat down at the table. The letter certainly explained why Burkhart hadn't hurried to escape the fire he'd set. Washy couldn't see any reason why anyone else had to know what had driven his friend to burn down Martone's house. Leave it a mystery, he thought. He'd tell Serena about the letter, no one else. Taking a wooden match from a container on the wall, Washy held Burkhart's last words over the sink. He struck the match, and in short order the letter was gone, the ash washed away in the swirl of tap water.

Martone showed up in town several days after the fire. He called Gordon Sylver incompetent and claimed he would sue the town for what had happened. Officials let him bluster for a while but didn't show much sympathy. "We did the best we could with the limited resources we have," was the answer he got from the selectmen.

The auto dealer declared that he was going to rebuild his summer home. "This time it's going to be even bigger," he told people who were willing to listen. But the rest of the winter went by and there was no activity at Martone's property. The next summer passed quietly with no sign that construction was imminent. Just after Labor Day, the phone rang at Sears Point. It was Larry Doyle.

"Seen the morning paper, Washy? The headlines in the *Boston Globe* say, 'Connecticut Car Dealer Indicted.'" Doyle went on, "Seems like Vincent Martone has a little bit of trouble back in Connecticut. The state attorney general is going after him for a kickback scheme he had going with the mayor of Bridgeport. There's a grand jury that's going to charge him with a whole list of things, not the least of which are jury tampering and tax avoidance. That will bring in the feds. I'm guessing that Martone won't be in a great hurry to do anything with his Brewster property. He'll be too busy trying to stay out of jail."

The legal problems that confronted Vincent Martone that fall were just the tip of the iceberg for the man who had for so long been making deals no one could refuse. He was eventually convicted along with other city officials in both Bridgeport and Stamford of schemes to defraud those cities. When the Internal Revenue Service got through with him, Martone faced additional fines and penalties. He spent Christmas at the federal prison in Danbury, Connecticut, along with his co-conspirators. As his appeals slowly wound their way through the judicial system, Martone's financial empire collapsed. His wife left him and the Brewster property was eventually put up for sale to satisfy outstanding legal and financial obligations. Washy and Serena worried about who might buy the property, so it was a great relief when a letter came to Sears Point from a group called The Conservation Alliance. As an abutter, Washy was by law in line to be notified. In the letter were the details of an arrangement worked out between the town of Brewster and the Commonwealth of Massachusetts, whereby Martone's property was being acquired by the Alliance as a perpetually protected area. The notice said the land would be returned to its natural state and managed by the Brewster natural resources department.

With the letter in his pocket, Washy drove to town hall. Larry Doyle was in the office. "Larry, did you know this was going on?"

"Of course I knew. Is there anything that goes on in town that I don't know?" Doyle, who rarely smiled, sat back in his chair and took off his dark-rimmed glasses, a smug look on his face.

"You could have told me," Washy said.

"I suppose I could have. But negotiations were difficult. I didn't want to get your hopes up. A lot of groups and individuals wanted that property. Our hope was to keep it from development. We were able to get the commonwealth to kick in a nice sum of money that was matched by the conservation group. The town's part of it will be overseeing the parcel and keeping it in its natural state. Anyway, Washy, you've got your peace and quiet back. And joined with your piece of protected property, it gives the town a nice green corridor to the shore. It's a win for everyone, except maybe Martone."

Driving back to Sears Point, Washy stopped at the cemetery at Red Top. He walked among the old markers. A red-tailed hawk soared above the pines, sharp eyes focused on the ground below in the raptor's endless search for food. Returning to his car, Washy drove back toward Sears

Point. The scenes were familiar. Occasional patches of blue water were visible in the breaks of the low hills that fronted the beach. Seagulls clustered in the marsh along Stony Brook down by Route 6A. White clouds were building above Quivet Neck. It was shaping up to be a spectacular fall day. As he pulled into his road, Washy Sears thought that this small piece of ground, not much in the eyes of the world but for so long his family home, had to be the most beautiful place on earth.

Serena's Shock

Brewster's population grew to more than four thousand in 1980. That number would double again in less than ten years. Brewster in that year had an assessed value approaching two hundred million dollars. The police budget was a quarter of a million dollars and money for educating the town's 450 elementary school children was almost seven hundred thousand dollars. When Fire Chief Gordon Sylver resigned in 1980, Roy Jones became the new chief. Jones had been a classmate of CJ's and after military service had worked his way up to captain. Now he was in charge of the entire department. Washy kidded Larry Doyle about the $29,000 annual salary that town meeting had approved for the selectmen. "I thought you were just doing it for your love of public service," he said to Doyle as he bumped into him one afternoon at Ken's Market.

Doyle smiled. "Actually, Washy, if you divided my hours into that salary, you'd come up with about a dollar an hour. I spend more time at town hall than I do with my business."

The board of selectmen changed again in the May town election of 1982 when, in a close election that pitted former selectman Bob Sawtelle against David Brownville, Sawtelle returned to the board. Fred Krapohl lost his position, finishing third in the race. After several years of debate, voters endorsed the idea of a town golf course, appropriating almost a half million dollars to take 170 acres of land off Freeman's Way by eminent domain. Designed by nationally renowned architects Cornish and Silva, it was to be named The Captains Course. As another sign that Brewster was changing, there was no significant opposition when the vote came to raising almost two million dollars to build it.

Ernie Gage, chairman of the Alewives Committee, reported that despite low levels of water in the mill ponds, there was a very good migration of herring up Stony Brook. The committee voted to not lease the herring rights to any commercial operation, and reported as well that the hordes of people coming to view the annual spring run of fish were ruining the landscape.

During this period, lengthy town meeting warrants dealt with bylaw changes that included a Peeping Tom ordinance, increased fines for sleeping in the open, and for using rude language in a public place. The old approach road to the dump was re-engineered, finally giving Rosamond Gage a chance to leave her front room windows open on hot summer days. There were still some old remnants of what Brewster had once been, with 54 horses, 6 ponies, 19 goats and 6 cows listed in the 1983 town report.

One thing that became more and more a regular part of Washy's routine was his attendance at funerals. Former selectman Jean Olmsted died in 1981, followed that same year by old classmate Connie Bragg and former moderator Grant Koch. Washy and Serena had attended the services for Lou Crocker a year earlier, and Lloyd Coggeshall, another of Washy's elementary school classmates, passed away in 1982. It was hard for Washy not to look in the mirror and see the years etched vividly in the face that looked back at him.

Shortly after Thanksgiving, almost two months after his seventy-fifth birthday, Washy arrived at Sears Point with a few Christmas packages. It was late in the afternoon and he'd expected to find Serena in the kitchen preparing supper. Instead, the house was quiet. Going to the bedroom, he found his wife propped up in bed on several pillows with a comforter pulled up around her.

"Early nap, sweetheart?" He went in and sat beside her on the bed.

"No, Washy. I just felt so tired. I've got quite a headache. I wanted to lie down."

"Well, I think you're entitled to do that once in a while, dear." He smoothed the covers over her. "I'll leave you for a bit."

In the shortened days of late November, the room was already dark. Leaving the door open, he quietly retreated to the living room. He didn't bother Serena for supper, fixing a sandwich and watching the evening news. After 7 p.m., Washy went back to the bedroom and found Serena still in the same position. He put on the light beside the bed. Her eyes were open but he couldn't seem to rouse her.

"Sweetheart, it's time to get up," he shook her. "If you stay in bed you'll be up half the night."

She moved a bit but appeared to have trouble speaking. Washy looked closely at his wife, and he could see that she was mouthing words that wouldn't come.

Calling the emergency telephone number, Washy told the dispatcher that his wife was barely responsive and they needed a rescue vehicle right away. Returning to the bedroom, he held Serena until they arrived.

The Waiting Game

At Cape Cod Hospital, doctors determined that Serena had suffered a stroke, and she was admitted immediately. Several doctors and nurses hovered around her until she was wheeled away for tests.

Washy sat alone in the waiting room for more than two hours before a doctor came out to speak with him. "Mr. Sears, your wife is alive but she's in very serious condition. From what we can see, she's had some type of a brain incident probably caused by a stroke. She doesn't appear to be able to speak, nor can she move much more than her right arm."

The news was stunning. Just a few hours ago he'd been talking with Serena. Now he was being told that his wife of more than thirty years was partially paralyzed and unable to communicate. It didn't seem possible. Everything had happened so fast.

After a few words of encouragement, the doctor left Washy alone, disappearing back into the institutional labyrinth of hospital corridors. Washy thought he'd maybe try and catch some sleep in the waiting area. He didn't want to leave Serena. But he realized that the doctor was right. He'd learn nothing until morning. Better to spend the night at home in his own bed than in an uncomfortable chair in a cold room. He decided to wait until the next morning to tell Mary what had happened. Instead, he called George Linehan, a friend who lived in East Dennis. Linehan came to pick him up and Washy was back home just after midnight.

Assuring Linehan that there was nothing more that could be done that night, Washy watched as his friend drove away. Once inside the dark house, it occurred to him that since he and Serena had been married, he couldn't remember ever spending a single night alone at Sears Point. He went into the bedroom and turned on the light, noting the disturbed coverlet as it had been left when the EMTs moved Serena. He smoothed it and lay on top of the bed fully clothed. Before he fell into a restless sleep, Washy did something that he rarely, if ever, did. He prayed.

In the morning he called Mary. She met him in the lobby of the hospital, where Washy told her about Serena. He reviewed what the doctors had said, not glossing over the seriousness of the diagnosis.

"They're not sure what caused the shock," he said. "We'll know more later this morning as to what we can expect."

Mary reached across and held Washy's hand. Choking back tears, she asked, "Will she ever be the same? How long before she can go home?"

Washy stood up and looked down the quiet corridor. "I don't know, Mary. I just don't know."

Around mid-morning, the doctor came out to meet them. Dressed in blue scrubs with his surgical mask dangling off to one side, he sat down between Washy and Serena. "Your wife had a reasonably good night." He looked at Washy. "She's stable and was able to sleep without problems. She doesn't appear to be in any pain." He put his hand on Washy's shoulder. "I know that you will want to see her, Mr. Sears. And you both can go up shortly. But you need to be aware that she may not respond to you. We've been trying to communicate with her but haven't had any success."

After the conference with the doctor, Washy and Mary went up to see Serena. A nurse excused herself and left as they entered. The single bed was quite high and had shiny metal railings standing like sentries along the sides. The sheets were plain and very white. Window blinds were drawn, preventing the morning sun from fully illuminating the room. Serena lay on her back in the center of the bed. A tube dangled from a bottle and ran down to her hand. Her breathing was steady but shallow and her eyes were closed.

"I don't think we should wake her," Washy said. Mary agreed and they both sat for a while looking at the small figure in the bed.

"I can move back to the house, Washy," Mary said quietly. "And I can stay and care for mother when she comes home. You'll need help."

"Let's wait a bit, Mary," Washy tried to comfort her. "A lot will depend on how your mother responds to therapy. I'm sure there is some kind of home care nursing help."

In truth, Washy wondered how he was going to manage. He'd never faced anything like this before. The Sears Point house wasn't set up for an invalid. If Serena couldn't walk, how would she be moved from room to room? Would she be able to feed or dress herself and use the bathroom on her own? A host of issues would have to be attended to. And as much as he tried to reassure Mary, Washy wasn't so confident that he knew how things would turn out.

A movement from the bed caught their attention. Serena's head shifted just a bit. Her right arm came haltingly out from beneath the covers and settled across her chest. Washy and Mary left their chairs and moved to her. Serena said nothing but when her eyes opened, it was clear that she recognized her husband and her daughter. Washy put his hand on Serena's face and gently began to stroke her hair. Mary held her mother's still outstretched hand.

"We're here, Serena, Mary and me. You're going to get well. And you'll be home again soon. The doctor says so. It will be just as it always was, sweetheart. The three of us. We love you very much."

Mary leaned across the bed and put her face next to Serena's. A tear fell from Serena's left eye, rolling softly down her cheek. In the distance, the shrill whistle of the departing Steamship Authority ferry left a haunting statement on the wind as the tall white ship eased past the Fish Hills.

A Long-Term Reality

As the doctor had told Washy and Mary, the brain is a mysterious and often unpredictable thing. Whatever one may predict, there are no certainties. And so it was with Serena. After her stay in the hospital, she was transferred to a local rehabilitation facility where therapists worked with her daily. After a month, she was able to sit up in bed and feed herself. Her left side, however, remained useless, and the aphasia that gripped her speech lessened only slightly. She slurred her words and it was difficult to understand her. It didn't appear that Serena would ever walk again.

At some point it was decided that no amount of continued therapy would achieve much more, and Serena was discharged and brought home to Sears Point. Ramps and support bars were added to the house, and a hospital bed was installed in the first floor bedroom. Another spring had arrived, and whenever the warmer days allowed, Serena was wheeled into a sunny spot on one of the porches that surrounded the house. Mary had moved back, and with the assistance of the VNA and home health aides, a routine was established to provide for Serena's care.

When he and Serena were alone, Washy told stories about the old days. He made her laugh when he recited a poem that they had both learned in elementary school.

"There was an old woman from Brewster.
Who had a very noisy rooster.
She chopped off its head until it was dead.
And now it don't crow like it uster!!!"

He read to Serena when the weather was such that they couldn't go outside. One morning as he searched the bookshelves for something that she might like, she let him know that she wanted her Bible. He went into the bedroom and picked up the well-worn book and brought it to her. "Do you want to read this, Serena?"

"No, Washy, I want *you* to read it to *me*."

Washy was a stranger to the scriptures, knowing perhaps just a couple of psalms and a few verses that he'd memorized in grammar school. "Where should I start?"

For perhaps the first time in a long time, Washy saw Serena smiling broadly. "At the beginning, silly, where else?"

Thus Washy began a journey through the King James Version of the Bible. From Genesis, Exodus and Deuteronomy and through the rest of the Old Testament, he read the scriptures to Serena every day. The psalms, proverbs, and words of the prophets passed in succession. After months, the New Testament followed. As he read to her, Serena sat with her eyes closed, but it was clear that his efforts, at first quite tentative, gave her considerable pleasure. She mouthed familiar passages as he read them. And when Washy allowed himself to admit it, he was finding a good deal of comfort himself in the ancient words on the worn pages.

The Nursing Home Decision

There are twenty-seven books in the New Testament. Somewhere between the First and Second Epistles of John, Washy noticed that Serena's focus had begun to wane. Despite all of the oblations to the Almighty, Serena's condition wasn't getting any better. It was more and more difficult to get her dressed in the morning, and she had ceased being able to feed herself. She spent much of each day sleeping. Mary stayed with her mother when Washy left the house. Other than doing necessary errands, he sat by Serena's bed for long periods of time talking softly to her even when she dozed off.

Mary first raised the idea that Serena needed to be moved to a place that could give her better care. Initially, Washy wouldn't hear of it. "I can't put Serena in a home," he told her. "Those places are just for people waiting to die. Your mother wouldn't get the personal care that she's getting here."

"Washy, we can't keep going on the way we have," Mary responded. "You're exhausted and mother isn't getting the nourishment she needs. Most days she's not even getting out of bed. We need to think about a nursing home."

As much as he tried to push the thought aside, Washy had to admit that Serena's care was taking a toll on him. It had been almost a year since she'd come back to Sears Point, and what had once seemed a plausible plan of care was now proving overwhelming.

"I stopped in at the new nursing home on Harwich Road," Mary continued. "It's an excellent care facility. People that I've talked to are pleased with how their relatives have been treated there. It's bright and clean and the staff is well trained. And it's close enough that we could visit mother every day. In an ideal world, we'd keep her here at Sears Point. But it's no longer possible. We need to do this, Washy."

With some time to think about it, Washy agreed to go with Mary to the nursing home. After meeting with the director and social worker, he signed the authorization to transfer Serena to the facility. On the drive back to Sears Point, Washy couldn't escape the feeling that somehow he had betrayed his partner of thirty-five years. In the house, he went into the bedroom where Serena lay in the semi-darkness. Holding her hand, he sat and told her what had been decided. He had expected some reaction. But as he looked at his partner, there was none. Serena appeared on the edge of a faraway world that was preparing for her arrival. Other than her labored breathing, she was silent. As Washy sat looking at his wife, her hand did not rise to wipe away his tears.

Reconnecting With a Friend

The nursing facility on Harwich Road was indeed bright and clean. Serena was in a three-person room with a window that looked out on a protected quadrangle where, when the weather was moderate, residents were wheeled outside. There was a shared bathroom and a pressed-wood bureau by each of the beds, each one covered with photographs of loved ones.

In the first weeks, the nursing staff made efforts to get Serena up and dressed so she could be taken to the day room. But she was so weak that it didn't seem worth the effort. Washy drove over in the morning to be with her, leaving only after he had fed Serena her supper, a pureed mix of something that resembled baby food. He watched his wife as she slept and he read to her when her eyes opened. It was hard to know even then if she knew he was beside her. Still, he never failed to tell Serena he loved her and always kissed her tenderly on the cheek when it was time to leave.

Partially as a way of varying his time at the facility, Washy volunteered to run the Friday bingo games. The contests were held after lunch and usually attracted a dozen or so residents. When he introduced the idea of paying ten cents a card and pooling the money as a prize for a winner, the participation tripled. It was on one of those Fridays that a man was wheeled into the day room by an aide. He had a shawl wrapped around his shoulders and an oxygen tank was tucked behind the wheelchair. A thin tube connected the tank to his nose. Washy was just setting out the bingo cards when he saw the man come in, and he recognized him right away.

"Bob Medeiros! I haven't seen you in a hoot's age. Come in to win some money?" The man pulled the shawl closer around him and looked hesitantly toward Washy. The once strong, muscular truck driver with the ready smile that Washy remembered from years ago was clearly not a well man.

It took a moment for Medeiros to recognize Washy. And when he did, he brightened immediately. The old smile came back, though with a few teeth missing. "I'll be damned. Washy Sears! Are you a resident here too?"

Washy explained about Serena and why he was at the nursing home. "She's been here a couple of months now," he told Medeiros. "No telling how long she'll be staying. I try to come over every day to keep her company. Calling the bingo games was just something I thought I could do to help out. Serena sleeps a lot."

At that point, the activities director for the facility came in with the numbered ping pong balls and began dumping them into the sorter. It was just about one o'clock in the afternoon. A bingo game that didn't start on time produced lots of grumbling from the players. Not all of it was good natured. They had their cards in place and were impatient to get going.

"Bob, I'll see you after we finish bingo. It will be good to catch up." Washy went to the front of the room to call the numbers.

After about an hour, the bingo session ended. The winners happily counted up their change. The losers voiced the usual complaints that Washy had intentionally avoided calling their numbers. He went over to where Bob Medeiros was sitting at one of the round tables. "Looks like you've got a good pile of dimes there. You did pretty well for a first-timer!"

Medeiros laughed. "Yeah, I better be careful not to spend it too fast."

When the aide came in, Washy motioned her away. "I'll take him back," he told her. He wheeled Medeiros down the hallway to a room similar to Serena's. It also had three beds. The one in the middle was stripped and the bureau next to it was clear of pictures. "Fellow in the middle died this morning," Medeiros said quietly. "It's not a place where you make long-term friends. People come and go pretty quick."

Washy waited for one of the nurses to come in and get Medeiros into bed. As the man was helped out of his wheelchair, Washy noticed how carefully the oxygen tank was kept attached to Medeiros.

"Want some TV?" the nurse asked.

"No, I'm going to take a nap. That bingo takes a lot out of a man," he smiled at the woman, who laughed as she left the room.

Looking at his watch, Washy told Medeiros that he was going to check in on Serena. "Tell you what, Bob. I'll come by tomorrow morning. We'll have more time to talk then." As he turned to leave the room, Bob Medeiros's eyes were closed. He was already asleep.

The Medeiros Story

The next morning after looking in on Serena, Washy found Medeiros in bed watching TV. The remains of a half-eaten breakfast were on the tray next to him. The oxygen tank was still connected. The middle bed in the room remained stripped and unmade.

"It's good to see you up and ready to start the day." Washy sat in a chair next to his friend.

"I'm up. That's true. But I don't have much on my schedule. One of my daughters is supposed to come and bring me some new socks. That might be the highlight of the day. How's your wife doing?"

"Pretty much as usual," Washy told him. "They can get a bit of food into her. She's losing weight. She was back to sleep when I left the room a few minutes ago. To be honest, she's not doing well. The doctor hasn't been encouraging."

"That's too bad, Washy. I'm sorry," Medeiros replied.

"So tell me, what are you doing in here?" Washy changed the subject.

"I've had emphysema for quite a while now. Comes from being a two-pack-a-day man for most of my life. I was able to handle things with the oxygen boost until about six months ago. I went for a checkup and my doctor spotted a shadow on my chest X-ray. A biopsy showed it to be cancer. They told me I had a couple of options. Surgery was one of them. Pretty nasty operation, they said, with a long recovery and no guarantee. They also said that radiation and chemotherapy might slow it down. I thought about it and figured that at my age, I'm sixty-two, I didn't want to go through it. It would have meant a lot of trips to Boston. And long-term survival rates for lung cancer are very low. So I made the decision to play out the string. I was home for a while but I got too weak to stay there, so here I am. It's where I probably should be at this stage. The last thing I want to do is put a burden on my kids."

"But sixty-two isn't that old, Bob. Not in my book anyway," Washy smiled. "My next big milestone is eighty. And it's not that far away. To me, you're still a kid!"

Medeiros laughed. "Maybe you think so, Washy. But when you can't breathe and you've got something inside that's eating away at your lungs, believe me, sixty-two is old. Most days I'm feeling more like I'm eighty."

Alternating his time with Serena, Washy arranged to bring Medeiros to the lounge area every day before lunch, where the two played cards. Washy learned that his friend had been born in New Bedford. His mother had come into the country as a teenager from Brava in the Azores.

From what she'd told him, Medeiros's father had been a white sailor. A fisherman, he thought. His mother had lived with the man for about a year, but they'd never married. Then his father went off on a sea voyage and didn't return. "Probably wrecked somewhere in the Atlantic. He never even knew my mother was pregnant when he shipped out," Medeiros said. "My mother wasn't sure how he'd react, so she'd held off telling him. She never told me much else about my father. After I was born, my mother couldn't afford to stay in New Bedford by herself, and she came to Harwich to live with some relatives. Louis Pina helped her out. He was also born in Brava. That's how I got to grow up here. My mother married one of his sons, and I've got a bunch of half-brothers in Harwich."

At one point, Medeiros mentioned that he'd been in the army during World War II. "Me and Rufus Pina were drafted together. I was just twenty. I think Rufus was maybe a year younger. We ended up in an anti-aircraft division and were sent to Britain. The army was segregated then, and we served in an all-black unit. I was white enough that some of the men thought I was an officer assigned to keep them in line. We got a big laugh out of that. Both of us drove trucks, worked in food service, and did maintenance on the guns. A couple of days after D-Day we landed in France. We followed the advance into Germany.

"At one point we were assigned to support the 99th Infantry Division. Because of the losses in the Battle of the Bulge, that unit had been integrated with black volunteers. Nothing like that had happened since the Civil

War. We were the first ones to cross the Rhine at Remagen in March of 1945. Just before the war ended, outside of Weimar we came across the Buchenwald Concentration Camp. We liberated it. What I saw there was unbelievable. I couldn't talk about it for years, it was so bad. After the war, I came home and got a job driving trucks for local contractors. I married Barbara Roderick and we had four kids. Because I could drive heavy equipment, I always had a job."

"What happened to your boy Greg?" Washy asked. "The one who played against my son in high school."

"He's done very well." Medeiros paused as a coughing spasm came over him. "But not at first. He got a basketball scholarship to a school in Maryland. He played four years there and got a teaching certificate. Being in school kept Greg out of the draft, so he missed Vietnam. None of us were sorry about that. When he finished college he came back to the Cape and applied for a teaching job in several school systems. Everyone wanted him to coach basketball, but they didn't offer him a permanent classroom job. For a couple of years he coached and substituted, hoping to get picked up when something opened up. By the third year, it was pretty clear to us that the schools were just playing him. And Greg knew it. They said they just didn't have any openings but we saw several cases where someone else got a job in the middle of the year even though Greg had better credentials. Unfortunately, he got his mother's genes, not mine. He just wasn't white enough. That's the real truth."

"But you say that things have worked out well for him?"

Medeiros nodded. "After a few years Greg saw that he was never going to be a full-time teacher on the Cape. He stopped looking. And he gave up coaching. For a while he hauled trash and pumped cesspools for Bobby Our. It was just about that time that the state began to enforce the Title V law that required new construction to build more environmentally sensitive septic systems. A lot of old cesspools needed upgrading and replacement too. Greg got himself certified as an installer. We took out some loans, remortgaged the house and purchased a couple of trucks and an excavator. From there, the business has just boomed. He's got about a dozen men working for him, and he owns a big steel building on Great Western Road. The shit business has paid very well. About three years ago, he and his wife built a big house right on Pleasant Lake. That's a long way from North Harwich."

Two Lives End

As spring approached, Washy grew to appreciate the company of this Portuguese man from Harwich, and he looked forward to their card games and conversations. As the days warmed, the two occasionally sat outside at a table in the quadrangle. It was during one of those afternoons that a nurse came out to get Washy. "Mr. Sears, you need to come with me. Your wife is quite agitated and we think you should be there."

Returning to Serena's room, the shades were drawn. Two nurses were near the head of Serena's bed when Washy entered. She lay on her back with her eyes closed and her mouth open. Unlike the shallow breaths that she'd routinely been taking, her intakes were much longer but spaced considerably apart. Her head shuddered convulsively with each breath. Every time Serena breathed there was a rattle from deep in her throat.

"Serena? It's me." Washy moved to the head of the bed. "I'm right here." Looking down at his wife, he was struck by how small she was. There seemed hardly anything to her. "Serena, it's all right. You can let go," he spoke softly while brushing back her hair, all the while gently rubbing the arm closest to him. "It's time, Serena. Time to go to Albion and Kay, and CJ. All the aunts and uncles, your brothers, they're waiting. You can do it. I love you very much and I always will."

After a time, Serena's breathing began to slow and gradually a peaceful calm seemed to descend over her. Both nurses left the room, closing the door behind them. As he looked at the woman who had been his partner for so long, Washy almost thought that he could detect a smile on Serena's face. Her head was no longer moving. There were a few more long breaths. Washy held his wife's hand, and in those last moments he could sense the final ebb of her life as it left her body. There were few occasions in Washy's life that had produced tears. He'd cried at the news of David's and CJ's deaths. Now as the woman that had shared almost half his life left him, the tears trickled freely down his face. Picking up the Bible from the nearby table, Washy placed it carefully in Serena's hand and curled her fingers around it. Wiping his eyes, he kissed her one last time and left the room.

A few days later, Serena Sears was laid to rest in the Foster Road Cemetery next to her father and mother. When Washy had called Clara to tell her of Serena's passing, his sister had told him that Serena should go up to Red Top. "That's where you will be, Washy," she said. "And it's where CJ is." But Washy knew how close Serena had been to her parents and decided to have her buried with them. "They ought to be together," he told Clara. Mary also agreed that it was the best thing to do. A fair number of people in town turned out for the funeral, and Pastor Mills preached a fine sermon. As Washy looked around at the people who gathered at the Baptist Church for the ceremony, he was struck by how few of them he knew well. There were so many new people in town. Serena came from a large and extended family, and many of them were in attendance and he and Mary sat with them. Later that afternoon, after everyone had left Sears Point and just before dusk, Washy drove back to the cemetery with Mary. They stood alone for a short time over the freshly turned earth. The flowers on Serena's grave were already beginning to wilt in the cool evening air.

It wasn't too long afterward that Bob Medeiros died. Washy had continued visiting his friend through the summer following Serena's death. The two played cards and reminisced about life in earlier days, remembering people they had worked with. Sometimes Greg Medeiros came by to visit his father and Washy saw what a handsome young man he'd become. On those occasions Washy thought about CJ and what might have been had his son lived. The elder Medeiros surprised Washy one day by revealing that his mother was still alive, living with one of her sisters in the old house in North Harwich. "She's in her eighties now," he told Washy. "She doesn't go out much. She's been angry with me for a while now because I let myself go. When I refused to have an operation, she said she wasn't going to visit me in the nursing home. And she never has."

"That seems strange that a mother wouldn't visit her son," Washy said.

"I believe that in her mind she thinks that as long as she stays away, I'll stay alive. She wants to remember me as I was, not as I am now. In a strange way, I think I understand. We talk on the phone."

On the day of the funeral, Holy Trinity Church in West Harwich was filled with the extensions of Bob Medeiros's family. Pinas, Lopes, Roses, Gomes, Raneos and Rodericks occupied the front pews. Washy seated himself toward the back. At the end of the service, as the coffin was being wheeled out, Washy watched as Greg Medeiros assisted a small, frail, white-haired woman toward the exit. It was his grandmother. On his way out of the church, Washy stopped to offer her his condolences. When Greg Medeiros whispered who he was, the old woman looked up and eyed Washy for a few moments, seemingly taking his full measure. She smiled and looked into his eyes as if she were perhaps trying to remember something. It was Sylvia Medeiros-Pina who broke the silence. "Thank you so much for coming, Mr. Sears. Robert spoke of you often when we talked on the phone. He enjoyed your company. He said you were like family." She smiled again at Washy. "I'm glad you were here today."

Leaving the church and driving back to Sears Point, Washy kept thinking about what Sylvia Medeiros-Pina had said about family. He wondered if he had maybe lived too long. Other than Mary and his sister, Clara, whom he rarely saw, he was pretty much alone. He knew he'd miss Bob Medeiros.

"I hated to see it go."

In 1986, Brewster voters approved an executive secretary form of government and the change to a five-member part-time board of selectmen. The decision was a recognition that the town had simply become too complex an entity for the old form of government to be effective. While the selectmen retained executive authority, Larry Doyle made it clear to Washy that he didn't like the change.

"I hated to see it go, Wash," Doyle told Washy one day when they happened to meet in the old town hall, which was undergoing renovations. "I think the old system was just fine as it was. I know that a lot of the new people in town wanted an executive secretary, and Harris Ivers and his committee convinced everyone that the full-time selectmen setup is outdated. But I said before the vote that I was going to vote against it, and I also said that if I was the only negative vote, my wife had better not come home after the meeting. As it was, the vote to change was very close."

Doyle revealed that he was not going to run for another term under the new system. "There are so many selectmen now that they'll be bumping into each other. I'd just be in the way. Anyway, Wash, as a private citizen I'll have the freedom to express my opinions any way I want." Doyle made his decision public at the December town employees' Christmas party.

That fall, Charles Sumner, who had been the town executive in Littleton, Massachusetts, was hired as the new executive secretary. Rita Lawler, a retired air force officer, had become the second woman elected to the board of selectmen the year before. Voters supported several non-binding ballot questions including a strong plea to the federal government to establish a universal health care plan. A study group was formed to look at an addition to the ten-year-old Stony Brook Elementary School. Twelve units of affordable housing were authorized for some town-owned property off Freeman's Way. In another sign that Brewster's population was continuing to grow, the town was divided into two voting precincts.

The Punkhorn

The pickup truck jounced along the dirt road that skirted Upper Mill Pond. Greg Hellyer, the natural resources coordinator for the Brewster Land Acquisition Committee, was in an expansive mood. "Washy, I wanted you to come out here with me so you could show me some of the old landmarks that are part of the Punkhorn. I can't think of anyone who knows the area better than you do. We've got some topographical maps and an aerial survey that was done after World War II. Other than that, there's not much to go on. I've walked most of it, but I wanted someone who had a history here, who remembers what it was. It's one thing to determine the old boundaries but quite another to know how this land was used. We've been doing deed research over at the county land court trying to see who owns it. Some property is 'owners unknown,' but other parts are held by people that we've identified."

Washy had met Hellyer earlier that year at the Museum of Natural History and had worked with the young naturalist as part of the committee that had recently secured the Eagle Point parcel on the eastern end of Upper Mill Pond. That piece, which included several hundred acres of bog and upland off Run Hill Road, was the first step in a plan for carving out a sizeable conservation area in the southwestern section of Brewster.

"My father and my brothers used to hunt out here when I was a teenager," Washy said. "A lot of families had woodlots and we used to cut firewood in the spring. That was probably sixty or seventy years ago. My father sold our woodlots back in the 1930s. We had maybe five or six, each about two acres apiece. We used to rotate the cutting, allowing the trees to grow back. A few people in town kept harvesting wood out here right through World War II when coal was hard to get."

Hellyer down-shifted the truck as the dirt road turned temporarily into a water-filled gully, a result of recent heavy rain. "That's why most of the trees in here are not much more than a half century old," the naturalist said. "It's relatively new growth even though some of the pines go up as high as thirty-five feet. I'm making an inventory of what's growing here and it will be part of the information package we submit to the conservation committee."

Washy looked out at the tangle of brush and vine that covered an old car engine on cement blocks that had once served as a water pump for a long abandoned cranberry bog. "It wasn't that long ago that these overgrown bogs were producing. I know Harry Alexander had a couple that he and his son Kenny worked, and Percie Newcomb owned bogs out here, too. I think Jack Nevin still owns some land that's been in his family for a long time."

The so-called Punkhorn section of Brewster was one of the few large undeveloped parcels left in the mid-Cape region, partly because it was relatively inaccessible. A few fire roads crossed the area. There were no electric poles, and restrictions on building on or near wetlands presented problems for any kind of development. The Punkhorn included numerous bogs and vernal pools, eventually backing up to Seymour's Pond near the Harwich line. Anyone who was thinking about subdividing any portion not only had to be creative, but also needed to spend considerable time unraveling the many title holders with claims there. But as the decade of the 1980s progressed and land values skyrocketed, speculators began eyeing the parcel for possible home lots and got busy researching old deeds in the hope that they could entice property owners to sell.

Hellyer pulled off the road and parked. The two men watched in silence as a doe and her fawn edged out onto the road from a thicket about fifty yards away. The animals seemed unaware of the presence of the men.

"That's what we want to save, Washy." Hellyer pointed at the deer. "If we can convince the town to buy the land out here, these animals have a future. The moratorium on homebuilding that we passed last year isn't permanent, and when it's over, the bulldozers won't be far behind. The pavement ends at the beginning of the Punkhorn."

The naturalist's concerns found no argument from Washy. He'd been working for more than a year now with land acquisition committee members Bob Finch and Dave Palmer in looking at undeveloped parcels that could be purchased by the town for conservation. In 1985, Finch and Palmer, along with Paul Wightman, were instrumental in getting voters to come up with almost two million dollars to purchase the property at Eagle Point. The state kicked in additional funding to bring down the overall cost, something the committee hoped would be the case with what they were planning next.

"We're going to sponsor a warrant article in the March 1987 annual town meeting that will ask voters to approve a bond issue for the purchase of about six hundred acres. That will be added to land we already have under conservation to make a really significant piece. It's going to cost almost six million dollars. What do you think, Washy, do you think we have a chance?"

Washy looked over at Hellyer. "You know, Greg, just a few years ago, I would have said there'd be absolutely no way that you could get such a proposal through town meeting. Brewster always held some of the tightest purse strings of any town on the Cape. And purchasing open space wasn't a priority. For a long time, people just couldn't see the need for it. It was hard enough just to get zoning approved. But there are a lot of new people in town. And they've seen what is happening with developments like Ocean Edge and The Villages, and frankly I think it scares them. We've got over seven thousand people living year-round in Brewster now. In the summer it seems like five times that number. I'm sensing that voters would be willing to support preserving a large piece."

"Would you speak in favor of the article?" Hellyer asked.

"I'm not sure I have that much influence anymore, if indeed I ever did," Washy replied. "Sure, I'd do it. But one person who could bring a lot of support would be Ernie Gage. He's been in favor of adding more conservation land for quite a while now. Get him to speak and a lot of people will listen."

"He's already said he will move the article when it comes up," Hilliard replied. "And he will speak in favor of it."

"That's good. Ernie has quite a following from his work at the herring run. People know and respect him."

When the annual town meeting took place in March, the duo of Finch and Palmer represented the land acquisition committee in explaining the proposed land-taking. A few voices were raised in opposition, mainly those who thought the price they were going to be paid for their land was far too low. Some worried about the effect of the bond issue on the tax rate. And there were threats of litigation. But the assembly didn't seem intimidated, and the vote to preserve the Punkhorn was overwhelmingly in favor. Washy never felt the need to rise and speak on the article, as it was clear that voters were more than ready to back the measure. Ernie Gage was unable to attend the meeting because of illness but his statement of support was read into the record. Right after the vote, Bob Finch raised his hand and asked that the action just taken by the voters be dedicated to Gage. As the crowd erupted in positive applause, Washy caught the eye of Greg Hellyer, who was sitting a few rows over. They both nodded and smiled at the same time.

A little over three weeks after the vote to preserve the Punkhorn, Washy ran into Hellyer. The naturalist mentioned that he'd heard that Ernie Gage had died a few days earlier. "I called Roz and visited with Ernie at his house about a week before he passed," Washy told Hellyer. "He was in a lot of pain. But one thing that made him smile was knowing that the Punkhorn had been saved. That gave him a lot of comfort. Ernie wanted you to know that he really appreciated what you and the rest of the committee did. He pointed out that some of the best preservation work done in the last few years had been done by people who weren't born in Brewster, people like you, Greg. You should be proud of what you've done."

Driving back to Sears Point, Washy reflected on a number of things. Brewster's newcomers, "washashores," as they were often derisively called, had brought something to town that was needed. He smiled, thinking about Win Burkhart and the antiques dealer's love of the town's history. Many of the newer residents were behind the decisions that were helping Brewster cope with change. Washy thought that the mix of old and new families was just about right. And he had a good feeling that whatever happened down the road, Brewster was headed in a good direction.

Hirschel Cohen

One day not long after the vote on the Punkhorn property, Barbara Nelson, Brewster's representative for the Conservation Alliance, called to talk with Washy about a new issue of concern.

"The proposal for putting in a bunch of condos between the north end of Cobb's Pond and the beach has come up again. We thought we had blocked it a year ago because of wetland concerns. It's a narrow piece of land. Sandy Side Realty Trust has come back this time with a scaled-down plan for the property, but it's still about forty units. The alliance had hoped we might be able to purchase the property if it looked like it would be a drawn-out permitting process for the developers. The owners are in a hurry to sell. There's a planning board hearing scheduled a week from tomorrow.

"The developers are hoping for a quick decision on the plan," she told him. "They've got a small window because of the complicated nature of the project's financing. They want approval to extend Governor Prence Road toward Sears Point to gain access into the property. The planning board will hear their argument next week."

"So what we need is something that will delay the permitting process. Is that right?" Washy shifted the phone to his other ear and took a pencil and pad off the shelf.

Nelson agreed that slowing things down was about the only chance they had to kill the project. "The backers of the development say they will move on to something else if it looks like it will be held up into the fall. The Sandy Side people have made a number of concessions in the hope they can get approval. At least two members of the planning board have said that they won't oppose the plan. Oh, and one more thing, Washy. Sandy Side has hired Hirsch Cohen to represent them at the hearing."

The mention of Hirschel Cohen wasn't a complete surprise. Whenever there was a development project that needed special legal attention to shepherd it through the permitting process, Hirsch Cohen was the attorney that got the call.

Cohen came from a family of merchants who had been doing business in Hyannis since the late nineteenth century. His extended family included Pearlsteins, Burmans, and Finklesteins, all of them prominent Hyannis retailers. A legendary athlete at Barnstable High School where he starred in football and basketball, Cohen had attended Boston University and stayed there to get his law degree. Unlike many of his college-educated contemporaries, Cohen volunteered for the army during the Vietnam War. He served his one year of combat duty there as a platoon leader.

After returning to the Cape, he opened an office in Hyannis specializing in real estate law. For two decades he had built a reputation as a capable attorney who could handle the most difficult projects for developers. He was the bane of local conservation and preservation groups. Planning boards hated to see his name on applications that were coming up for review, because it usually signaled a long night of data, statistics, and references to the general laws of the commonwealth, some of them quite obscure but nonetheless always pertinent.

When he was asked how it felt to be characterized as a hired gun for off-Cape developers, Cohen would just shrug while pointedly reminding his critics that everyone deserved competent legal representation. "I do the work that I'm paid for," he would say. "And I make sure that my clients get a fair hearing when they go before local boards in any real estate matter. That is what I do, no more, no less."

Even opponents admitted that Cohen was consistent and fair. If challenged on a point of real estate law, he usually had the answers. People either loved or hated Hirsch Cohen. But all of them respected him. And if nothing else, they agreed that Cohen was a gentleman.

"Hirsch Cohen will come to that hearing with everything in order," Washy noted. "He'll be prepared. You can count on that. What we have to do is find something that will catch him by surprise. Something that he doesn't anticipate. That won't be easy. Give me a little time to think about it, and I'll see what I can come up with."

Washy went into the living room where Mary was sitting. "You heard the conversation. We've got about a week to think of something that will force the planning board to hold up its recommendation. Got any friends who might be holding some endangered species that we could put on the property?"

Mary laughed. "If only we had some spotted salamanders or maybe a few box turtles. That might do it. But I can't think of anyone who might have anything like that."

Washy looked out of the living room window toward Paine's Creek. "You know, Mary, I'm thinking we just might have something that could do it. Maybe even better than box turtles. Get in the car and let's go see Fred Dunford at the natural history museum."

Dunford was the staff archaeologist for the museum. A Harwich native, Dunford held a doctorate from Harvard University and lived in Brewster on Round Pond up near the five corners. He'd done a number of surveys analyzing early Native American habitation sites on various parts of Cape Cod. He was familiar with the Stony Brook Valley and Wing's Island and had just finished some site work at Eagle Point.

"Fred, I'm sure that you've heard about the condo development that's been proposed near Sears Point."

Dunford nodded. "Yes, I've heard about it. I thought it was shot down a year ago because of potential pollution problems that might affect Cobb's Pond."

"Well it's back, a scaled-down version of it anyway. The developers are going to try and get approval next week when they go before the planning board. They've got a short term option on the property. It's got a good chance of passing unless we can find something that will slow it down."

"So how does that involve me?" Dunford asked.

"I got to thinking about when my brother David and I were kids and would play around that area. We always found a lot of Indian arrowheads. I'm wondering if you might come and take a look to see if the site of the proposed development might contain significant artifacts. It's about all we've got."

Dunford considered. "I do have an intern that might be able to come over and take a good look. He's here for the summer and he'd be a good person to do it."

“Well, see if you can set it up, will you, Fred? If possible, we need him to come over in a day or so. I can show him where we used to find the arrowheads.”

“I'll tell him, Wash. And I'll have him call you when he's ready to go.”

More Than an Artifact

Two days later, as Washy worked on the bog, a Jeep drove up and a young man got out. “You must be Washy Sears. I'm Andrew Leska. Fred Dunford told me you wanted me to look at a possible Indian artifact site.”

“Thanks for coming out, Andrew. Yes, I told Fred that I'd come across a number of Indian points and tools around here, and I thought it might be worthwhile to have a professional take a look around.” Washy pointed toward the slope leading down to Cobb's Pond. “My brother and I used to play over there near that clearing and we always came up with something, especially in the spring when the ground thawed out and arrowheads came to the surface.”

With Washy leading, the two walked down from the bog into the line of pines that bordered the pond.

“Here's that clearing I told you about. It's probably best to start here.”

Setting up a grid across the gentle slope, Leska began sifting through carefully measured twelve-inch-deep holes that were placed about six feet apart. Just after noon, Washy was bringing a cold drink down to the site when he heard a whoop. Rushing forward, he found Leska on his knees over a small depression.

“Look at this, will you!!” Leska pointed excitedly toward the ground. “Mr. Sears, you've got an Indian grave here, definitely a pre-colonial burial. I found some points nearby, and as I was moving my trowel, I hit something. It's definitely a group of human bones. Can I use your phone? I want to call Fred. We'll want to photograph this find *in situ*.”

After the call from Leska, Fred Dunford drove out to Sears Point. As Washy watched the two archaeologists, they carefully brushed away the soil surrounding the bones, taking a series of photographs. Eventually what remained of the skeleton was exposed.

“See how the bones are arranged?” Dunford said. “It's a conventional Indian burial with the head toward the east and the body in a fetal position. At first glance it looks to be Woodland Period. Pre-colonial to be sure. Some of the bones are missing, probably disturbed by animals shortly after the burial. It's a shallow grave.”

A tarp was put over the excavation and Dunford told Washy that he would contact the county medical examiner. “After certifying that the bones are older than a hundred years, jurisdiction then moves to the state archaeologist,” Dunford explained. “He'll send someone down here from his office to assess the site. The Commission of Indian Affairs also has to be notified. It's going to take some time to do everything. There's a lot of paperwork."

"So we're looking at a couple of weeks?"

Dunford laughed. "Washy, I think I can be pretty certain that it will take a couple of months. You know how the state works. I'm going to call Chief Ehrhart just to let him know that we've found human remains out here. He may want to have a look."

After Dunford and Leska left, Washy went back to the house. Mary had supper ready and when they finished, Washy called Barbara Nelson. "Hi, Barbara. I hope I'm not interrupting anything. I think we are going to be all right for the Sandy Side hearing on Wednesday. I've just come up with something that I'm pretty sure Hirsch Cohen won't be ready for."

On the night of the hearing, Washy and Mary sat with a number of people who were there to speak against the proposed development. Hirsch Cohen was also in the room along with two representatives of the Sandy Side group. Wearing his usual rumpled brown suit, Cohen set up an easel with a map of the development. Several architectural sketches of the proposed condo complex showing a tennis court and large outside pool were on the table next to the easel. He was reaching into his briefcase for additional documents when Barbara Nelson asked to be recognized.

"Members of the board, I would like to call your attention to the fact that in the past week it was determined that that the location of the proposed development is in fact a significant Native American site. Numerous artifacts have been located on the property including arrowheads, stone tools, and pottery bits. We would request that any decision on the application by the board be postponed until a complete survey as required by law is done by the state archaeologist."

Cohen didn't seem to be overly concerned by what he was hearing. He smiled at Barbara Nelson and asked permission to respond. "Mr. Chairman." He pointed to Steve Eldredge. "It's not an uncommon thing for an area faced with development to be salted with common Indian artifacts in order to hold up a project. I'm not saying this is the case here, but in our surveys of the property, we've found no such objects. And even if there are Native American artifacts out there, the law gives us the provision to move ahead as long as we make an effort to identify and record these artifacts. Their presence should have no bearing on my client's application."

Nelson was immediately up again. "I'll grant that the presence of artifacts alone cannot hold up a development. But an Indian grave certainly will." Walking forward, she placed the photos taken by Dunford and Leska on the table next to the Sandy Side drawings.

The revelation that an Indian grave had been discovered on the site was clearly something that Cohen hadn't anticipated. As his clients looked to him for some kind of response, he had no reply.

Nelson continued, "Because the commonwealth has very specific laws on the jurisdiction and handling of Indian gravesites, I would suggest that the planning board postpone a decision on the Sandy Side project. Perhaps the developers would like to withdraw their application and submit it later. It will take considerable time for the site to be surveyed and the Indian remains removed, if indeed they are removed."

On an unanimous voice vote, the planning board agreed to postpone the Sandy Side hearing to a date to be later determined. "We'll consider the proposal withdrawn temporarily. Without prejudice, of course," said Eldredge.

The Sandy Side people seemed stunned. Cohen moved slowly to wrap up his presentation materials, shaking his head. He folded his charts and stowed his documents in his briefcase. For just a moment Washy made eye contact with Cohen. He thought he saw a slight smile on the attorney's face. Washy, Mary and Barbara Nelson gathered up the rest of those who had come to oppose the project, and they all adjourned to the Brewster Inn for a victory celebration.

A few days later Washy heard a knock on the door. It was Hirschel Cohen. "May I come in for a minute, Mr. Sears?"

Washy welcomed the attorney into the living room.

Cohen's eyes took in the simple furnishings, and then he walked over to the window and looked across the landscape. "You know, Mr. Sears, I didn't make the connection until the night of the hearing. There are a lot of Sears over in this part of the Cape. You're the father of CJ Sears, am I correct?"

"Yes, that's right. CJ was my son," Washy acknowledged.

Cohen turned from the window and sat down. "I knew your son when I was in high school. We played against each other a few times in basketball, and he and I attended Boys State at the University of Massachusetts when we were juniors. I was at college when he was killed in Vietnam. In a way, your son was one of the reasons I decided to join the army. I didn't get over there until the last stages of the war, but it was important for me to serve my country. I was a company commander with the Fourth Division. We operated in the Central Highlands, Dragon Mountain south of Pleiku.

"Men like your son never had the advantages that I had," Cohen continued. "It wasn't the well-off who went to Vietnam. A lot of my law school friends ducked it completely or took refuge getting assigned to the judge advocate's office. I felt I owed it to everyone who signed up or who'd been drafted that I should volunteer. And I'm glad I did. The army taught me a lot about people and a lot about myself."

Cohen hadn't taken his coat off and it was clear that he wasn't planning to spend a long morning talking. He looked around the room and then stood up to leave, pausing momentarily by the fireplace mantle with its collection of family pictures. His eyes lingered on the photograph of CJ in his marine uniform.

"Another thing, Mr. Sears." Cohen had his hand on the door. "The army taught me to always respect and learn from people who are smarter than I am. I talked to Barbara Nelson the day after the hearing, and she told me how you brought the archaeologists out here. It was an angle I never expected. I probably should have. I don't know how the Indian grave got there, or how the archaeologists found it, but it was the deal breaker. With the long delay that will come with the survey, Sandy Side has folded. Barbara told me that the property owners are listening to an offer from the Conservation Alliance, and it looks like they might take it. From a personal standpoint, I actually think that would be a better use for the land. Mind you, I wouldn't want to be quoted on that." Cohen was now smiling broadly. "You are a very smart man, Mr. Sears."

The door was open. Washy still hadn't said anything when Cohen reached into his coat pocket. The lawyer placed a small piece of dirt-covered quartz on the kitchen counter. "Take a look at this. It's an arrowhead. I found it in the driveway as I was walking up to your house. Yes, Mr. Sears, you are a very smart man indeed."

Death of an Old Friend

Larry Doyle died in March of 1990. He was eighty years old. In the weeks before Doyle passed, Washy spent quite a bit of time visiting with the former selectman. A little more than two years apart in age, they had witnessed the changes of the last half century together. Both had seen Brewster transformed from a rural small town to a suburban home for almost nine thousand people. The two had not always agreed, but they'd been drawn to each other in old age, survivors of a time that few people in town still remembered. A little more than two years from his last stint in town hall, Doyle still wasn't a convert to Brewster's new form of government.

"I can't see how the town is run any better now that we have five selectmen instead of the three we always had," Doyle said one afternoon. "We've got more boards and regulations than you can shake a stick at. Now they're talking about a town planner. What's he going to do? Today, you can't build a house unless you've got about an acre and a half. And we are looking at a limit on commercial development along Route 6A. Where are people going to work? As much as I supported some planning, I'm more and more feeling like a museum character on display for the tourists who come down here looking for those quaint little villages."

"Times are different, Larry. That's for sure. We've come a long way from when your father and Tom Tubman were highway surveyors. Imagine if they could come back now."

"They wouldn't recognize the place," Doyle replied. "Don't know as I do myself."

Washy reminded Doyle that the bridge over Route 6 on Freeman's Way had been named after him. "You've got a permanent marker here, Larry. Everyone headed over to Pleasant Bay will remember you as an important person in Brewster when they see that sign."

Doyle wasn't impressed. "You know, Washy, I didn't say anything at the time they dedicated that bridge to me. I probably should have. It was a nice thing. But the name should have really gone to Fobe Foster. The whole idea of putting in the road and getting that bridge built was his. He had to endure a lot of snide remarks about 'Fobe's Folley' all through those years when nothing was happening there. Today, it's the biggest growth area in town. And the thing is, nobody now besides you and me even knows who the hell Fobe was. I'd say that Fobe got the last laugh on that bridge to nowhere. And I suspect he, or at least someone in his family, made a fair amount of money on it, too."

Over the remainder of the decade, other friends and a few relatives finished out their days, having navigated their own long journeys through life. Clara died in 1992 at age eighty. There hadn't been much contact between Washy and his sister after Serena's death, and he took her passing in the spirit of losing a longtime acquaintance. Clara had left instructions that she wanted to be buried with her husband in their family plot in Newton. There would be no visit to Red Top.

Jack Sheehan

The air conditioning in the Brewster Ladies' Library was barely holding its own against the August heat as a large crowd took seats in the meeting room. They'd come to listen to four Brewster veterans of World War II as part of the commemoration of the fiftieth anniversary of the end of that conflict. At the long table at the north end of the hall sat Henry Wittemore, John Latham, Washington Chase, and Washington Sears. Washy was a reluctant participant, only agreeing to come after repeated entreaties from Wittemore and a push from Mary, who was going to drive him there. Washy was the oldest of the four, at eighty-eight. But not by that much. He'd grown up with all three of the other men.

When the conversation ended after a good hour, a young man approached Washy. He introduced himself as Jack Sheehan. "Mr. Sears, I'm a teacher in Harwich. I live in Brewster on Tubman Road near Buddy Bassett's animal farm. I'm interested in Cape history and I'd like to know if we could get together sometime, and you could tell me a bit about

Brewster's past. I've already spoken to quite a few longtime residents – Doris Ulm, Larry Crocker, Mertis Foster, and Tommy Gage." He pointed at the other three veterans. "And I've spoken to them, too."

Washy smiled at the mention of those people, some of whom had passed on. "Certainly, you're welcome to come out to my house at Sears Point. I'm not going far these days, and you could catch me just about any time. Give me a call when you want to come."

A week later, Sheehan arrived out at Sears Point with a pad of paper and a small tape recorder. "You don't mind if I put you on tape, do you?" He asked. "It lets me go back and check my notes later."

"It's not a problem for me," Washy told him as he ushered the younger man into the living room. "I hope your batteries are charged."

As the two sat drinking coffee that morning, the first of many conversations took place. They were for the most part unscripted, with Sheehan occasionally asking a specific question about something. Otherwise, Washy simply sat back and recounted what he remembered about his life in Brewster, now almost nine decades. Sheehan listened. He was particularly interested in the history of the weirs that once dotted the flats from Dennis toward Orleans. Washy told him how his father and grandfather had worked the flats for decades, making a living from the sea, something that was much more difficult to do in the present age. When the weather was good and they could get outside, Washy walked with Sheehan as far as the bluff overlooking the beach and pointed out some of the still visible stubs of the old traps, their classic configuration still recognizable at low tide. "I wish I could take you out there and show you things more close up," he told Sheehan. "But I just can't do it anymore."

"So you're an Irishman, are you?" Washy asked Sheehan during one of their meetings. When Sheehan acknowledged that indeed he was, Washy laughed. "One time there weren't many Irish on the Cape. A few in Sandwich, maybe Woods Hole, but not out here. There's a Brewster story that when an Irishman named O'Brien was appointed as a postmaster here in the 1800s, the townspeople protested to high heaven and had him removed. They said he was a foreigner. To them, at least, he was. O'Brien had been born in Boston."

Sheehan chuckled at the story. "I've only been in town for a few years myself, but I'll admit that I look at people who are retiring here now as being foreigners. I can only imagine how you feel, Washy."

"One thing you learn when you get older, Jack. Nothing stays the same. And I don't say that in a bad way. It's just what it is. My father and grandfather grew up in this house. Even being part of this same place, they still lived the bulk of their lives in very different worlds. It's like that for me."

Sheehan switched off the recorder. He walked over to the window that looked west toward Crowe's Pasture. "I guess I feel that something gets lost when people don't have at least some sense of where they came from. I doubt that any more than a handful of people living in Brewster today have any idea of what you've told me about earlier times. We live our lives at such a pace that the past seems almost meaningless, maybe even irrelevant. I think that's sad."

Washy poured a cup of coffee. "If you're as good a historian as I think you are, you'll write something that will let people fill in those gaps. They'll end up knowing how it all came to be."

Sheehan picked up the recorder and moved to leave. "Perhaps you're right, Washy. Maybe there is a book in all this. But for me, at least, I think it's most important that I know. And because of you, I do."

The New Millennium

Brewster entered the twenty-first century with a population of just over ten thousand people. There were three voting precincts to handle the increasing number of new residents. No less than eight political parties were listed under registered voters. Town offices and various boards were filled with names like Przygocki, Sedlewicz, Guazzaloca and Hirschman. There were over fifty boards, authorities, and committees managing everything from handicapped citizens' access to public facilities to water quality. Steve Eldridge held a selectman position and Steve Doyle remained as moderator. Other than those two and Rollie Bassett's long run as constable, the former dominance of town affairs by the old families was now just a memory.

The town's annual budget was well over thirty million dollars. There were only two cows registered in town as the century turned, but there were five llamas. Surprisingly, there were more horses in Brewster than when Washy had been born. Operating out of its new station on Route 124, the police department reported logging over three hundred thousand miles in the year 2000 while dealing with routine matters, but also with 15 attempted suicides, 108 instances of vandalism and a 119 cases of larceny and theft. The lack of affordable housing was a continuing topic of concern, and the town was already in the process of putting together plans for a celebration of Brewster's two hundred years of existence.

As a means of preserving Sears Point, Washy met with the Brewster Conservation Alliance shortly after the Sandy Side decision and completed an agreement that allowed for the non-profit trust group to take title to the property with the proviso that Washy and Mary would have a lifetime tenancy at the house. Sears Point would never see a developer's spade. David's two sons had long ago severed ties with the Cape, and Clara's daughters were living in other states. And while there continued to be no shortage of Sears in the area, Washy's branch of the family was at an end.

Now, in his mid-nineties, Washy's daily routine was pretty much set. The visiting nurse arrived every morning. She fixed lunch and straightened up the house while making sure Washy took his pills. If someone from the Council on Aging wasn't coming to take him to an activity at the Senior Center, he'd be down for a nap by early afternoon. On weekends, Jack Sheehan would sometimes stop by to continue talking about Brewster's past. Washy hoped that someday something would come of all the things he'd told the young writer.

This particular September morning was warm and the living room windows were open. An occasional bug bumbled awkwardly into the screens. The familiar pungent smell of the flats rode in on the breeze from the beach. Gulls soared and light fluffy clouds moved across the sky. The television programming was suddenly interrupted by a news report that a plane had hit a building in New York City. It was soon clear that the crash was no accident. As terrible images of destruction unfolded in New York, Washy sat watching in shock as the twin World Trade Center towers, the tallest buildings in the city, were engulfed in smoke and flame. The news commentator reported that it was a terrorist attack from the air.

The phone rang. It was Mary.

"Are you watching television, Washy?" she asked, quite certain that indeed he was. "It's horrible. How could something like this happen? What does it mean?"

Washy didn't have an immediate answer, but his thoughts went back to the luncheonette in Falmouth where sixty years ago he had first heard about the attack on Pearl Harbor. It was the same feeling of fear and uncertainty. No one had answers then. There were none now. He didn't reply.

"I'll be coming home early," Mary continued. "They're telling people to leave. Everything seems to be shutting down. You stay right where you are."

As he continued to watch the scenes of destruction unfold on television, the thought struck Washy that he'd lived too long. For a moment he almost envied those sleeping in the ground at Red Top. School shootings, rampant drug use, crime that used to be confined to urban areas now common on the Cape, professional athletes getting millions of dollars for hitting or throwing a ball. There were too many unanswered questions like the ones that Mary had just voiced. What, indeed, did it all mean? He couldn't say. The world was spinning in a different orbit, a new direction, unpredictable and ominous. There seemed a new vulnerability. The only surety was that there was really no safe place anymore.

Pleasant Lake Manor

As nursing homes go, Pleasant Lake Manor was better than most. Considerably older than the two facilities built in Brewster in the 1980s, it was still a place where a relative could feel comfortable leaving a loved one for an extended time. Mary decided to see if she could get Washy a place there. On a spring morning in 2006 she sat with one of the administrators in the garden that connected the two wings of the flat-roofed building. The atmosphere was quiet and relaxed. A small statue of some Greek god stood in the middle of the brick patio, surrounded by early season daffodils. A sign beside it said it was a memorial to someone's parents. The two wings, while identical on the outside, were quite different inside. The north section, called the Satucket wing, housed the so-called private pay "clients." Residents were in single rooms. Maid service was frequent and people had a measure of independence that pretty much mirrored the way they had lived in their own homes. Some married couples lived there and a few residents had small pets. Residents took their meals in a small, nicely appointed and carpeted dining room with sturdy oaken tables.

The Nauset wing on the south side of the complex was set up dormitory-style. The floors throughout were linoleum. The inside air was heavy with lemon disinfectant. The white walls sported pictures that might have come from a Motel 6. All of the rooms in the Nauset wing housed three people. The nurses' station was where the wheelchair-bound residents crowded, most of them looking for some kind of attention. It was a clinical atmosphere, not much different from a hospital. And it was like this because all of the residents that lived on this side of the manor were very needy.

It had been obvious for some time that Washy needed more care than just the occasional visiting nurse at Sears Point. His decline was particularly noticeable after several falls. When Mary discussed it with him, Washy was neither surprised nor angry. At ninety-eight he was a realist. At first, Mary thought she could get Washy into one of the newer care facilities in town. But they had waiting lists and she'd turned to an available space at Pleasant Lake Manor after a friend told her that her mother had had a good experience there.

"I'd like my father to be in the north wing if that is possible," Mary told the administrator as they sat in the garden. "His mind is sharp but he has difficulty getting around."

But after a series of questions about Washy's mobility, or lack of it, the choice quickly narrowed to the south wing. "I'm sure it would work best if your father were with the people in the Nauset side," the administrator said. "The nursing staff is trained to assist people who need the extra help. And at his age, it's better that he not be by himself. You are describing a man who is quite frail."

Mary knew it was true. There wasn't much more to do other than accept it. When a few weeks later a private ambulance brought Washy over from Sears Point to Pleasant Lake Manor, it delivered him directly to the south wing.

Room 137

On the Nauset side of Pleasant Lake Manor the doors to the rooms were always open. The only time this wasn't the case was when someone made their final journey out of the place. Then all doors were closed. "We don't want to unduly disturb the residents," was the official line. But the residents surely knew. The closed doors were like a signal. After all, except for the severely demented, everyone in the Nauset wing knew that they were living on borrowed time.

Washy wasn't surprised that both of his roommates had lived most of their lives in places away from Cape Cod. Just about everyone in the facility had been born somewhere else.

In contrast to his two roommates, who rarely saw visitors, Washy did have company. Mary tried to stop in after work, and when the weather was good she took him out for rides on weekends. Jack Sheehan also was a regular, continuing to fill his notebook with stories that he'd collected about Brewster. He'd been reading a lot of documents in the archives of the historical society as well as microfilm copies of old newspapers at the Snow Library in Orleans. One day, just after school had started up in September, Sheehan came in with a large binder and set it on the table next to Washy's bed. "This is the draft of a book I wasn't sure I'd ever get to write," he said. "It's a history of Brewster. It's just a draft right now. I've got a number of people looking it over for accuracy. I expect they'll add some stories of their own when they read it. I hope so. I haven't set any date for publication, but when it comes out, Washy, you are going to get the first copy."

Washy had never been one to dwell on death. But as he lay in bed he occasionally wondered how it would all end. Would there be a bright glow? Angels singing? Or might his life simply switch off like an old black-and-white TV, collapsing to a tiny spot of light that burned at the center of the screen, before dimming and disappearing forever. Washy didn't know. He'd lived more than his share, and he was very aware that his failing body wasn't going to get better. He was connected to Brewster's past, not its future. Washy's friends were gone. He'd outlived them all. When it came right down to it, there wasn't all that much more to live for. The town that he'd grown up in was now a stranger to him. Other than Mary, there was no close family left. She would certainly be better off without having to worry about him. The door that his father, mother, David, Clara, Serena,

CJ and Win Burkhart had already passed through was now very close. He could almost touch it. What lay beyond was a mystery, and Washy wondered for a moment if it was a sin to be looking forward to what was on the other side.

Going Home

"They're going to throw you a big birthday party," Mary announced on a Wednesday in early October. She was sitting in a chair next to Washy's bed. "You're quite a celebrity! The director was telling me that the manor has never celebrated a one-hundredth birthday before. Everyone is really excited."

"I don't want anything like that," Washy told her. "See if you can get them to back off."

"But Washy, they are going to have a special dinner for all the residents. There will be a cake. They've got a photographer. You will be the guest of honor."

"Mary, you know how I feel about these kinds of things. I never want any notoriety. It seems foolish to celebrate a man just because he survived a century. Tell them I don't want it."

"I think it's probably too late, Washy. Your birthday is next week. They've already lined up the caterer and the cake's been ordered. You'll just have to put up with it. It'll be fun."

Like many other things in his life at the manor, this was just something else that Washy realized he had no way to control. At this stage, things just happened. It was like being a game piece on a checker board. Someone else made the moves. Making a fuss would serve no purpose. He smiled at Mary and said it would be all right.

"I'm going to pick you up after lunch on Friday and take you out to Sears Point," Mary told him. "The forecast is for some clouds and a bit of light rain. But it's going to be warm. We can have some tea or cocoa out on the porch. Before I run you back here, we can drive up to Red Top and visit the graves. There will still be plenty enough light."

And so it was on the Friday before his one-hundredth birthday, Washy found himself sitting on the porch in an Adirondack chair at the house at Sears Point. It was warm enough that he almost called to Mary to forget the blanket. But he knew as the afternoon wore on and the sun got lower, the cover would be useful. And he wanted to be outside. The air was fresh and the seat was comfortable. As he looked across the bay toward the outer Cape, the timeless and unchanging vista of sea and sand spread out before him.

The eastern sky gave a hint of clearing. The rain had stopped and the water in the bay was blue-green. Washy could see several fishing boats working the water over toward Rock Harbor. They were just white specks near the horizon. In the short time Washy had been sitting on the porch, the outlines of some sandbars off toward Point of Rocks were beginning to show. The tide was going out.

Listening to Mary move around in the house, Washy caught himself thinking that Serena was inside fixing supper. He wondered for a moment if CJ was home from school yet. What roads would need to be fixed come spring? Did he have enough in the budget to handle snow removal? Couldn't abide Albion Rogers getting upset if his street wasn't plowed. That was certain. He smiled as his mind remembered finding Let and Tiny playing pool behind the stage at town hall. An image of Windsor Burkett buying something that looked like a lamp at Harry Snow's store almost made Washy laugh out loud. A similar reaction came when he recalled Kay Rogers' surprise announcement about a new baby at town meeting. Avery Taggart appeared, stirring a cup of coffee across from him at the Blue Parrot. There was an image of Sparrow Higgins driving an old Ford on a dirt track out in the woods of South Harwich. A young man whose life was still ahead of him sat in the passenger seat. A dimly lit roadhouse loomed ahead. And far back, but still there in Washy's memory, was the presence of a pretty young figure skater silhouetted against a rising moon, her cheeks red, dark hair flowing and blue eyes flashing, being whisked across a frozen cranberry bog by his father.

And then he saw his father coming in from the flats. Two small boys skipped through the tide pools beside him as the sorrel horse pulled the fish cart ashore. Washy's mother stood on the bluffs fronting the house at Sears Point. She was waving to the three of them. It all seemed so very real. Like a drawer in an old desk that hadn't been opened in a very long time, a continuously changing kaleidoscope of images spilled across his consciousness.

In the comfort of the Adirondack chair, Washy closed his eyes. The smell of the sea filled his head. It was sweet and familiar, like an old friend. He could see the door now, right in front of him. It was open. Without leaving his chair, Washy stepped easily through it. There were familiar voices calling to him. He didn't look back. In the air above Sears Point, the gulls wheeled and soared over the newly emerging sandbars, looking for something to scavenge. The clouds were giving up to the afternoon sun. The tide in the bay was now in full retreat.

Acknowledgements

My deepest gratitude goes to the people who were willing to take the time to read and comment on this novel while in its draft stage. These early readers include: Sandra Hall Tubman, Susan Eldridge Smithwick, Jean Bates Sears, Robert Bates, Ellen Chahey, Vicky West Warburton, Steve Doyle, Jack Latham, Rob Williams, Judi Gallant Leck, Lawren Cowen, Gerard Golden, Corinne Cowen, Katie Duff, and Judy Friend. My long-time writing partner Jack Sheedy and Ed Maroney, former editor of the *Barnstable Patriot* newspaper, provided excellent guidance in the areas of syntax, punctuation, style, organization, and tone. As the manuscript's editor, Barbara Clark gave me a generous helping of her professional insight and spent long hours reining in my tendency to occasionally lose sight of the story's main objectives. She helped me to focus on what the novel was supposed to be about – the story of Brewster in the twentieth century. For her patience and encouragement, I thank her. Once again, as she's done for so many of our books, Kristen vonHentschel contributed her outstanding design and layout work to prepare the manuscript for printing. I am also indebted to my wife, Beth, who has been my sounding board on just about any piece of writing I've done in the past twenty-five years. Hopefully this novel will, at least to some degree, make up for all of the time I spent in my office writing while neglecting things around the house.

I want to give a shout out to the staff at the Snow Library in Orleans for giving me access to the microfilm of the *Cape Codder* newspaper. I also very much appreciated the cooperation of the town clerk's office in Brewster, in letting me use the bound copies of town reports from 1907 through 2007. I hope I wasn't a nuisance showing up as I usually did without an appointment. The oral history tapes housed in the Brewster Ladies Library gave me original source material for the novel's story line.

Finally, I have to thank my parents who took a chance and moved to Brewster in 1949. They gave me the experience of growing up in the place that served to provide the direction my life has taken ever since.

Karen North Wells, the cover artist for *Sears Point*, is well known locally and nationally for her high quality work. Her studio, Underground Art Gallery, is located at 673 Satucket Road, Brewster, Massachusetts. www.undergroundgallery.com